Four Great Tragedies

DOVER • **GIANT THRIFT** • EDITIONS

Four Great Tragedies

Hamlet, Macbeth, Othello, and Romeo and Juliet

WILLIAM SHAKESPEARE

DOVER PUBLICATIONS, INC.
Mineola, New York

DOVER GIANT THRIFT EDITIONS

GENERAL EDITOR: MARY CAROLYN WALDREP
EDITOR OF THIS VOLUME: T. N. R. ROGERS

Copyright

Theatrical Rights

Bibliographical Note

This Dover edition, first published in 2005, contains the unabridged texts of four plays: *Hamlet* as published in Volume VII of the second edition of *The Works of William Shakespeare* by Macmillan and Company, London, in 1892, and republished as a Dover Thrift Edition in 1992; *Macbeth* as published in Volume VII of the second edition of *The Works of William Shakespeare* by Macmillan and Company, London, in 1892, and republished as a Dover Thrift Edition in 1993; *Othello* as published in Volume XVI of *The Caxton Edition of the Complete Works of William Shakespeare* by the Caxton Publishing Company, London (n.d.), and republished as a Dover Thrift Edition in 1996; and *Romeo and Juliet* as published in Volume VI of the second edition of *The Works of William Shakespeare* by Macmillan and Company, London, in 1892, and republished as a Dover Thrift Edition in 1993. Introductory Notes were written, and footnotes revised or written anew, specially for the Dover editions.

Library of Congress Cataloging-in-Publication Data

Shakespeare, William, 1564–1616.
  [Plays Selections]
  Four great tragedies : Hamlet, Macbeth, Othello, and Romeo and Juliet / William Shakespeare.
      p. cm. — (Dover giant thrift editions)
  Contents: Hamlet—Macbeth—Othello—Romeo and Juliet.
  ISBN 0-486-44083-4 (pbk.)
   1. Macbeth, King of Scotland, 11th cent.—Drama. 2. Othello (Fictitious character)—Drama. 3. Juliet (Fictitious character)—Drama. 4. Hamlet (Legendary character)—Drama. 5. Romeo (Fictitious character)—Drama. I. Title. II. Series.

PR2763 2005
822.3'3—dc22

                                                                    2005041289

Manufactured in the United States of America
Dover Publications, Inc., 31 East 2nd Street, Mineola, N.Y. 11501

Contents

Hamlet 1
  Note 3
  Dramatis Personæ 4
  Act I 5
  Act II 33
  Act III 55
  Act IV 83
  Act V 105

Macbeth 127
  Note 129
  Dramatis Personæ 130
  Act I 131
  Act II 149
  Act III 163
  Act IV 181
  Act V 199

Othello 213
  Note 215
  Dramatis Personæ 216
  Act I 217
  Act II 236
  Act III 255
  Act IV 276
  Act V 293

Romeo and Juliet 309
  Note 311
  Dramatis Personæ 312
  Prologue 313
  Act I 314
  Act II 335
  Act III 355
  Act IV 379
  Act V 392

Hamlet

Hamlet

WILLIAM SHAKESPEARE (1564–1616) wrote *Hamlet* between 1599 and 1601, creating one of the very greatest and most discussed works in English literature. The playwright did not, however, invent his eponymous hero or the basic features of the plot. Hamlet, the avenging son, was a figure from Danish legend dating back at least as far as the twelfth-century *Historiae Danicae* by Saxo Grammaticus. The Elizabethans were familiar with Saxo through Belleforest's French translation. The immediate source for Shakespeare's play is thought to have been a lost play now known as the *Ur-Hamlet,* possibly written by Thomas Kyd. Influenced by Seneca's tragedies, Kyd was instrumental in securing a place for the revenge drama on the English stage. Although *Hamlet* does incorporate all the stock elements of the revenge tragedy—murder, madness, revenge, and supernatural intervention—the play transfigures the form, developing complex characters out of stage types, interweaving philosophical questions with a compelling narrative, and offering a brilliant commentary on contemporary stagecraft.

The edition reprinted here is that of the "Cambridge Shakespeare," which combines the texts of the Second Quarto (1604) and the First Folio (1623). Punctuation and orthography have been modernized. The annotations are based on those given in the third edition of Alexander Schmidt's *Shakespeare Lexicon.*

SHANE WELLER

Dramatis Personae

CLAUDIUS, King of Denmark.
HAMLET, son to the late, and nephew to the present king.
POLONIUS, Lord Chamberlain.
HORATIO, friend to Hamlet.
LAERTES, son to Polonius.
VOLTIMAND,
CORNELIUS,
ROSENCRANTZ,
GUILDENSTERN, } courtiers.
OSRIC,
A Gentleman,
A Priest.
MARCELLUS, } officers.
BERNARDO,
FRANCISCO, a soldier.
REYNALDO, servant to Polonius.
Players.
Two Clowns, grave-diggers.
FORTINBRAS, Prince of Norway.
A Captain.
English Ambassadors.

GERTRUDE, Queen of Denmark, and mother to Hamlet.
OPHELIA, daughter to Polonius.

Lords, Ladies, Officers, Soldiers, Sailors, Messengers,
and other Attendants.

Ghost of Hamlet's Father.

SCENE: *Denmark*.

ACT I.

SCENE I. *Elsinore. A platform before the castle.*

FRANCISCO *at his post. Enter to him* BERNARDO.

BER.	Who's there?
FRAN.	Nay, answer me. Stand and unfold yourself.
BER.	Long live the King!
FRAN.	Bernardo?
BER.	He.
FRAN.	You come most carefully upon your hour.
BER.	'Tis now struck twelve. Get thee to bed, Francisco.
FRAN.	For this relief much thanks. 'Tis bitter cold,
	And I am sick at heart.
BER.	Have you had quiet guard?
FRAN.	Not a mouse stirring.
BER.	Well, good night.
	If you do meet Horatio and Marcellus,
	The rivals[1] of my watch, bid them make haste.
FRAN.	I think I hear them. Stand, ho! Who is there?

Enter HORATIO *and* MARCELLUS.

HOR.	Friends to this ground.
MAR.	And liegemen to the Dane.
FRAN.	Give you good night.
MAR.	O, farewell, honest soldier.
	Who hath relieved you?
FRAN.	Bernardo hath my place.
	Give you good night. [*Exit.*
MAR	Holla, Bernardo!
BER.	Say,

[1] *rivals*] partners.

	What, is Horatio there?
HOR.	A piece of him.
BER.	Welcome, Horatio. Welcome, good Marcellus.
MAR.	What, has this thing appear'd again tonight?
BER.	I have seen nothing.
MAR.	Horatio says 'tis but our fantasy,
	And will not let belief take hold of him
	Touching this dreaded sight, twice seen of us.
	Therefore I have entreated him along
	With us to watch the minutes of this night,
	That if again this apparition come
	He may approve our eyes[2] and speak to it.
HOR.	Tush, tush, 'twill not appear.
BER.	Sit down awhile,
	And let us once again assail your ears,
	That are so fortified against our story,
	What we have two nights seen.
HOR.	Well, sit we down,
	And let us hear Bernardo speak of this.
BER.	Last night of all,
	When yond same star that's westward from the pole[3]
	Had made his course to illume that part of heaven
	Where now it burns, Marcellus and myself,
	The bell then beating one—

Enter GHOST.

MAR.	Peace, break thee off. Look where it comes again.
BER.	In the same figure like the King that's dead.
MAR.	Thou art a scholar; speak to it, Horatio.
BER.	Looks it not like the King? Mark it, Horatio.
HOR.	Most like. It harrows me with fear and wonder.
BER.	It would be spoke to.
MAR.	Question it, Horatio.
HOR.	What art thou that usurp'st this time of night,
	Together with that fair and warlike form
	In which the majesty of buried Denmark
	Did sometimes[4] march? By heaven I charge thee, speak!
MAR.	It is offended.
BER.	See, it stalks away.

[2] *approve our eyes*] confirm what we have seen.
[3] *pole*] polestar.
[4] *sometimes*] formerly.

HOR.   Stay! speak, speak! I charge thee, speak!   [*Exit* GHOST.

MAR.   'Tis gone, and will not answer.

BER.   How now, Horatio? You tremble and look pale.
         Is not this something more than fantasy?
         What think you on't?

HOR.   Before my God, I might not this believe
         Without the sensible and true avouch
         Of mine own eyes.

MAR.   Is it not like the King?

HOR.   As thou art to thyself.
         Such was the very armour he had on
         When he the ambitious Norway combated;
         So frown'd he once, when, in an angry parle,[5]
         He smote the sledded Polacks on the ice.
         'Tis strange.

MAR.   Thus twice before, and jump[6] at this dead hour,
         With martial stalk hath he gone by our watch.

HOR.   In what particular thought to work I know not;
         But, in the gross and scope[7] of my opinion,
         This bodes some strange eruption to our state.

MAR.   Good now, sit down, and tell me, he that knows,
         Why this same strict and most observant watch
         So nightly toils the subject of the land,[8]
         And why such daily cast[9] of brazen cannon,
         And foreign mart[10] for implements of war,
         Why such impress[11] of shipwrights, whose sore task
         Does not divide the Sunday from the week.
         What might be toward, that this sweaty haste
         Doth make the night joint-labourer with the day,
         Who is't that can inform me?

HOR.   That can I—
         At least the whisper goes so. Our last King,
         Whose image even but now appear'd to us,
         Was, as you know, by Fortinbras of Norway,
         Thereto prick'd on by a most emulate[12] pride,

[5] *parle*] parley, exchange.
[6] *jump*] exactly.
[7] *gross and scope*] general drift.
[8] *toils . . . land*] causes the people of this land to toil.
[9] *cast*] casting.
[10] *mart*] trading.
[11] *impress*] conscription.
[12] *emulate*] jealous, ambitious.

Dared to the combat; in which our valiant Hamlet—
For so this side of our known world esteem'd him—
Did slay this Fortinbras; who by a seal'd compact,
Well ratified by law and heraldry,
Did forfeit, with his life, all those his lands
Which he stood seized[13] of, to the conqueror;
Against the which, a moiety competent[14]
Was gaged by our King; which had return'd
To the inheritance of Fortinbras,
Had he been vanquisher; as, by the same covenant
And carriage of the article design'd,[15]
His fell to Hamlet. Now, sir, young Fortinbras,
Of unimproved[16] metal hot and full,
Hath in the skirts of Norway here and there
Shark'd up[17] a list of lawless resolutes,[18]
For food and diet to some enterprise
That hath a stomach in't; which is no other—
As it doth well appear unto our state—
But to recover of us, by strong hand
And terms compulsatory, those foresaid lands
So by his father lost. And this, I take it,
Is the main motive of our preparations,
The source of this our watch and the chief head
Of this post-haste and romage[19] in the land.

BER.   I think it be no other but e'en so.
Well may it sort[20] that this portentous figure
Comes armed through our watch, so like the King
That was and is the question of these wars.

HOR.   A mote it is to trouble the mind's eye.
In the most high and palmy[21] state of Rome,
A little ere the mightiest Julius fell,
The graves stood tenantless, and the sheeted dead
Did squeak and gibber in the Roman streets;
As stars with trains of fire and dews of blood,

---

[13] *seized*] possessed.
[14] *moiety competent*] sufficient portion.
[15] *carriage . . . design'd*] import of the aforementioned article.
[16] *unimproved*] unemployed, latent.
[17] *Shark'd up*] recruited haphazardly and illegally.
[18] *resolutes*] desperadoes.
[19] *romage*] bustle, activity.
[20] *sort*] be fitting.
[21] *palmy*] glorious.

Disasters[22] in the sun; and the moist star,[23]
Upon whose influence Neptune's empire stands,
Was sick almost to doomsday with eclipse.
And even the like precurse[24] of feared events,
As harbingers preceding still[25] the fates
And prologue to the omen coming on,
Have heaven and earth together demonstrated
Unto our climatures and countrymen.

Enter GHOST.

But soft, behold! Lo, where it comes again.
I'll cross[26] it, though it blast me. Stay, illusion.
If thou hast any sound or use of voice,
Speak to me;
If there be any good thing to be done,
That may to thee do ease and grace to me,
Speak to me;
If thou art privy to thy country's fate,
Which, happily,[27] foreknowing may avoid,
O, speak!
Or if thou hast uphoarded in thy life
Extorted treasure in the womb of earth,
For which, they say, you spirits oft walk in death,
Speak of it; stay and speak. [*The cock crows.*] Stop it, Marcellus.

MAR. Shall I strike at it with my partisan?[28]
HOR. Do, if it will not stand.
BER.   'Tis here.
HOR.   'Tis here.
MAR. 'Tis gone.   [*Exit* GHOST.
We do it wrong, being so majestical,
To offer it the show of violence;
For it is, as the air, invulnerable,
And our vain blows malicious mockery.[29]
BER. It was about to speak, when the cock crew.

---

[22] *Disasters*] ominous signs.
[23] *the moist star*] the moon.
[24] *precurse*] forerunning.
[25] *still*] always.
[26] *cross*] confront.
[27] *happily*] haply, by chance.
[28] *partisan*] long-handled spear.
[29] *malicious mockery*] a mere semblance of malice.

HOR. And then it started like a guilty thing
      Upon a fearful summons. I have heard,
      The cock, that is the trumpet to the morn,
      Doth with his lofty and shrill-sounding throat
      Awake the god of day, and at his warning,
      Whether in sea or fire, in earth or air,
      The extravagant and erring[30] spirit hies
      To his confine;[31] and of the truth herein
      This present object made probation.[32]

MAR. It faded on the crowing of the cock.
      Some say that ever 'gainst[33] that season comes
      Wherein our Saviour's birth is celebrated,
      The bird of dawning singeth all night long;
      And then, they say, no spirit dare stir abroad,
      The nights are wholesome, then no planets strike,[34]
      No fairy takes[35] nor witch hath power to charm,
      So hallow'd and so gracious[36] is the time.

HOR. So have I heard and do in part believe it.
      But look, the morn, in russet mantle clad,
      Walks o'er the dew of yon high eastward hill.
      Break we our watch up; and by my advice,
      Let us impart what we have seen tonight
      Unto young Hamlet; for, upon my life,
      This spirit, dumb to us, will speak to him.
      Do you consent we shall acquaint him with it,
      As needful in our loves, fitting our duty?

MAR. Let's do't, I pray; and I this morning know
      Where we shall find him most conveniently.   [*Exeunt.*

---

[30] *extravagant and erring*] wandering.
[31] *confine*] appointed territory.
[32] *probation*] proof.
[33] *'gainst*] just before.
[34] *strike*] blast, destroy.
[35] *takes*] charms.
[36] *gracious*] blessed.

SCENE II. *A room of state in the castle.*

Flourish. Enter the KING, QUEEN, HAMLET, POLONIUS, LAERTES, VOLTIMAND, CORNELIUS, Lords, *and* Attendants.

KING.   Though yet of Hamlet our dear brother's death
    The memory be green, and that it us befitted
    To bear our hearts in grief and our whole kingdom
    To be contracted in one brow of woe,
    Yet so far hath discretion fought with nature
    That we with wisest sorrow think on him
    Together with remembrance of ourselves.
    Therefore our sometime sister, now our queen,
    The imperial jointress[1] to this warlike state,
    Have we, as 'twere with a defeated joy,
    With an auspicious and a dropping eye,
    With mirth in funeral and with dirge in marriage,
    In equal scale weighing delight and dole,
    Taken to wife. Nor have we herein barr'd
    Your better wisdoms, which have freely gone
    With this affair along. For all, our thanks.
    Now follows, that you know, young Fortinbras,
    Holding a weak supposal[2] of our worth,
    Or thinking by our late dear brother's death
    Our state to be disjoint and out of frame,
    Colleagued with this dream of his advantage,
    He hath not fail'd to pester us with message,
    Importing the surrender of those lands
    Lost by his father, with all bonds of law,
    To our most valiant brother. So much for him.
    Now for ourself, and for this time of meeting,
    Thus much the business is: we have here writ
    To Norway, uncle of young Fortinbras—
    Who, impotent and bed-rid, scarcely hears
    Of this his nephew's purpose—to suppress

---

[1] *jointress*] dowager.
[2] *weak supposal*] low opinion.

His further gait[3] herein, in that the levies,
The lists and full proportions, are all made
Out of his subject;[4] and we here dispatch
You, good Cornelius, and you, Voltimand,
For bearers of this greeting to old Norway,
Giving to you no further personal power
To business with the King more than the scope
Of these dilated[5] articles allow.
Farewell, and let your haste commend your duty.

COR. }
VOL. }   In that and all things will we show our duty.

KING.   We doubt it nothing. Heartily farewell.
                              [*Exeunt* VOLTIMAND *and* CORNELIUS.
And now, Laertes, what's the news with you?
You told us of some suit; what is't, Laertes?
You cannot speak of reason to the Dane,[6]
And lose your voice.[7] What wouldst thou beg, Laertes,
That shall not be my offer, not thy asking?
The head is not more native to the heart,
The hand more instrumental to the mouth,
Than is the throne of Denmark to thy father.
What wouldst thou have, Laertes?

LAER.   My dread lord,
Your leave and favour to return to France,
From whence though willingly I came to Denmark,
To show my duty in your coronation,
Yet now, I must confess, that duty done,
My thoughts and wishes bend again toward France
And bow them to your gracious leave and pardon.

KING.   Have you your father's leave? What says Polonius?

POL.   He hath, my lord, wrung from me my slow leave
By laboursome petition, and at last
Upon his will I seal'd my hard[8] consent.
I do beseech you, give him leave to go.

KING.   Take thy fair hour, Laertes; time be thine,
And thy best graces spend it at thy will.

---

[3] *gait*] proceeding.
[4] *Out of his subject*] at the expense of his people.
[5] *dilated*] detailed, copious.
[6] *the Dane*] the King of Denmark.
[7] *lose your voice*] speak in vain.
[8] *hard*] reluctant.

	But now, my cousin[9] Hamlet, and my son—
HAM.	[*Aside*] A little more than kin, and less than kind.
KING.	How is it that the clouds still hang on you?
HAM.	Not so, my lord; I am too much i' the sun.
QUEEN.	Good Hamlet, cast thy nighted colour off,

       And let thine eye look like a friend on Denmark.
       Do not for ever with thy vailed[10] lids
       Seek for thy noble father in the dust.
       Thou know'st 'tis common: all that lives must die,
       Passing through nature to eternity.

HAM.   Ay, madam, it is common.

QUEEN.   If it be,
       Why seems it so particular with thee?

HAM.   Seems, madam? Nay, it is. I know not 'seems.'
       'Tis not alone my inky cloak, good mother,
       Nor customary suits of solemn black,
       Nor windy suspiration of forced breath,
       No, nor the fruitful river in the eye,
       Nor the dejected haviour of the visage,
       Together with all forms, moods, shapes of grief,
       That can denote me truly. These indeed seem,
       For they are actions that a man might play;
       But I have that within which passeth show,
       These but the trappings and the suits of woe.

KING.   'Tis sweet and commendable in your nature, Hamlet,
       To give these mourning duties to your father;
       But, you must know, your father lost a father,
       That father lost, lost his, and the survivor bound
       In filial obligation for some term
       To do obsequious sorrow.[11] But to persever
       In obstinate condolement is a course
       Of impious stubbornness; 'tis unmanly grief;
       It shows a will most incorrect[12] to heaven,
       A heart unfortified, a mind impatient,
       An understanding simple and unschool'd;
       For what we know must be and is as common
       As any the most vulgar[13] thing to sense,

---

[9] *cousin*] close relation.
[10] *vailed*] lowered.
[11] *obsequious sorrow*] i.e., mourning appropriate for obsequies.
[12] *incorrect*] recalcitrant.
[13] *vulgar*] ordinary, commonplace.

Why should we in our peevish opposition
Take it to heart? Fie! 'tis a fault to heaven,
A fault against the dead, a fault to nature,
To reason most absurd, whose common theme
Is death of fathers, and who still[14] hath cried,
From the first corse till he that died today,
'This must be so.' We pray you, throw to earth
This unprevailing[15] woe, and think of us
As of a father; for let the world take note,
You are the most immediate[16] to our throne,
And with no less nobility of love
Than that which dearest father bears his son
Do I impart toward you. For your intent
In going back to school in Wittenberg,
It is most retrograde[17] to our desire,
And we beseech you, bend you to remain
Here in the cheer and comfort of our eye,
Our chiefest courtier, cousin and our son.

QUEEN. Let not thy mother lose her prayers, Hamlet.
     I pray thee, stay with us; go not to Wittenberg.
HAM. I shall in all my best obey you, madam.
KING. Why, 'tis a loving and a fair reply.
     Be as ourself in Denmark. Madam, come;
     This gentle and unforced accord of Hamlet
     Sits smiling to my heart; in grace whereof,
     No jocund health that Denmark drinks today,
     But the great cannon to the clouds shall tell,
     And the King's rouse[18] the heaven shall bruit[19] again,
     Re-speaking earthly thunder. Come away.

              [Flourish. Exeunt all but HAMLET.

HAM. O, that this too too sullied flesh would melt,
     Thaw and resolve itself into a dew,
     Or that the Everlasting had not fix'd
     His canon 'gainst self-slaughter! O God! God!
     How weary, stale, flat and unprofitable
     Seem to me all the uses of this world!

Soliloquy (handwritten note in margin)

[14] *still*] always.
[15] *unprevailing*] unavailing, pointless.
[16] *most immediate*] next in succession.
[17] *retrograde*] contrary.
[18] *rouse*] drink, toast.
[19] *bruit*] announce.

Fie on't! ah fie! 'Tis an unweeded garden
That grows to seed; things rank and gross in nature
Possess it merely.[20] That it should come to this!
But two months dead—nay, not so much, not two—
So excellent a king, that was to this
Hyperion to a satyr, so loving to my mother
That he might not beteem[21] the winds of heaven
Visit her face too roughly. Heaven and earth,
Must I remember? Why, she would hang on him
As if increase of appetite had grown
By what it fed on; and yet, within a month—
Let me not think on't—Frailty, thy name is woman—
A little month, or ere those shoes were old
With which she follow'd my poor father's body,
Like Niobe, all tears—why she, even she—
O God! a beast that wants discourse of reason
Would have mourn'd longer—married with my uncle,
My father's brother, but no more like my father
Than I to Hercules. Within a month,
Ere yet the salt of most unrighteous tears
Had left the flushing in her galled eyes,
She married. O, most wicked speed, to post
With such dexterity to incestuous sheets!
It is not, nor it cannot come to good.
But break, my heart, for I must hold my tongue.

Enter HORATIO, MARCELLUS, *and* BERNARDO.

HOR.   Hail to your lordship.
HAM.   I am glad to see you well.
         Horatio—or I do forget myself.
HOR.   The same, my lord, and your poor servant ever.
HAM.   Sir, my good friend; I'll change that name[22] with you.
         And what make you from Wittenberg, Horatio?—
         Marcellus.
MAR.   My good lord.
HAM.   I am very glad to see you.—[*To* BER.] Good even, sir.—
         But what, in faith, make you from Wittenberg?
HOR.   A truant disposition, good my lord.
HAM.   I would not hear your enemy say so,

---

[20] *merely*] entirely.
[21] *beteem*] permit.
[22] *change that name*] exchange the name "servant."

Nor shall you do my ear that violence,
To make it truster of your own report
Against yourself. I know you are no truant.
But what is your affair in Elsinore?
We'll teach you to drink deep ere you depart.

HOR. My lord, I came to see your father's funeral.

HAM. I pray thee, do not mock me, fellow-student;
I think it was to see my mother's wedding.

HOR. Indeed, my lord, it follow'd hard upon.

HAM. Thrift, thrift, Horatio. The funeral baked meats
Did coldly furnish forth the marriage tables.
Would I had met my dearest[23] foe in heaven
Or ever[24] I had seen that day, Horatio.
My father—Methinks I see my father.

HOR. O where, my lord?

HAM. In my mind's eye, Horatio.

HOR. I saw him once; he was a goodly king.

HAM. He was a man, take him for all in all;
I shall not look upon his like again.

HOR. My lord, I think I saw him yesternight.

HAM. Saw? Who?

HOR. My lord, the King your father.

HAM. The King my father?

HOR. Season your admiration[25] for a while
With an attent ear, till I may deliver,
Upon the witness of these gentlemen,
This marvel to you.

HAM. For God's love, let me hear!

HOR. Two nights together had these gentlemen,
Marcellus and Bernardo, on their watch,
In the dead vast and middle of the night,
Been thus encounter'd. A figure like your father,
Armed at point exactly,[26] cap-à-pie,[27]
Appears before them, and with solemn march
Goes slow and stately by them. Thrice he walk'd
By their oppress'd and fear-surprised eyes
Within his truncheon's length, whilst they, distill'd

---

[23] *dearest*] direst.
[24] *Or ever*] before.
[25] *Season your admiration*] temper your astonishment.
[26] *at point exactly*] correctly.
[27] *cap-à-pie*] head to foot.

Almost to jelly with the act[28] of fear,
Stand dumb, and speak not to him. This to me
In dreadful secrecy impart they did;
And I with them the third night kept the watch,
Where, as they had deliver'd, both in time,
Form of the thing, each word made true and good,
The apparition comes. I knew your father;
These hands are not more like.

HAM.   But where was this?
MAR.   My lord, upon the platform where we watch'd.
HAM.   Did you not speak to it?
HOR.   My lord, I did,
But answer made it none. Yet once methought
It lifted up it head and did address
Itself to motion, like as it would speak.
But even then the morning cock crew loud,
And at the sound it shrunk in haste away
And vanish'd from our sight.

HAM.   'Tis very strange.
HOR.   As I do live, my honour'd lord, 'tis true,
And we did think it writ down in our duty
To let you know of it.

HAM.   Indeed, indeed, sirs; but this troubles me.
Hold you the watch tonight?

MAR. ⎱
BER. ⎰   We do, my lord.

HAM.   Arm'd, say you?

MAR. ⎱
BER. ⎰   Arm'd, my lord.

HAM.   From top to toe?

MAR. ⎱
BER. ⎰   My lord, from head to foot.

HAM.   Then saw you not his face?
HOR.   O, yes, my lord; he wore his beaver[29] up.
HAM.   What look'd he, frowningly?
HOR.   A countenance more in sorrow than in anger.
HAM.   Pale, or red?
HOR.   Nay, very pale.
HAM.   And fix'd his eyes upon you?

---

[28] act] effect.
[29] beaver] visor (covering lower part of the face).

HOR.	Most constantly.
HAM.	I would I had been there.
HOR.	It would have much amazed you.
HAM.	Very like, very like. Stay'd it long?
HOR.	While one with moderate haste might tell a hundred.
MAR. ⎫ BER. ⎭	Longer, longer.
HOR.	Not when I saw't.
HAM.	His beard was grizzled, no?
HOR.	It was as I have seen it in his life, A sable silver'd.
HAM.	I will watch tonight; Perchance 'twill walk again.
HOR.	I warrant it will.
HAM.	If it assume my noble father's person, I'll speak to it, though hell itself should gape And bid me hold my peace. I pray you all, If you have hitherto conceal'd this sight, Let it be tenable in your silence still, And whatsoever else shall hap tonight, Give it an understanding, but no tongue. I will requite your loves. So fare you well. Upon the platform, 'twixt eleven and twelve, I'll visit you.
ALL.	Our duty to your honour.
HAM.	Your loves, as mine to you. Farewell.

          [Exeunt all but HAMLET.

My father's spirit in arms! All is not well.
I doubt[30] some foul play. Would the night were come.
Till then sit still, my soul. Foul deeds will rise,
Though all the earth o'erwhelm them, to men's eyes. *[Exit.*

---

[30] *doubt*] suspect.

SCENE III. *A room in Polonius's house.*

Enter LAERTES *and* OPHELIA.

LAER.   My necessaries are embark'd. Farewell.
        And, sister, as the winds give benefit
        And convoy is assistant,[1] do not sleep,
        But let me hear from you.
OPH.   Do you doubt that?
LAER.   For Hamlet, and the trifling of his favour,
        Hold it a fashion, and a toy in blood,[2]
        A violet in the youth of primy[3] nature,
        Forward,[4] not permanent, sweet, not lasting,
        The perfume and suppliance[5] of a minute,
        No more.
OPH.   No more but so?
LAER.   Think it no more.
        For nature crescent[6] does not grow alone
        In thews[7] and bulk, but, as this temple[8] waxes,
        The inward service of the mind and soul
        Grows wide withal. Perhaps he loves you now,
        And now no soil nor cautel[9] doth besmirch
        The virtue of his will; but you must fear,
        His greatness weigh'd,[10] his will is not his own;
        For he himself is subject to his birth.
        He may not, as unvalued persons do,
        Carve for himself, for on his choice depends
        The safety and health of this whole state;
        And therefore must his choice be circumscribed

---

[1] *convoy is assistant*] means of conveyance are available.
[2] *toy in blood*] amorous whim.
[3] *primy*] flourishing.
[4] *Forward*] premature.
[5] *suppliance*] pastime, gratification.
[6] *crescent*] growing.
[7] *thews*] strength.
[8] *temple*] i.e., human body.
[9] *cautel*] deceit.
[10] *His greatness weigh'd*] his important position being considered.

Unto the voice and yielding[11] of that body
Whereof he is the head. Then if he says he loves you,
It fits your wisdom so far to believe it
As he in his particular act and place
May give his saying deed; which is no further
Than the main[12] voice of Denmark goes withal.
Then weigh what loss your honour may sustain
If with too credent ear you list[13] his songs,
Or lose your heart, or your chaste treasure open
To his unmaster'd importunity.
Fear it, Ophelia, fear it, my dear sister,
And keep you in the rear of your affection,
Out of the shot and danger of desire.
The chariest[14] maid is prodigal enough
If she unmask her beauty to the moon.
Virtue itself 'scapes not calumnious strokes.
The canker galls the infants of the spring
Too oft before their buttons[15] be disclosed,
And in the morn and liquid[16] dew of youth
Contagious blastments[17] are most imminent.
Be wary then; best safety lies in fear.
Youth to itself rebels, though none else near.

OPH.   I shall the effect of this good lesson keep
As watchman to my heart. But, good my brother,
Do not, as some ungracious[18] pastors do,
Show me the steep and thorny way to heaven,
Whilst, like a puff'd and reckless libertine,
Himself the primrose path of dalliance treads
And recks not his own rede.[19]

LAER.   O, fear me not.
I stay too long. But here my father comes.

Enter POLONIUS.

A double blessing is a double grace;

---

[11] *yielding*] consent.
[12] *main*] general.
[13] *list*] listen to.
[14] *chariest*] most modest.
[15] *buttons*] buds.
[16] *liquid*] pure, limpid.
[17] *blastments*] blights.
[18] *ungracious*] impious.
[19] *recks not his own rede*] does not heed his own advice.

	Occasion smiles upon a second leave.
POL.	Yet here, Laertes? Aboard, aboard, for shame!
	The wind sits in the shoulder of your sail,
	And you are stay'd for. There, my blessing with thee.
	And these few precepts in thy memory
	Look thou character.[20] Give thy thoughts no tongue,
	Nor any unproportion'd thought his act.
	Be thou familiar, but by no means vulgar.
	Those friends thou hast, and their adoption tried,[21]
	Grapple them to thy soul with hoops of steel,
	But do not dull thy palm with entertainment
	Of each new-hatch'd unfledged comrade. Beware
	Of entrance to a quarrel; but being in,
	Bear't, that the opposed may beware of thee.
	Give every man thy ear, but few thy voice;
	Take each man's censure,[22] but reserve thy judgement.
	Costly thy habit[23] as thy purse can buy,
	But not express'd in fancy; rich, not gaudy;
	For the apparel oft proclaims the man;
	And they in France of the best rank and station
	Are of a most select and generous chief[24] in that.
	Neither a borrower nor a lender be;
	For loan oft loses both itself and friend,
	And borrowing dulls the edge of husbandry.[25]
	This above all: to thine own self be true,
	And it must follow, as the night the day,
	Thou canst not then be false to any man.
	Farewell. My blessing season this in thee.
LAER.	Most humbly do I take my leave, my lord.
POL.	The time invites you; go, your servants tend.
LAER.	Farewell, Ophelia, and remember well
	What I have said to you.
OPH.	'Tis in my memory lock'd,
	And you yourself shall keep the key of it.
LAER.	Farewell. [*Exit.*
POL.	What is't, Ophelia, he hath said to you?

[20] *character*] inscribe.
[21] *tried*] justified
[22] *censure*] opinion.
[23] *habit*] dress.
[24] *chief*] excellence.
[25] *husbandry*] economy, saving.

OPH.	So please you, something touching the Lord Hamlet.
POL.	Marry, well bethought.
	'Tis told me, he hath very oft of late
	Given private time to you, and you yourself
	Have of your audience been most free and bounteous.
	If it be so—as so 'tis put on[26] me,
	And that in way of caution—I must tell you,
	You do not understand yourself so clearly
	As it behoves my daughter and your honour.
	What is between you? Give me up the truth.
OPH.	He hath, my lord, of late made many tenders
	Of his affection to me.
POL.	Affection? Pooh! You speak like a green girl,
	Unsifted[27] in such perilous circumstance.
	Do you believe his tenders, as you call them?
OPH.	I do not know, my lord, what I should think.
POL.	Marry, I'll teach you. Think yourself a baby,
	That you have ta'en these tenders for true pay,
	Which are not sterling.[28] Tender yourself more dearly;[29]
	Or—not to crack the wind of the poor phrase,
	Running it thus—you'll tender me a fool.
OPH.	My lord, he hath importuned me with love
	In honourable fashion.
POL.	Ay, fashion you may call it. Go to, go to.
OPH.	And hath given countenance[30] to his speech, my lord,
	With almost all the holy vows of heaven.
POL.	Ay, springes[31] to catch woodcocks. I do know,
	When the blood burns, how prodigal the soul
	Lends the tongue vows. These blazes, daughter,
	Giving more light than heat, extinct in both,
	Even in their promise, as it is a-making,
	You must not take for fire. From this time
	Be something scanter of your maiden presence;
	Set your entreatments[32] at a higher rate

[26] *put on*] impressed upon.

[27] *unsifted*] inexperienced.

[28] *sterling*] of genuine value. Polonius is playing on two meanings of "tender": (1) to proffer affection; (2) to pay money.

[29] *Tender . . . dearly*] (1) Take care of yourself; (2) set a higher price on yourself.

[30] *countenance*] authority.

[31] *springes*] snares.

[32] *entreatments*] exchanges.

Than a command to parley.[33] For Lord Hamlet,
Believe so much in him, that he is young,
And with a larger tether may he walk
Than may be given you. In few,[34] Ophelia,
Do not believe his vows; for they are brokers,[35]
Not of that dye which their investments[36] show,
But mere implorators[37] of unholy suits,
Breathing[38] like sanctified and pious bawds,
The better to beguile. This is for all:
I would not, in plain terms, from this time forth,
Have you so slander any moment leisure,
As to give words or talk with the Lord Hamlet.
Look to't, I charge you. Come your ways.

OPH.   I shall obey, my lord.   [*Exeunt.*

SCENE IV. *The platform.*

Enter HAMLET, HORATIO, *and* MARCELLUS.

HAM.   The air bites shrewdly;[1] it is very cold.
HOR.   It is a nipping and an eager[2] air.
HAM.   What hour now?
HOR.   I think it lacks of twelve.
MAR.   No, it is struck.
HOR.   Indeed? I heard it not. It then draws near the season
         Wherein the spirit held his wont to walk.
             [*A flourish of trumpets, and ordnance shot off within.*
         What doth this mean, my lord?
HAM.   The King doth wake tonight and takes his rouse,[3]

[33] *command to parley*] invitation to talk.
[34] *In few*] in short.
[35] *brokers*] go-betweens, panders.
[36] *investments*] clothes.
[37] *implorators*] implorers.
[38] *Breathing*] speaking.

---

[1] *shrewdly*] keenly.
[2] *eager*] biting, bitter.
[3] *takes his rouse*] carouses.

Keeps wassail,[4] and the swaggering upspring[5] reels;
And as he drains his draughts of Rhenish down,
The kettle-drum and trumpet thus bray out
The triumph[6] of his pledge.

HOR.   Is it a custom?
HAM.   Ay, marry, is't;
But to my mind, though I am native here
And to the manner born, it is a custom
More honour'd in the breach than the observance.
This heavy-headed revel east and west
Makes us traduced and tax'd of[7] other nations.
They clepe[8] us drunkards, and with swinish phrase
Soil our addition;[9] and indeed it takes
From our achievements, though perform'd at height,
The pith and marrow of our attribute.[10]
So, oft it chances in particular men,[11]
That for some vicious mole of nature in them,
As in their birth—wherein they are not guilty,
Since nature cannot choose his origin—
By the o'ergrowth of some complexion,[12]
Oft breaking down the pales[13] and forts of reason,
Or by some habit that too much o'er-leavens[14]
The form of plausive[15] manners, that these men—
Carrying, I say, the stamp of one defect,
Being Nature's livery, or Fortune's star—
Their virtues else—be they as pure as grace,
As infinite as man may undergo—[16]
Shall in the general censure take corruption
From that particular fault. The dram of evil
Doth all the noble substance of a doubt[17]

[4] *keeps wassail*] carouses.
[5] *upspring*] wild German dance.
[6] *triumph*] celebration.
[7] *tax'd of*] censured by.
[8] *clepe*] call.
[9] *with swinish . . . addition*] by calling us swine sully our reputation.
[10] *attribute*] reputation.
[11] *particular men*] individuals.
[12] *complexion*] humor, trait.
[13] *pales*] palings.
[14] *o'er-leavens*] corrupts.
[15] *plausive*] pleasing.
[16] *undergo*] sustain.
[17] *of a doubt*] the text seems to be corrupt here.

To his own scandal.

Enter GHOST.

HOR.   Look, my lord, it comes.
HAM.   Angels and ministers of grace defend us!
            Be thou a spirit of health or goblin damn'd,
            Bring with thee airs from heaven or blasts from hell,
            Be thy intents wicked or charitable,
            Thou comest in such a questionable[18] shape
            That I will speak to thee. I'll call thee Hamlet,
            King, father, royal Dane. O, answer me!
            Let me not burst in ignorance, but tell
            Why thy canonized bones, hearsed[19] in death,
            Have burst their cerements, why the sepulchre,
            Wherein we saw thee quietly inurn'd,
            Hath oped his ponderous and marble jaws,
            To cast thee up again. What may this mean,
            That thou, dead corse, again, in complete steel,
            Revisits thus the glimpses of the moon,
            Making night hideous, and we fools of nature[20]
            So horridly to shake our disposition
            With thoughts beyond the reaches of our souls?
            Say, why is this? Wherefore? What should we do?
                                    [GHOST *beckons* HAMLET.
HOR.   It beckons you to go away with it,
            As if it some impartment[21] did desire
            To you alone.
MAR.   Look, with what courteous action
            It waves you to a more removed ground.
            But do not go with it.
HOR.   No, by no means.
HAM.   It will not speak. Then I will follow it.
HOR.   Do not, my lord.
HAM.   Why, what should be the fear?
            I do not set my life at a pin's fee;
            And for my soul, what can it do to that,
            Being a thing immortal as itself?
            It waves me forth again. I'll follow it.

18 *questionable*] inviting question.
19 *hearsed*] coffined.
20 *fools of nature*] beings limited to the understanding of things natural.
21 *impartment*] communication.

HOR.   What if it tempt you toward the flood, my lord,
           Or to the dreadful summit of the cliff
           That beetles o'er[22] his base into the sea,
           And there assume some other horrible form,
           Which might deprive your sovereignty of reason
           And draw you into madness? Think of it.
           The very place puts toys of desperation,[23]
           Without more motive, into every brain
           That looks so many fathoms to the sea
           And hears it roar beneath.

HAM.   It waves me still.
           Go on; I'll follow thee.

MAR.   You shall not go, my lord.

HAM.   Hold off your hands.

HOR.   Be ruled; you shall not go.

HAM.   My fate cries out,
           And makes each petty artery in this body
           As hardy as the Nemean lion's[24] nerve.
           Still am I call'd. Unhand me, gentlemen.
           By heaven, I'll make a ghost of him that lets[25] me.
           I say, away! Go on; I'll follow thee.
                        [*Exeunt* GHOST *and* HAMLET.

HOR.   He waxes desperate with imagination.

MAR.   Let's follow. 'Tis not fit thus to obey him.

HOR.   Have after. To what issue will this come?

MAR.   Something is rotten in the state of Denmark.

HOR.   Heaven will direct it.

MAR.   Nay, let's follow him.   [*Exeunt.*

---

[22] *beetles o'er*] overhangs.
[23] *toys of desperation*] freakish thoughts of suicide.
[24] *Nemean lion's*] The Nemean lion was slain by Hercules as the first of his twelve labors.
[25] *lets*] hinders.

SCENE V. *Another part of the platform.*

Enter GHOST *and* HAMLET.

HAM.	Whither wilt thou lead me? Speak; I'll go no further.
GHOST.	Mark me.
HAM.	I will.
GHOST.	My hour is almost come,

When I to sulphurous and tormenting flames
Must render up myself.

HAM.   Alas, poor ghost!

GHOST. Pity me not, but lend thy serious hearing
To what I shall unfold.

HAM.   Speak; I am bound to hear.

GHOST. So art thou to revenge, when thou shalt hear.

HAM. What?

GHOST. I am thy father's spirit,
Doom'd for a certain term to walk the night,
And for the day confined to fast in fires,
Till the foul crimes done in my days of nature
Are burnt and purged away. But that I am forbid
To tell the secrets of my prison-house,
I could a tale unfold whose lightest word
Would harrow up thy soul, freeze thy young blood,
Make thy two eyes, like stars, start from their spheres,
Thy knotted and combined locks to part
And each particular hair to stand an end,
Like quills upon the fretful porpentine.
But this eternal blazon[1] must not be
To ears of flesh and blood. List, list, O, list!
If thou didst ever thy dear father love—

HAM. O God!

GHOST. Revenge his foul and most unnatural murder.

HAM. Murder?

GHOST. Murder most foul, as in the best it is,
But this most foul, strange, and unnatural.

HAM. Haste me to know't, that I, with wings as swift

---

[1] *eternal blazon*] description of the afterlife.

GHOST.

As meditation or the thoughts of love,
May sweep to my revenge.
                I find thee apt;
And duller shouldst thou be than the fat weed
That roots itself in ease on Lethe[2] wharf,
Wouldst thou not stir in this. Now, Hamlet, hear.
'Tis given out that, sleeping in my orchard,[3]
A serpent stung me; so the whole ear of Denmark
Is by a forged process[4] of my death
Rankly abused. But know, thou noble youth,
The serpent that did sting thy father's life
Now wears his crown.

Biblical allusion

HAM.   O my prophetic soul! My uncle!

GHOST.   Ay, that incestuous, that adulterate beast,
With witchcraft of his wit, with traitorous gifts—
O wicked wit and gifts that have the power
So to seduce!—won to his shameful lust
The will of my most seeming-virtuous queen.
O Hamlet, what a falling off was there!
From me, whose love was of that dignity
That it went hand in hand even with the vow
I made to her in marriage; and to decline
Upon a wretch, whose natural gifts were poor
To those of mine.
But virtue, as it never will be moved,
Though lewdness court it in a shape of heaven,
So lust, though to a radiant angel link'd,
Will sate itself in a celestial bed
And prey on garbage.
But, soft! methinks I scent the morning air;
Brief let me be. Sleeping within my orchard,
My custom always of the afternoon,
Upon my secure[5] hour thy uncle stole,
With juice of cursed hebenon in a vial,
And in the porches of my ears did pour
The leperous distilment, whose effect
Holds such an enmity with blood of man
That swift as quicksilver it courses through

---

[2] *Lethe*] the river of forgetfulness in the underworld.
[3] *orchard*] garden.
[4] *process*] account.
[5] *secure*] free from apprehension, unsuspecting.

The natural gates and alleys of the body,
And with a sudden vigour it doth posset[6]
And curd, like eager[7] droppings into milk,
The thin and wholesome blood. So did it mine;
And a most instant tetter[8] bark'd about,
Most lazar-like,[9] with vile and loathsome crust,
All my smooth body.
Thus was I, sleeping, by a brother's hand
Of life, of crown, of queen, at once dispatch'd,[10]
Cut off even in the blossoms of my sin,
Unhousel'd, disappointed, unaneled,[11]
No reckoning made, but sent to my account
With all my imperfections on my head.
O, horrible! O, horrible! most horrible!
If thou hast nature in thee, bear it not.
Let not the royal bed of Denmark be
A couch for luxury[12] and damned incest.
But, howsoever thou pursuest this act,
Taint not thy mind, nor let thy soul contrive
Against thy mother aught. Leave her to heaven,
And to those thorns that in her bosom lodge,
To prick and sting her. Fare thee well at once.
The glow-worm shows the matin[13] to be near,
And 'gins to pale his uneffectual fire.
Adieu, adieu, adieu. Remember me.   *[Exit.*

HAM.   O all you host of heaven! O earth! What else?
And shall I couple[14] hell? O, fie! Hold, hold, my heart;
And you, my sinews, grow not instant old,
But bear me stiffly up. Remember thee?
Ay, thou poor ghost, while memory holds a seat
In this distracted globe.[15] Remember thee?
Yea, from the table[16] of my memory

---

[6] *posset*] curdle, in the manner of a posset (a hot drink of spiced milk mixed with wine or ale).
[7] *eager*] sour.
[8] *tetter*] skin disease.
[9] *lazar-like*] like a leper.
[10] *dispatch'd*] deprived.
[11] *Unhousel'd, disappointed, unaneled*] not having received the sacrament, unprepared and not having received extreme unction.
[12] *luxury*] lechery.
[13] *matin*] morning.
[14] *couple*] include.
[15] *globe*] head.
[16] *table*] (writing) tablet.

I'll wipe away all trivial fond[17] records,
All saws[18] of books, all forms, all pressures[19] past,
That youth and observation copied there;
And thy commandment all alone shall live
Within the book and volume of my brain,
Unmix'd with baser matter. Yes, by heaven!
O most pernicious woman!
O villain, villain, smiling, damned villain!
My tables[20]—meet it is I set it down
That one may smile, and smile, and be a villain;
At least I'm sure it may be so in Denmark.   [*Writing.*
So, uncle, there you are. Now to my word.[21]
It is 'Adieu, adieu, remember me.'
I have sworn't.

HOR. ⎱
MAR. ⎰   [*Within*] My lord, my lord.

Enter HORATIO *and* MARCELLUS.

MAR.   Lord Hamlet.
HOR.   Heaven secure[22] him!
HAM.   So be it.
MAR.   Illo, ho, ho, my lord.
HAM.   Hillo, ho, ho, boy. Come, bird, come.
MAR.   How is't, my noble lord?
HOR.   What news, my lord?
HAM.   O, wonderful!
HOR.   Good my lord, tell it.
HAM.   No; you will reveal it.
HOR.   Not I, my lord, by heaven.
MAR.   Nor I, my lord.
HAM.   How say you, then; would heart of man once think it?
        But you'll be secret?

HOR. ⎱
MAR. ⎰   Ay, by heaven, my lord.

HAM.   There's ne'er a villain dwelling in all Denmark
        But he's an arrant knave.
HOR.   There needs no ghost, my lord, come from the grave

---

[17] *fond*] foolish.
[18] *saws*] maxims.
[19] *pressures*] impressions.
[20] *tables*] portable writing-tablets.
[21] *word*] watchword, motto.
[22] *secure*] protect.

	To tell us this.
HAM.	Why, right, you are i' the right;

HAM.   Why, right, you are i' the right;
And so, without more circumstance at all,
I hold it fit that we shake hands and part,
You, as your business and desire shall point you—
For every man hath business and desire,
Such as it is—and for my own poor part,
Look you, I'll go pray.

HOR. These are but wild and whirling words, my lord.

HAM. I'm sorry they offend you, heartily;
Yes, faith, heartily.

HOR.   There's no offence, my lord.

HAM. Yes, by Saint Patrick,[23] but there is, Horatio,
And much offence too. Touching this vision here,
It is an honest[24] ghost, that let me tell you.
For your desire to know what is between us,
O'ermaster't as you may. And now, good friends,
As you are friends, scholars and soldiers,
Give me one poor request.

HOR. What is't, my lord? We will.

HAM. Never make known what you have seen tonight.

HOR. ⎫
MAR. ⎭ My lord, we will not.

HAM.   Nay, but swear't.

HOR.   In faith,
My lord, not I.

MAR.   Nor I, my lord, in faith.

HAM. Upon my sword.[25]

MAR.   We have sworn, my lord, already.

HAM. Indeed, upon my sword, indeed.

GHOST. [*Beneath*] Swear.

HAM. Ah, ha, boy, say'st thou so? Art thou there, truepenny?[26]
Come on. You hear this fellow in the cellarage.
Consent to swear.

HOR.   Propose the oath, my lord.

HAM. Never to speak of this that you have seen,
Swear by my sword.

GHOST. [*Beneath*] Swear.

---

[23] *Saint Patrick*] The Irish saint was said to be the keeper of Purgatory.
[24] *honest*] real.
[25] *sword*] The sword's hilt forms a cross.
[26] *truepenny*] honest fellow.

HAM.   *Hic et ubique?*[27] Then we'll shift our ground.
         Come hither, gentlemen,
         And lay your hands again upon my sword.
         Never to speak of this that you have heard,
         Swear by my sword.

GHOST.   [*Beneath*] Swear.

HAM.   Well said, old mole. Canst work i' the earth so fast?
         A worthy pioner![28] Once more remove, good friends.

HOR.   O day and night, but this is wondrous strange.

HAM.   And therefore as a stranger give it welcome.
         There are more things in heaven and earth, Horatio,
         Than are dreamt of in your philosophy.
         But come;
         Here, as before, never, so help you mercy,
         How strange or odd soe'er I bear myself—
         As I perchance hereafter shall think meet
         To put an antic[29] disposition on—
         That you, at such times seeing me, never shall,
         With arms encumber'd[30] thus, or this head-shake,
         Or by pronouncing of some doubtful phrase,
         As 'Well, we know,' or 'We could, an if we would,'
         Or 'If we list to speak,' or 'There be, an if they might,'
         Or such ambiguous giving out,[31] to note[32]
         That you know aught of me; this not to do,
         So grace and mercy at your most need help you,
         Swear.

GHOST.   [*Beneath*] Swear.

HAM.   Rest, rest, perturbed spirit. [*They swear.*] So, gentlemen,
         With all my love I do commend me to you;
         And what so poor a man as Hamlet is
         May do to express his love and friending to you,
         God willing, shall not lack. Let us go in together;
         And still[33] your fingers on your lips, I pray.
         The time is out of joint. O cursed spite,
         That ever I was born to set it right!
         Nay, come, let's go together.   [*Exeunt.*

---

[27] *Hic et ubique*] here and everywhere.
[28] *pioner*] miner, digger.
[29] *antic*] odd, strange.
[30] *encumber'd*] folded.
[31] *giving out*] intimation.
[32] *note*] show.
[33] *still*] always.

ACT II.

SCENE I. *A room in Polonius's house.*

Enter POLONIUS *and* REYNALDO.

POL.   Give him this money and these notes, Reynaldo.
REY.   I will, my lord.
POL.   You shall do marvellous wisely, good Reynaldo,
       Before you visit him, to make inquire
       Of his behaviour.
REY.   My lord, I did intend it.
POL.   Marry, well said, very well said. Look you, sir,
       Inquire me first what Danskers[1] are in Paris,
       And how, and who, what means, and where they keep,[2]
       What company, at what expense, and finding
       By this encompassment[3] and drift of question
       That they do know my son, come you more nearer
       Than your particular demands will touch it.[4]
       Take[5] you, as 'twere, some distant knowledge of him,
       As thus, 'I know his father and his friends,
       And in part him.' Do you mark this, Reynaldo?
REY.   Ay, very well, my lord.
POL.   'And in part him; but,' you may say, 'not well;
       But if't be he I mean, he's very wild,
       Addicted so and so;' and there put on him
       What forgeries you please—marry, none so rank
       As may dishonour him, take heed of that—
       But, sir, such wanton, wild and usual slips

---

[1] *Danskers*] Danes.
[2] *keep*] dwell.
[3] *encompassment*] roundabout way of talking.
[4] *come . . . it*] you will find out more than by asking direct questions.
[5] *Take*] assume.

As are companions noted and most known
To youth and liberty.

REY.   As gaming, my lord?

POL.   Ay, or drinking, fencing, swearing, quarrelling,
Drabbing.[6] You may go so far.

REY.   My lord, that would dishonour him.

POL.   'Faith, no; as you may season it in the charge.
You must not put another scandal on him,
That he is open to incontinency.[7]
That's not my meaning; but breathe his faults so quaintly[8]
That they may seem the taints of liberty,
The flash and outbreak of a fiery mind,
A savageness in unreclaimed[9] blood,
Of general assault.[10]

REY.   But, my good lord—

POL.   Wherefore should you do this?

REY.   Ay, my lord,
I would know that.

POL.   Marry, sir, here's my drift,
And I believe it is a fetch of warrant:[11]
You laying these slight sullies on my son,
As 'twere a thing a little soil'd i' the working,
Mark you,
Your party in converse,[12] him you would sound,
Having ever seen in the prenominate[13] crimes
The youth you breathe of guilty, be assured
He closes[14] with you in this consequence:
'Good sir,' or so, or 'friend,' or 'gentleman,'
According to the phrase or the addition[15]
Of man and country.

REY.   Very good, my lord.

POL.   And then, sir, does he this—he does—what was I about to say?
By the mass, I was about to say something. Where did I leave?

---

[6] *Drabbing*] whoring.
[7] *incontinency*] habitual licentiousness.
[8] *quaintly*] skillfully, delicately.
[9] *unreclaimed*] untamed.
[10] *Of general assault*] to which all young men are liable.
[11] *fetch of warrant*] justified stratagem.
[12] *converse*] conversation.
[13] *prenominate*] aforementioned.
[14] *closes*] agrees.
[15] *addition*] title.

REY.   At 'closes in the consequence,' at 'friend or so,' and 'gentle-
           man.'

POL.   At 'closes in the consequence,' ay, marry.
           He closes with you thus: 'I know the gentleman;
           I saw him yesterday,' or 't'other day,'
           Or then, or then, with such, or such, 'and, as you say,
           There was a[16] gaming,' 'there o'ertook in's rouse,'[17]
           'There falling out at tennis;' or perchance,
           'I saw him enter such a house of sale,'
           Videlicet,[18] a brothel, or so forth.
           See you now;
           Your bait of falsehood takes this carp of truth;
           And thus do we of wisdom and of reach,[19]
           With windlasses[20] and with assays of bias,[21]
           By indirections find directions out.
           So, by my former lecture and advice,
           Shall you my son. You have me, have you not?

REY.   My lord, I have.

POL.   God be wi' ye. Fare ye well.

REY.   Good my lord.

POL.   Observe his inclination in yourself.[22]

REY.   I shall, my lord.

POL.   And let him ply his music.

REY.   Well, my lord.

POL.   Farewell.   [*Exit* REYNALDO.

Enter OPHELIA.

           How now, Ophelia, what's the matter?

OPH.   O, my lord, my lord, I have been so affrighted.

POL.   With what, i' the name of God?

OPH.   My lord, as I was sewing in my closet,
           Lord Hamlet, with his doublet all unbraced,[23]
           No hat upon his head, his stockings foul'd,
           Ungarter'd and down-gyved[24] to his ankle,

---

[16] *a*] he.

[17] *o'ertook in's rouse*] overcome by drinking.

[18] *Videlicet*] namely.

[19] *reach*] ability.

[20] *windlasses*] indirect advances.

[21] *assays of bias*] assays that resemble the curved path of a bowling ball

[22] *Observe . . . yourself*](?) Behave as he does.

[23] *unbraced*] unbuttoned.

[24] *down-gyved*] fallen down and thereby resembling gyves (fetters).

        Pale as his shirt, his knees knocking each other,
        And with a look so piteous in purport
        As if he had been loosed out of hell
        To speak of horrors, he comes before me.

POL.   Mad for thy love?

OPH.   My lord, I do not know,
        But truly I do fear it.

POL.   What said he?

OPH.   He took me by the wrist and held me hard;
        Then goes he to the length of all his arm,[25]
        And with his other hand thus o'er his brow,
        He falls to such perusal of my face
        As he would draw it. Long stay'd he so.
        At last, a little shaking of mine arm,
        And thrice his head thus waving up and down,
        He raised a sigh so piteous and profound
        As it did seem to shatter all his bulk[26]
        And end his being. That done, he lets me go,
        And with his head over his shoulder turn'd,
        He seem'd to find his way without his eyes;
        For out o' doors he went without their helps,
        And to the last bended their light on me.

POL.   Come, go with me. I will go seek the King.
        This is the very ecstasy[27] of love,
        Whose violent property fordoes itself[28]
        And leads the will to desperate undertakings
        As oft as any passion under heaven
        That does afflict our natures. I am sorry.
        What, have you given him any hard words of late?

OPH.   No, my good lord, but, as you did command,
        I did repel his letters and denied
        His access to me.

POL.   That hath made him mad.
        I am sorry that with better heed and judgement
        I had not quoted[29] him. I fear'd he did but trifle
        And meant to wrack thee. But beshrew my jealousy![30]

---

[25] *goes . . . arm*] withdraws to arm's length.
[26] *bulk*] body, in particular the trunk.
[27] *ecstasy*] madness.
[28] *Whose . . . itself*] the violent nature of which destroys itself.
[29] *quoted*] observed.
[30] *jealousy*] suspicion.

By heaven, it is as proper to our age
To cast beyond ourselves in our opinions
As it is common for the younger sort
To lack discretion. Come, go we to the King.
This must be known, which, being kept close, might move
More grief to hide than hate to utter love.[31]
Come.   [*Exeunt.*

SCENE II. *A room in the castle.*

Flourish. Enter KING, QUEEN, ROSENCRANTZ, GUILDENSTERN, *and*
Attendants.

KING.   Welcome, dear Rosencrantz and Guildenstern.
        Moreover[1] that we much did long to see you,
        The need we have to use you did provoke
        Our hasty sending. Something have you heard
        Of Hamlet's transformation—so call it,
        Sith[2] nor the exterior nor the inward man
        Resembles that it was. What it should be,
        More than his father's death, that thus hath put him
        So much from the understanding of himself,
        I cannot dream of. I entreat you both
        That, being of so young days brought up with him
        And sith so neighbour'd to his youth and haviour,
        That you vouchsafe your rest[3] here in our court
        Some little time: so by your companies
        To draw him on to pleasures, and to gather
        So much as from occasion[4] you may glean,
        Whether aught to us unknown afflicts him thus
        That open'd lies within our remedy.
QUEEN. Good gentlemen, he hath much talk'd of you,

[31] *might move . . . love*] might cause more grief by being concealed than hatred by being
exposed as love.

[1] *Moreover*] besides the fact.
[2] *Sith*] since.
[3] *vouchsafe your rest*] agree to stay.
[4] *occasion*] opportunity.

And sure I am two men there are not living
To whom he more adheres. If it will please you
To show us so much gentry[5] and good will
As to expend your time with us awhile
For the supply and profit[6] of our hope,
Your visitation shall receive such thanks
As fits a king's remembrance.

Ros.   Both your Majesties
Might, by the sovereign power you have of us,
Put your dread pleasures more into command
Than to entreaty.

GUIL.   But we both obey,
And here give up ourselves, in the full bent[7]   *Servants of*
To lay our service freely at your feet,   *Jesus*
To be commanded.

KING.   Thanks, Rosencrantz and gentle Guildenstern.
QUEEN.   Thanks, Guildenstern and gentle Rosencrantz.
And I beseech you instantly to visit
My too much changed son. Go, some of you,
And bring these gentlemen where Hamlet is.

GUIL.   Heavens make our presence and our practices
Pleasant and helpful to him.

QUEEN.   Ay, amen.
[*Exeunt* ROSENCRANTZ, GUILDENSTERN, *and some* Attendants.

Enter POLONIUS.

POL.   The ambassadors from Norway, my good lord,
Are joyfully return'd.
KING.   Thou still[8] hast been the father of good news.
POL.   Have I, my lord? I assure my good liege,
I hold my duty as I hold my soul,
Both to my God and to my gracious King.
And I do think, or else this brain of mine
Hunts not the trail of policy so sure
As it hath used to do, that I have found
The very cause of Hamlet's lunacy.
KING.   O, speak of that; that do I long to hear.
POL.   Give first admittance to the ambassadors.

---

[5] *gentry*] courtesy.
[6] *supply and profit*] support and fulfillment.
[7] *in the full bent*] to the utmost extent.
[8] *still*] always.

               My news shall be the fruit to that great feast.

KING.   Thyself do grace to them, and bring them in.

                                      [*Exit* POLONIUS.

               He tells me, my dear Gertrude, he hath found

               The head and source of all your son's distemper.

QUEEN.   I doubt[9] it is no other but the main:

               His father's death and our o'erhasty marriage.

KING.   Well, we shall sift him.[10]

Enter POLONIUS, *with* VOLTIMAND *and* CORNELIUS.

                        Welcome, my good friends.

               Say, Voltimand, what from our brother Norway?

VOLT.   Most fair return of greetings and desires.

               Upon our first,[11] he sent out to suppress

               His nephew's levies, which to him appear'd

               To be a preparation 'gainst the Polack,[12]

               But better look'd into, he truly found

               It was against your Highness; whereat grieved,

               That so his sickness, age and impotence

               Was falsely borne in hand,[13] sends out arrests

               On Fortinbras; which he, in brief, obeys,

               Receives rebuke from Norway, and in fine[14]

               Makes vow before his uncle never more

               To give the assay of arms[15] against your Majesty.

               Whereon old Norway, overcome with joy,

               Gives him three thousand crowns in annual fee

               And his commission to employ those soldiers,

               So levied as before, against the Polack,

               With an entreaty, herein further shown,   [*Giving a paper.*

               That it might please you to give quiet pass

               Through your dominions for this enterprise,

               On such regards of safety and allowance[16]

---

[9] *doubt*] suspect.

[10] *sift him*] question him (Polonius).

[11] *our first*] i.e., our first mentioning the actions of Fortinbras.

[12] *the Polack*] the King of Poland.

[13] *borne in hand*] abused, deluded.

[14] *in fine*] in the end.

[15] *assay of arms*] attack.

[16] *safety and allowance*] safety of Denmark and permission for the Norwegian troops to pass through.

.As therein are set down.

KING.   It likes us well,
And at our more consider'd time[17] we'll read,
Answer, and think upon this business.
Meantime we thank you for your well-took labour.
Go to your rest; at night we'll feast together.
Most welcome home.   [*Exeunt* VOLTIMAND *and* CORNELIUS.

POL.   This business is well ended.
My liege, and madam, to expostulate
What majesty should be, what duty is,
Why day is day, night night, and time is time,
Were nothing but to waste night, day and time.
Therefore, since brevity is the soul of wit
And tediousness the limbs and outward flourishes,
I will be brief. Your noble son is mad.
Mad call I it; for, to define true madness,
What is't but to be nothing else but mad?
But let that go.

QUEEN.   More matter, with less art.

POL.   Madam, I swear I use no art at all.
That he is mad, 'tis true; 'tis true 'tis pity;
And pity 'tis 'tis true—a foolish figure;
But farewell it, for I will use no art.
Mad let us grant him then. And now remains
That we find out the cause of this effect,
Or rather say, the cause of this defect,
For this effect defective comes by cause.
Thus it remains and the remainder thus:
Perpend;[18]
I have a daughter—have while she is mine—
Who in her duty and obedience, mark,
Hath given me this. Now gather and surmise.   [*Reads.*

To the celestial, and my soul's idol, the most beautified Ophelia—

That's an ill phrase, a vile phrase; 'beautified' is a vile phrase.
    But you shall hear: [*Reads.*

In her excellent white bosom, these, &c.

QUEEN. Came this from Hamlet to her?
POL.   Good madam, stay awhile. I will be faithful.   [*Reads.*

---

[17] *more consider'd time*] convenience.
[18] *Perpend*] consider.

> Doubt thou the stars are fire,
> Doubt that the sun doth move,
> Doubt[19] truth to be a liar,
> But never doubt I love.

O dear Ophelia, I am ill at these numbers.[20] I have not art to reckon[21] my groans. But that I love thee best, O most best, believe it. Adieu.

Thine evermore, most dear lady, whilst this
machine[22] is to him, HAMLET.

This in obedience hath my daughter shown me;
And more above, hath his solicitings,
As they fell out by time, by means and place,
All given to mine ear.

KING.   But how hath she
Received his love?

POL.   What do you think of me?

KING. As of a man faithful and honourable.

POL. I would fain prove so. But what might you think,
When I had seen this hot love on the wing—
As I perceived it, I must tell you that,
Before my daughter told me—what might you,
Or my dear Majesty your queen here, think,
If I had play'd the desk or table-book,[23]
Or given my heart a winking,[24] mute and dumb,
Or look'd upon this love with idle sight;[25]
What might you think? No, I went round[26] to work,
And my young mistress thus I did bespeak:
'Lord Hamlet is a prince, out of thy star.
This must not be.' And then I prescripts gave her,
That she should lock herself from his resort,
Admit no messengers, receive no tokens.
Which done, she took the fruits of my advice;
And he, repulsed—a short tale to make—
Fell into a sadness, then into a fast,
Thence to a watch,[27] thence into a weakness,

---

[19] *Doubt*] suspect.
[20] *ill at these numbers*] not gifted in versifying.
[21] *reckon*] (1) count; (2) put into verse.
[22] *machine*] body.
[23] *play'd . . . table-book*] served as a go-between.
[24] *given . . . winking*] shut my eyes deliberately.
[25] *idle sight*] thoughtlessly.
[26] *round*] straight.
[27] *a watch*] insomnia.

Thence to a lightness,[28] and by this declension[29]
Into the madness wherein now he raves
And all we mourn for.

KING.   Do you think 'tis this?

QUEEN.   It may be; very like.

POL.   Hath there been such a time—I'ld fain know that—
That I have positively said ' 'Tis so,'
When it proved otherwise?

KING.   Not that I know.

POL.   [*Pointing to his head and shoulder*] Take this from this, if this
        be otherwise.
If circumstances lead me, I will find
Where truth is hid, though it were hid indeed
Within the centre.[30]

KING.   How may we try it further?

POL.   You know, sometimes he walks four hours together
Here in the lobby.

QUEEN.   So he does, indeed.

POL.   At such a time I'll loose my daughter to him.
Be you and I behind an arras[31] then;
Mark the encounter. If he love her not,
And be not from his reason fall'n thereon,[32]
Let me be no assistant for a state,
But keep a farm and carters.

KING.   We will try it.

QUEEN.   But look where sadly the poor wretch comes reading.

POL.   Away, I do beseech you both, away.
I'll board[33] him presently.[34] O, give me leave.

                    [*Exeunt* KING, QUEEN, *and* Attendants.

Enter HAMLET, *reading.*

How does my good Lord Hamlet?

HAM.   Well, God-a-mercy.

POL.   Do you know me, my lord?

HAM.   Excellent well. You are a fishmonger.

POL.   Not I, my lord.

---

[28] *lightness*] lightheadedness, mental derangement.
[29] *declension*] deterioration.
[30] *centre*] i.e., of the earth.
[31] *arras*] tapestry, named after the French town of Arras.
[32] *thereon*] on that account.
[33] *board*] accost, address.
[34] *presently*] immediately.

HAM.   Then I would you were so honest a man.

POL.   Honest, my lord?

HAM.   Ay, sir. To be honest, as this world goes, is to be one man picked out of ten thousand.

POL.   That's very true, my lord.

HAM.   For if the sun breed maggots in a dead dog, being a good kissing carrion[35]—Have you a daughter?

POL.   I have, my lord.

HAM.   Let her not walk i' the sun. Conception[36] is a blessing, but as your daughter may conceive—friend, look to't.

POL.   [Aside] How say you by that? Still[37] harping on my daughter. Yet he knew me not at first; he said I was a fishmonger. He is far gone. And truly in my youth I suffered much extremity for love, very near this. I'll speak to him again.—What do you read, my lord?

HAM.   Words, words, words.

POL.   What is the matter, my lord?

HAM.   Between who?

POL.   I mean, the matter that you read, my lord.

HAM.   Slanders, sir. For the satirical rogue says here that old men have grey beards, that their faces are wrinkled, their eyes purging[38] thick amber and plum-tree gum, and that they have a plentiful lack of wit, together with most weak hams—all which, sir, though I most powerfully and potently believe, yet I hold it not honesty[39] to have it thus set down; for yourself, sir, shall grow old as I am, if like a crab you could go backward.

POL.   [Aside] Though this be madness, yet there is method in't.— Will you walk out of the air, my lord?

HAM.   Into my grave?

POL.   Indeed, that's out of the air. [Aside] How pregnant sometimes his replies are!—a happiness that often madness hits on, which reason and sanity could not so prosperously be delivered of. I will leave him, and suddenly[40] contrive the means of meeting between him and my daughter.—My honourable lord, I will take my leave of you.

---

[35] *a good kissing carrion*] carrion good for kissing. "Carrion" can also have the meaning "live flesh."

[36] *Conception*] (1) forming concepts; (2) becoming pregnant.

[37] *Still*] always.

[38] *purging*] discharging.

[39] *honesty*] decency.

[40] *suddenly*] immediately.

HAM.	You cannot, sir, take from me anything that I will more willingly part withal—except my life, except my life, except my life.
POL.	Fare you well, my lord.
HAM.	These tedious old fools!

Enter ROSENCRANTZ *and* GUILDENSTERN.

POL.	You go to seek the Lord Hamlet. There he is.
ROS.	[*To Polonius*] God save you, sir. [*Exit* POLONIUS.
GUIL.	My honoured lord.
ROS.	My most dear lord.
HAM.	My excellent good friends. How dost thou, Guildenstern? Ah, Rosencrantz. Good lads, how do you both?
ROS.	As the indifferent[41] children of the earth.
GUIL.	Happy, in that we are not over-happy; on Fortune's cap we are not the very button.
HAM.	Nor the soles of her shoe?
ROS.	Neither, my lord.
HAM.	Then you live about her waist, or in the middle of her favours?
GUIL.	Faith, her privates[42] we.
HAM.	In the secret parts of Fortune? O, most true; she is a strumpet. What's the news?
ROS.	None, my lord; but that the world's grown honest.
HAM.	Then is doomsday near. But your news is not true. Let me question more in particular. What have you, my good friends, deserved at the hands of Fortune that she sends you to prison hither?
GUIL.	Prison, my lord?
HAM.	Denmark's a prison.
ROS.	Then is the world one.
HAM.	A goodly one, in which there are many confines, wards and dungeons, Denmark being one o' the worst.
ROS.	We think not so, my lord.
HAM.	Why, then 'tis none to you; for there is nothing either good or bad but thinking makes it so. To me it is a prison.
ROS.	Why, then your ambition makes it one: 'tis too narrow for your mind.
HAM.	O God, I could be bounded in a nutshell and count myself a king of infinite space were it not that I have bad dreams.

[41] *indifferent*] ordinary.
[42] *privates*] (1) persons not holding a public office; (2) genitalia.

GUIL.	Which dreams indeed are ambition; for the very substance of the ambitious is merely the shadow of a dream.
HAM.	A dream itself is but a shadow.
ROS.	Truly, and I hold ambition of so airy and light a quality that it is but a shadow's shadow.
HAM.	Then are our beggars bodies, and our monarchs and outstretched heroes the beggars' shadows. Shall we to the court? For, by my fay, I cannot reason.
ROS. GUIL.	We'll wait upon[43] you.
HAM.	No such matter. I will not sort[44] you with the rest of my servants; for, to speak to you like an honest man, I am most dreadfully attended. But, in the beaten way of friendship,[45] what make you at Elsinore?
ROS.	To visit you, my lord, no other occasion.
HAM.	Beggar that I am, I am even poor in thanks, but I thank you. And sure, dear friends, my thanks are too dear a halfpenny. Were you not sent for? Is it your own inclining? Is it a free visitation? Come, deal justly with me. Come, come. Nay, speak.
GUIL.	What should we say, my lord?
HAM.	Why, anything, but to the purpose. You were sent for; and there is a kind of confession in your looks which your modesties have not craft enough to colour. I know the good King and Queen have sent for you.
ROS.	To what end, my lord?
HAM.	That you must teach me. But let me conjure[46] you by the rights of our fellowship, by the consonancy of our youth, by the obligation of our ever-preserved love, and by what more dear a better proposer could charge you withal, be even[47] and direct with me whether you were sent for or no.
ROS.	[Aside to GUIL.] What say you?
HAM.	[Aside] Nay then, I have an eye of[48] you.—If you love me, hold not off.
GUIL.	My lord, we were sent for.
HAM.	I will tell you why. So shall my anticipation prevent your discovery,[49] and your secrecy to the King and Queen moult

---

[43] *wait upon*] escort.
[44] *sort*] class.
[45] *in the . . . friendship*] in the kind of plain language used among friends
[46] *conjure*] entreat.
[47] *even*] honest.
[48] *of*] on.
[49] *prevent your discovery*] forestall your confession.

no feather. I have of late—but wherefore I know not—lost
all my mirth, forgone all custom of exercises, and indeed
it goes so heavily with my disposition that this goodly
frame,[50] the earth, seems to me a sterile promontory. This
most excellent canopy, the air, look you, this brave[51]
o'erhanging firmament, this majestical roof fretted[52] with
golden fire, why, it appears no other thing to me than a
foul and pestilent congregation of vapours. What a piece of
work is a man! How noble in reason, how infinite in
faculty, in form and moving how express and admirable, in
action how like an angel, in apprehension how like a
god—the beauty of the world, the paragon of animals! And
yet, to me, what is this quintessence of dust? Man delights
not me—no, nor woman neither, though by your smiling
you seem to say so.

ROS.   My lord, there was no such stuff in my thoughts.

HAM.   Why did you laugh then, when I said man delights not me?

ROS.   To think, my lord, if you delight not in man, what lenten
entertainment[53] the players shall receive from you. We
coted[54] them on the way, and hither are they coming to offer
you service.

HAM.   He that plays the king shall be welcome; his Majesty shall have
tribute of me. The adventurous knight shall use his foil and
target,[55] the lover shall not sigh gratis, the humorous man[56]
shall end his part in peace, the clown shall make those laugh
whose lungs are tickle o' the sere,[57] and the lady shall say her
mind freely, or the blank verse shall halt for't. What players
are they?

ROS.   Even those you were wont to take such delight in, the trage-
dians of the city.

HAM.   How chances it they travel? Their residence, both in reputation
and profit, was better both ways.

ROS.   I think their inhibition[58] comes by the means of the late
innovation.

---

[50] *frame*] structure.
[51] *brave*] beautiful.
[52] *fretted*] adorned.
[53] *lenten entertainment*] poor reception.
[54] *coted*] passed by.
[55] *foil and target*] fencing sword and targe (light shield)
[56] *humorous man*] stage character representing the effect of one of the four "humours,"
particularly that of "choler."
[57] *are tickle o' the sere*] have a hair trigger; i.e., will laugh at anything.
[58] *inhibition*] prohibition (from acting in the town).

HAM.   Do they hold the same estimation they did when I was in the city? Are they so followed?

ROS.   No, indeed, are they not.

HAM.   How comes it? Do they grow rusty?

ROS.   Nay, their endeavour keeps in the wonted pace. But there is, sir, an eyrie of children, little eyases,[59] that cry out on the top of question and are most tyrannically[60] clapped for't. These are now the fashion, and so berattle the common stages[61]— so they call them—that many wearing rapiers are afraid of goose-quills,[62] and dare scarce come thither.

HAM.   What, are they children? Who maintains 'em? How are they escoted?[63] Will they pursue the quality[64] no longer than they can sing? Will they not say afterwards, if they should grow themselves to common players—as it is most like, if their means are no better—their writers do them wrong to make them exclaim against their own succession?[65]

ROS.   Faith, there has been much to do on both sides, and the nation holds it no sin to tarre[66] them to controversy. There was for a while no money bid for argument[67] unless the poet and the player went to cuffs[68] in the question.[69]

HAM.   Is't possible?

GUIL.   O, there has been much throwing about of brains.

HAM.   Do the boys carry it away?[70]

ROS.   Ay, that they do, my lord, Hercules and his load[71] too.

HAM.   It is not very strange; for my uncle is King of Denmark, and those that would make mows[72] at him while my father lived, give twenty, forty, fifty, a hundred ducats apiece for his picture in little. 'Sblood, there is something in this more than natural, if philosophy could find it out.

[Flourish of trumpets within.

---

[59] *eyases*] young hawks.

[60] *tyrannically*] violently.

[61] *berattle the common stages*] berate the public playhouses.

[62] *many . . . goose-quills*] gallants are afraid of being satirized.

[63] *escoted*] supported.

[64] *quality*] (acting) profession.

[65] *succession*] i.e., future profession.

[66] *tarre*] incite.

[67] *argument*] plots for plays.

[68] *went to cuffs*] attacked one another.

[69] *in the question*] concerning the controversy.

[70] *carry it away*] win.

[71] *Hercules and his load*] perhaps a reference to the Globe theatre, the sign of which portrayed Hercules supporting the earth.

[72] *mows*] faces.

GUIL.   There are the players.

HAM.   Gentlemen, you are welcome to Elsinore. Your hands, come
         then. The appurtenance of welcome is fashion and cere-
         mony. Let me comply with you in this garb,[73] lest my
         extent[74] to the players—which, I tell you, must show fairly
         outwards—should more appear like entertainment than
         yours. You are welcome. But my uncle-father and aunt-
         mother are deceived.

GUIL.   In what, my dear lord?

HAM.   I am but mad north-north-west. When the wind is southerly I
         know a hawk from a handsaw.

Enter POLONIUS.

POL.   Well be with you, gentlemen.

HAM.   Hark you, Guildenstern, and you too—at each ear a hearer.
         That great baby you see there is not yet out of his swaddling
         clouts.

ROS.   Happily[75] he's the second time come to them; for they say an
         old man is twice a child.

HAM.   I will prophesy he comes to tell me of the players. Mark it. You
         say right, sir; o' Monday morning; 'twas so, indeed.

POL.   My lord, I have news to tell you.

HAM.   My lord, I have news to tell you. When Roscius[76] was an actor
         in Rome—

POL.   The actors are come hither, my lord.

HAM.   Buzz, buzz.

POL.   Upon my honour—

HAM.   Then came each actor on his ass—

POL.   The best actors in the world, either for tragedy, comedy, history,
         pastoral, pastoral-comical, historical-pastoral, tragical-
         historical, tragical-comical-historical-pastoral, scene indi-
         vidable,[77] or poem unlimited.[78] Seneca cannot be too
         heavy, nor Plautus too light. For the law of writ and the
         liberty, these are the only men.

HAM.   O Jephthah, judge of Israel,[79] what a treasure hadst thou!

POL.   What a treasure had he, my lord?

---

[73] *garb*] manner.
[74] *extent*] welcome.
[75] *Happily*] haply, perhaps.
[76] *Roscius*] the most celebrated actor of ancient Rome.
[77] *individable*] unclassifiable.
[78] *unlimited*] undefined.
[79] *Jephthah, judge of Israel*] a Biblical figure who sacrificed his own daughter.

HAM.   Why,

> One fair daughter, and no more,
> The which he loved passing[80] well.

POL.   [*Aside*] Still on my daughter.
HAM.   Am I not i' the right, old Jephthah?
POL.   If you call me Jephthah, my lord, I have a daughter that I love passing well.
HAM.   Nay, that follows not.
POL.   What follows, then, my lord?
HAM.   Why,

> As by lot God wot,

and then, you know,

> It came to pass, as most like it was—

The first row[81] of the pious chanson will show you more; for look where my abridgement[82] comes.

Enter the Players.

You are welcome, masters. Welcome, all. I am glad to see thee well. Welcome, good friends. O, my old friend! Why, thy face is valanced[83] since I saw thee last. Comest thou to beard[84] me in Denmark? What, my young lady[85] and mistress! By'r lady, your ladyship is nearer to heaven than when I saw you last, by the altitude of a chopine.[86] Pray God, your voice, like a piece of uncurrent gold, be not cracked within the ring.[87] Masters, you are all welcome. We'll e'en to't like French falconers, fly at any thing we see.[88] We'll have a speech straight. Come, give us a taste of your quality. Come, a passionate speech.
FIRST PLAY.   What speech, my good lord?

---

[80] *passing*] exceedingly.
[81] *row*] stanza.
[82] *abridgement*] (1) entertainment; (2) reason for cutting short the conversation with Polonius.
[83] *valanced*] fringed (bearded).
[84] *beard*] face, defy (with the obvious pun on the actor's new facial hair).
[85] *my young lady*] a boy who would play a woman's role.
[86] *chopine*] a woman's thick-soled shoe.
[87] *cracked within the ring*] A coin that had been clipped within the ring surrounding the sovereign's head was not legal tender.
[88] *French . . . see*] Falcons were trained to attack only one kind of quarry. Hamlet is thus expressing his overenthusiasm.

HAM.   I heard thee speak me a speech once, but it was never acted, or,
if it was, not above once; for the play, I remember, pleased
not the million, 'twas caviare to the general.[89] But it was—
as I received it, and others, whose judgements in such
matters cried in the top of[90] mine—an excellent play, well
digested[91] in the scenes, set down with as much modesty[92]
as cunning.[93] I remember, one said there were no sallets[94]
in the lines to make the matter savoury, nor no matter in
the phrase that might indict the author of affection,[95] but
called it an honest method, as wholesome as sweet, and by
very much more handsome than fine. One speech in it I
chiefly loved: 'twas Æneas' tale to Dido, and thereabout
of it especially where he speaks of Priam's slaughter.[96] If it
live in your memory, begin at this line—let me see, let
me see—
The rugged Pyrrhus, like th' Hyrcanian beast—[97]
It is not so. It begins with Pyrrhus—
The rugged Pyrrhus, he whose sable arms,[98]
Black as his purpose, did the night resemble
When he lay couched in the ominous horse,[99]
Hath now this dread and black complexion smear'd
With heraldry more dismal. Head to foot
Now is he total gules,[100] horridly trick'd[101]
With blood of fathers, mothers, daughters, sons,
Baked and impasted with the parching streets,
That lend a tyrannous and a damned light
To their lord's murder. Roasted in wrath and fire,
And thus o'er-sized[102] with coagulate gore,
With eyes like carbuncles, the hellish Pyrrhus
Old grandsire Priam seeks.
So, proceed you.

[89] *caviare to the general*] i.e., too rich for common taste.
[90] *in the top of*] with more authority than.
[91] *digested*] arranged.
[92] *modesty*] restraint.
[93] *cunning*] skill.
[94] *sallets*] salad, relish; here, offensive language.
[95] *affection*] affectation.
[96] *Priam's slaughter*] for the account of the sacking of Troy, see Virgil's *Aeneid*, II.
[97] *Hyrcanian beast*] tiger (from Hyrcania, a region on the southeast coast of the Caspian sea).
[98] *sable arms*] black armor.
[99] *the ominous horse*] the Trojan horse.
[100] *gules*] a heraldic term for red.
[101] *trick'd*] a heraldic term; here, adorned.
[102] *o'ersized*] smeared.

POL.   'Fore God, my lord, well spoken, with good accent and good
             discretion.

FIRST PLAY.   Anon he finds him
             Striking too short at Greeks. His antique sword,
             Rebellious to his arm, lies where it falls,
             Repugnant[103] to command. Unequal match'd,
             Pyrrhus at Priam drives, in rage strikes wide,
             But with the whiff and wind of his fell[104] sword
             The unnerved father falls. Then senseless[105] Ilium,
             Seeming to feel this blow, with flaming top
             Stoops to his base, and with a hideous crash
             Takes prisoner Pyrrhus' ear. For, lo! his sword,
             Which was declining on the milky head
             Of reverend Priam, seem'd i' the air to stick.
             So, as a painted tyrant, Pyrrhus stood,
             And like a neutral to his will and matter,[106]
             Did nothing.
             But as we often see, against[107] some storm,
             A silence in the heavens, the rack[108] stand still,
             The bold winds speechless and the orb below
             As hush as death, anon the dreadful thunder
             Doth rend the region,[109] so after Pyrrhus' pause
             Aroused vengeance[110] sets him new a-work,
             And never did the Cyclops' hammers fall
             On Mars's armour, forged for proof[111] eterne,
             With less remorse[112] than Pyrrhus' bleeding sword
             Now falls on Priam.
             Out, out, thou strumpet, Fortune! All you gods,
             In general synod take away her power,
             Break all the spokes and fellies[113] from her wheel,
             And bowl the round nave[114] down the hill of heaven
             As low as to the fiends.

POL.   This is too long.

103 *Repugnant*] refractory.
104 *fell*] fierce.
105 *senseless*] insensate.
106 *matter*] purpose, aim.
107 *against*] before.
108 *rack*] clouds.
109 *region*] sky, air.
110 *vengeance*] Achilles, Pyrrhus' father, had been killed by Paris, Priam's son.
111 *proof*] tested and found impenetrable.
112 *remorse*] compassion.
113 *fellies*] rim.
114 *nave*] hub.

HAM.   It shall to the barber's, with your beard. Prithee, say on. He's for a jig[115] or a tale of bawdry, or he sleeps. Say on; come to Hecuba.

FIRST PLAY.   But who, O, who had seen the mobled[116] queen—

HAM.   'The mobled queen?'

POL.   That's good; 'mobled queen' is good.

FIRST PLAY.   Run barefoot up and down, threatening the flames
With bisson rheum,[117] a clout upon that head
Where late the diadem stood, and for a robe,
About her lank and all o'er-teemed[118] loins,
A blanket, in the alarm of fear caught up;
Who this had seen, with tongue in venom steep'd
'Gainst Fortune's state would treason have pronounced.
But if the gods themselves did see her then,
When she saw Pyrrhus make malicious sport
In mincing with his sword her husband's limbs,
The instant burst of clamour that she made,
Unless things mortal move them not at all,
Would have made milch[119] the burning eyes of heaven
And passion in the gods.

POL.   Look whether he has not turned his colour and has tears in's eyes. Prithee, no more.

HAM.   'Tis well. I'll have thee speak out the rest of this soon. Good my lord, will you see the players well bestowed?[120] Do you hear, let them be well used, for they are the abstract[121] and brief chronicles of the time. After your death you were better have a bad epitaph than their ill report while you live.

POL.   My lord, I will use them according to their desert.

HAM.   God's bodykins, man, much better. Use every man after his desert, and who shall 'scape whipping? Use them after your own honour and dignity: the less they deserve, the more merit is in your bounty. Take them in.

POL.   Come, sirs.

HAM.   Follow him, friends. We'll hear a play tomorrow.
     [*Exit* POLONIUS *with all the* Players *but the* First.]
Dost thou hear me, old friend? Can you play *The Murder of Gonzago?*

---

[115] *jig*] a farcical metrical composition with singing and dancing.
[116] *mobled*] with head muffled.
[117] *bisson rheum*] blinding tears.
[118] *o'er-teemed*] worn out by childbearing.
[119] *milch*] shed milky tears.
[120] *bestowed*] lodged.
[121] *abstract*] summary.

FIRST PLAY.   Ay, my lord.
HAM.   We'll ha't tomorrow night. You could, for a need,[122] study a
               speech of some dozen or sixteen lines, which I would set
               down and insert in't, could you not?
FIRST PLAY.   Ay, my lord.
HAM.   Very well. Follow that lord, and look you mock him not. [*Exit*
               FIRST PLAYER.] My good friends, I'll leave you till night.
               You are welcome to Elsinore.
ROS.   Good my lord.
HAM.   Ay, so. God be wi' ye.
                              [*Exeunt* ROSENCRANTZ *and* GUILDENSTERN.
                              Now I am alone.
               O, what a rogue and peasant slave am I!
               Is it not monstrous that this player here,
               But in a fiction, in a dream of passion,
               Could force his soul so to his own conceit
               That from her working all his visage wann'd,
               Tears in his eyes, distraction in's aspect,
               A broken voice, and his whole function suiting
               With forms to his conceit?[123] And all for nothing!
               For Hecuba!
               What's Hecuba to him, or he to Hecuba,
               That he should weep for her? What would he do,
               Had he the motive and the cue for passion
               That I have? He would drown the stage with tears
               And cleave the general ear with horrid speech,
               Make mad the guilty and appal the free,[124]
               Confound the ignorant, and amaze[125] indeed
               The very faculties of eyes and ears.
               Yet I,
               A dull and muddy-mettled[126] rascal, peak,[127]
               Like John-a-dreams, unpregnant of[128] my cause,
               And can say nothing; no, not for a king,
               Upon whose property and most dear life
               A damn'd defeat was made. Am I a coward?
               Who calls me villain, breaks my pate across,
               Plucks off my beard and blows it in my face,

---

[122] *for a need*] if necessary.
[123] *his whole . . . conceit*] his entire being producing gestures to match his conception.
[124] *free*] innocent.
[125] *amaze*] confuse.
[126] *muddy-mettled*] dull-spirited.
[127] *peak*] mope.
[128] *unpregnant of*] indifferent to.

Tweaks me by the nose, gives me the lie i' the throat,
As deep as to the lungs? Who does me this?
Ha!
'Swounds, I should take it: for it cannot be
But I am pigeon-liver'd and lack gall
To make oppression bitter,[129] or ere this
I should have fatted all the region kites[130]
With this slave's offal. Bloody, bawdy villain!
Remorseless, treacherous, lecherous, kindless[131] villain!
Why, what an ass am I! This is most brave,
That I, the son of a dear father murder'd,
Prompted to my revenge by heaven and hell,
Must, like a whore, unpack my heart with words,
And fall a-cursing, like a very drab,[132]
A scullion![133] Fie upon't! Foh!
About,[134] my brain! Hum, I have heard
That guilty creatures, sitting at a play,
Have by the very cunning of the scene
Been struck so to the soul that presently[135]
They have proclaim'd their malefactions.
For murder, though it have no tongue, will speak
With most miraculous organ. I'll have these players
Play something like the murder of my father
Before mine uncle. I'll observe his looks,
I'll tent[136] him to the quick. If he but blench,[137]
I know my course. The spirit that I have seen
May be the devil, and the devil hath power
To assume a pleasing shape, yea, and perhaps
Out of my weakness and my melancholy,
As he is very potent with such spirits,[138]
Abuses me to damn me. I'll have grounds
More relative[139] than this. The play's the thing
Wherein I'll catch the conscience of the King.　　　*[Exit.*

---

[129] *pigeon-liver'd . . . bitter*] Pigeons were thought not to produce gall, and therefore to be without malice.
[130] *region kites*] kites of the air.
[131] *kindless*] unnatural.
[132] *drab*] prostitute.
[133] *scullion*] kitchen servant.
[134] *About*] get active.
[135] *presently*] immediately.
[136] *tent*] probe, search.
[137] *blench*] start, flinch.
[138] *spirits*] humors.
[139] *relative*] to the purpose, conclusive.

ACT III.

SCENE I. *A room in the castle.*

Enter KING, QUEEN, POLONIUS, OPHELIA, ROSENCRANTZ, *and* GUILDENSTERN.

KING.   And can you by no drift of conference[1]
        Get from him why he puts on this confusion,
        Grating so harshly all his days of quiet
        With turbulent and dangerous lunacy?

ROS.   He does confess he feels himself distracted,
        But from what cause he will by no means speak.

GUIL.   Nor do we find him forward to be sounded;
        But, with a crafty madness, keeps aloof,
        When we would bring him on to some confession
        Of his true state.

QUEEN.   Did he receive you well?

ROS.   Most like a gentleman.

GUIL.   But with much forcing of his disposition.

ROS.   Niggard of question,[2] but of our demands
        Most free in his reply.

QUEEN.   Did you assay him
        To any pastime?[3]

ROS.   Madam, it so fell out that certain players
        We o'er-raught[4] on the way. Of these we told him,
        And there did seem in him a kind of joy
        To hear of it. They are about the court,
        And, as I think, they have already order

---

[1] *drift of conference*] turn of conversation.
[2] *Niggard of question*] sparing in conversation.
[3] *assay . . . pastime*] tempt him with any form of entertainment.
[4] *o'er-raught*] overtook.

This night to play before him.

POL.   'Tis most true;
And he beseech'd me to entreat your Majesties
To hear and see the matter.

KING.   With all my heart; and it doth much content me
To hear him so inclined.
Good gentlemen, give him a further edge, [5]
And drive his purpose on to these delights.

ROS.   We shall, my lord.

               [*Exeunt* ROSENCRANTZ *and* GUILDENSTERN.

KING.   Sweet Gertrude, leave us too;
For we have closely[6] sent for Hamlet hither,
That he, as 'twere by accident, may here
Affront[7] Ophelia.
Her father and myself, lawful espials, [8]
Will so bestow ourselves that, seeing unseen,
We may of their encounter frankly judge,
And gather by him, as he is behaved,
If't be the affliction of his love or no
That thus he suffers for.

QUEEN.   I shall obey you.
And for your part, Ophelia, I do wish
That your good beauties be the happy cause
Of Hamlet's wildness; so shall I hope your virtues
Will bring him to his wonted way again,
To both your honours.

OPH.   Madam, I wish it may. [*Exit* QUEEN.

POL.   Ophelia, walk you here. Gracious,[9] so please you,
We will bestow ourselves. [*To* OPHELIA.] Read on this book,
That show of such an exercise[10] may colour
Your loneliness. [11] We are oft to blame in this—
'Tis too much proved—that with devotion's visage
And pious action we do sugar o'er
The devil himself.

KING.   [*Aside*] O, 'tis too true.

---

[5] *edge*] incitement.
[6] *closely*] secretly.
[7] *Affront*] encounter.
[8] *espials*] spies.
[9] *Gracious*] Your Grace.
[10] *exercise*] act of religious devotion.
[11] *colour Your loneliness*] make your being alone seem plausible.

> How smart a lash that speech doth give my conscience.
> The harlot's cheek, beautied with plastering art,
> Is not more ugly to the thing that helps it
> Than is my deed to my most painted word.
> O heavy burden!

POL. ' I hear him coming. Let's withdraw, my lord.

> *[Exeunt* KING *and* POLONIUS.*

Enter HAMLET.

HAM. To be, or not to be, that is the question:
> Whether 'tis nobler in the mind to suffer
> The slings and arrows of outrageous fortune,
> Or to take arms against a sea of troubles, *Nature*
> And by opposing end them. To die: to sleep;
> No more; and by a sleep to say we end *Pain of life*
> The heart-ache and the thousand natural shocks
> That flesh is heir to; 'tis a consummation
> Devoutly to be wish'd. To die, to sleep;
> To sleep; perchance to dream. Ay, there's the rub;[12]
> For in that sleep of death what dreams may come,
> When we have shuffled off[13] this mortal coil,[14] *Ornaments*
> Must give us pause—there's the respect
> That makes calamity of so long life.[15]
> For who would bear the whips and scorns of time,
> The oppressor's wrong, the proud man's contumely,
> The pangs of disprized[16] love, the law's delay,
> The insolence of office, and the spurns
> That patient merit of the unworthy takes,
> When he himself might his quietus[17] make
> With a bare bodkin?[18] Who would fardels[19] bear,
> To grunt and sweat under a weary life,
> But that the dread of something after death,
> The undiscover'd country from whose bourn[20]
> No traveller returns, puzzles the will,

---

[12] *rub]* obstacle (a bowling term for anything blocking or deflecting the course of the bowl).
[13] *shuffled off]* cast off.
[14] *coil]* (1) turmoil; (2) (?) rope.
[15] *of so long life]* so long-lived.
[16] *disprized]* undervalued.
[17] *quietus]* final settlement of an account.
[18] *bare bodkin]* mere dagger.
[19] *fardels]* burdens, packs.
[20] *bourn]* boundary.

And makes us rather bear those ills we have
Than fly to others that we know not of?
Thus conscience[21] does make cowards of us all,
And thus the native hue of resolution
Is sicklied o'er with the pale cast of thought,
And enterprises of great pitch[22] and moment
With this regard their currents turn awry
And lose the name of action. Soft you now,
The fair Ophelia! Nymph, in thy orisons[23]
Be all my sins remember'd.

OPH.   Good my lord,
How does your honour for this many a day?

HAM.   I humbly thank you: well.

OPH.   My lord, I have remembrances of yours
That I have longed long to redeliver.
I pray you, now receive them.

HAM.   No, not I.
I never gave you aught.

OPH.   My honour'd lord, you know right well you did;
And with them words of so sweet breath composed
As made the things more rich. Their perfume lost,
Take these again; for to the noble mind
Rich gifts wax poor when givers prove unkind.
There, my lord.

HAM.   Ha, ha! Are you honest?[24]

OPH.   My lord?

HAM.   Are you fair?

OPH.   What means your lordship?

HAM.   That if you be honest and fair, your honesty should admit no
discourse to your beauty.

OPH.   Could beauty, my lord, have better commerce than with honesty?

HAM.   Ay, truly; for the power of beauty will sooner transform honesty from what it is to a bawd than the force of honesty can translate beauty into his likeness. This was sometime a paradox, but now the time gives it proof. I did love you once.

OPH.   Indeed, my lord, you made me believe so.

---

[21] *conscience*] (1) consciousness; (2) conscience.
[22] *pitch*] height.
[23] *orisons*] prayers.
[24] *honest*] (1) truthful; (2) chaste.

HAM.   You should not have believed me; for virtue cannot so inoculate[25] our old stock but we shall relish of it. [26] I loved you not.

OPH.   I was the more deceived.

HAM.   Get thee to a nunnery. Why, wouldst thou be a breeder of sinners? I am myself indifferent[27] honest, but yet I could accuse me of such things that it were better my mother had not borne me. I am very proud, revengeful, ambitious, with more offences at my beck[28] than I have thoughts to put them in, imagination to give them shape, or time to act them in. What should such fellows as I do crawling between heaven and earth? We are arrant knaves all. Believe none of us. Go thy ways to a nunnery. Where's your father?

OPH.   At home, my lord.

HAM.   Let the doors be shut upon him, that he may play the fool nowhere but in's own house. Farewell.

OPH.   O, help him, you sweet heavens!

HAM.   If thou dost marry, I'll give thee this plague for thy dowry: be thou as chaste as ice, as pure as snow, thou shalt not escape calumny. Get thee to a nunnery, farewell. Or, if thou wilt needs marry, marry a fool; for wise men know well enough what monsters[29] you make of them. To a nunnery, go; and quickly too. Farewell.

OPH.   O heavenly powers, restore him!

HAM.   I have heard of your paintings too, well enough. God hath given you one face, and you make yourselves another. You jig, you amble, and you lisp, and nickname God's creatures, and make your wantonness your ignorance. Go to, I'll no more on't; it hath made me mad. I say, we will have no more marriages. Those that are married already—all but one—shall live; the rest shall keep as they are. To a nunnery, go. [Exit.

OPH.   O, what a noble mind is here o'erthrown!
        The courtier's, soldier's, scholar's, eye, tongue, sword,
        The expectancy and rose of the fair state,
        The glass of fashion and the mould of form,
        The observed[30] of all observers, quite, quite down!
        And I, of ladies most deject and wretched,

---

[25] *inoculate*] graft.
[26] *of it*] i.e., of the old, sinful nature.
[27] *indifferent*] moderately.
[28] *at my beck*] ready to be committed.
[29] *monsters*] i.e., cuckolds (having grown horns).
[30] *observed*] revered, respected.

That suck'd the honey of his music vows,
Now see that noble and most sovereign reason
Like sweet bells jangled out of tune and harsh,
That unmatch'd form and feature of blown[31] youth
Blasted with ecstasy.[32] O, woe is me,
To have seen what I have seen, see what I see!

Enter KING *and* POLONIUS.

KING.   Love? His affections do not that way tend;
         Nor what he spake, though it lack'd form a little,
         Was not like madness. There's something in his soul
         O'er which his melancholy sits on brood,
         And I do doubt[33] the hatch and the disclose
         Will be some danger; which for to prevent,
         I have in quick determination
         Thus set it down: he shall with speed to England,
         For the demand of our neglected tribute.
         Haply the seas and countries different
         With variable objects shall expel
         This something-settled matter in his heart,
         Whereon his brains still[34] beating puts him thus
         From fashion of himself.[35] What think you on't?
POL.   It shall do well. But yet do I believe
         The origin and commencement of his grief
         Sprung from neglected love. How now, Ophelia?
         You need not tell us what Lord Hamlet said;
         We heard it all. My lord, do as you please;
         But, if you hold it fit, after the play,
         Let his queen mother all alone entreat him
         To show his grief. Let her be round[36] with him;
         And I'll be placed, so please you, in the ear
         Of all their conference. If she find him not,
         To England send him, or confine him where
         Your wisdom best shall think.
KING.   It shall be so.
         Madness in great ones must not unwatch'd go.   [*Exeunt.*

---

[31] *blown*] in full blossom.
[32] *ecstasy*] madness.
[33] *doubt*] fear.
[34] *still*] constantly.
[35] *From fashion of himself*] out of his normal manner.
[36] *be round*] speak plainly.

SCENE II. *A hall in the castle.*

Enter HAMLET *and* Players.

HAM. Speak the speech, I pray you, as I pronounced it to you,
trippingly on the tongue. But if you mouth it, as many of
your players do, I had as lief the town-crier spoke my lines.
Nor do not saw the air too much with your hand, thus; but
use all gently: for in the very torrent, tempest, and, as I may
say, whirlwind of your passion, you must acquire and beget a
temperance that may give it smoothness. O, it offends me to
the soul to hear a robustious periwig-pated fellow tear a
passion to tatters, to very rags, to split the ears of the groundlings,[1] who, for the most part, are capable of[2] nothing but
inexplicable dumb-shows and noise. I would have such a
fellow whipped for o'erdoing Termagant.[3] It out-Herods
Herod.[4] Pray you, avoid it.

FIRST PLAY. I warrant your honour.

HAM. Be not too tame neither, but let your own discretion be your
tutor. Suit the action to the word, the word to the action,
with this special observance, that you o'erstep not the modesty of nature. For anything so overdone is from the purpose
of playing, whose end, both at the first and now, was and is,
to hold, as 'twere, the mirror up to nature, to show virtue
her own feature, scorn her own image, and the very age
and body of the time his form and pressure.[5] Now this
overdone or come tardy off,[6] though it make the unskilful
laugh, cannot but make the judicious grieve, the censure[7]
of the which one must in your allowance o'erweigh a whole
theatre of others. O, there be players that I have seen play,
and heard others praise, and that highly, not to speak it pro-
fanely, that neither having the accent of Christians nor the

---

[1] *groundlings*] those spectators who stood in the pit of the theater.

[2] *capable of*] responsive to.

[3] *Termagant*] a legendary Muslim deity, presented as a violently noisy character in medieval
dramas.

[4] *Herod*] Herod was presented as a ranting tyrant in medieval dramas.

[5] *pressure*] stamped impression.

[6] *come tardy off*] performed inadequately.

[7] *censure*] critical judgement.

gait of Christian, pagan, nor man, have so strutted and
bellowed, that I have thought some of Nature's journeymen[8]
had made men, and not made them well, they imitated
humanity so abominably.

FIRST PLAY.   I hope we have reformed that indifferently[9] with us, sir.

HAM.   O, reform it altogether. And let those that play your clowns
speak no more than is set down for them; for there be of
them that will themselves laugh, to set on some quantity of
barren spectators to laugh too, though in the meantime
some necessary question of the play be then to be considered. That's villanous, and shows a most pitiful ambition in
the fool that uses it. Go, make you ready. [*Exeunt* Players.

Enter POLONIUS, ROSENCRANTZ, *and* GUILDENSTERN.

How now, my lord! Will the King hear this piece of work?

POL.   And the Queen too, and that presently.[10]

HAM.   Bid the players make haste.   [*Exit* POLONIUS.
Will you two help to hasten them?

ROS. ⎫
GUIL. ⎭   We will, my lord.

                    [*Exeunt* ROSENCRANTZ *and* GUILDENSTERN.

HAM.   What ho, Horatio!

Enter HORATIO.

HOR.   Here, sweet lord, at your service.

HAM.   Horatio, thou art e'en as just a man
As e'er my conversation coped[11] withal.

HOR.   O, my dear lord—

HAM.   Nay, do not think I flatter;
For what advancement may I hope from thee,
That no revenue hast but thy good spirits,
To feed and clothe thee? Why should the poor be flatter'd?
No, let the candied tongue lick absurd[12] pomp,
And crook the pregnant[13] hinges of the knee
Where thrift[14] may follow fawning. Dost thou hear?

---

[8] *journeymen*] hired workmen.
[9] *indifferently*] tolerably well.
[10] *presently*] immediately.
[11] *coped*] encountered.
[12] *absurd*] insipid.
[13] *pregnant*] ready.
[14] *thrift*] profit.

Since my dear soul was mistress of her choice,
And could of men distinguish her election,
Sh'hath seal'd thee for herself; for thou hast been
As one, in suffering all, that suffers nothing,
A man that Fortune's buffets and rewards
Hast ta'en with equal thanks; and blest are those
Whose blood[15] and judgement are so well commeddled[16]
That they are not a pipe for Fortune's finger
To sound what stop she please. Give me that man
That is not passion's slave, and I will wear him
In my heart's core, ay, in my heart of heart,
As I do thee. Something too much of this.
There is a play tonight before the King.
One scene of it comes near the circumstance
Which I have told thee of my father's death.
I prithee, when thou seest that act afoot,
Even with the very comment[17] of thy soul
Observe my uncle. If his occulted guilt
Do not itself unkennel in one speech,
It is a damned ghost that we have seen,
And my imaginations are as foul
As Vulcan's stithy.[18] Give him heedful note;
For I mine eyes will rivet to his face,
And after we will both our judgements join
In censure of his seeming.[19]

HOR.   Well, my lord.
If he steal aught the whilst this play is playing,
And 'scape detecting, I will pay the theft.

HAM.   They are coming to the play. I must be idle.[20]
Get you a place.

Danish march. A flourish. *Enter* KING, QUEEN, POLONIUS, OPHELIA, ROSENCRANTZ, GUILDENSTERN, *and other Lords attendant, with the Guard carrying torches.*

KING.   How fares our cousin Hamlet?

---

15 *blood*] passion.
16 *commeddled*] commingled.
17 *the very comment*] the most searching judgment.
18 *Vulcan's stithy*] the smithy of Vulcan, god of fire and metalworking.
19 *In censure of his seeming*] in judgment of his behavior.
20 *idle*] unoccupied, distracted.

HAM.   Excellent, i' faith; of the chameleon's dish.[21] I eat the air, promise-crammed. You cannot feed capons so.

KING.   I have nothing with this answer, Hamlet. These words are not mine.[22]

HAM.   No, nor mine now. [*To* POLONIUS] My lord, you played once i' the university, you say?

POL.   That did I, my lord, and was accounted a good actor.

HAM.   What did you enact?

POL.   I did enact Julius Cæsar. I was killed i' the Capitol. Brutus killed me.

HAM.   It was a brute part of him to kill so capital a calf there. Be the players ready?

ROS.   Ay, my lord; they stay upon your patience.

QUEEN.   Come hither, my dear Hamlet, sit by me.

HAM.   No, good mother, here's metal more attractive.

POL.   [*To the* KING] O, ho! do you mark that?

HAM.   Lady, shall I lie in your lap? [*Lying down at* OPHELIA's *feet*.

OPH.   No, my lord.

HAM.   I mean, my head upon your lap?

OPH.   Ay, my lord.

HAM.   Do you think I meant country matters?

OPH.   I think nothing, my lord.

HAM.   That's a fair thought to lie between maids' legs.

OPH.   What is, my lord?

HAM.   Nothing.

OPH.   You are merry, my lord.

HAM.   Who, I?

OPH.   Ay, my lord.

HAM.   O God, your only jig-maker. What should a man do but be merry? For, look you, how cheerfully my mother looks, and my father died within's two hours.

OPH.   Nay, 'tis twice two months, my lord.

HAM.   So long? Nay then, let the devil wear black, for I'll have a suit of sables. O heavens, die two months ago, and not forgotten yet! Then there's hope a great man's memory may outlive his life half a year. But, by'r lady, he must build churches then, or else shall he suffer not thinking on, with the hobby-horse,[23] whose epitaph is, 'For, O, for, O, the hobby-horse is forgot.'

---

[21] *the chameleon's dish*] Chameleons were said to feed on air. Hamlet deliberately misinterprets "fare" to mean "feed."

[22] *are not mine*] do not correspond to my question.

[23] *hobby-horse*] a character in the morris dance.

Hautboys play. The dumb-show enters.

Enter a King *and a* Queen *very lovingly, the* Queen *embracing him, and he her. She kneels and makes show of protestation unto him. He takes her up and declines his head upon her neck; lays him down upon a bank of flowers. She, seeing him asleep, leaves him. Anon comes in a fellow, takes off his crown, kisses it, and pours poison in the* King's *ears, and exit. The* Queen *returns, finds the* King *dead, and makes passionate action. The* Poisoner, *with some two or three* Mutes, *comes in again, seeming to lament with her. The dead body is carried away. The* Poisoner *wooes the* Queen *with gifts. She seems loath and unwilling awhile, but in the end accepts his love.*   [*Exeunt.*

OPH.	What means this, my lord?
HAM.	Marry, this is miching mallecho.[24] It means mischief.
OPH.	Belike this show imports the argument[25] of the play.

Enter PROLOGUE.

HAM.	We shall know by this fellow. The players cannot keep counsel; they'll tell all.
OPH.	Will he tell us what this show meant?
HAM.	Ay, or any show that you'll show him. Be not you ashamed to show, he'll not shame to tell you what it means.
OPH.	You are naught,[26] you are naught. I'll mark the play.
PRO.	For us, and for our tragedy,
	Here stooping to your clemency,
	We beg your hearing patiently.
HAM.	Is this a prologue, or the posy[27] of a ring?
OPH.	'Tis brief, my lord.
HAM.	As woman's love.

Enter two Players, KING *and* QUEEN.

P. KING.	Full thirty times hath Phœbus' cart[28] gone round
	Neptune's salt wash and Tellus' orbed ground,[29]
	And thirty dozen moons with borrowed sheen
	About the world have times twelve thirties been,
	Since love our hearts and Hymen[30] did our hands
	Unite commutual in most sacred bands.

[24] *miching mallecho*] insidious mischief.
[25] *argument*] plot.
[26] *naught*] worthless, indecent.
[27] *posy*] a motto inscribed on a ring.
[28] *Phœbus' cart*] the chariot of the sun-god.
[29] *Tellus' orbed ground*] the earth.
[30] *Hymen*] the god of marriage.

P. QUEEN. So many journeys may the sun and moon
    Make us again count o'er ere love be done.
    But, woe is me, you are so sick of late,
    So far from cheer and from your former state,
    That I distrust[31] you. Yet, though I distrust,
    Discomfort you, my lord, it nothing must.
    For women's fear and love hold quantity,[32]
    In neither aught, or in extremity.
    Now, what my love is, proof hath made you know,
    And as my love is sized, my fear is so.
    Where love is great, the littlest doubts are fear,
    Where little fears grow great, great love grows there.
P. KING. Faith, I must leave thee, love, and shortly too.
    My operant[33] powers their functions leave to do,[34]
    And thou shalt live in this fair world behind,
    Honour'd, beloved; and haply one as kind
    For husband shalt thou—
P. QUEEN.   O, confound the rest!
    Such love must needs be treason in my breast.
    In second husband let me be accurst,
    None wed the second but who kill'd the first.
HAM. [*Aside*] Wormwood, wormwood.
P. QUEEN. The instances[35] that second marriage move
    Are base respects of thrift,[36] but none of love.
    A second time I kill my husband dead
    When second husband kisses me in bed.
P. KING. I do believe you think what now you speak,
    But what we do determine oft we break.
    Purpose is but the slave to memory,
    Of violent birth but poor validity,
    Which now, like fruit unripe, sticks on the tree,
    But fall unshaken when they mellow be.
    Most necessary 'tis that we forget
    To pay ourselves what to ourselves is debt.
    What to ourselves in passion we propose,
    The passion ending, doth the purpose lose.

[31] *distrust*] feel concern for.
[32] *hold quantity*] are in proportion to one another.
[33] *operant*] active.
[34] *leave to do*] cease to carry out.
[35] *instances*] motives.
[36] *thrift*] profit, gain.

The violence of either grief or joy
Their own enactures[37] with themselves destroy.
Where joy most revels, grief doth most lament;
Grief joys, joy grieves, on slender accident.
This world is not for aye, nor 'tis not strange
That even our loves should with our fortunes change,
For 'tis a question left us yet to prove,
Whether love lead fortune or else fortune love.
The great man down, you mark his favourite flies,
The poor advanced makes friends of enemies.
And hitherto doth love on fortune tend;
For who not needs shall never lack a friend,
And who in want a hollow friend doth try
Directly seasons him[38] his enemy.
But, orderly to end where I begun,
Our wills and fates do so contrary run,
That our devices still[39] are overthrown;
Our thoughts are ours, their ends none of our own.
So think thou wilt no second husband wed,
But die thy thoughts when thy first lord is dead.

P. QUEEN.   Nor earth to me give food nor heaven light,
Sport and repose lock from me day and night,
To desperation turn my trust and hope,
An anchor's cheer[40] in prison be my scope,
Each opposite, that blanks[41] the face of joy,
Meet what I would have well and it destroy,
Both here and hence pursue me lasting strife,
If, once a widow, ever I be wife.

HAM.   If she should break it now.

P. KING.   'Tis deeply sworn. Sweet, leave me here awhile.
My spirits grow dull, and fain I would beguile
The tedious day with sleep.   [Sleeps.

P. QUEEN.   Sleep rock thy brain,
And never come mischance between us twain.   [Exit.

HAM.   Madam, how like you this play?

QUEEN.   The lady doth protest too much, methinks.

HAM.   O, but she'll keep her word.

---

[37] *enactures*] fulfillments.
[38] *seasons him*] ripens him into.
[39] *still*] always.
[40] *anchor's cheer*] anchorite's fare.
[41] *blanks*] blanches, makes pale.

KING.   Have you heard the argument? Is there no offence in't?

HAM.   No, no, they do but jest, poison in jest. No offence i' the world.

KING.   What do you call the play?

HAM.   *The Mousetrap.* Marry, how? Tropically.[42] This play is the image of a murder done in Vienna. Gonzago is the Duke's name; his wife, Baptista. You shall see anon. 'Tis a knavish piece of work, but what o' that? Your Majesty, and we that have free[43] souls, it touches us not. Let the galled jade[44] wince, our withers are unwrung.[45]

Enter LUCIANUS.

         This is one Lucianus, nephew to the King.

OPH.   You are as good as a chorus, my lord.

HAM.   I could interpret between you and your love, if I could see the puppets dallying.

OPH.   You are keen,[46] my lord, you are keen.

HAM.   It would cost you a groaning[47] to take off my edge.[48]

OPH.   Still better, and worse.

HAM.   So you mistake[49] your husbands. Begin, murderer. Pox, leave thy damnable faces and begin. Come, the croaking raven doth bellow for revenge.

LUC.   Thoughts black, hands apt, drugs fit, and time agreeing,
         Confederate season, else no creature seeing;
         Thou mixture rank, of midnight weeds collected,
         With Hecate's ban[50] thrice blasted, thrice infected,
         Thy natural magic and dire property,
         On wholesome life usurp[51] immediately.
                              [*Pours the poison into the sleeper's ear.*

HAM.   He poisons him i' the garden for his estate. His name's Gonzago. The story is extant, and written in very choice Italian. You shall see anon how the murderer gets the love of Gonzago's wife.

OPH.   The King rises.

[42] *Tropically*] metaphorically.
[43] *free*] innocent.
[44] *galled jade*] horse rubbed sore (by a saddle or harness).
[45] *unwrung*] not pinched.
[46] *keen*] bitter.
[47] *groaning*] i.e., sexual intercourse.
[48] *edge*] i.e., sexual appetite.
[49] *mistake*] take in error.
[50] *Hecate's ban*] the curse of Hecate, goddess of magic and the underworld.
[51] *usurp*] encroach.

HAM.   What, frighted with false fire?[52]
QUEEN.   How fares my lord?
POL.   Give o'er the play.
KING.   Give me some light. Away!
POL.   Lights, lights, lights! [*Exeunt all but* HAMLET *and* HORATIO.
HAM.   Why, let the stricken deer go weep,
                             The hart ungalled play;
                        For some must watch, while some must sleep,
                             Thus runs the world away.

           Would not this, sir, and a forest of feathers—if the rest of my
                fortunes turn Turk with me—with two Provincial roses[53] on
                my razed[54] shoes, get me a fellowship in a cry[55] of players,
                sir?
HOR.   Half a share.
HAM   A whole one, I.

                        For thou dost know, O Damon dear,
                             This realm dismantled was
                        Of Jove himself; and now reigns here
                             A very, very—pajock.[56]

HOR.   You might have rhymed.
HAM.   O good Horatio, I'll take the ghost's word for a thousand pound.
                Didst perceive?
HOR.   Very well, my lord.
HAM.   Upon the talk of the poisoning?
HOR.   I did very well note him.
HAM.   Ah, ha! Come, some music; come, the recorders.

                        For if the King like not the comedy,
                        Why then, belike, he likes it not, perdy.[57]

           Come, some music.

Enter ROSENCRANTZ *and* GUILDENSTERN.

GUIL.   Good my lord, vouchsafe me a word with you.
HAM.   Sir, a whole history.

---

[52] *false fire*] discharge of blank shots.
[53] *Provincial roses*] roses from Provins or from Provence.
[54] *razed*] slashed (in patterns). The feathers and decorated shoes were regularly part of an
      actor's costume.
[55] *cry*] pack.
[56] *pajock*] (?) peacock.
[57] *perdy*] a colloquial form of *pardieu*.

GUIL.	The King, sir—
HAM.	Ay, sir, what of him?
GUIL.	Is in his retirement marvellous distempered.
HAM.	With drink, sir?
GUIL.	No, my lord, rather with choler.
HAM.	Your wisdom should show itself more richer to signify this to the doctor; for, for me to put him to his purgation would perhaps plunge him into far more choler.
GUIL.	Good my lord, put your discourse into some frame, and start not so wildly from my affair.
HAM.	I am tame, sir. Pronounce.
GUIL.	The Queen, your mother, in most great affliction of spirit, hath sent me to you.
HAM.	You are welcome.
GUIL.	Nay, good my lord, this courtesy is not of the right breed. If it shall please you to make me a wholesome answer, I will do your mother's commandment; if not, your pardon and my return shall be the end of my business.
HAM.	Sir, I cannot.
GUIL.	What, my lord?
HAM.	Make you a wholesome answer. My wit's diseased. But, sir, such answer as I can make, you shall command, or rather, as you say, my mother. Therefore no more, but to the matter. My mother, you say—
ROS.	Then thus she says: your behaviour hath struck her into amazement and admiration.[58]
HAM.	O wonderful son, that can so astonish a mother! But is there no sequel at the heels of this mother's admiration? Impart.
ROS.	She desires to speak with you in her closet, ere you go to bed.
HAM.	We shall obey, were she ten times our mother. Have you any further trade with us?
ROS.	My lord, you once did love me.
HAM.	So I do still, by these pickers and stealers.[59]
ROS.	Good my lord, what is your cause of distemper? You do surely bar the door upon your own liberty if you deny your griefs to your friend.
HAM.	Sir, I lack advancement.
ROS.	How can that be, when you have the voice of the King himself for your succession in Denmark?

[58] *admiration*] astonishment.
[59] *pickers and stealers*] i.e., hands.

HAM.   Ay, sir, but 'while the grass grows'—the proverb is something
        musty.

Enter Players *with recorders.*

        O, the recorders! Let me see one. To withdraw[60] with you:—
        why do you go about to recover the wind of[61] me, as if you
        would drive me into a toil?[62]
GUIL.   O, my lord, if my duty be too bold, my love is too unmannerly.
HAM.   I do not well understand that. Will you play upon this pipe?
GUIL.   My lord, I cannot.
HAM.   I pray you.
GUIL.   Believe me, I cannot.
HAM.   I do beseech you.
GUIL.   I know no touch of it, my lord.
HAM.   It is as easy as lying. Govern these ventages with your fingers
        and thumb, give it breath with your mouth, and it will
        discourse most eloquent music. Look you, these are the
        stops.
GUIL.   But these cannot I command to any utterance of harmony. I
        have not the skill.
HAM.   Why, look you now, how unworthy a thing you make of me.
        You would play upon me, you would seem to know my
        stops, you would pluck out the heart of my mystery, you
        would sound me from my lowest note to the top of my
        compass; and there is much music, excellent voice, in this
        little organ; yet cannot you make it speak. 'Sblood, do you
        think I am easier to be played on than a pipe? Call me what
        instrument you will, though you can fret me, yet you cannot
        play upon me.

Enter POLONIUS.

        God bless you, sir.
POL.   My lord, the Queen would speak with you, and presently.[63]
HAM.   Do you see yonder cloud that's almost in shape of a camel?
POL.   By the mass, and 'tis like a camel, indeed.
HAM.   Methinks it is like a weasel.
POL.   It is backed like a weasel.
HAM.   Or like a whale?

60 *withdraw*] i e , to speak a word in private
61 *recover the wind of*] a hunting metaphor meaning "to get upwind of."
62 *toil*] net.
63 *presently*] immediately.

POL.　　Very like a whale.
HAM.　　Then I will come to my mother by and by. [*Aside*] They fool
　　　　　me to the top of my bent.[64]—I will come by and by.
POL.　　I will say so.　　　　　　　　　　　　　[*Exit* POLONIUS.
HAM.　　'By and by' is easily said. Leave me, friends.
　　　　　　　　　　　　　　　　　[*Exeunt all but* HAMLET.
　　　　'Tis now the very witching time of night,
　　　　When churchyards yawn, and hell itself breathes out
　　　　Contagion to this world. Now could I drink hot blood,
　　　　And do such bitter business as the day
　　　　Would quake to look on. Soft, now to my mother.
　　　　O heart, lose not thy nature. Let not ever
　　　　The soul of Nero[65] enter this firm bosom.
　　　　Let me be cruel, not unnatural.
　　　　I will speak daggers to her, but use none.
　　　　My tongue and soul in this be hypocrites;
　　　　How in my words soever she be shent,[66]
　　　　To give them seals never my soul consent.　　　　　[*Exit*.

SCENE III. *A room in the castle.*

Enter KING, ROSENCRANTZ, *and* GUILDENSTERN.

KING.　　I like him not, nor stands it safe with us
　　　　　To let his madness range. Therefore prepare you.
　　　　　I your commission will forthwith dispatch,
　　　　　And he to England shall along with you.
　　　　　The terms of our estate may not endure
　　　　　Hazard so near us as doth hourly grow
　　　　　Out of his brows.
GUIL.　　　　　　　　　　We will ourselves provide.[1]
　　　　　Most holy and religious fear it is
　　　　　To keep those many many bodies safe

---

[64] *the top of my bent*] to the utmost limit.
[65] *Nero*] the Roman emperor who put his mother, Agrippina, to death.
[66] *shent*] reproached.

---

[1] *provide*] equip.

	That live and feed upon your Majesty.

Ros.   The single and peculiar[2] life is bound
With all the strength and armour of the mind
To keep itself from noyance,[3] but much more
That spirit upon whose weal depends and rests
The lives of many. The cess[4] of majesty
Dies not alone, but like a gulf[5] doth draw
What's near it with it. It is a massy wheel,
Fix'd on the summit of the highest mount,
To whose huge spokes ten thousand lesser things
Are mortised and adjoin'd; which, when it falls,
Each small annexment, petty consequence,
Attends the boisterous ruin. Never alone
Did the King sigh, but with a general groan.

KING.   Arm you,[6] I pray you, to this speedy voyage,
For we will fetters put about this fear,
Which now goes too free-footed.

Ros. ⎫
GUIL. ⎭   We will haste us.

[*Exeunt* ROSENCRANTZ *and* GUILDENSTERN.

Enter POLONIUS.

POL.   My lord, he's going to his mother's closet.
Behind the arras I'll convey myself,
To hear the process.[7] I'll warrant she'll tax him home.
And, as you said, and wisely was it said,
'Tis meet that some more audience than a mother,
Since nature makes them partial, should o'erhear
The speech, of vantage.[8] Fare you well, my liege.
I'll call upon you ere you go to bed,
And tell you what I know.

KING.   Thanks, dear my lord.

[*Exit* POLONIUS.

O, my offence is rank, it smells to heaven.
It hath the primal eldest curse upon't,
A brother's murder. Pray can I not,

---

[2] *peculiar*] particular, individual.
[3] *noyance*] harm.
[4] *cess*] decease.
[5] *gulf*] whirlpool.
[6] *Arm you*] prepare, equip yourselves.
[7] *process*] proceedings.
[8] *of vantage*] besides.

Though inclination be as sharp as will;
My stronger guilt defeats my strong intent,
And, like a man to double business bound,
I stand in pause where I shall first begin,
And both neglect. What if this cursed hand
Were thicker than itself with brother's blood,
Is there not rain enough in the sweet heavens
To wash it white as snow? Whereto serves mercy
But to confront the visage of offence?
And what's in prayer but this twofold force,
To be forestalled ere we come to fall,
Or pardon'd being down? Then I'll look up.
My fault is past. But O, what form of prayer
Can serve my turn? 'Forgive me my foul murder?'
That cannot be, since I am still possess'd
Of those effects for which I did the murder—
My crown, mine own ambition and my queen.
May one be pardon'd and retain the offence?[9]
In the corrupted currents of this world
Offence's gilded hand may shove by justice,
And oft 'tis seen the wicked prize itself
Buys out the law. But 'tis not so above:
There is no shuffling,[10] there the action lies
In his true nature, and we ourselves compell'd
Even to the teeth and forehead of[11] our faults
To give in evidence. What then? What rests?
Try what repentance can. What can it not?
Yet what can it when one can not repent?
O wretched state, O bosom black as death,
O limed soul, that struggling to be free
Art more engaged! Help, angels! Make assay.
Bow, stubborn knees, and, heart with strings of steel,
Be soft as sinews of the new-born babe.
All may be well.   *[Retires and kneels.*

Enter HAMLET.

HAM. Now might I do it pat, now he is praying.
    And now I'll do't. And so he goes to heaven;

---

[9] *offence*] the fruits of the crime.
[10] *shuffling*] trickery.
[11] *to the teeth and forehead of*] face to face with.

And so am I revenged. That would be scann'd:[12]
A villain kills my father, and for that,
I, his sole son, do this same villain send
To heaven.
O, this is hire and salary, not revenge.
He took my father grossly, full of bread,
With all his crimes broad blown,[13] as flush[14] as May;
And how his audit stands who knows save heaven?
But in our circumstance[15] and course of thought,
'Tis heavy with him. And am I then revenged,
To take him in the purging of his soul,
When he is fit and season'd for his passage?
No.
Up, sword, and know thou a more horrid hent.[16]
When he is drunk asleep, or in his rage,
Or in the incestuous pleasure of his bed,
At game, a-swearing, or about some act
That has no relish of salvation in't,
Then trip him, that his heels may kick at heaven
And that his soul may be as damn'd and black
As hell, whereto it goes. My mother stays.
This physic[17] but prolongs thy sickly days.   [*Exit.*

KING.   [*Rising*] My words fly up, my thoughts remain below.
Words without thoughts never to heaven go.   [*Exit.*

---

[12] *would be scann'd*] needs to be examined.
[13] *broad blown*] in full bloom.
[14] *flush*] lusty, in its prime.
[15] *in our circumstance*] viewed from our earthly perspective.
[16] *hent*] seizing, opportunity for seizing.
[17] *physic*] i.e., praying.

SCENE IV. *The Queen's closet.*

Enter QUEEN *and* POLONIUS.

POL. He will come straight. Look you lay home to him.[1]
   Tell him his pranks have been too broad[2] to bear with,
   And that your grace hath screen'd and stood between
   Much heat and him. I'll silence me even here.
   Pray you, be round[3] with him.

QUEEN.   I'll warrant you,
   Fear me not. Withdraw, I hear him coming.
          [POLONIUS *hides behind the arras.*

Enter HAMLET.

HAM. Now, mother, what's the matter?
QUEEN. Hamlet, thou hast thy father much offended.
HAM. Mother, you have my father much offended.
QUEEN. Come, come, you answer with an idle tongue.
HAM. Go, go, you question with a wicked tongue.
QUEEN. Why, how now, Hamlet?
HAM.   What's the matter now?
QUEEN. Have you forgot me?
HAM.   No, by the rood, not so.
   You are the Queen, your husband's brother's wife,
   And—would it were not so—you are my mother.
QUEEN. Nay, then, I'll set those to you that can speak.
HAM. Come, come, and sit you down; you shall not budge.
   You go not till I set you up a glass
   Where you may see the inmost part of you.
QUEEN. What wilt thou do? Thou wilt not murder me?
   Help, help, ho!
POL. [*Behind*] What, ho! Help, help, help!
HAM. [*Drawing*] How now, a rat? Dead for a ducat, dead.
        [*Makes a pass through the arras.*
POL. [*Behind*] O, I am slain!   [*Falls and dies.*
QUEEN.   O me, what hast thou done?

[1] *lay home to him*] speak bluntly with him.
[2] *broad*] unrestrained.
[3] *round*] plain-spoken.

HAM.	Nay, I know not. Is it the King?
QUEEN.	O, what a rash and bloody deed is this!
HAM.	A bloody deed. Almost as bad, good mother,
	As kill a king and marry with his brother.
QUEEN.	As kill a king?
HAM.	Ay, lady, 'twas my word.

          [*Lifts up the arras and discovers* POLONIUS.

Thou wretched, rash, intruding fool, farewell.
I took thee for thy better. Take thy fortune.
Thou find'st to be too busy is some danger.—
Leave wringing of your hands. Peace, sit you down,
And let me wring your heart; for so I shall,
If it be made of penetrable stuff,
If damned custom have not braz'd[4] it so,
That it be proof[5] and bulwark against sense.[6]

QUEEN. What have I done, that thou darest wag thy tongue
In noise so rude against me?

HAM.   Such an act
That blurs the grace and blush of modesty,
Calls virtue hypocrite, takes off the rose
From the fair forehead of an innocent love,
And sets a blister[7] there, makes marriage vows
As false as dicers' oaths—O, such a deed
As from the body of contraction[8] plucks
The very soul, and sweet religion makes
A rhapsody[9] of words. Heaven's face doth glow,
Yea, this solidity and compound mass
With tristful visage, as against the doom,[10]
Is thought-sick at the act.

QUEEN.   Ay me, what act,
That roars so loud and thunders in the index?[11]

HAM. Look here upon this picture, and on this,
The counterfeit presentment[12] of two brothers.
See what a grace was seated on this brow:

---

[4] *braz'd*] coated with brass, hardened.
[5] *proof*] impenetrable.
[6] *sense*] reason.
[7] *blister*] prostitutes were branded on the forehead.
[8] *contraction*] the marriage contract.
[9] *rhapsody*] cento, amalgam of empty words.
[10] *against the doom*] in expectation of the Judgment Day.
[11] *index*] preface, prologue.
[12] *counterfeit presentment*] representation, portrait.

Hyperion's curls, the front[13] of Jove himself,
An eye like Mars, to threaten and command,
A station[14] like the herald Mercury
New-lighted on a heaven-kissing hill,
A combination and a form indeed
Where every god did seem to set his seal
To give the world assurance of a man.
This was your husband. Look you now, what follows.
Here is your husband: like a mildew'd ear,
Blasting[15] his wholesome brother. Have you eyes?
Could you on this fair mountain leave[16] to feed,
And batten on this moor? Ha, have you eyes?
You cannot call it love, for at your age
The heyday in the blood is tame, it's humble,
And waits upon the judgement; and what judgement
Would step from this to this? Sense[17] sure you have,
Else could you not have motion, but sure that sense
Is apoplex'd, for madness would not err,
Nor sense to ecstasy[18] was ne'er so thrall'd
But it reserved some quantity of choice,
To serve in such a difference. What devil was't
That thus hath cozen'd you at hoodman-blind?[19]
Eyes without feeling, feeling without sight,
Ears without hands or eyes, smelling sans all,
Or but a sickly part of one true sense
Could not so mope.[20]
O shame, where is thy blush? Rebellious hell,
If thou canst mutine in a matron's bones,
To flaming youth let virtue be as wax
And melt in her own fire. Proclaim no shame
When the compulsive ardour gives the charge,[21]
Since frost itself as actively doth burn,
And reason panders will.

QUEEN.   O Hamlet, speak no more.

13 *front*] forehead.
14 *station*] stance.
15 *Blasting*] blighting, causing to wither.
16 *leave*] cease.
17 *Sense*] the faculties and act of perception.
18 *ecstasy*] delusion, madness.
19 *hoodman-blind*] blindman's buff.
20 *mope*] act without thought.
21 *gives the charge*] attacks.

Thou turn'st mine eyes into my very soul,
And there I see such black and grained[22] spots
As will not leave their tinct.

HAM.   Nay, but to live
In the rank sweat of an enseamed[23] bed,
Stew'd in corruption, honeying and making love
Over the nasty sty—

QUEEN.   O, speak to me no more.
These words like daggers enter in my ears.
No more, sweet Hamlet.

HAM.   A murderer and a villain,
A slave that is not twentieth part the tithe
Of your precedent lord, a vice[24] of kings,
A cutpurse of the empire and the rule,
That from a shelf the precious diadem stole
And put it in his pocket—

QUEEN. No more.
HAM.   A king of shreds and patches—

Enter GHOST.

Save me, and hover o'er me with your wings,
You heavenly guards! What would your gracious figure?

QUEEN. Alas, he's mad.
HAM.   Do you not come your tardy son to chide,
That, lapsed in time and passion, lets go by
The important[25] acting of your dread command?
O, say!

GHOST. Do not forget. This visitation
Is but to whet thy almost blunted purpose.
But look, amazement on thy mother sits.
O, step between her and her fighting soul.
Conceit[26] in weakest bodies strongest works.
Speak to her, Hamlet.

HAM.   How is it with you, lady?
QUEEN. Alas, how is't with you,
That you do bend your eye on vacancy
And with the incorporal air do hold discourse?

---

[22] *grained*] dyed in grain, which was a red dye made from the dried bodies of insects.
[23] *enseamed*] filthy.
[24] *vice*] the buffoon-like character of Morality plays.
[25] *important*] urgent.
[26] *Conceit*] imagination.

Forth at your eyes your spirits wildly peep,
And, as the sleeping soldiers in the alarm,[27]
Your bedded hair, like life in excrements,[28]
Start up and stand an end. O gentle son,
Upon the heat and flame of thy distemper
Sprinkle cool patience. Whereon do you look?

HAM.   On him, on him. Look you how pale he glares.
His form and cause conjoin'd, preaching to stones,
Would make them capable.[29]—Do not look upon me,
Lest with this piteous action you convert
My stern effects.[30] Then what I have to do
Will want true colour—tears perchance for blood.

QUEEN.   To whom do you speak this?

HAM.   Do you see nothing there?

QUEEN.   Nothing at all; yet all that is I see.

HAM.   Nor did you nothing hear?

QUEEN.   No, nothing but ourselves.

HAM.   Why, look you there. Look how it steals away.
My father, in his habit[31] as he lived.
Look where he goes, even now, out at the portal. [*Exit* GHOST.

QUEEN.   This is the very coinage of your brain.
This bodily creation ecstasy[32]
Is very cunning in.

HAM.   Ecstasy?
My pulse, as yours, doth temperately keep time,
And makes as healthful music. It is not madness
That I have utter'd. Bring me to the test,
And I the matter will re-word, which madness
Would gambol[33] from. Mother, for love of grace,
Lay not that flattering unction[34] to your soul,
That not your trespass but my madness speaks.
It will but skin[35] and film the ulcerous place,
Whiles rank corruption, mining all within,
Infects unseen. Confess yourself to heaven,
Repent what's past, avoid what is to come,

---

[27] *in the alarm*] at the call to arms.
[28] *excrements*] growths out from the body.
[29] *capable*] responsive.
[30] *effects*] intended actions.
[31] *his habit*] appearance.
[32] *ecstasy*] madness.
[33] *gambol*] skip, shy away.
[34] *unction*] salve, ointment.
[35] *skin*] cover with skin.

And do not spread the compost on the weeds,
To make them ranker. Forgive me this my virtue,
For in the fatness of these pursy[36] times
Virtue itself of vice must pardon beg,
Yea, curb[37] and woo for leave to do him good.

QUEEN.   O Hamlet, thou hast cleft my heart in twain.

HAM.   O, throw away the worser part of it
And live the purer with the other half.
Good night. But go not to my uncle's bed.
Assume[38] a virtue, if you have it not.
That monster, custom, who all sense doth eat,
Of habits evil, is angel yet in this,
That to the use of actions fair and good
He likewise gives a frock or livery,
That aptly is put on. Refrain tonight
And that shall lend a kind of easiness
To the next abstinence, the next more easy;
For use almost can change the stamp of nature
And either master the devil, or throw him out
With wondrous potency. Once more, good night;
And when you are desirous to be blest,
I'll blessing beg of you. For this same lord, [*Pointing to* POLONIUS.
I do repent. But heaven hath pleased it so,
To punish me with this, and this with me,
That I must be their scourge and minister.
I will bestow[39] him, and will answer well
The death I gave him. So, again, good night.
I must be cruel, only to be kind.
This bad begins, and worse remains behind.[40]
One word more, good lady.

QUEEN.   What shall I do?

HAM.   Not this, by no means, that I bid you do:
Let the bloat King tempt you again to bed,
Pinch wanton on your cheek, call you his mouse,
And let him, for a pair of reechy[41] kisses,
Or paddling[42] in your neck with his damn'd fingers,
Make you to ravel all this matter out,

---

[36] *pursy*] flabby.
[37] *curb*] bow.
[38] *Assume*] take on, adopt.
[39] *bestow*] dispose of.
[40] *behind*] i.e., to come.
[41] *reechy*] filthy, stinking.
[42] *paddling*] playing amorously.

That I essentially am not in madness,
But mad in craft. 'Twere good you let him know;
For who, that's but a queen, fair, sober, wise,
Would from a paddock,[43] from a bat, a gib,[44]
Such dear concernings hide? Who would do so?
No, in despite of sense and secrecy,
Unpeg the basket on the house's top,
Let the birds fly, and like the famous ape,[45]
To try conclusions, in the basket creep
And break your own neck down.

QUEEN. Be thou assured, if words be made of breath
And breath of life, I have no life to breathe
What thou hast said to me.

HAM. I must to England; you know that?

QUEEN.   Alack,
I had forgot. 'Tis so concluded on.

HAM. There's letters seal'd, and my two schoolfellows,
Whom I will trust as I will adders fang'd,
They bear the mandate. They must sweep my way,
And marshal me to knavery.[46] Let it work;
For 'tis the sport to have the enginer[47]
Hoist[48] with his own petard;[49] and't shall go hard
But I will delve one yard below their mines,
And blow them at the moon. O, 'tis most sweet
When in one line[50] two crafts[51] directly meet.
This man shall set me packing.[52]
I'll lug the guts into the neighbour room.
Mother, good night indeed. This counsellor
Is now most still, most secret and most grave,
Who was in life a foolish prating knave.
Come, sir, to draw toward an end with you.
Good night, mother.

          [*Exeunt severally;* HAMLET *dragging in* POLONIUS.

---

[43] *paddock*] toad.
[44] *gib*] tomcat.
[45] *famous ape*] the ape, seeing the birds flying, imitates them and ends badly.
[46] *marshal me to knavery*] lead me to suffer knavery.
[47] *enginer*] creator of military hardware.
[48] *Hoist*] blown up.
[49] *petard*] explosive device.
[50] *in one line*] head on.
[51] *crafts*] plots.
[52] *packing*] (1) off in a hurry; (2) plotting.

ACT IV.

Scene I. *A room in the castle.*

Enter King, Queen, Rosencrantz, *and* Guildenstern.

KING.   There's matter in these sighs, these profound heaves;
        You must translate. 'Tis fit we understand them.
        Where is your son?
QUEEN.   Bestow this place on us a little while.
                            [*Exeunt* Rosencrantz *and* Guildenstern.
        Ah, mine own lord, what have I seen tonight!
KING.   What, Gertrude? How does Hamlet?
QUEEN.   Mad as the sea and wind, when both contend
        Which is the mightier. In his lawless fit,
        Behind the arras hearing something stir,
        Whips out his rapier, cries 'A rat, a rat!'
        And in this brainish[1] apprehension kills
        The unseen good old man.
KING.   O heavy deed!
        It had been so with us, had we been there.
        His liberty is full of threats to all,
        To you yourself, to us, to everyone.
        Alas, how shall this bloody deed be answer'd?
        It will be laid to us, whose providence
        Should have kept short,[2] restrain'd and out of haunt,[3]
        This mad young man. But so much was our love,
        We would not understand what was most fit,
        But, like the owner of a foul disease,
        To keep it from divulging,[4] let it feed

---

[1] *brainish*] brainsick.
[2] *short*] i.e., on a short leash.
[3] *out of haunt*] away from any public place.
[4] *divulging*] becoming known.

Even on the pith of life. Where is he gone?

QUEEN. To draw apart the body he hath kill'd,
      O'er whom—his very madness, like some ore[5]
      Among a mineral[6] of metals base,
      Shows itself pure—he weeps for what is done.

KING.   O Gertrude, come away.
      The sun no sooner shall the mountains touch,
      But we will ship him hence; and this vile deed
      We must, with all our majesty and skill,
      Both countenance and excuse. Ho, Guildenstern!

Enter ROSENCRANTZ *and* GUILDENSTERN.

      Friends both, go join you with some further aid.
      Hamlet in madness hath Polonius slain,
      And from his mother's closet hath he dragg'd him.
      Go seek him out, speak fair, and bring the body
      Into the chapel. I pray you, haste in this.
                  [*Exeunt* ROSENCRANTZ *and* GUILDENSTERN.
      Come, Gertrude, we'll call up our wisest friends,
      And let them know, both what we mean to do,
      And what's untimely done. So . . . slander,[7]
      Whose whisper o'er the world's diameter
      As level[8] as the cannon to his blank[9]
      Transports his poison'd shot, may miss our name
      And hit the woundless[10] air. O, come away.
      My soul is full of discord and dismay.   [*Exeunt.*

---

[5] *ore*] precious metal, perhaps gold.
[6] *mineral*] mine.
[7] *So . . . slander*] a defective line.
[8] *level*] straight.
[9] *blank*] target.
[10] *woundless*] invulnerable.

SCENE II. *Another room in the castle.*

Enter HAMLET.

HAM.   Safely stowed.

ROS. ⎫
GUIL. ⎭   [*Within*] Hamlet! Lord Hamlet!

HAM.   But soft, what noise? Who calls on Hamlet? O, here they
           come.

Enter ROSENCRANTZ *and* GUILDENSTERN.

ROS.   What have you done, my lord, with the dead body?

HAM.   Compounded it with dust, whereto 'tis kin.

ROS.   Tell us where 'tis, that we may take it thence and bear it to the
           chapel.

HAM.   Do not believe it.

ROS.   Believe what?

HAM.   That I can keep your counsel and not mine own. Besides, to be
           demanded of a sponge—what replication[1] should be made
           by the son of a king?

ROS.   Take you me for a sponge, my lord?

HAM.   Ay, sir, that soaks up the King's countenance,[2] his rewards, his
           authorities. But such officers do the King best service in the
           end. He keeps them, like an ape, in the corner of his jaw—
           first mouthed, to be last swallowed. When he needs what
           you have gleaned, it is but squeezing you, and, sponge, you
           shall be dry again.

ROS.   I understand you not, my lord.

HAM.   I am glad of it. A knavish speech sleeps in a foolish ear.

ROS.   My lord, you must tell us where the body is, and go with us to
           the King.

HAM.   The body is with the King, but the King is not with the body.
           The King is a thing—

GUIL.   A thing, my lord?

HAM.   Of nothing. Bring me to him.   [*Exeunt.*

---

[1] *replication*] reply.
[2] *countenance*] patronage, favor.

SCENE III. *Another room in the castle.*

Enter KING, *attended.*

KING. I have sent to seek him, and to find the body.
How dangerous is it that this man goes loose!
Yet must not we put the strong law on him.
He's loved of the distracted[1] multitude,
Who like not in their judgement, but their eyes;
And where 'tis so, the offender's scourge[2] is weigh'd,
But never the offence. To bear all smooth and even,
This sudden sending him away must seem
Deliberate pause.[3] Diseases desperate grown
By desperate appliance[4] are relieved,
Or not at all.

Enter ROSENCRANTZ.

How now, what hath befall'n?
ROS. Where the dead body is bestow'd, my lord,
We cannot get from him.
KING. But where is he?
ROS. Without, my lord; guarded, to know your pleasure.
KING. Bring him before us.
ROS. Ho, Guildenstern! Bring in my lord.

Enter HAMLET *and* GUILDENSTERN.

KING. Now, Hamlet, where's Polonius?
HAM. At supper.
KING. At supper? Where?
HAM. Not where he eats, but where he is eaten. A certain convoca-
tion of politic worms are e'en at him. Your worm is your
only emperor for diet. We fat all creatures else to fat us, and
we fat ourselves for maggots. Your fat king and your lean
beggar is but variable service,[5] two dishes, but to one table.
That's the end.

---

[1] *distracted*] irrational, unthinking.
[2] *scourge*] punishment.
[3] *Deliberate pause*] the result of careful consideration.
[4] *appliance*] cure, treatment.
[5] *service*] course (of food).

KING.   Alas, alas!
HAM.   A man may fish with the worm that hath eat of a king, and eat
         of the fish that hath fed of that worm.
KING.   What dost thou mean by this?
HAM.   Nothing but to show you how a king may go a progress[6]
         through the guts of a beggar.
KING.   Where is Polonius?
HAM.   In heaven. Send thither to see. If your messenger find him not
         there, seek him i' the other place yourself. But indeed, if you
         find him not within this month, you shall nose him as you
         go up the stairs into the lobby.
KING.   [*To some* Attendants] Go seek him there.
HAM.   He will stay till you come.   [*Exeunt* Attendants.
KING.   Hamlet, this deed, for thine especial safety—
         Which we do tender,[7] as we dearly grieve
         For that which thou hast done—must send thee hence
         With fiery quickness. Therefore prepare thyself.
         The bark is ready and the wind at help,[8]
         The associates tend,[9] and everything is bent
         For England.
HAM.   For England?
KING.   Ay, Hamlet.
HAM.   Good.
KING.   So is it, if thou knew'st our purposes.
HAM.   I see a cherub that sees them. But, come; for England. Fare-
         well, dear mother.
KING.   Thy loving father, Hamlet.
HAM.   My mother. Father and mother is man and wife, man and wife
         is one flesh, and so, my mother. Come, for England. [*Exit.*
KING.   Follow him at foot.[10] Tempt him with speed aboard.
         Delay it not. I'll have him hence tonight.
         Away, for every thing is seal'd and done
         That else leans on the affair. Pray you, make haste.
                          [*Exeunt* ROSENCRANTZ *and* GUILDENSTERN.
         And, England,[11] if my love thou hold'st at aught—
         As my great power thereof may give thee sense,
         Since yet thy cicatrice looks raw and red

---

[6] *progress*] journey made by a sovereign.
[7] *tender*] hold dear.
[8] *at help*] favorable.
[9] *tend*] attend, are in waiting.
[10] *at foot*] closely.
[11] *England*] the King of England.

After the Danish sword, and thy free awe
Pays homage to us—thou mayst not coldly set[12]
Our sovereign process;[13] which imports at full,
By letters congruing to[14] that effect,
The present[15] death of Hamlet. Do it, England;
For like the hectic[16] in my blood he rages,
And thou must cure me. Till I know 'tis done,
Howe'er my haps, my joys were ne'er begun.   [*Exit.*

SCENE IV. *A plain in Denmark.*

Enter FORTINBRAS, *a* Captain *and* Soldiers, *marching*.

FOR.   Go, captain, from me greet the Danish king.
Tell him that by his license Fortinbras
Craves the conveyance of a promised march
Over his kingdom. You know the rendezvous.
If that his Majesty would aught with us,
We shall express our duty in his eye;[1]
And let him know so.

CAP.   I will do't, my lord.

FOR.   Go softly on.   [*Exeunt* FORTINBRAS *and* Soldiers.

Enter HAMLET, ROSENCRANTZ, GUILDENSTERN, *and others*.

HAM.   Good sir, whose powers are these?
CAP.   They are of Norway, sir.
HAM.   How purposed, sir, I pray you?
CAP.   Against some part of Poland.
HAM.   Who commands them, sir?
CAP.   The nephew to old Norway, Fortinbras.
HAM.   Goes it against the main of Poland, sir,
Or for some frontier?

---

[12] *coldly set*] regard with indifference.
[13] *process*] mandate.
[14] *congruing to*] in accordance with.
[15] *present*] immediate.
[16] *hectic*] fever.

---

[1] *express . . . eye*] pay our respects to him in person.

CAP.   Truly to speak, and with no addition,
         We go to gain a little patch of ground
         That hath in it no profit but the name.
         To pay five ducats, five, I would not farm[2] it,
         Nor will it yield to Norway or the Pole
         A ranker[3] rate, should it be sold in fee.[4]

HAM.   Why, then the Polack never will defend it.

CAP.   Yes, it is already garrison'd.

HAM.   Two thousand souls and twenty thousand ducats
         Will not debate the question of this straw!
         This is the imposthume[5] of much wealth and peace,
         That inward breaks, and shows no cause without
         Why the man dies. I humbly thank you, sir.

CAP.   God be wi' you, sir.   [Exit.

ROS.   Will't please you go, my lord?

HAM.   I'll be with you straight. Go a little before.
                         [Exeunt all but HAMLET.

         How all occasions do inform against me,
         And spur my dull revenge. What is a man,
         If his chief good and market of his time
         Be but to sleep and feed? A beast, no more.
         Sure, he that made us with such large discourse,[6]
         Looking before and after, gave us not
         That capability and godlike reason
         To fust[7] in us unused. Now, whether it be
         Bestial oblivion, or some craven scruple
         Of thinking too precisely on the event—
         A thought which, quarter'd, hath but one part wisdom
         And ever three parts coward—I do not know
         Why yet I live to say this thing's to do,
         Sith I have cause, and will, and strength, and means,
         To do't. Examples gross as earth exhort me:
         Witness this army, of such mass and charge,[8]
         Led by a delicate and tender prince,
         Whose spirit with divine ambition puff'd
         Makes mouths at the invisible event,

---

[2] *farm*] take the lease of.
[3] *ranker*] greater.
[4] *in fee*] outright, freehold.
[5] *imposthume*] abscess.
[6] *discourse*] faculty of reason.
[7] *fust*] grow moldy.
[8] *charge*] expense, cost.

Exposing what is mortal and unsure
To all that fortune, death and danger dare,
Even for an eggshell. Rightly to be great
Is not to stir without great argument,
But greatly to find quarrel in a straw
When honour's at the stake. How stand I then,
That have a father kill'd, a mother stain'd,
Excitements of my reason and my blood,
And let all sleep, while to my shame I see
The imminent death of twenty thousand men,
That for a fantasy and trick[9] of fame
Go to their graves like beds, fight for a plot
Whereon the numbers cannot try the cause,[10]
Which is not tomb enough and continent
To hide the slain? O, from this time forth,
My thoughts be bloody, or be nothing worth.   [*Exit.*

SCENE V. *Elsinore. A room in the castle.*

Enter QUEEN, HORATIO, *and a* Gentleman.

QUEEN.   I will not speak with her.
GENT.   She is importunate,
    Indeed distract.[1] Her mood will needs be pitied.
QUEEN.   What would she have?
GENT.   She speaks much of her father, says she hears
    There's tricks i' the world, and hems and beats her heart,
    Spurns enviously[2] at straws, speaks things in doubt,[3]
    That carry but half sense. Her speech is nothing,
    Yet the unshaped use of it doth move
    The hearers to collection.[4] They aim at it,
    And botch the words up fit to their own thoughts,
    Which, as her winks and nods and gestures yield them,

[9] *trick*] trifle.
[10] *Whereon . . . cause*] i.e., the disputed territory is not large enough to be the battlefield.

[1] *distract*] mad.
[2] *enviously*] spitefully.
[3] *in doubt*] ambiguously.
[4] *collection*] make inferences.

        Indeed would make one think there might be thought,
        Though nothing sure, yet much unhappily.[5]
HOR.   'Twere good she were spoken with, for she may strew
        Dangerous conjectures in ill-breeding minds.
QUEEN. Let her come in.   [*Exit* Gentleman.
        [*Aside*] To my sick soul, as sin's true nature is,
        Each toy[6] seems prologue to some great amiss.[7]
        So full of artless jealousy[8] is guilt,
        It spills[9] itself in fearing to be spilt.

Enter Gentleman, *with* OPHELIA.

OPH.   Where is the beauteous Majesty of Denmark?
QUEEN. How now, Ophelia?
OPH.   [*Sings*] How should I your true love know
               From another one?
            By his cockle hat and staff
            And his sandal shoon.[10]

QUEEN. Alas, sweet lady, what imports this song?
OPH.   Say you? Nay, pray you, mark.

        [*Sings*] He is dead and gone, lady,
            He is dead and gone;
           At his head a grass-green turf,
           At his heels a stone.

        Oh, oh!
QUEEN. Nay, but, Ophelia—
OPH.   Pray you, mark.

        [*Sings*] White his shroud as the mountain snow—

Enter KING.

QUEEN. Alas, look here, my lord.
OPH.   [*Sings*]   Larded[11] with sweet flowers,
             Which bewept to the grave did go
             With true-love showers.

---

[5] *unhappily*] mischievously.
[6] *toy*] trifle.
[7] *great amiss*] calamity.
[8] *jealousy*] apprehension.
[9] *spills*] destroys.
[10] *cockle hat . . . shoon*] The lover is dressed as a pilgrim. *Shoon* is the archaic plural of "shoe."
[11] *Larded*] garnished, adorned.

KING.   How do you, pretty lady?
OPH.   Well, God 'ild you. [12] They say the owl was a baker's daughter.
        Lord, we know what we are, but know not what we may be.
        God be at your table.
KING.   Conceit upon her father.
OPH.   Pray you, let's have no words of this; but when they ask you
        what it means, say you this:

        [*Sings*] Tomorrow is Saint Valentine's day,
                All in the morning betime,
             And I a maid at your window,
                To be your Valentine.

        Then up he rose, and donn'd his clothes,
                And dupp'd[13] the chamber door,
             Let in the maid, that out a maid
                Never departed more.

KING.   Pretty Ophelia—
OPH.   Indeed, without an oath, I'll make an end on't.

        [*Sings*] By Gis[14] and by Saint Charity,
                Alack, and fie for shame!
             Young men will do't, if they come to't,
                By Cock,[15] they are to blame.

        Quoth she, 'Before you tumbled me,
                You promised me to wed.'

        He answers:

        'So would I ha' done, by yonder sun,
                An thou hadst not come to my bed.'

KING.   How long hath she been thus?
OPH.   I hope all will be well. We must be patient. But I cannot
        choose but weep, to think they should lay him i' the cold
        ground. My brother shall know of it. And so I thank you for
        your good counsel. Come, my coach. Good night, ladies;
        good night, sweet ladies; good night, good night.   [*Exit*.
KING.   Follow her close. Give her good watch, I pray you.
                                                [*Exit* HORATIO.
        O, this is the poison of deep grief; it springs

---

[12] *God 'ild you*] God yield (reward) you.
[13] *dupp'd*] opened.
[14] *Gis*] a corruption of "Jesus."
[15] *Cock*] a corruption of "God."

All from her father's death. O Gertrude, Gertrude,
When sorrows come, they come not single spies, [16]
But in battalions. First, her father slain;
Next, your son gone, and he most violent author
Of his own just remove; the people muddied,
Thick and unwholesome in their thoughts and whispers,
For good Polonius' death; and we have done but greenly, [17]
In hugger-mugger[18] to inter him; poor Ophelia
Divided from herself and her fair judgement,
Without the which we are pictures, or mere beasts;
Last, and as much containing as all these,
Her brother is in secret come from France,
Feeds on his wonder, [19] keeps himself in clouds,
And wants not buzzers[20] to infect his ear
With pestilent speeches of his father's death;
Wherein necessity, of matter beggar'd,
Will nothing stick[21] our person to arraign[22]
In ear and ear. O my dear Gertrude, this,
Like to a murdering-piece, [23] in many places
Gives me superfluous death.   [A *noise within.*

QUEEN.   Alack, what noise is this?
KING.   Where are my Switzers?[24] Let them guard the door.

Enter another Gentleman.

          What is the matter?
GENT.   Save yourself, my lord.
The ocean, overpeering of his list, [25]
Eats not the flats with more impetuous haste.
Than young Laertes, in a riotous head, [26]
O'erbears your officers. The rabble call him lord;
And, as the world were now but to begin,
Antiquity forgot, custom not known—

[16] *spies*] advance guards.
[17] *greenly*] foolishly.
[18] *In hugger-mugger*] clandestinely.
[19] *wonder*] bewilderment.
[20] *wants not buzzers*] does not lack rumor-mongers.
[21] *nothing stick*] not hesitate.
[22] *arraign*] accuse.
[23] *murdering-piece*] a type of cannon firing grapeshot.
[24] *Switzers*] Swiss mercenaries, used as a personal bodyguard.
[25] *overpeering of his list*] rising above its boundary.
[26] *head*] armed force.

The ratifiers and props of every word—
They cry 'Choose we! Laertes shall be king.'
Caps, hands and tongues applaud it to the clouds,
'Laertes shall be king, Laertes king.'

QUEEN. How cheerfully on the false trail they cry.[27]
O, this is counter, you false Danish dogs!   [*Noise within.*
KING. The doors are broke.

Enter LAERTES, *armed*; Danes *following.*

LAER. Where is this King? Sirs, stand you all without.
DANES. No, let's come in.
LAER.   I pray you, give me leave.
DANES. We will, we will.
LAER. I thank you. Keep the door.   [*They retire without the door.*
                         O thou vile king,
Give me my father.
QUEEN.   Calmly, good Laertes.
LAER. That drop of blood that's calm proclaims me bastard,
Cries cuckold to my father, brands the harlot
Even here, between the chaste unsmirched brows
Of my true mother.
KING.   What is the cause, Laertes,
That thy rebellion looks so giant-like?
Let him go, Gertrude. Do not fear[28] our person.
There's such divinity doth hedge a king
That treason can but peep to what it would,
Acts little of his will. Tell me, Laertes,
Why thou art thus incensed. Let him go, Gertrude.
Speak, man.
LAER. Where is my father?
KING.   Dead.
QUEEN.   But not by him.
KING. Let him demand his fill.
LAER. How came he dead? I'll not be juggled with.
To hell, allegiance! Vows, to the blackest devil!
Conscience and grace, to the profoundest pit!
I dare damnation. To this point I stand,
That both the worlds I give to negligence,

---

[27] *cry*] make the sound of hounds.
[28] *fear*] fear for.

Let come what comes; only I'll be revenged
Most throughly[29] for my father.
KING.   Who shall stay you?
LAER.   My will, not all the world.
And for my means, I'll husband them so well,
They shall go far with little.
KING.   Good Laertes,
If you desire to know the certainty
Of your dear father's death, is't writ in your revenge
That, swoopstake,[30] you will draw both friend and foe,
Winner and loser?
LAER.   None but his enemies.
KING.   Will you know them then?
LAER.   To his good friends thus wide I'll ope my arms,
And, like the kind[31] life-rendering pelican,
Repast them with my blood.
KING.   Why, now you speak
Like a good child and a true gentleman.
That I am guiltless of your father's death,
And am most sensibly[32] in grief for it,
It shall as level to your judgement pierce
As day does to your eye.
DANES.   [*Within*]   Let her come in.
LAER.   How now, what noise is that?

Enter OPHELIA.

O heat, dry up my brains! Tears seven times salt,
Burn out the sense and virtue[33] of mine eye!
By heaven, thy madness shall be paid with weight,
Till our scale turn the beam. O rose of May!
Dear maid, kind sister, sweet Ophelia!
O heavens, is't possible a young maid's wits
Should be as mortal as an old man's life?
Nature is fine in love, and where 'tis fine
It sends some precious instance[34] of itself
After the thing it loves.

---

[29] *throughly*] thoroughly.
[30] *swoopstake*] sweepstake; i.e., indiscriminately.
[31] *kind*] behaving in accordance with its nature
[32] *sensibly*] feelingly.
[33] *virtue*] power.
[34] *instance*] specimen, sample.

OPH.   [*Sings*] They bore him barefaced on the bier;
                       And in his grave rain'd many a tear—

            Fare you well, my dove.
LAER.   Hadst thou thy wits, and didst persuade revenge,
            It could not move thus.
OPH.   You must sing 'down a-down,' and you 'Call him a-down-a.'
            O, how the wheel[35] becomes it! It is the false steward that
            stole his master's daughter.
LAER.   This nothing's more than matter.
OPH.   There's rosemary, that's for remembrance. Pray you, love, re-
            member. And there is pansies, that's for thoughts.
LAER.   A document in madness: thoughts and remembrance fitted.
OPH.   There's fennel for you, and columbines.[36] There's rue for you,
            and here's some for me. We may call it herb of grace[37] o'
            Sundays. O, you must wear your rue with a difference.[38]
            There's a daisy.[39] I would give you some violets,[40] but they
            withered all when my father died. They say a made a good
            end—

            [*Sings*] For bonny sweet Robin is all my joy.

LAER.   Thought[41] and affliction, passion,[42] hell itself,
            She turns to favour and to prettiness.
OPH.   [*Sings*] And will a not come again?
                              And will a not come again?
                                 No, no, he is dead,
                                 Go to thy death-bed,
                              He never will come again.

                              His beard was as white as snow,
                              All flaxen was his poll.
                                 He is gone, he is gone,
                                 And we cast away moan.
                              God ha' mercy on his soul.

            And of[43] all Christian souls, I pray God. God be wi' you.
                                                                    [*Exit.*

---

[35] *wheel*] poetic refrain, burden.
[36] *fennel . . . columbines*] plants signifying infidelity.
[37] *rue . . . herb of grace*] plant signifying repentance.
[38] *a difference*] a mark of distinction, in heraldry.
[39] *daisy*] signifying unhappy love.
[40] *violets*] signifying faithfulness.
[41] *Thought*] sorrow, melancholy thought.
[42] *passion*] grief.
[43] *of*] on.

LAER.   Do you see this, O God?
KING.   Laertes, I must commune with your grief,
         Or you deny me right. Go but apart,
         Make choice of whom your wisest friends you will,
         And they shall hear and judge 'twixt you and me.
         If by direct or by collateral[44] hand
         They find us touch'd,[45] we will our kingdom give,
         Our crown, our life, and all that we call ours,
         To you in satisfaction. But if not,
         Be you content to lend your patience to us,
         And we shall jointly labour with your soul
         To give it due content.
LAER.   Let this be so.
         His means of death, his obscure funeral—
         No trophy,[46] sword, nor hatchment[47] o'er his bones,
         No noble rite nor formal ostentation—[48]
         Cry to be heard, as 'twere from heaven to earth,
         That I must call't in question.
KING.   So you shall.
         And where the offence is, let the great axe fall.
         I pray you, go with me.   [*Exeunt.*

SCENE VI. *Another room in the castle.*

Enter HORATIO *and a* Servant.

HOR.   What are they that would speak with me?
SERV.   Seafaring men, sir. They say they have letters for you.
HOR.   Let them come in.   [*Exit* Servant.
         I do not know from what part of the world
         I should be greeted, if not from Lord Hamlet.

Enter Sailors.

FIRST SAIL.   God bless you, sir.

44 collateral] indirect.
45 *touch'd*] implicated.
46 *trophy*] memorial.
47 *hatchment*] armorial escutcheon.
48 *ostentation*] ceremony.

HOR. Let him bless thee too.

FIRST SAIL. He shall, sir, an't please him. There's a letter for you, sir. It comes from the ambassador that was bound for England—if your name be Horatio, as I am let to know it is.

HOR. [*Reads*] Horatio, when thou shalt have overlooked[1] this, give these fellows some means to the King. They have letters for him. Ere we were two days old at sea, a pirate of very warlike appointment gave us chase. Finding ourselves too slow of sail, we put on a compelled valour, and in the grapple I boarded them. On the instant they got clear of our ship; so I alone became their prisoner. They have dealt with me like thieves of mercy; but they knew what they did: I am to do a turn for them. Let the King have the letters I have sent, and repair thou to me with as much speed as thou wouldest fly death. I have words to speak in thine ear will make thee dumb, yet are they much too light for the bore[2] of the matter. These good fellows will bring thee where I am. Rosencrantz and Guildenstern hold their course for England. Of them I have much to tell thee. Farewell.

> He that thou knowest thine, HAMLET.

Come, I will make you way for these your letters,
And do't the speedier, that you may direct me
To him from whom you brought them.   [*Exeunt.*

SCENE VII. *Another room in the castle.*

Enter KING *and* LAERTES.

KING. Now must your conscience my acquittance seal,
And you must put me in your heart for friend,
Sith you have heard, and with a knowing ear,
That he which hath your noble father slain
Pursued my life.

LAER.   It well appears. But tell me
Why you proceeded not against these feats,[1]
So crimeful and so capital[2] in nature,

---

[1] *overlooked*] looked over, read.
[2] *too light for the bore*] i.e., Hamlet's words are like shot too light for the bore of the gun.

---

[1] *feats*] wicked deeds.
[2] *capital*] punishable by death.

As by your safety, wisdom, all things else,
You mainly[3] were stirr'd up.

KING.   O, for two special reasons,
Which may to you perhaps seem much unsinew'd,
But yet to me they're strong. The Queen his mother
Lives almost by his looks; and for myself—
My virtue or my plague, be it either which—
She's so conjunctive[4] to my life and soul
That, as the star moves not but in his sphere,
I could not but by her. The other motive,
Why to a public count[5] I might not go,
Is the great love the general gender[6] bear him,
Who, dipping all his faults in their affection,
Would, like the spring that turneth wood to stone,
Convert his gyves[7] to graces; so that my arrows,
Too slightly timber'd for so loud a wind,
Would have reverted to my bow again
And not where I had aim'd them.

LAER.   And so have I a noble father lost,
A sister driven into desperate terms,[8]
Whose worth, if praises may go back again,[9]
Stood challenger on mount of all the age
For her perfections. But my revenge will come.

KING.   Break not your sleeps for that. You must not think
That we are made of stuff so flat and dull
That we can let our beard be shook with danger
And think it pastime. You shortly shall hear more.
I loved your father, and we love ourself.
And that, I hope, will teach you to imagine—

Enter a Messenger, *with letters.*

How now? What news?

MESS.   Letters, my lord, from Hamlet.
This to your Majesty; this to the Queen.

KING.   From Hamlet? Who brought them?

MESS.   Sailors, my lord, they say. I saw them not.

---

[3] *mainly*] mightily.
[4] *conjunctive*] closely joined.
[5] *count*] reckoning, account.
[6] *general gender*] common people.
[7] *gyves*] chains, fetters; here, deficiencies.
[8] *terms*] circumstances.
[9] *go back again*] i.e., to what she was before she lapsed into madness.

They were given me by Claudio. He received them
Of him that brought them.

KING. Laertes, you shall hear them.—
Leave us. [*Exit* Messenger.

[*Reads*] High and mighty, you shall know I am set naked[10] on your kingdom. Tomorrow shall I beg leave to see your kingly eyes, when I shall, first asking your pardon, thereunto recount the occasion of my sudden and more strange return.

HAMLET.

What should this mean? Are all the rest come back?
Or is it some abuse,[11] and no such thing?

LAER. Know you the hand?

KING. 'Tis Hamlet's character.[12] 'Naked'—
And in a postscript here, he says 'Alone.'
Can you advise me?

LAER. I'm lost in it, my lord. But let him come.
It warms the very sickness in my heart
That I shall live and tell him to his teeth,
'Thus diest thou.'

KING. If it be so, Laertes—
As how should it be so, how otherwise?—
Will you be ruled by me?

LAER. Ay, my lord,
So you will not o'errule me to a peace.

KING. To thine own peace. If he be now return'd,
As checking at[13] his voyage, and that he means
No more to undertake it, I will work him
To an exploit now ripe in my device,
Under the which he shall not choose but fall;
And for his death no wind of blame shall breathe,
But even his mother shall uncharge[14] the practice,[15]
And call it accident.

LAER. My lord, I will be ruled;
The rather, if you could devise it so
That I might be the organ.

KING. It falls right.

---

[10] *naked*] destitute.
[11] *abuse*] deception.
[12] *character*] handwriting.
[13] *checking at*] turning from.
[14] *uncharge*] acquit of blame.
[15] *practice*] devious stratagem.

You have been talk'd of since your travel much,
And that in Hamlet's hearing, for a quality
Wherein, they say, you shine. Your sum of parts
Did not together pluck such envy from him,
As did that one, and that in my regard
Of the unworthiest siege.[16]

LAER.   What part is that, my lord?

KING.   A very ribbon in the cap of youth,
Yet needful too; for youth no less becomes
The light and careless livery that it wears
Than settled age his sables and his weeds,
Importing health and graveness. Two months since,
Here was a gentleman of Normandy—
I've seen myself, and served against, the French,
And they can well[17] on horseback; but this gallant
Had witchcraft in't. He grew unto his seat,
And to such wondrous doing brought his horse
As had he been incorpsed and demi-natured
With the brave beast. So far he topp'd my thought
That I, in forgery[18] of shapes and tricks,
Come short of what he did.

LAER.   A Norman was't?

KING.   A Norman.

LAER.   Upon my life, Lamord.

KING.   The very same.

LAER.   I know him well. He is the brooch indeed
And gem of all the nation.

KING.   He made confession of[19] you,
And gave you such a masterly report,
For art and exercise in your defence,[20]
And for your rapier most especial,
That he cried out, 'twould be a sight indeed
If one could match[21] you. The scrimers[22] of their nation,
He swore, had neither motion, guard, nor eye,
If you opposed them. Sir, this report of his

---

[16] *siege*] rank.
[17] *can well*] are skillful.
[18] *forgery*] invention.
[19] *made confession of*] spoke of.
[20] *defence*] swordsmanship.
[21] *match*] engage in a match with.
[22] *scrimers*] fencers.

Did Hamlet so envenom with his envy
That he could nothing do but wish and beg
Your sudden coming o'er, to play with him.
Now, out of this—

LAER.   What out of this, my lord?
KING. Laertes, was your father dear to you?
Or are you like the painting of a sorrow,
A face without a heart?

LAER.   Why ask you this?
KING. Not that I think you did not love your father,
But that I know love is begun by time,
And that I see, in passages of proof,[23]
Time qualifies[24] the spark and fire of it.
There lives within the very flame of love
A kind of wick or snuff that will abate it;
And nothing is at a like goodness still,[25]
For goodness, growing to a pleurisy,
Dies in his own too much. That we would do,
We should do when we would; for this 'would' changes
And hath abatements and delays as many
As there are tongues, are hands, are accidents,
And then this 'should' is like a spendthrift sigh
That hurts by easing. But, to the quick o' the ulcer:
Hamlet comes back; what would you undertake
To show yourself your father's son in deed
More than in words?

LAER.   To cut his throat i' the church.
KING. No place indeed should murder sanctuarize.[26]
Revenge should have no bounds. But, good Laertes,
Will you do this, keep close within your chamber.
Hamlet return'd shall know you are come home.
We'll put on[27] those shall praise your excellence
And set a double varnish on the fame
The Frenchman gave you, bring you in fine[28] together
And wager on your heads. He, being remiss,[29]
Most generous and free from all contriving,

---

[23] *passages of proof*] reliable instances.
[24] *qualifies*] diminishes.
[25] *still*] always.
[26] *sanctuarize*] give sanctuary to.
[27] *put on*] set to work.
[28] *in fine*] in the end.
[29] *remiss*] unsuspecting.

                    Will not peruse the foils, so that with ease,
                    Or with a little shuffling, you may choose
                    A sword unbated,[30] and in a pass[31] of practice
                    Requite him for your father.

LAER.   I will do't.
                    And for that purpose I'll anoint my sword.
                    I bought an unction[32] of a mountebank,
                    So mortal that but dip a knife in it,
                    Where it draws blood no cataplasm[33] so rare,
                    Collected from all simples[34] that have virtue
                    Under the moon, can save the thing from death
                    That is but scratch'd withal. I'll touch my point
                    With this contagion that, if I gall[35] him slightly,
                    It may be death.

KING.   Let's further think of this,
                    Weigh what convenience both of time and means
                    May fit us to our shape.[36] If this should fail,
                    And that our drift[37] look through our bad performance,
                    'Twere better not assay'd. Therefore this project
                    Should have a back or second that might hold
                    If this did blast in proof.[38] Soft, let me see.
                    We'll make a solemn wager on your cunnings—[39]
                    I ha't!
                    When in your motion you are hot and dry—
                    As make your bouts more violent to that end—
                    And that he calls for drink, I'll have prepared him
                    A chalice for the nonce; whereon but sipping,
                    If he by chance escape your venom'd stuck,[40]
                    Our purpose may hold there. But stay, what noise?

Enter QUEEN.

                    How now, sweet Queen?
QUEEN.   One woe doth tread upon another's heel,

---

[30] *unbated*] unblunted (without a button on the point).
[31] *pass*] a single thrust or a bout.
[32] *unction*] ointment.
[33] *cataplasm*] plaster, poultice.
[34] *simples*] medicinal herbs.
[35] *gall*] wound.
[36] *shape*] form of proceeding.
[37] *drift*] scheme.
[38] *blast in proof*] fail when put to the test.
[39] *your cunnings*] your respective skill.
[40] *stuck*] thrust.

So fast they follow. Your sister's drown'd, Laertes.
LAER. Drown'd? O, where?
QUEEN. There is a willow grows aslant a brook,
That shows his hoary leaves in the glassy stream.
Therewith fantastic garlands did she make
Of crow-flowers,[41] nettles, daisies, and long purples,[42]
That liberal[43] shepherds give a grosser name,
But our cold[44] maids do dead men's fingers call them.
There, on the pendent boughs her crownet weeds
Clambering to hang, an envious[45] sliver broke;
When down her weedy trophies and herself
Fell in the weeping brook. Her clothes spread wide,
And mermaid-like awhile they bore her up;
Which time she chanted snatches of old lauds,[46]
As one incapable[47] of her own distress,
Or like a creature native and indued
Unto[48] that element. But long it could not be
Till that her garments, heavy with their drink,
Pull'd the poor wretch from her melodious lay
To muddy death.
LAER.   Alas, then she is drown'd.
QUEEN. Drown'd, drown'd.
LAER. Too much of water hast thou, poor Ophelia,
And therefore I forbid my tears. But yet
It is our trick;[49] nature her custom holds,
Let shame say what it will. When these are gone,
The woman will be out.[50] Adieu, my lord.
I have a speech of fire that fain would blaze,
But that this folly douts it.[51]   [*Exit.*
KING.   Let's follow, Gertrude.
How much I had to do to calm his rage.
Now fear I this will give it start again;
Therefore let's follow.   [*Exeunt.*

[41] *crow-flowers*] ragged robins.
[42] *long purples*] Orchis mascula.
[43] *liberal*] licentious.
[44] *cold*] chaste.
[45] *envious*] spiteful.
[46] *lauds*] hymns.
[47] *incapable*] unaware.
[48] *indued Unto*] suited to live in.
[49] *our trick*] in our nature.
[50] *When . . . out*] i.e., when I have shed these tears the woman in me will have been cast off, too.
[51] *this folly douts it*] this weeping extinguishes it.

ACT V.

SCENE I. *A churchyard.*

Enter two Clowns, *with spades, &c.*

FIRST CLO.   Is she to be buried in Christian burial that wilfully seeks
her own salvation?[1]

SEC. CLO.   I tell thee she is; and therefore make her grave straight.[2] The
crowner[3] hath sat on her, and finds it Christian burial.

FIRST CLO.   How can that be, unless she drowned herself in her own
defence?

SEC. CLO.   Why, 'tis found so.

FIRST CLO.   It must be *se offendendo*;[4] it cannot be else. For here lies the
point: if I drown myself wittingly, it argues an act, and an act
hath three branches: it is to act, to do, and to perform;
argal,[5] she drowned herself wittingly.

SEC. CLO.   Nay, but hear you, Goodman Delver—

FIRST CLO.   Give me leave. Here lies the water—good. Here stands the
man—good. If the man go to this water and drown himself,
it is, will he, nill he, he goes. Mark you that. But if the water
come to him and drown him, he drowns not himself; argal,
he that is not guilty of his own death shortens not his own
life.

SEC. CLO.   But is this law?

FIRST CLO.   Ay, marry, is't; crowner's quest[6] law.

---

[1] *Christian burial . . . salvation*] The Clowns assume that Ophelia has committed suicide
and that therefore she cannot be buried in consecrated ground. *Salvation* is a blunder for
"damnation."

[2] *straight*] straightaway.

[3] *crowner*] coroner.

[4] *se offendendo*] a blunder for *se defendendo* (in self-defense).

[5] *argal*] an uneducated pronunciation of "ergo."

[6] *quest*] inquest.

SEC. CLO.   Will you ha' the truth on't? If this had not been a gentle-woman, she should have been buried out o' Christian burial.

FIRST CLO.   Why, there thou say'st. And the more pity that great folk should have countenance in this world to drown or hang themselves, more than their even[7] Christian. Come, my spade. There is no ancient gentlemen but gardeners, ditchers and grave-makers: they hold up[8] Adam's profession.

SEC. CLO.   Was he a gentleman?

FIRST CLO.   A was the first that ever bore arms.

SEC. CLO.   Why, he had none.

FIRST CLO.   What, art a heathen? How dost thou understand the Scripture? The Scripture says Adam digged. Could he dig without arms? I'll put another question to thee. If thou answerest me not to the purpose, confess thyself—

SEC. CLO.   Go to.

FIRST CLO.   What is he that builds stronger than either the mason, the shipwright, or the carpenter?

SEC. CLO.   The gallows-maker; for that frame outlives a thousand tenants.

FIRST CLO.   I like thy wit well, in good faith. The gallows does well. But how does it well? It does well to those that do ill. Now, thou dost ill to say the gallows is built stronger than the church; argal, the gallows may do well to thee. To't again, come.

SEC. CLO.   'Who builds stronger than a mason, a shipwright, or a carpenter?'

FIRST CLO.   Ay, tell me that, and unyoke.[9]

SEC. CLO.   Marry, now I can tell.

FIRST CLO.   To't.

SEC. CLO.   Mass, I cannot tell.

Enter HAMLET *and* HORATIO, *afar off.*

FIRST CLO.   Cudgel thy brains no more about it, for your dull ass will not mend his pace with beating, and when you are asked this question next, say 'A grave-maker.' The houses that he makes last till doomsday. Go, get thee to Yaughan. Fetch me a stoup of liquor.

                [*Exit* Sec. Clown; First Clown *digs, and sings.*

---

[7] *even*] fellow.
[8] *hold up*] continue.
[9] *unyoke*] i.e., then your work is done.

> In youth, when I did love, did love,
>> Methought it was very sweet,
> To contract,[10] O, the time, for-a my behove,[11]
>> O, methought, there-a was nothing-a meet.

HAM.   Has this fellow no feeling of his business, that he sings at grave-
          making?
HOR.   Custom hath made it in him a property of easiness.[12]
HAM.   'Tis e'en so. The hand of little employment hath the daintier
          sense.
FIRST CLO.   [Sings] But age, with his stealing steps,
>> Hath claw'd me in his clutch,
> And hath shipped me intil[13] the land,
>> As if I had never been such. [Throws up a skull.]

HAM.   That skull had a tongue in it, and could sing once. How the
          knave jowls[14] it to the ground, as if it were Cain's jawbone,
          that did the first murder. It might be the pate of a politician,
          which this ass now o'er-offices,[15] one that would circum-
          vent God, might it not?
HOR.   It might, my lord.
HAM.   Or of a courtier, which could say 'Good morrow, sweet lord.
          How dost thou, sweet lord?' This might be my Lord Such-
          a-one, that praised my Lord Such-a-one's horse, when he
          meant to beg it, might it not?
HOR.   Ay, my lord.
HAM.   Why, e'en so; and now my Lady Worm's, chapless,[16] and
          knocked about the mazard[17] with a sexton's spade. Here's
          fine revolution, an we had the trick[18] to see't. Did these
          bones cost no more the breeding, but to play at loggats[19]
          with 'em? Mine ache to think on't.
FIRST CLO.   [Sings] A pickaxe, and a spade, a spade,
>> For and[20] a shrouding-sheet;
> O, a pit of clay for to be made
>> For such a guest is meet. [Throws up another skull.]

---

[10] contract] shorten (probably a blunder by the Clown).
[11] behove] behoof, advantage.
[12] property of easiness] activity that does not trouble the mind.
[13] intil] to.
[14] jowls] throws, dashes.
[15] o'er-offices] lords over (by virtue of his office as grave digger).
[16] chapless] without a jaw.
[17] mazard] head.
[18] trick] knack, art.
[19] loggats] a game in which small logs are thrown at a stake.
[20] For and] and moreover.

HAM. There's another. Why may not that be the skull of a lawyer? Where be his quiddities now, his quillets,[21] his cases, his tenures, and his tricks? Why does he suffer this rude knave now to knock him about the sconce with a dirty shovel, and will not tell him of his action of battery? Hum! This fellow might be in's time a great buyer of land, with his statutes, his recognizances, his fines, his double vouchers, his recoveries.[22] Is this the fine[23] of his fines and the recovery of his recoveries, to have his fine pate full of fine dirt? Will his vouchers vouch[24] him no more of his purchases, and double ones too, than the length and breadth of a pair of indentures?[25] The very conveyances of his lands will hardly lie in this box;[26] and must the inheritor[27] himself have no more, ha?

HOR. Not a jot more, my lord.

HAM. Is not parchment made of sheepskins?

HOR. Ay, my lord, and of calfskins too.

HAM. They are sheep and calves which seek out assurance in that. I will speak to this fellow. Whose grave's this, sirrah?

FIRST CLO. Mine, sir.

     [Sings] O, a pit of clay for to be made
       For such a guest is meet.

HAM. I think it be thine indeed, for thou liest in't.

FIRST CLO. You lie out on't, sir, and therefore 'tis not yours. For my part, I do not lie in't, and yet it is mine.

HAM. Thou dost lie in't, to be in't and say 'tis thine. 'Tis for the dead, not for the quick; therefore thou liest.

FIRST CLO. 'Tis a quick lie, sir; 'twill away again from me to you.

HAM. What man dost thou dig it for?

FIRST CLO. For no man, sir.

HAM. What woman then?

FIRST CLO. For none, neither.

HAM. Who is to be buried in't?

FIRST CLO. One that was a woman, sir, but, rest her soul, she's dead.

---

[21] *quiddities . . . quillets*] subtle arguments.
[22] *statutes . . . recoveries*] legal terms relating to the transfer and mortgaging of land.
[23] *fine*] end.
[24] *vouch*] guarantee.
[25] *indentures*] contracts.
[26] *box*] coffin.
[27] *inheritor*] possessor, owner.

HAM.   How absolute[28] the knave is! We must speak by the card,[29] or
           equivocation will undo us. By the Lord, Horatio, this three
           years I have taken note of it: the age is grown so picked[30] that
           the toe of the peasant comes so near the heel of the courtier,
           he galls his kibe.[31] How long hast thou been a grave-maker?

FIRST CLO.   Of all the days i' the year, I came to't that day that our last
           King Hamlet o'ercame Fortinbras.

HAM.   How long is that since?

FIRST CLO.   Cannot you tell that? Every fool can tell that. It was that
           very day that young Hamlet was born—he that is mad and
           sent into England.

HAM.   Ay, marry, why was he sent into England?

FIRST CLO.   Why, because a was mad. A shall recover his wits there; or,
           if a do not, 'tis no great matter there.

HAM.   Why?

FIRST CLO.   'Twill not be seen in him there. There the men are as mad
           as he.

HAM.   How came he mad?

FIRST CLO.   Very strangely, they say.

HAM.   How 'strangely'?

FIRST CLO.   Faith, e'en with losing his wits.

HAM.   Upon what ground?

FIRST CLO.   Why, here in Denmark. I have been sexton here, man and
           boy, thirty years.

HAM.   How long will a man lie i' the earth ere he rot?

FIRST CLO.   I'faith, if a be not rotten before a die—as we have many
           pocky corses nowadays that will scarce hold the laying
           in[32]—a will last you some eight year or nine year. A tanner
           will last you nine year.

HAM.   Why he more than another?

FIRST CLO.   Why, sir, his hide is so tanned with his trade that a will
           keep out water a great while; and your water is a sore decayer
           of your whoreson dead body. Here's a skull, now. This skull
           has lain in the earth three and twenty years.

HAM.   Whose was it?

FIRST CLO.   A whoreson mad fellow's it was. Whose do you think it
           was?

---

[28] *absolute*] strict.
[29] *by the card*] with the utmost precision.
[30] *picked*] refined.
[31] *galls his kibe*] chafes the sore on his heel.
[32] *hold the laying in*] remain in one piece until after the burial.

HAM.   Nay, I know not.

FIRST CLO.   A pestilence on him for a mad rogue! A poured a flagon of
            Rhenish on my head once. This same skull, sir, was Yorick's
            skull, the King's jester.

HAM.   [*Takes the skull*] This?

FIRST CLO.   E'en that.

HAM.   Alas, poor Yorick. I knew him, Horatio: a fellow of infinite jest,
            of most excellent fancy. He hath borne me on his back a
            thousand times; and now, how abhorred in my imagination
            it is! My gorge rises at it. Here hung those lips that I have
            kissed I know not how oft. Where be your gibes now, your
            gambols, your songs, your flashes of merriment, that were
            wont to set the table on a roar? Not one now to mock your
            own grinning? Quite chop-fallen? Now get you to my lady's
            chamber, and tell her, let her paint an inch thick, to this
            favour[33] she must come. Make her laugh at that. Prithee,
            Horatio, tell me one thing.

HOR.   What's that, my lord?

HAM.   Dost thou think Alexander looked o' this fashion i' the earth?

HOR.   E'en so.

HAM.   And smelt so? Pah!   [*Puts down the skull.*

HOR.   E'en so, my lord.

HAM.   To what base uses we may return, Horatio! Why, may not
            imagination trace the noble dust of Alexander till he find it
            stopping a bung-hole?

HOR.   'Twere to consider too curiously[34] to consider so.

HAM.   No, faith, not a jot; but to follow him thither with modesty[35]
            enough and likelihood to lead it, as thus: Alexander died,
            Alexander was buried, Alexander returneth into dust, the
            dust is earth, of earth we make loam, and why of that loam,
            whereto he was converted, might they not stop a beer-barrel?
            Imperious[36] Cæsar, dead and turn'd to clay,
            Might stop a hole to keep the wind away.
            O, that that earth, which kept the world in awe,
            Should patch a wall to expel the winter's flaw![37]
            But soft, but soft awhile! Here comes the King,
            The Queen, the courtiers.

---

[33] *favour*] appearance.
[34] *curiously*] minutely.
[35] *modestly*] moderation.
[36] *Imperious*] imperial.
[37] *flaw*] gust of wind.

Enter Priests, &c. *in procession; the Corpse of Ophelia*, LAERTES, *and*
Mourners *following;* KING, QUEEN, *their trains*, &c.

	Who is this they follow?
	And with such maimed rites? This doth betoken
	The corse they follow did with desperate hand
	Fordo[38] its own life. 'Twas of some estate.[39]
	Couch we[40] awhile and mark. [*Retiring with* HORATIO.
LAER.	What ceremony else?
HAM.	That is Laertes, a very noble youth. Mark.
LAER.	What ceremony else?
PRIEST.	Her obsequies have been as far enlarged
	As we have warranty. Her death was doubtful;
	And, but that great command o'ersways the order,
	She should in ground unsanctified have lodged
	Till the last trumpet; for charitable prayers,
	Shards,[41] flints and pebbles should be thrown on her.
	Yet here she is allow'd her virgin crants,[42]
	Her maiden strewments[43] and the bringing home
	Of bell and burial.[44]
LAER.	Must there no more be done?
PRIEST.	No more be done.
	We should profane the service of the dead
	To sing a requiem and such rest to her
	As to peace-parted souls.
LAER.	Lay her i' the earth,
	And from her fair and unpolluted flesh
	May violets spring. I tell thee, churlish priest,
	A ministering angel shall my sister be
	When thou liest howling.
HAM.	What, the fair Ophelia!
QUEEN.	[*Scattering flowers*] Sweets to the sweet. Farewell.
	I hoped thou shouldst have been my Hamlet's wife;
	I thought thy bride-bed to have deck'd, sweet maid,
	And not have strew'd thy grave.
LAER.	O, treble woe

---

[38] *Fordo*] destroy.
[39] *estate*] rank.
[40] *Couch we*] let us remain hidden.
[41] *Shards*] fragments of pottery.
[42] *crants*] garlands.
[43] *strewments*] strewing of flowers.
[44] *bringing home . . . burial*] laying to rest to the sound of the knell.

Fall ten times treble on that cursed head
Whose wicked deed thy most ingenious sense
Deprived thee of! Hold off the earth awhile,
Till I have caught her once more in mine arms.

                             [Leaps into the grave.

Now pile your dust upon the quick and dead,
Till of this flat a mountain you have made
To o'ertop old Pelion or the skyish head
Of blue Olympus.

HAM.   *[Advancing]* What is he whose grief
Bears such an emphasis, whose phrase of sorrow
Conjures the wandering stars[45] and makes them stand
Like wonder-wounded hearers? This is I,
Hamlet the Dane.

LAER.   The devil take thy soul!   *[Grappling with him.*
HAM.   Thou pray'st not well.
I prithee, take thy fingers from my throat;
For, though I am not splenative[46] and rash,
Yet have I in me something dangerous,
Which let thy wisdom fear. Hold off thy hand.

KING.   Pluck them asunder.
QUEEN. Hamlet, Hamlet!
ALL.   Gentlemen!
HOR.   Good my lord, be quiet.
HAM.   Why, I will fight with him upon this theme
Until my eyelids will no longer wag.

QUEEN. O my son, what theme?
HAM.   I loved Ophelia. Forty thousand brothers
Could not, with all their quantity of love,
Make up my sum. What wilt thou do for her?

KING.   O, he is mad, Laertes.
QUEEN. For love of God, forbear[47] him.
HAM.   'Swounds, show me what thou'lt do.
Woo't[48] weep, woo't fight, woo't fast, woo't tear thyself,
Woo't drink up eisel,[49] eat a crocodile?
I'll do't. Dost thou come here to whine,
To outface me with leaping in her grave?

---

[45] *wandering stars*] planets.
[46] *splenative*] hot-tempered, impetuous.
[47] *forbear*] leave alone.
[48] *Woo't*] will you.
[49] *eisel*] vinegar.

Be buried quick[50] with her, and so will I.
And, if thou prate of mountains, let them throw
Millions of acres on us, till our ground,
Singeing his pate against the burning zone,[51]
Make Ossa like a wart. Nay, an thou'lt mouth,
I'll rant as well as thou.

QUEEN.   This is mere madness;
And thus awhile the fit will work on him.
Anon, as patient as the female dove
When that her golden couplets are disclosed,[52]
His silence will sit drooping.

HAM.   Hear you, sir;
What is the reason that you use me thus?
I loved you ever. But it is no matter.
Let Hercules himself do what he may,
The cat will mew, and dog will have his day.   [Exit.

KING.   I pray thee, good Horatio, wait upon him. [Exit HORATIO.
[To LAERTES] Strengthen your patience in our last night's
    speech;
We'll put the matter to the present push.—[53]
Good Gertrude, set some watch over your son.
This grave shall have a living monument.
An hour of quiet shortly shall we see;
Till then, in patience our proceeding be.   [Exeunt.

SCENE II. *A hall in the castle.*

Enter HAMLET *and* HORATIO.

HAM.   So much for this, sir. Now shall you see the other.
          You do remember all the circumstance?
HOR.   Remember it, my lord!
HAM.   Sir, in my heart there was a kind of fighting
          That would not let me sleep. Methought I lay

---

[50] *quick*] alive.
[51] *burning zone*] sun's sphere or orbit.
[52] *disclosed*] hatched.
[53] *to the present push*] into immediate action.

Worse than the mutines in the bilboes.[1] Rashly—
And praised be rashness for it: let us know
Our indiscretion sometime serves us well
When our deep plots do pall; and that should learn us
There's a divinity that shapes our ends,
Rough-hew them how we will—

HOR.   That is most certain.

HAM.   Up from my cabin,
My sea-gown scarf'd about me, in the dark
Groped I to find out them,[2] had my desire,
Finger'd[3] their packet, and in fine[4] withdrew
To mine own room again, making so bold,
My fears forgetting manners, to unseal
Their grand commission, where I found, Horatio—
O royal knavery!—an exact command,
Larded[5] with many several sorts of reasons
Importing Denmark's health and England's too,
With, ho! such bugs and goblins in my life,[6]
That on the supervise,[7] no leisure bated,[8]
No, not to stay the grinding of the axe,
My head should be struck off.

HOR.   Is't possible?

HAM.   Here's the commission. Read it at more leisure.
But wilt thou hear now how I did proceed?

HOR.   I beseech you.

HAM.   Being thus benetted round with villanies—
Or[9] I could make a prologue to my brains,
They had begun the play—I sat me down,
Devised a new commission, wrote it fair.[10]
I once did hold it, as our statists[11] do,
A baseness to write fair, and labour'd much
How to forget that learning; but, sir, now
It did me yeoman's service. Wilt thou know

---

[1] *mutines in the bilboes*] mutineers in shackles.
[2] *them*] Rosencrantz and Guildenstern.
[3] *Finger'd*] pilfered.
[4] *in fine*] finally.
[5] *Larded*] garnished.
[6] *such bugs . . . life*] such imaginary dangers, should I be allowed to live.
[7] *supervise*] perusal (of Claudius' missive).
[8] *no leisure bated*] with no delay.
[9] *Or*] before.
[10] *fair*] in a legible hand.
[11] *statists*] statesmen.

	The effect of what I wrote?
HOR.	Ay, good my lord.
HAM.	An earnest conjuration from the King,

As England was his faithful tributary,
As love between them like the palm might flourish,
As peace should still[12] her wheaten garland wear
And stand a comma 'tween their amities,
And many such-like 'As'es of great charge,[13]
That on the view and knowing of these contents,
Without debatement further, more or less,
He should the bearers put to sudden death,
Not shriving-time[14] allow'd.

HOR.	How was this seal'd?
HAM.	Why, even in that was heaven ordinant.[15]

I had my father's signet in my purse,
Which was the model of that Danish seal;
Folded the writ up in the form of the other,
Subscribed it, gave't the impression, placed it safely,
The changeling never known. Now, the next day
Was our sea-fight; and what to this was sequent
Thou know'st already.

HOR.	So Guildenstern and Rosencrantz go to't.
HAM.	Why, man, they did make love to this employment.

They are not near my conscience. Their defeat
Does by their own insinuation grow.
'Tis dangerous when the baser nature comes
Between the pass[16] and fell incensed points
Of mighty opposites.

HOR.	Why, what a king is this!
HAM.	Does it not, think thee, stand me now upon—[17]

He that hath kill'd my king and whored my mother,
Popp'd in between the election and my hopes,
Thrown out his angle[18] for my proper[19] life,
And with such cozenage[20]—is't not perfect conscience
To quit him with this arm? And is't not to be damn'd

---

12 *still*] always.
13 *charge*] importance. There is a pun on "asses," and the load they carry.
14 *shriving-time*] time for absolution.
15 *ordinant*] ordaining, directing.
16 *pass*] sword thrust.
17 *stand me now upon*] put me under obligation.
18 *angle*] fishhook.
19 *proper*] own.
20 *cozenage*] deceit.

	To let this canker of our nature come

              To let this canker of our nature come
              In further evil?

HOR.   It must be shortly known to him from England
              What is the issue of the business there.

HAM.   It will be short. The interim is mine;
              And a man's life's no more than to say 'One.'
              But I am very sorry, good Horatio,
              That to Laertes I forgot myself;
              For by the image of my cause I see
              The portraiture of his. I'll court his favours.
              But, sure, the bravery[21] of his grief did put me
              Into a towering passion.

HOR.   Peace, who comes here?

Enter OSRIC.

OSR.   Your lordship is right welcome back to Denmark.

HAM.   I humbly thank you, sir. Dost know this water-fly?

HOR.   No, my good lord.

HAM.   Thy state is the more gracious,[22] for 'tis a vice to know him. He hath much land, and fertile. Let a beast be lord of beasts, and his crib[23] shall stand at the king's mess. 'Tis a chuff,[24] but, as I say, spacious in the possession of dirt.

OSR.   Sweet lord, if your lordship were at leisure, I should impart a thing to you from his Majesty.

HAM.   I will receive it, sir, with all diligence of spirit. Put your bonnet to his right use: 'tis for the head.

OSR.   I thank your lordship, it is very hot.

HAM.   No, believe me, 'tis very cold; the wind is northerly.

OSR.   It is indifferent[25] cold, my lord, indeed.

HAM.   But yet methinks it is very sultry and hot for my complexion.[26]

OSR.   Exceedingly, my lord. It is very sultry, as 'twere—I cannot tell how. But, my lord, his Majesty bade me signify to you that he has laid a great wager on your head. Sir, this is the matter—

HAM.   I beseech you, remember—

                     [HAMLET *moves him to put on his hat.*

---

[21] *bravery*] bravado, ostentation.
[22] *gracious*] virtuous.
[23] *crib*] manger, trough.
[24] *chuff*] a wealthy, but dull, person.
[25] *indifferent*] moderately.
[26] *complexion*] temperament, constitution.

OSR.   Nay, good my lord; for mine ease, in good faith. Sir, here is
       newly come to court Laertes—believe me, an absolute gen-
       tleman, full of most excellent differences,[27] of very soft
       society and great showing.[28] Indeed, to speak feelingly[29] of
       him, he is the card or calendar of gentry,[30] for you shall find
       in him the continent[31] of what part a gentleman would see.

HAM.   Sir, his definement suffers no perdition[32] in you, though, I
       know, to divide him inventorially would dizzy the arithme-
       tic of memory, and yet but yaw neither,[33] in respect of his
       quick sail. But, in the verity of extolment, I take him to be a
       soul of great article,[34] and his infusion[35] of such dearth[36]
       and rareness as, to make true diction of him, his semblable
       is his mirror,[37] and who else would trace[38] him, his um-
       brage,[39] nothing more.

OSR.   Your lordship speaks most infallibly of him.

HAM.   The concernancy,[40] sir? Why do we wrap the gentleman in our
       more rawer breath?[41]

OSR.   Sir?

HOR.   Is't not possible to understand in another tongue?[42] You will
       do't, sir, really.

HAM.   What imports the nomination[43] of this gentleman?

OSR.   Of Laertes?

HOR.   His purse is empty already; all's golden words are spent.

HAM.   Of him, sir.

OSR.   I know you are not ignorant—

HAM.   I would you did, sir. Yet, in faith, if you did, it would not much
       approve[44] me. Well, sir?

---

[27] *differences*] extraordinary qualities.
[28] *soft society . . . showing*] distinguished appearance.
[29] *feelingly*] perceptively.
[30] *card or calendar of gentry*] epitome of courtesy.
[31] *continent*] container.
[32] *perdition*] loss.
[33] *but yaw neither*] steer out of course nevertheless.
[34] *article*] i.e., matter to be listed on an inventory.
[35] *infusion*] quality.
[36] *dearth*] rarity.
[37] *his semblable is his mirror*] the only person like him is his own reflection.
[38] *trace*] follow.
[39] *umbrage*] shadow.
[40] *concernancy*] import, significance.
[41] *more rawer breath*] inadequate language.
[42] *another tongue*] i.e., simpler terms.
[43] *nomination*] mentioning.
[44] *approve*] commend.

OSR.   You are not ignorant of what excellence Laertes is—
HAM.   I dare not confess that, lest I should compare with him in
         excellence; but, to know a man well were to know himself.
OSR.   I mean, sir, for his weapon; but in the imputation[45] laid on
         him by them in his meed,[46] he's unfellowed.
HAM.   What's his weapon?
OSR.   Rapier and dagger.
HAM.   That's two of his weapons. But, well.
OSR.   The King, sir, hath wagered with him six Barbary horses,
         against the which he has impawned,[47] as I take it, six French
         rapiers and poniards,[48] with their assigns,[49] as girdle,
         hanger,[50] and so. Three of the carriages, in faith, are very
         dear to fancy, very responsive[51] to the hilts, most delicate
         carriages, and of very liberal conceit.[52]
HAM.   What call you the carriages?
HOR.   I knew you must be edified by the margent[53] ere you had done.
OSR.   The carriages, sir, are the hangers.
HAM.   The phrase would be more german[54] to the matter if we could
         carry a cannon by our sides. I would it might be hangers till
         then. But, on. Six Barbary horses against six French swords,
         their assigns, and three liberal-conceited carriages—that's
         the French bet against the Danish. Why is this 'impawned,'
         as you call it?
OSR.   The King, sir, hath laid, sir, that in a dozen passes[55] between
         yourself and him, he shall not exceed you three hits. He
         hath laid on twelve for nine. And it would come to immedi-
         ate trial, if your lordship would vouchsafe the answer.
HAM.   How if I answer no?
OSR.   I mean, my lord, the opposition of your person in trial.
HAM.   Sir, I will walk here in the hall. If it please his Majesty, it is the
         breathing time[56] of day with me. Let the foils be brought,

---

[45] *imputation*] reputation.
[46] *meed*] service.
[47] *impawned*] wagered.
[48] *poniards*] daggers.
[49] *assigns*] accessories.
[50] *hanger*] part of a belt to which the scabbard is attached.
[51] *responsive*] matching, suited.
[52] *liberal conceit*] (?) tasteful design.
[53] *margent*] margin (of a book, on which could be written explanatory notes).
[54] *german*] germane, appropriate.
[55] *passes*] bouts.
[56] *breathing time*] exercise period.

the gentleman willing, and the King hold his purpose, I will
win for him an I can. If not, I will gain nothing but my
shame and the odd hits.

OSR.   Shall I redeliver you e'en so?

HAM.   To this effect, sir, after what flourish your nature will.

OSR.   I commend my duty to your lordship.

HAM.   Yours, yours. [*Exit* OSRIC.] He does well to commend it himself; there are no tongues else for's turn.

HOR.   This lapwing runs away with the shell on his head.[57]

HAM.   He did comply with his dug[58] before he sucked it. Thus has
he—and many more of the same breed that I know the
drossy[59] age dotes on—only got the tune of the time and
outward habit of encounter, a kind of yesty[60] collection,
which carries them through and through the most fanned
and winnowed[61] opinions; and do but blow them to their
trial, the bubbles are out.[62]

Enter a Lord.

LORD.   My lord, his Majesty commended him to you by young Osric,
who brings back to him that you attend him in the hall. He
sends to know if your pleasure hold to play with Laertes or
that you will take longer time.

HAM.   I am constant to my purposes; they follow the King's pleasure.
If his fitness[63] speaks, mine is ready; now or whensoever,
provided I be so able as now.

LORD.   The King and Queen and all are coming down.

HAM.   In happy time.

LORD.   The Queen desires you to use some gentle entertainment[64] to
Laertes before you fall to play.

HAM.   She well instructs me.   [*Exit* Lord.

HOR.   You will lose this wager, my lord.

HAM.   I do not think so. Since he went into France, I have been in

---

[57] *This lapwing . . . head*] Horatio refers to the fact that Osric has put his hat back on.
Lapwings were said to leave the nest shortly after hatching and therefore came to signify
precocity and pretension.

[58] *did comply . . . dug*] was courteous to his mother's breast.

[59] *drossy*] frivolous.

[60] *yesty*] frothy.

[61] *fanned and winnowed*] tried and sifted.

[62] *do but blow . . . out*] i.e., when you put them to the test by conversing with them their
expressions are found to be empty.

[63] *fitness*] convenience.

[64] *gentle entertainment*] courtesy.

	continual practice. I shall win at the odds. But thou wouldst not think how ill all's here about my heart; but it is no matter.
HOR.	Nay, good my lord—
HAM.	It is but foolery; but it is such a kind of gain-giving[65] as would perhaps trouble a woman.
HOR.	If your mind dislike anything, obey it. I will forestall their repair hither and say you are not fit.
HAM.	Not a whit. We defy augury. There is special providence in the fall of a sparrow. If it be now, 'tis not to come; if it be not to come, it will be now; if it be not now, yet it will come. The readiness is all. Since no man has aught of what he leaves, what is't to leave betimes? Let be.

Enter KING, QUEEN, LAERTES, *and* Lords, OSRIC *and other* Attendants *with foils and gauntlets; a table and flagons of wine on it.*

KING.	Come, Hamlet, come, and take this hand from me.
	[*The* KING *puts* LAERTES' *hand into* HAMLET'S.
HAM.	Give me your pardon, sir. I've done you wrong;
	But pardon't as you are a gentleman.
	This presence[66] knows,
	And you must needs have heard, how I am punish'd
	With sore distraction. What I have done
	That might your nature, honour and exception[67]
	Roughly awake, I here proclaim was madness.
	Was't Hamlet wrong'd Laertes? Never Hamlet.
	If Hamlet from himself be ta'en away,
	And when he's not himself does wrong Laertes,
	Then Hamlet does it not, Hamlet denies it.
	Who does it then? His madness. If't be so,
	Hamlet is of the faction that is wrong'd;
	His madness is poor Hamlet's enemy.
	Sir, in this audience,
	Let my disclaiming from a purposed evil
	Free me so far in your most generous thoughts
	That I have shot mine arrow o'er the house
	And hurt my brother.
LAER.	I am satisfied in nature,
	Whose motive in this case should stir me most
	To my revenge; but in my terms of honour

[65] *gain-giving*] misgiving.
[66] *presence*] noble assembly.
[67] *exception*] disapproval.

I stand aloof, and will no reconcilement
Till by some elder masters of known honour
I have a voice[68] and precedent of peace
To keep my name ungored. But till that time
I do receive your offer'd love like love
And will not wrong it.

HAM.   I embrace it freely,
And will this brother's wager frankly play.—
Give us the foils. Come on.

LAER.   Come, one for me.

HAM.   I'll be your foil,[69] Laertes. In mine ignorance
Your skill shall, like a star i' the darkest night,
Stick fiery off[70] indeed.

LAER.   You mock me, sir.

HAM.   No, by this hand.

KING.   Give them the foils, young Osric. Cousin Hamlet,
You know the wager?

HAM.   Very well, my lord.
Your Grace has laid the odds o' the weaker side.

KING.   I do not fear it; I have seen you both,
But since he is better'd, we have therefore odds.

LAER.   This is too heavy; let me see another.

HAM.   This likes me well. These foils have all a length?

                        [*They prepare to play.*

OSR.   Ay, my good lord.

KING.   Set me the stoups of wine upon that table.
If Hamlet give the first or second hit,
Or quit in answer of the third exchange,
Let all the battlements their ordnance fire:
The King shall drink to Hamlet's better breath,
And in the cup an union[71] shall he throw,
Richer than that which four successive kings
In Denmark's crown have worn. Give me the cups;
And let the kettle to the trumpet speak,
The trumpet to the cannoneer without,
The cannons to the heavens, the heaven to earth,
'Now the King drinks to Hamlet.' Come, begin.
And you, the judges, bear a wary eye.

---

[68] *voice*] authoritative judgment.
[69] *foil*] background on which a jewel is placed.
[70] *Stick fiery off*] stand out brightly.
[71] *union*] pearl.

HAM.	Come on, sir.
LAER.	Come, my lord. *[They play.*
HAM.	One.
LAER.	No.
HAM.	Judgement.
OSR.	A hit, a very palpable hit.
LAER.	Well, again.
KING.	Stay; give me drink. Hamlet, this pearl is thine.

         Here's to thy health.

                 [Trumpets sound, and cannon shot off within.
                    Give him the cup.

HAM.	I'll play this bout first. Set it by awhile.

         Come. *[They play.]* Another hit. What say you?

LAER.	A touch, a touch, I do confess.
KING.	Our son shall win.
QUEEN.	He's fat[72] and scant of breath.

         Here, Hamlet, take my napkin, rub thy brows.
         The Queen carouses to thy fortune, Hamlet.

HAM.	Good madam.
KING.	Gertrude, do not drink.
QUEEN.	I will, my lord; I pray you, pardon me.
KING.	*[Aside]* It is the poison'd cup; it is too late.
HAM.	I dare not drink yet, madam—by and by.
QUEEN.	Come, let me wipe thy face.
LAER.	My lord, I'll hit him now.
KING.	I do not think't.
LAER.	*[Aside]* And yet it is almost against my conscience.
HAM.	Come, for the third, Laertes. You but dally.

         I pray you, pass[73] with your best violence.
         I am afeard you make a wanton of me.[74]

LAER.	Say you so? Come on. *[They play.*
OSR.	Nothing, neither way.
LAER.	Have at you now!

         [Laertes wounds HAMLET; then, in scuffling, they change
                 rapiers, and HAMLET wounds LAERTES.

KING.	Part them; they are incensed.
HAM.	Nay, come, again. *[The QUEEN falls.*
OSR.	Look to the Queen there, ho!
HOR.	They bleed on both sides. How is it, my lord?

---

[72] *fat*] unfit.
[73] *pass*] thrust.
[74] *make a wanton of me*] treat me like a spoiled child.

OSR.   How is't, Laertes?
LAER.   Why, as a woodcock to mine own springe,[75] Osric.
        I am justly kill'd with mine own treachery.
HAM.   How does the Queen?
KING.   She swoons to see them bleed.
QUEEN. No, no, the drink, the drink—O my dear Hamlet—
        The drink, the drink! I am poison'd.   [Dies.
HAM.   O villany! Ho! Let the door be lock'd.
        Treachery! Seek it out.   [Exit OSRIC; LAERTES falls.
LAER.   It is here, Hamlet. Hamlet, thou art slain.
        No medicine in the world can do thee good;
        In thee there is not half an hour of life.
        The treacherous instrument is in thy hand,
        Unbated and envenom'd. The foul practice[76]
        Hath turn'd itself on me. Lo, here I lie,
        Never to rise again. Thy mother's poison'd.
        I can no more. The King, the King's to blame.
HAM.   The point envenom'd too? Then, venom, to thy work.
                                              [Stabs the KING.
ALL.   Treason! treason!
KING.   O, yet defend me, friends. I am but hurt.
HAM.   Here, thou incestuous, murderous, damned Dane,
        Drink off this potion. Is thy union here?
        Follow my mother.   [KING dies.
LAER.   He is justly served.
        It is a poison temper'd[77] by himself.
        Exchange forgiveness with me, noble Hamlet.
        Mine and my father's death come not upon thee,
        Nor thine on me.   [Dies.
HAM.   Heaven make thee free of it. I follow thee.
        I am dead, Horatio. Wretched[78] Queen, adieu!
        You that look pale and tremble at this chance,
        That are but mutes or audience to this act,
        Had I but time—as this fell sergeant,[79] Death,
        Is strict in his arrest—O, I could tell you—
        But let it be. Horatio, I am dead,
        Thou livest. Report me and my cause aright

[75] springe] snare.
[76] practice] strategem, insidious device.
[77] temper'd] mixed.
[78] Wretched] unhappy.
[79] sergeant] sheriff's officer.

	To the unsatisfied.
HOR.	Never believe it.

I am more an antique Roman[80] than a Dane.
Here's yet some liquor left.

HAM.   As thou'rt a man,
Give me the cup. Let go. By heaven, I'll have't.
O God, Horatio, what a wounded name,
Things standing thus unknown, shall live behind me!
If thou didst ever hold me in thy heart,
Absent thee from felicity awhile,
And in this harsh world draw thy breath in pain
To tell my story.   [*March afar off, and shot within.*

Enter OSRIC.

What warlike noise is this?

OSR. Young Fortinbras, with conquest come from Poland,
To the ambassadors of England gives
This warlike volley.

HAM.   O, I die, Horatio.
The potent poison quite o'er-crows[81] my spirit.
I cannot live to hear the news from England;
But I do prophesy the election lights
On Fortinbras. He has my dying voice.
So tell him, with the occurrents,[82] more and less,
Which have solicited.[83] The rest is silence.   [*Dies.*

HOR. Now cracks a noble heart. Good night, sweet prince,
And flights of angels sing thee to thy rest.   [*March within.*
Why does the drum come hither?

Enter FORTINBRAS, *and the* English Ambassadors, *with drum, colours,
and* Attendants.

FORT. Where is this sight?

HOR.   What is it you would see?
If aught of woe or wonder,[84] cease your search.

FORT. This quarry cries on havoc.[85] O proud Death,
What feast is toward in thine eternal cell,
That thou so many princes at a shot

---

[80] *antique Roman*] i.e., one who chooses suicide rather than a dishonorable life.
[81] *o'er-crows*] triumphs over.
[82] *occurrents*] occurrences.
[83] *solicited*] moved (me to choose him).
[84] *wonder*] destruction, grief.
[85] *This quarry cries on havoc*] This heap of dead proclaims indiscriminate slaughter.

So bloodily hast struck?
FIRST AMB.   The sight is dismal;[86]
And our affairs from England come too late.
The ears are senseless that should give us hearing
To tell him his commandment is fulfill'd,
That Rosencrantz and Guildenstern are dead.
Where should we have our thanks?
HOR.   Not from his mouth,
Had it the ability of life to thank you.
He never gave commandment for their death.
But since so jump upon this bloody question[87]
You from the Polack wars, and you from England,
Are here arrived, give order that these bodies
High on a stage[88] be placed to the view;
And let me speak to the yet unknowing world
How these things came about. So shall you hear
Of carnal, bloody and unnatural acts,
Of accidental judgements, casual[89] slaughters,
Of deaths put on[90] by cunning and forced[91] cause,
And, in this upshot, purposes mistook
Fall'n on the inventors' heads. All this can I
Truly deliver.
FORT.   Let us haste to hear it,
And call the noblest to the audience.
For me, with sorrow I embrace my fortune.
I have some rights of memory[92] in this kingdom,
Which now to claim my vantage doth invite me.
HOR.   Of that I shall have also cause to speak,
And from his mouth whose voice will draw on more.[93]
But let this same[94] be presently perform'd,
Even while men's minds are wild, lest more mischance
On[95] plots and errors happen.
FORT.   Let four captains
Bear Hamlet like a soldier to the stage;

86 *dismal*] horrifying.
87 *jump . . . question*] immediately after this bloody business.
88 *stage*] platform.
89 *casual*] accidental.
90 *put on*] instigated.
91 *forced*] violent.
92 *of memory*] traditional, remembered.
93 *draw on more*] influence others (to vote for Fortinbras).
94 *this same*] the aforementioned.
95 *On*] in addition to; (?) as a result of.

For he was likely, had he been put on,
To have proved most royal; and, for his passage,[96]
The soldiers' music and the rites of war
Speak loudly for him.
Take up the bodies. Such a sight as this
Becomes the field, but here shows much amiss.
Go, bid the soldiers shoot.

> [A *dead march. Exeunt, bearing off the bodies;*
> *after which a peal of ordnance is shot off.*

[96] *passage*] passing, death.

Macbeth

Macbeth

In Macbeth, the story of a catastrophic regicide, Shakespeare offers his most harrowing depiction of evil and the guilt and madness to which it can give rise. Thought to have been written between 1603 and 1606 (after both *Hamlet* and *Othello*), *Macbeth* was most probably first performed in 1606, at Hampton Court, in the presence of King James I (who was reputed to be a descendant of Banquo, one of the victims of Macbeth, an eleventh-century Scottish king). The play is considerably shorter than any of the other great tragedies of Shakespeare's middle period, and the text as it now exists is possibly a truncated and somewhat revised version (with interpolations by other hands) of a lost version. Shakespeare's principal source was Raphael Holinshed's *Chronicles of Scotland*, although there are also numerous allusions to contemporary historical events, most significantly to the notorious Gunpowder Plot of 1605 and the trials that followed the plot's discovery.

The text reprinted here is that of the "Cambridge Shakespeare"; the explanatory footnotes are based on the glosses given in the third edition of Alexander Schmidt's *Shakespeare Lexicon*.

Shane Weller

ACT I.

SCENE I. *A desert place.*

Thunder and lightning. Enter three Witches.

FIRST WITCH.   When shall we three meet again
　　　　　In thunder, lightning, or in rain?
SEC. WITCH.   When the hurlyburly's done,
　　　　　When the battle's lost and won.
THIRD WITCH.   That will be ere the set of sun.
FIRST WITCH.   Where the place?
SEC. WITCH.　　　　　　　　Upon the heath.
THIRD WITCH.   There to meet with Macbeth.
FIRST WITCH.   I come, Graymalkin. [1]
ALL.　　Paddock[2] calls:—anon!
　　　　　Fair is foul, and foul is fair.
　　　　　Hover through the fog and filthy air.　　　　　[*Exeunt.*

SCENE II. *A camp near Forres.*

Alarum within. Enter DUNCAN, MALCOLM, DONALBAIN, LENNOX, *with*
Attendants, *meeting a bleeding* Sergeant.

DUN.　　What bloody man is that? He can report,
　　　　　As seemeth by his plight, of the revolt
　　　　　The newest state.

---

[1] *Graymalkin*] a witches' familiar in the shape of a cat.
[2] *Paddock*] a toad (another witches' familiar).

131

MAL.   This is the sergeant
              Who like a good and hardy soldier fought
              'Gainst my captivity. Hail, brave friend!
              Say to the king the knowledge of the broil
              As thou didst leave it.
SER.   Doubtful it stood;
              As two spent swimmers, that do cling together
              And choke their art. The merciless Macdonwald—
              Worthy to be a rebel, for to that
              The multiplying villanies of nature
              Do swarm upon him—from the western isles
              Of kerns and gallowglasses[1] is supplied;
              And fortune, on his damned quarrel smiling,
              Show'd like a rebel's whore: but all's too weak:
              For brave Macbeth—well he deserves that name—
              Disdaining fortune, with his brandish'd steel,
              Which smoked with bloody execution,
              Like valour's minion carved out his passage
              Till he faced the slave;
              Which ne'er shook hands, nor bade farewell to him,
              Till he unseam'd him from the nave to the chaps,[2]
              And fix'd his head upon our battlements.
DUN.   O valiant cousin! worthy gentleman!
SER.   As whence the sun 'gins his reflection
              Shipwrecking storms and direful thunders break,
              So from that spring whence comfort seem'd to come
              Discomfort swells. Mark, king of Scotland, mark:
              No sooner justice had, with valour arm'd,
              Compell'd these skipping kerns to trust their heels,
              But the Norweyan lord, surveying vantage,[3]
              With furbish'd arms and new supplies of men,
              Began a fresh assault.
DUN.   Dismay'd not this
              Our captains, Macbeth and Banquo?
SER.   Yes;
              As sparrows eagles, or the hare the lion.

---

[1] *kerns and gallowglasses*] Irish foot soldiers.
[2] *nave to the chaps*] navel to the jaw.
[3] *surveying vantage*] seeing his opportunity.

        If I say sooth, I must report they were
        As cannons overcharged with double cracks;
        So they
        Doubly redoubled strokes upon the foe:
        Except they meant to bathe in reeking wounds,
        Or memorize another Golgotha,[4]
        I cannot tell—
        But I am faint; my gashes cry for help.

DUN.   So well thy words become thee as thy wounds;
        They smack of honour both. Go get him surgeons.
                      [Exit Sergeant, attended.
        Who comes here?

Enter ROSS.

MAL.   The worthy thane of Ross.
LEN.   What a haste looks through his eyes! So should he look
        That seems to speak things strange.
ROSS.   God save the king!
DUN.   Whence camest thou, worthy thane?
ROSS.   From Fife, great king;
        Where the Norweyan banners flout the sky
        And fan our people cold.
        Norway himself, with terrible numbers,
        Assisted by that most disloyal traitor
        The thane of Cawdor, began a dismal[5] conflict;
        Till that Bellona's[6] bridegroom, lapp'd in proof,[7]
        Confronted him with self-comparisons,[8]
        Point against point rebellious, arm 'gainst arm,
        Curbing his lavish spirit: and, to conclude,
        The victory fell on us.
DUN.   Great happiness!
ROSS.   That now
        Sweno, the Norways' king, craves composition;[9]

---

[4] *Golgotha*] the place of execution outside Jerusalem; also known as Calvary.
[5] *dismal*] fatal.
[6] *Bellona*] goddess of war.
[7] *lapp'd in proof*] clad in impenetrable armor.
[8] *self-comparisons*] equal force and skill.
[9] *composition*] accord, peace.

Nor would we deign him burial of his men
Till he disbursed, at Saint Colme's inch, [10]
Ten thousand dollars to our general use.

DUN. No more that thane of Cawdor shall deceive
Our bosom interest: go pronounce his present death,
And with his former title greet Macbeth.

ROSS. I'll see it done.

DUN. What he hath lost, noble Macbeth hath won. [*Exeunt.*

SCENE III. *A heath.*

Thunder. Enter the three Witches.

FIRST WITCH. Where hast thou been, sister?

SEC. WITCH. Killing swine.

THIRD WITCH. Sister, where thou?

FIRST WITCH. A sailor's wife had chestnuts in her lap,
And mounch'd, [1] and mounch'd, and mounch'd. 'Give me,'
quoth I:
'Aroint thee, [2] witch!' the rump-fed ronyon [3] cries.
Her husband's to Aleppo gone, master o' the Tiger:
But in a sieve I'll thither sail,
And, like a rat without a tail,
I'll do, I'll do, and I'll do.

SEC. WITCH. I'll give thee a wind.

FIRST WITCH. Thou'rt kind.

THIRD WITCH. And I another.

FIRST WITCH. I myself have all the other;
And the very ports they blow,
All the quarters that they know
I' the shipman's card. [4]
I will drain him dry as hay:

[10] *inch*] island.
[1] *mounch'd*] munched.
[2] *Aroint thee*] begone.
[3] *ronyon*] mangy creature.
[4] *shipman's card*] compass or chart.

             Sleep shall neither night nor day
             Hang upon his pent-house lid;[5]
             He shall live a man forbid:
             Weary se'nnights nine times nine
             Shall he dwindle, peak,[6] and pine:
             Though his bark cannot be lost,
             Yet it shall be tempest-tost.
             Look what I have.

SEC. WITCH.   Show me, show me.

FIRST WITCH.   Here I have a pilot's thumb,
             Wreck'd as homeward he did come.   [*Drum within.*

THIRD WITCH.   A drum, a drum!
             Macbeth doth come.

ALL.   The weird sisters, hand in hand,
             Posters[7] of the sea and land,
             Thus do go about, about:
             Thrice to thine, and thrice to mine,
             And thrice again, to make up nine.
             Peace! the charm's wound up.

Enter MACBETH *and* BANQUO.

MACB.   So foul and fair a day I have not seen.

BAN.   How far is't call'd to Forres? What are these
             So wither'd, and so wild in their attire,
             That look not like the inhabitants o' the earth,
             And yet are on't? Live you? or are you aught
             That man may question? You seem to understand me,
             By each at once her choppy[8] finger laying
             Upon her skinny lips: you should be women,
             And yet your beards forbid me to interpret
             That you are so.

MACB.   Speak, if you can: what are you?

FIRST WITCH.   All hail, Macbeth! hail to thee, thane of Glamis!

SEC. WITCH.   All hail, Macbeth! hail to thee, thane of Cawdor!

---

[5] *pent-house lid*] eyelid.
[6] *peak*] grow thin.
[7] *Posters*] swift travelers.
[8] *choppy*] chapped.

THIRD WITCH.   All hail, Macbeth, that shalt be king hereafter!
BAN.   Good sir, why do you start, and seem to fear
            Things that do sound so fair? I' the name of truth,
            Are ye fantastical,[9] or that indeed
            Which outwardly ye show? My noble partner
            You greet with present grace and great prediction
            Of noble having[10] and of royal hope,
            That he seems rapt withal: to me you speak not:
            If you can look into the seeds of time,
            And say which grain will grow and which will not,
            Speak then to me, who neither beg nor fear
            Your favours nor your hate.
FIRST WITCH.   Hail!
SEC. WITCH.   Hail!
THIRD WITCH.   Hail!
FIRST WITCH.   Lesser than Macbeth, and greater.
SEC. WITCH.   Not so happy, yet much happier.
THIRD WITCH.   Thou shalt get kings, though thou be none:
            So all hail, Macbeth and Banquo!
FIRST WITCH.   Banquo and Macbeth, all hail!
MACB.   Stay, you imperfect speakers, tell me more:
            By Sinel's death I know I am thane of Glamis;
            But how of Cawdor? the thane of Cawdor lives,
            A prosperous gentleman; and to be king
            Stands not within the prospect of belief,
            No more than to be Cawdor. Say from whence
            You owe[11] this strange intelligence? or why
            Upon this blasted heath you stop our way
            With such prophetic greeting? Speak, I charge you.
                                            [*Witches vanish.*
BAN.   The earth hath bubbles as the water has,
            And these are of them: whither are they vanish'd?
MACB.   Into the air, and what seem'd corporal melted
            As breath into the wind. Would they had stay'd!
BAN.   Were such things here as we do speak about?

[9] *fantastical*] imaginary.
[10] *having*] estate, property.
[11] *owe*] possess.

Or have we eaten on the insane root
That takes the reason prisoner?
MACB.   Your children shall be kings.
BAN.   You shall be king.
MACB.   And thane of Cawdor too: went it not so?
BAN.   To the selfsame tune and words. Who's here?

Enter ROSS *and* ANGUS.

ROSS.   The king hath happily received, Macbeth,
          The news of thy success: and when he reads
          Thy personal venture in the rebels' fight,
          His wonders and his praises do contend
          Which should be thine or his: silenced with that,
          In viewing o'er the rest o' the selfsame day,
          He finds thee in the stout Norweyan ranks,
          Nothing afeard of what thyself didst make,
          Strange images of death. As thick as hail
          Came post with post, and every one did bear
          Thy praises in his kingdom's great defence,
          And pour'd them down before him.
ANG.   We are sent
          To give thee, from our royal master, thanks;
          Only to herald thee into his sight,
          Not pay thee.
ROSS.   And for an earnest[12] of a greater honour,
          He bade me, from him, call thee thane of Cawdor:
          In which addition,[13] hail, most worthy thane!
          For it is thine.
BAN.   What, can the devil speak true?
MACB.   The thane of Cawdor lives: why do you dress me
          In borrow'd robes?
ANG.   Who was the thane lives yet,
          But under heavy judgement bears that life
          Which he deserves to lose. Whether he was combined
          With those of Norway, or did line[14] the rebel
          With hidden help and vantage, or that with both

[12] *earnest*] portion paid as a pledge.
[13] *addition*] title.
[14] *line*] strengthen.

He labour'd in his country's wreck, I know not;
But treasons capital, confess'd and proved,
Have overthrown him.

MACB.   [*Aside*] Glamis, and thane of Cawdor:
The greatest is behind.—Thanks for your pains.—
Do you not hope your children shall be kings,
When those that gave the thane of Cawdor to me
Promised no less to them?

BAN.   That, trusted home,
Might yet enkindle you unto the crown,
Besides the thane of Cawdor. But 'tis strange:
And oftentimes, to win us to our harm,
The instruments of darkness tell us truths,
Win us with honest trifles, to betray's
In deepest consequence.
Cousins, a word, I pray you.

MACB.   [*Aside*] Two truths are told,
As happy prologues to the swelling act
Of the imperial theme.—I thank you, gentlemen.—
[*Aside*] This supernatural soliciting
Cannot be ill; cannot be good: if ill,
Why hath it given me earnest of success,
Commencing in a truth? I am thane of Cawdor:
If good, why do I yield to that suggestion
Whose horrid image doth unfix my hair
And make my seated heart knock at my ribs,
Against the use of nature? Present fears
Are less than horrible imaginings:
My thought, whose murder yet is but fantastical,
Shakes so my single state of man that function
Is smother'd in surmise, and nothing is
But what is not.

BAN.   Look, how our partner's rapt.

MACB.   [*Aside*] If chance will have me king, why, chance may crown
          me,
Without my stir.

BAN.   New honours come upon him,
Like our strange garments, cleave not to their mould
But with the aid of use.

MACB.   [*Aside*] Come what come may,

         Time and the hour runs through the roughest day.
BAN.   Worthy Macbeth, we stay upon your leisure.
MACB.   Give me your favour:[15] my dull brain was wrought
         With things forgotten. Kind gentlemen, your pains
         Are register'd where every day I turn
         The leaf to read them. Let us toward the king.
         Think upon what hath chanced, and at more time,
         The interim having weigh'd it, let us speak
         Our free hearts each to other.
BAN.   Very gladly.
MACB.   Till then, enough. Come, friends.   [*Exeunt.*

SCENE IV. *Forres. The palace.*

Flourish. Enter DUNCAN, MALCOLM, DONALBAIN, LENNOX, *and* Attendants.

DUN.   Is execution done on Cawdor? Are not
         Those in commission yet return'd?
MAL.   My liege,
         They are not yet come back. But I have spoke
         With one that saw him die, who did report
         That very frankly he confess'd his treasons,
         Implored your highness' pardon and set forth
         A deep repentance: nothing in his life
         Became him like the leaving it; he died
         As one that had been studied in his death,
         To throw away the dearest thing he owed
         As 'twere a careless trifle.
DUN.   There's no art
         To find the mind's construction in the face:
         He was a gentleman on whom I built
         An absolute trust.

---

[15] *favour*] pardon.

Enter MACBETH, BANQUO, ROSS, *and* ANGUS.

O worthiest cousin!

The sin of my ingratitude even now
Was heavy on me: thou art so far before,
That swiftest wing of recompense is slow
To overtake thee. Would thou hadst less deserved,
That the proportion both of thanks and payment
Might have been mine! only I have left to say,
More is thy due than more than all can pay.

MACB. The service and the loyalty I owe,
In doing it, pays itself. Your highness' part
Is to receive our duties: and our duties
Are to your throne and state children and servants;
Which do but what they should, by doing every thing
Safe toward[1] your love and honour.

DUN.   Welcome hither:
I have begun to plant thee, and will labour
To make thee full of growing. Noble Banquo,
That hast no less deserved, nor must be known
No less to have done so: let me infold thee
And hold thee to my heart.

BAN.   There if I grow,
The harvest is your own.

DUN.   My plenteous joys,
Wanton in fulness, seek to hide themselves
In drops of sorrow. Sons, kinsmen, thanes,
And you whose places are the nearest, know,
We will establish our estate upon
Our eldest, Malcolm, whom we name hereafter
The Prince of Cumberland: which honour must
Not unaccompanied invest him only,
But signs of nobleness, like stars, shall shine
On all deservers. From hence to Inverness,
And bind us further to you.

MACB. The rest is labour, which is not used for you:
I'll be myself the harbinger, and make joyful
The hearing of my wife with your approach;

---

[1] *Safe toward*] to secure (or consistent with).

So humbly take my leave.

DUN.   My worthy Cawdor!

MACB.   [*Aside*] The Prince of Cumberland! that is a step
         On which I must fall down, or else o'erleap,
         For in my way it lies. Stars, hide your fires;
         Let not light see my black and deep desires:
         The eye wink at the hand; yet let that be
         Which the eye fears, when it is done, to see.   [*Exit.*

DUN.   True, worthy Banquo; he is full so valiant,
         And in his commendations I am fed;
         It is a banquet to me. Let's after him,
         Whose care is gone before to bid us welcome:
         It is a peerless kinsman.   [*Flourish. Exeunt.*

SCENE V. *Inverness. Macbeth's castle.*

Enter LADY MACBETH, *reading a letter.*

LADY M. 'They met me in the day of success; and I have learned by the
        perfectest report, they have more in them than mortal knowledge.
        When I burned in desire to question them further, they made them-
        selves air, into which they vanished. Whiles I stood rapt in the wonder
        of it, came missives[1] from the king, who all-hailed me "Thane of
        Cawdor"; by which title, before, these weird sisters saluted me, and
        referred me to the coming on of time, with "Hail, king that shalt be!"
        This have I thought good to deliver thee, my dearest partner of
        greatness, that thou mightst not lose the dues of rejoicing, by being
        ignorant of what greatness is promised thee. Lay it to thy heart, and
        farewell.'

        Glamis thou art, and Cawdor, and shalt be
        What thou art promised: yet do I fear thy nature;
        It is too full o' the milk of human kindness
        To catch the nearest way: thou wouldst be great;
        Art not without ambition, but without

---

[1] *missives*] messengers

The illness[2] should attend it: what thou wouldst highly,
That wouldst thou holily; wouldst not play false,
And yet wouldst wrongly win: thou 'ldst have, great Glamis,
That which cries 'Thus thou must do, if thou have it;
And that which rather thou dost fear to do
Than wishest should be undone.' Hie thee hither,
That I may pour my spirits in thine ear,
And chastise with the valour of my tongue
All that impedes thee from the golden round,
Which fate and metaphysical[3] aid doth seem
To have thee crown'd withal.

Enter a MESSENGER.

                                    What is your tidings?
MESS. The king comes here to-night.
LADY M.   Thou'rt mad to say it:
Is not thy master with him? who, were't so,
Would have inform'd for preparation.
MESS. So please you, it is true: our thane is coming:
One of my fellows had the speed of him,
Who, almost dead for breath, had scarcely more
Than would make up his message.
LADY M.   Give him tending;
He brings great news.   *[Exit Messenger.*
                    The raven himself is hoarse
That croaks the fatal entrance of Duncan
Under my battlements. Come, you spirits
That tend on mortal[4] thoughts, unsex me here,
And fill me, from the crown to the toe, top-full
Of direst cruelty! make thick my blood,
Stop up the access and passage to remorse,[5]
That no compunctious visitings of nature
Shake my fell purpose, nor keep peace between
The effect and it! Come to my woman's breasts,

[2] *illness*] wickedness.
[3] *metaphysical*] supernatural.
[4] *mortal*] deadly, murderous.
[5] *remorse*] pity, tenderness.

And take[6] my milk for gall, you murdering ministers,
Wherever in your sightless[7] substances
You wait on nature's mischief! Come, thick night,
And pall thee in the dunnest smoke of hell,
That my keen knife see not the wound it makes,
Nor heaven peep through the blanket of the dark,
To cry 'Hold, hold!'

Enter MACBETH.

                            Great Glamis! worthy Cawdor!
Greater than both, by the all-hail hereafter!
Thy letters have transported me beyond
This ignorant present, and I feel now
The future in the instant.
MACB.   My dearest love,
Duncan comes here to-night.
LADY M.   And when goes hence?
MACB.   To-morrow, as he purposes.
LADY M.   O, never
Shall sun that morrow see!
Your face, my thane, is as a book where men
May read strange matters. To beguile the time,[8]
Look like the time; bear welcome in your eye,
Your hand, your tongue: look like the innocent flower,
But be the serpent under't. He that's coming
Must be provided for: and you shall put
This night's great business into my dispatch;
Which shall to all our nights and days to come
Give solely sovereign sway and masterdom.
MACB.   We will speak further.
LADY M.   Only look up clear;
To alter favour[9] ever is to fear:
Leave all the rest to me.   [*Exeunt.*

[6] *take*] exchange.
[7] *sightless*] invisible.
[8] *time*] world, others.
[9] *favour*] expression, countenance

SCENE VI. *Before Macbeth's castle.*

Hautboys and torches. Enter DUNCAN, MALCOLM, DONALBAIN, BAN-
QUO, LENNOX, MACDUFF, ROSS, ANGUS, *and* Attendants.

DUN. This castle hath a pleasant seat; the air
   Nimbly and sweetly recommends itself
   Unto our gentle senses.

BAN.   This guest of summer,
   The temple-haunting martlet,[1] does approve[2]
   By his loved mansionry that the heaven's breath
   Smells wooingly here: no jutty,[3] frieze,
   Buttress, nor coign[4] of vantage, but this bird
   Hath made his pendent bed and procreant cradle:
   Where they most breed and haunt, I have observed
   The air is delicate.

Enter LADY MACBETH.

DUN.   See, see, our honour'd hostess!
   The love that follows us sometime is our trouble,
   Which still we thank as love. Herein I teach you
   How you shall bid God 'ild[5] us for your pains,
   And thank us for your trouble.

LADY M.   All our service
   In every point twice done, and then done double,
   Were poor and single business to contend
   Against those honours deep and broad wherewith
   Your majesty loads our house: for those of old,
   And the late dignities heap'd up to them,
   We rest your hermits.[6]

DUN.   Where's the thane of Cawdor?
   We coursed him at the heels, and had a purpose

---

[1] *martlet*] house-martin.
[2] *approve*] prove.
[3] *jutty*] projection.
[4] *coign*] corner.
[5] *'ild*] reward.
[6] *hermits*] beadsmen, those who pray for another.

To be his purveyor:[7] but he rides well,
And his great love, sharp as his spur, hath holp him
To his home before us. Fair and noble hostess,
We are your guest to-night.

LADY M.   Your servants ever
Have theirs, themselves, and what is theirs, in compt,[8]
To make their audit at your highness' pleasure,
Still to return your own.

DUN.   Give me your hand;
Conduct me to mine host: we love him highly,
And shall continue our graces towards him.
By your leave, hostess.   [Exeunt.

SCENE VII. *Macbeth's castle.*

Hautboys and torches. Enter a Sewer,[1] *and divers* Servants *with dishes and service, and pass over the stage. Then enter* MACBETH.

MACB.   If it were done when 'tis done, then 'twere well
It were done quickly: if the assassination
Could trammel up[2] the consequence, and catch,
With his surcease,[3] success; that but this blow
Might be the be-all and the end-all here,
But here, upon this bank and shoal of time,
We'ld jump the life to come. But in these cases
We still have judgement here; that we but teach
Bloody instructions, which being taught return
To plague the inventor: this even-handed justice
Commends the ingredients of our poison'd chalice
To our own lips. He's here in double trust:
First, as I am his kinsman and his subject,

[7] *purveyor*] provider.
[8] *compt*] account.

---

[1] *Sewer*] head servant.
[2] *trammel up*] tie up or catch in a net.
[3] *surcease*] death.

Strong both against the deed; then, as his host,
Who should against his murderer shut the door,
Not bear the knife myself. Besides, this Duncan
Hath borne his faculties[4] so meek, hath been
So clear[5] in his great office, that his virtues
Will plead like angels trumpet-tongued against
The deep damnation of his taking-off;
And pity, like a naked new-born babe,
Striding[6] the blast, or heaven's cherubin horsed
Upon the sightless couriers of the air,
Shall blow the horrid deed in every eye,
That tears shall drown the wind. I have no spur
To prick the sides of my intent, but only
Vaulting ambition, which o'erleaps itself
And falls on the other.[7]

Enter LADY MACBETH.

                            How now! what news?
LADY M. He has almost supp'd: why have you left the chamber?
MACB. Hath he ask'd for me?
LADY M.   Know you not he has?
MACB. We will proceed no further in this business:
     He hath honour'd me of late; and I have bought
     Golden opinions from all sorts of people,
     Which would be worn now in their newest gloss,
     Not cast aside so soon.
LADY M.   Was the hope drunk
     Wherein you dress'd yourself? hath it slept since?
     And wakes it now, to look so green and pale
     At what it did so freely? From this time
     Such I account thy love. Art thou afeard
     To be the same in thine own act and valour
     As thou art in desire? Wouldst thou have that
     Which thou esteem'st the ornament of life,
     And live a coward in thine own esteem,

[4] *faculties*] powers.
[5] *clear*] irreproachable.
[6] *Striding*] bestriding, mounting.
[7] *other*] other side (of the horse).

　　　　　　　　Letting 'I dare not' wait upon 'I would,'
　　　　　　　　Like the poor cat i' the adage?

MACB.　　　　　　　　　　　　　　　Prithee, peace:
　　　　　　　　I dare do all that may become a man;
　　　　　　　　Who dares do more is none.

LADY M.　　　　　　　　　　　　What beast was't then
　　　　　　　　That made you break this enterprise to me?
　　　　　　　　When you durst do it, then you were a man;
　　　　　　　　And, to be more than what you were, you would
　　　　　　　　Be so much more the man. Nor time nor place
　　　　　　　　Did then adhere, and yet you would make both:
　　　　　　　　They have made themselves, and that their fitness now
　　　　　　　　Does unmake you. I have given suck, and know
　　　　　　　　How tender 'tis to love the babe that milks me:
　　　　　　　　I would, while it was smiling in my face,
　　　　　　　　Have pluck'd my nipple from his boneless gums,
　　　　　　　　And dash'd the brains out, had I so sworn as you
　　　　　　　　Have done to this.

MACB.　　　　　　　　　　If we should fail?

LADY M.　　　　　　　　　　　　　　We fail!
　　　　　　　　But screw your courage to the sticking-place,
　　　　　　　　And we'll not fail. When Duncan is asleep—
　　　　　　　　Whereto the rather shall his day's hard journey
　　　　　　　　Soundly invite him—his two chamberlains
　　　　　　　　Will I with wine and wassail so convince,[8]
　　　　　　　　That memory, the warder of the brain,
　　　　　　　　Shall be a fume, and the receipt of reason
　　　　　　　　A limbec[9] only: when in swinish sleep
　　　　　　　　Their drenched natures lie as in a death,
　　　　　　　　What cannot you and I perform upon
　　　　　　　　The unguarded Duncan? what not put upon
　　　　　　　　His spongy officers, who shall bear the guilt
　　　　　　　　Of our great quell?[10]

MACB.　　　　　　　　　Bring forth men-children only;
　　　　　　　　For thy undaunted mettle should compose
　　　　　　　　Nothing but males. Will it not be received,

---

[8] *convince*] overcome.
[9] *limbec*] alembic, still.
[10] *quell*] murder.

When we have mark'd with blood those sleepy two
Of his own chamber, and used their very daggers,
That they have done't?

LADY M.   Who dares receive it other,
As we shall make our griefs and clamour roar
Upon his death?

MACB.   I am settled, and bend up
Each corporal agent to this terrible feat.
Away, and mock the time with fairest show:
False face must hide what the false heart doth know. [*Exeunt.*

ACT II.

Scene I. *Inverness. Court of Macbeth's castle.*

Enter Banquo, *and* Fleance *bearing a torch before him.*

Ban. How goes the night, boy?
Fle. The moon is down; I have not heard the clock.
Ban. And she goes down at twelve.
Fle.   I take't, 'tis later, sir.
Ban. Hold, take my sword. There's husbandry in heaven,
     Their candles are all out. Take thee that too.
     A heavy summons lies like lead upon me,
     And yet I would not sleep. Merciful powers,
     Restrain in me the cursed thoughts that nature
     Gives way to in repose!

Enter Macbeth, *and a* Servant *with a torch.*

                                    Give me my sword.
     Who's there?
Macb. A friend.
Ban. What, sir, not yet at rest? The king's a-bed:
     He hath been in unusual pleasure, and
     Sent forth great largess to your offices:[1]
     This diamond he greets your wife withal,
     By the name of most kind hostess; and shut up
     In measureless content.
Macb.   Being unprepared,
     Our will became the servant to defect,
     Which else should free have wrought.
Ban.   All's well.

[1] *offices*] servants' quarters.

149

I dreamt last night of the three weird sisters:
To you they have show'd some truth.

MACB.   I think not of them:
Yet, when we can entreat an hour to serve,
We would spend it in some words upon that business,
If you would grant the time.

BAN.   At your kind'st leisure.

MACB. If you shall cleave to my consent, when 'tis,
It shall make honour for you.

BAN.   So I lose none
In seeking to augment it, but still keep
My bosom franchised and allegiance clear,
I shall be counsell'd.

MACB.   Good repose the while!

BAN. Thanks, sir: the like to you!   [*Exeunt Banquo and Fleance.*

MACB. Go bid thy mistress, when my drink is ready,
She strike upon the bell. Get thee to bed.   [*Exit Servant.*
Is this a dagger which I see before me,
The handle toward my hand? Come, let me clutch thee.
I have thee not, and yet I see thee still.
Art thou not, fatal vision, sensible
To feeling as to sight? or art thou but
A dagger of the mind, a false creation,
Proceeding from the heat-oppressed brain?
I see thee yet, in form as palpable
As this which now I draw.
Thou marshall'st me the way that I was going;
And such an instrument I was to use.
Mine eyes are made the fools o' the other senses,
Or else worth all the rest: I see thee still;
And on thy blade and dudgeon[2] gouts[3] of blood,
Which was not so before. There's no such thing:
It is the bloody business which informs
Thus to mine eyes. Now o'er the one half-world
Nature seems dead, and wicked dreams abuse
The curtain'd sleep; witchcraft celebrates
Pale Hecate's offerings; and wither'd murder,

[2] *dudgeon*] handle.
[3] *gouts*] drops.

Alarum'd by his sentinel, the wolf,
Whose howl's his watch, thus with his stealthy pace,
With Tarquin's ravishing strides, towards his design
Moves like a ghost. Thou sure and firm-set earth,
Hear not my steps, which way they walk, for fear
Thy very stones prate of my whereabout,
And take the present horror from the time,
Which now suits with it. Whiles I threat, he lives:
Words to the heat of deeds too cold breath gives. [*A bell rings.*
I go, and it is done: the bell invites me.
Hear it not, Duncan, for it is a knell
That summons thee to heaven, or to hell.   [*Exit.*

SCENE II. *The same.*

Enter LADY MACBETH.

LADY M. That which hath made them drunk hath made me bold;
       What hath quench'd them hath given me fire. Hark! Peace!
       It was the owl that shriek'd, the fatal bellman,
       Which gives the stern'st good-night. He is about it:
       The doors are open, and the surfeited grooms[1]
       Do mock their charge with snores: I have drugg'd their pos-
         sets,[2]
       That death and nature do contend about them,
       Whether they live or die.
MACB.   [*Within*] Who's there? what, ho!
LADY M. Alack, I am afraid they have awaked
       And 'tis not done: the attempt and not the deed
       Confounds us. Hark! I laid their daggers ready;
       He could not miss 'em. Had he not resembled
       My father as he slept, I had done't.

---

[1] *grooms*] menials.
[2] *possets*] bedtime drink of hot milk curdled with ale.

Enter MACBETH.

                                             My husband!
MACB.   I have done the deed. Didst thou not hear a noise?
LADY M. I heard the owl scream and the crickets cry.
         Did not you speak?
MACB.   When?
LADY M.   Now.
MACB.   As I descended?
LADY M. Ay.
MACB.   Hark!
         Who lies i' the second chamber?
LADY M.   Donalbain.
MACB.   This is a sorry sight.   [*Looking on his hands.*
LADY M. A foolish thought, to say a sorry sight.
MACB.   There's one did laugh in's sleep, and one cried 'Murder!'
         That they did wake each other: I stood and heard them:
         But they did say their prayers, and address'd them[3]
         Again to sleep.
LADY M.   There are two lodged together.
MACB.   One cried 'God bless us!' and 'Amen' the other,
         As they had seen me with these hangman's hands:
         Listening their fear, I could not say 'Amen,'
         When they did say 'God bless us!'
LADY M. Consider it not so deeply.
MACB.   But wherefore could not I pronounce 'Amen'?
         I had most need of blessing, and 'Amen'
         Stuck in my throat.
LADY M.   These deeds must not be thought
         After these ways; so, it will make us mad.
MACB.   Methought I heard a voice cry 'Sleep no more!
         Macbeth does murder sleep'—the innocent sleep,
         Sleep that knits up the ravell'd sleave[4] of care,
         The death of each day's life, sore labour's bath,
         Balm of hurt minds, great nature's second course,
         Chief nourisher in life's feast,—

[3] *address'd them*] made themselves ready.
[4] *sleave*] silk.

LADY M.   What do you mean?
MACB.   Still it cried 'Sleep no more!' to all the house:
          'Glamis hath murder'd sleep, and therefore Cawdor
          Shall sleep no more: Macbeth shall sleep no more.'
LADY M.   Who was it that thus cried? Why, worthy thane,
          You do unbend your noble strength, to think
          So brainsickly of things. Go get some water,
          And wash this filthy witness from your hand.
          Why did you bring these daggers from the place?
          They must lie there: go carry them, and smear
          The sleepy grooms with blood.
MACB.   I'll go no more:
          I am afraid to think what I have done;
          Look on't again I dare not.
LADY M   Infirm of purpose!
          Give me the daggers: the sleeping and the dead
          Are but as pictures: 'tis the eye of childhood
          That fears a painted devil. If he do bleed,
          I'll gild the faces of the grooms withal,
          For it must seem their guilt.   [Exit. Knocking within.
MACB.   Whence is that knocking?
          How is't with me, when every noise appals me?
          What hands are here? ha! they pluck out mine eyes!
          Will all great Neptune's ocean wash this blood
          Clean from my hand? No; this my hand will rather
          The multitudinous seas incarnadine,
          Making the green one red.

Re-enter LADY MACBETH.

LADY M.   My hands are of your colour, but I shame
          To wear a heart so white. [Knocking within.] I hear a knocking
          At the south entry: retire we to our chamber:
          A little water clears us of this deed:
          How easy is it then! Your constancy
          Hath left you unattended.[5] [Knocking within.] Hark! more
              knocking:
          Get on your nightgown, lest occasion call us
          And show us to be watchers: be not lost

---

[5] left you unattended] abandoned you

> So poorly in your thoughts.

MACB.   To know my deed, 'twere best not know myself.

                                        [*Knocking within.*

Wake Duncan with thy knocking! I would thou couldst!

                                              [*Exeunt.*

SCENE III. *The same.*

Enter a Porter. *Knocking within.*

PORTER.   Here's a knocking indeed! If a man were porter of hell-gate, he
should have old[1] turning the key. [*Knocking within.*] Knock,
knock, knock! Who's there, i' the name of Beelzebub? Here's
a farmer, that hanged himself on th' expectation of plenty:[2]
come in time; have napkins enow about you; here you'll
sweat for't. [*Knocking within.*] Knock, knock! Who's there, in
th' other devil's name? Faith, here's an equivocator, that
could swear in both the scales against either scale; who committed treason enough for God's sake, yet could not equivocate to heaven: O, come in, equivocator. [*Knocking within.*]
Knock, knock, knock! Who's there? Faith, here's an English
tailor come hither, for stealing out of a French hose: come in,
tailor; here you may roast your goose.[3] [*Knocking within.*]
Knock, knock; never at quiet! What are you? But this place is
too cold for hell. I'll devil-porter it no further: I had thought
to have let in some of all professions, that go the primrose way
to the everlasting bonfire. [*Knocking within.*] Anon, anon! I
pray you, remember the porter.   [*Opens the gate.*

Enter MACDUFF *and* LENNOX.

MACD.   Was it so late, friend, ere you went to bed,
That you do lie so late?

---

[1] *old*] too much.
[2] *expectation of plenty*] i.e., low prices.
[3] *goose*] smoothing iron.

PORT.　Faith, sir, we were carousing till the second cock: and drink,
　　　　sir, is a great provoker of three things.
MACD.　What three things does drink especially provoke?
PORT.　Marry, sir, nose-painting, sleep and urine. Lechery, sir, it
　　　　provokes and unprovokes; it provokes the desire, but it takes
　　　　away the performance: therefore much drink may be said to
　　　　be an equivocator with lechery: it makes him and it mars
　　　　him; it sets him on and it takes him off; it persuades him and
　　　　disheartens him; makes him stand to and not stand to; in
　　　　conclusion, equivocates him in a sleep, and giving him the
　　　　lie, leaves him.
MACD.　I believe drink gave thee the lie last night.
PORT.　That it did, sir, i' the very throat on me: but I requited him for
　　　　his lie, and, I think, being too strong for him, though he
　　　　took up my legs sometime, yet I made a shift[4] to cast him.
MACD.　Is thy master stirring?

Enter MACBETH.

　　　　Our knocking has awaked him; here he comes.
LEN.　　Good morrow, noble sir.
MACB.　　　　　　　　　　　　Good morrow, both.
MACD.　Is the king stirring, worthy thane?
MACB.　　　　　　　　　　　　　　Not yet.
MACD.　He did command me to call timely on him:
　　　　I have almost slipp'd the hour.
MACB.　　　　　　　　　　　　I'll bring you to him.
MACD.　I know this is a joyful trouble to you;
　　　　But yet 'tis one.
MACB.　The labour we delight in physics pain.
　　　　This is the door.
MACD.　　　　　　　　　　I'll make so bold to call,
　　　　For 'tis my limited[5] service.　　　　　　　　　　[*Exit.*
LEN.　　Goes the king hence to-day?
MACB.　　　　　　　　　　　He does: he did appoint so.
LEN.　　The night has been unruly: where we lay,
　　　　Our chimneys were blown down, and, as they say,
　　　　Lamentings heard i' the air, strange screams of death,

―――――――――

[4] *made a shift*] contrived.
[5] *limited*] appointed.

> And prophesying with accents terrible
> Of dire combustion and confused events
> New hatch'd to the woful time: the obscure bird
> Clamour'd the livelong night: some say, the earth
> Was feverous and did shake.

MACB.   'Twas a rough night.
LEN.   My young remembrance cannot parallel
         A fellow to it.

Re-enter MACDUFF.

MACD.   O horror, horror, horror! Tongue nor heart
         Cannot conceive nor name thee.

MACB. ⎫
LEN. ⎬   What's the matter?
MACD.   Confusion now hath made his masterpiece.
         Most sacrilegious murder hath broke ope
         The Lord's anointed temple, and stole thence
         The life o' the building.

MACB.   What is't you say? the life?
LEN.   Mean you his majesty?
MACD.   Approach the chamber, and destroy your sight
         With a new Gorgon: do not bid me speak;
         See, and then speak yourselves. [*Exeunt Macbeth and Lennox.*
                                   Awake, awake!
         Ring the alarum-bell. Murder and treason!
         Banquo and Donalbain! Malcolm! awake!
         Shake off this downy sleep, death's counterfeit,
         And look on death itself! up, up, and see
         The great doom's image! Malcolm! Banquo!
         As from your graves rise up, and walk like sprites,
         To countenance[6] this horror. Ring the bell.   [*Bell rings.*

Enter LADY MACBETH.

LADY M. What's the business,
         That such a hideous trumpet calls to parley
         The sleepers of the house? speak, speak!
MACD.   O gentle lady,

---

[6] *countenance*] be in keeping with and behold.

'Tis not for you to hear what I can speak:
The repetition, in a woman's ear,
Would murder as it fell.

Enter BANQUO.

                         O Banquo, Banquo!
Our royal master's murder'd.
LADY M.   Woe, alas!
What, in our house?
BAN.   Too cruel any where.
Dear Duff, I prithee, contradict thyself,
And say it is not so.

Re-enter MACBETH *and* LENNOX, *with* ROSS.

MACB.   Had I but died an hour before this chance,
I had lived a blessed time; for from this instant
There's nothing serious in morality:[7]
All is but toys: renown and grace is dead;
The wine of life is drawn, and the mere lees
Is left this vault to brag of.

Enter MALCOLM *and* DONALBAIN.

DON.   What is amiss?
MACB.   You are, and do not know't:
The spring, the head, the fountain of your blood
Is stopp'd; the very source of it is stopp'd.
MACD.   Your royal father's murder'd.
MAL.   O, by whom?
LEN.   Those of his chamber, as it seem'd, had done't:
Their hands and faces were all badged with blood;
So were their daggers, which unwiped we found
Upon their pillows:
They stared, and were distracted; no man's life
Was to be trusted with them.
MACB.   O, yet I do repent me of my fury,
That I did kill them.
MACD.   Wherefore did you so?

---

mortality] human life.

MACB.   Who can be wise, amazed, temperate and furious,
             Loyal and neutral, in a moment? No man:
             The expedition of my violent love
             Outrun the pauser reason. Here lay Duncan,
             His silver skin laced with his golden blood,
             And his gash'd stabs look'd like a breach in nature
             For ruin's wasteful[8] entrance: there, the murderers,
             Steep'd in the colours of their trade, their daggers
             Unmannerly breech'd[9] with gore: who could refrain,
             That had a heart to love, and in that heart
             Courage to make's love known?

LADY M.   Help me hence, ho!

MACD.   Look to the lady.

MAL.   [*Aside to Don.*] Why do we hold our tongues,
             That most may claim this argument for ours?

DON.   [*Aside to Mal.*] What should be spoken here, where our fate,
             Hid in an auger-hole, may rush, and seize us?
             Let's away;
             Our tears are not yet brew'd.

MAL.   [*Aside to Don.*] Nor our strong sorrow
             Upon the foot of motion.

BAN.   Look to the lady:
                         [*Lady Macbeth is carried out.*
             And when we have our naked frailties hid,
             That suffer in exposure, let us meet,
             And question this most bloody piece of work,
             To know it further. Fears and scruples[10] shake us:
             In the great hand of God I stand, and thence
             Against the undivulged pretence[11] I fight
             Of treasonous malice.

MACD.   And so do I.

ALL.   So all.

MACB.   Let's briefly put on manly readiness,
             And meet i' the hall together.

---

[8] *wasteful*] destructive.
[9] *breech'd*] sheathed, covered.
[10] *scruples*] doubts.
[11] *pretence*] purpose, design.

ALL.	Well contented.

[Exeunt all but Malcolm and Donalbain.

MAL.   What will you do? Let's not consort with them:
        To show an unfelt sorrow is an office
        Which the false man does easy. I'll to England.
DON.   To Ireland, I; our separated fortune
        Shall keep us both the safer: where we are
        There's daggers in men's smiles: the near in blood,
        The nearer bloody.
MAL.   This murderous shaft that's shot
        Hath not yet lighted, and our safest way
        Is to avoid the aim. Therefore to horse;
        And let us not be dainty of leave-taking,
        But shift away:[12] there's warrant in that theft
        Which steals itself when there's no mercy left.   *[Exeunt.*

SCENE IV. *Outside Macbeth's castle.*

Enter ROSS *with an* old Man.

OLD M. Threescore and ten I can remember well:
        Within the volume of which time I have seen
        Hours dreadful and things strange, but this sore night
        Hath trifled former knowings.
ROSS.   Ah, good father,
        Thou seest, the heavens, as troubled with man's act,
        Threaten his bloody stage: by the clock 'tis day,
        And yet dark night strangles the travelling lamp:
        Is't night's predominance, or the day's shame,
        That darkness does the face of earth entomb,
        When living light should kiss it?
OLD M.   'Tis unnatural,

12 *shift away*] contrive to get away

Even like the deed that's done. On Tuesday last
A falcon towering in her pride of place
Was by a mousing owl hawk'd at and kill'd.

ROSS. And Duncan's horses—a thing most strange and certain—
Beauteous and swift, the minions[1] of their race,
Turn'd wild in nature, broke their stalls, flung out,
Contending 'gainst obedience, as they would make
War with mankind.

OLD M.   'Tis said they eat each other.

ROSS. They did so, to the amazement of mine eyes,
That look'd upon't.

Enter MACDUFF.

                              Here comes the good Macduff.
How goes the world, sir, now?

MACD.   Why, see you not?

ROSS. Is't known who did this more than bloody deed?

MACD. Those that Macbeth hath slain.

ROSS.   Alas, the day!
What good could they pretend?[2]

MACD.   They were suborn'd:
Malcolm and Donalbain, the king's two sons,
Are stol'n away and fled, which puts upon them
Suspicion of the deed.

ROSS.   'Gainst nature still:
Thriftless ambition, that wilt ravin up
Thine own life's means! Then 'tis most like
The sovereignty will fall upon Macbeth.

MACD. He is already named, and gone to Scone
To be invested.

ROSS.   Where is Duncan's body?

MACD. Carried to Colme-kill,
The sacred storehouse of his predecessors
And guardian of their bones.

ROSS.   Will you to Scone?

MACD. No, cousin, I'll to Fife.

---

[1] *minions*] darlings, favorites.
[2] *pretend*] intend.

ROSS.   Well, I will thither.
MACD.   Well, may you see things well done there: adieu!
         Lest our old robes sit easier than our new!
ROSS.   Farewell, father.
OLD M.   God's benison go with you, and with those
         That would make good of bad and friends of foes! [*Exeunt.*

ACT III.

SCENE I. *Forres. The palace.*

Enter BANQUO.

BAN. Thou hast it now: king, Cawdor, Glamis, all,
As the weird women promised, and I fear
Thou play'dst most foully for't: yet it was said
It should not stand in thy posterity,
But that myself should be the root and father
Of many kings. If there come truth from them—
As upon thee, Macbeth, their speeches shine—
Why, by the verities on thee made good,
May they not be my oracles as well
And set me up in hope? But hush, no more.

Sennet sounded. Enter MACBETH, *as king;* LADY MACBETH, *as queen;*
LENNOX, ROSS, Lords, Ladies, *and* Attendants.

MACB. Here's our chief guest.
LADY M. If he had been forgotten,
It had been as a gap in our great feast,
And all-thing[1] unbecoming.
MACB. To-night we hold a solemn[2] supper, sir,
And I'll request your presence.
BAN. Let your highness
Command upon me, to the which my duties
Are with a most indissoluble tie
For ever knit.
MACB. Ride you this afternoon?
BAN. Ay, my good lord.

[1] *all-thing*] altogether.
[2] *solemn*] formal.

163

MACB.   We should have else desired your good advice,
         Which still[3] hath been both grave and prosperous,
         In this day's council; but we'll take to-morrow.
         Is't far you ride?
BAN.   As far, my lord, as will fill up the time
         'Twixt this and supper: go not my horse the better,
         I must become a borrower of the night
         For a dark hour or twain.
MACB.   Fail not our feast.
BAN.   My lord, I will not.
MACB.   We hear our bloody cousins are bestow'd
         In England and in Ireland, not confessing
         Their cruel parricide, filling their hearers
         With strange invention: but of that to-morrow,
         When therewithal we shall have cause[4] of state
         Craving us jointly. Hie you to horse: adieu,
         Till you return at night. Goes Fleance with you?
BAN.   Ay, my good lord: our time does call upon's.
MACB.   I wish your horses swift and sure of foot,
         And so I do commend you to their backs.
         Farewell.   [*Exit Banquo.*
         Let every man be master of his time
         Till seven at night; to make society
         The sweeter welcome, we will keep ourself
         Till supper-time alone: while[5] then, God be with you!

               [*Exeunt all but Macbeth and an Attendant.*

         Sirrah, a word with you: attend those men
         Our pleasure?
ATTEND.   They are, my lord, without the palace-gate.
MACB.   Bring them before us.   [*Exit Attendant.*
               To be thus is nothing;
         But to be safely thus: our fears in Banquo
         Stick deep; and in his royalty of nature

---

[3] *still*] always.
[4] *cause*] affairs.
[5] *while*] until.

Reigns that which would be fear'd: 'tis much he dares,
And, to that dauntless temper of his mind,
He hath a wisdom that doth guide his valour
To act in safety. There is none but he
Whose being I do fear: and under him
My Genius is rebuked, as it is said
Mark Antony's was by Cæsar. He chid the sisters,
When first they put the name of king upon me,
And bade them speak to him; then prophet-like
They hail'd him father to a line of kings:
Upon my head they placed a fruitless crown
And put a barren sceptre in my gripe,
Thence to be wrench'd with an unlineal hand,
No son of mine succeeding. If't be so,
For Banquo's issue have I filed[6] my mind;
For them the gracious Duncan have I murder'd;
Put rancours in the vessel of my peace
Only for them, and mine eternal jewel
Given to the common enemy of man,
To make them kings, the seed of Banquo kings!
Rather than so, come, fate, into the list,
And champion me to the utterance![7] Who's there?

Re-enter Attendant, *with two* Murderers.

Now go to the door, and stay there till we call. [*Exit Attendant.*
Was it not yesterday we spoke together?
FIRST MUR.   It was, so please your highness.
MACB.   Well then, now
Have you consider'd of my speeches? Know
That it was he in the times past which held you
So under fortune, which you thought had been
Our innocent self: this I made good to you
In our last conference; pass'd in probation with you,
How you were borne in hand,[8] how cross'd, the instruments,
Who wrought with them, and all things else that might

---

[6] *filed*] defiled.
[7] *utterance*] uttermost.
[8] *borne in hand*] tricked.

> To half a soul and to a notion[9] crazed
> Say 'Thus did Banquo.'

FIRST MUR.   You made it known to us.

MACB.   I did so; and went further, which is now
> Our point of second meeting. Do you find
> Your patience so predominant in your nature,
> That you can let this go? Are you so gospell'd,[10]
> To pray for this good man and for his issue,
> Whose heavy hand hath bow'd you to the grave
> And beggar'd yours for ever?

FIRST MUR.   We are men, my liege.

MACB.   Ay, in the catalogue ye go for men;
> As hounds and greyhounds, mongrels, spaniels, curs,
> Shoughs, water-rugs[11] and demi-wolves, are clept[12]
> All by the name of dogs: the valued file
> Distinguishes the swift, the slow, the subtle,
> The housekeeper, the hunter, every one
> According to the gift which bounteous nature
> Hath in him closed, whereby he does receive
> Particular addition, from the bill
> That writes them all alike: and so of men.
> Now if you have a station in the file,
> Not i' the worst rank of manhood, say it,
> And I will put that business in your bosoms
> Whose execution takes your enemy off,
> Grapples you to the heart and love of us,
> Who wear our health but sickly in his life,
> Which in his death were perfect.

SEC. MUR.   I am one, my liege,
> Whom the vile blows and buffets of the world
> Have so incensed that I am reckless what
> I do to spite the world.

FIRST MUR.   And I another
> So weary with disasters, tugg'd with fortune,
> That I would set my life on any chance,

---

[9] *notion*] mind.
[10] *gospell'd*] inclined to act according to the precepts of the Gospels.
[11] *Shoughs, water-rugs*] shaggy dogs, poodles.
[12] *clept*] called.

To mend it or be rid on 't.
MACB.   Both of you
Know Banquo was your enemy.
BOTH MUR.   True, my lord.
MACB.   So is he mine, and in such bloody distance
That every minute of his being thrusts
Against my near'st of life: and though I could
With barefaced power sweep him from my sight
And bid my will avouch it, yet I must not,
For certain friends that are both his and mine,
Whose loves I may not drop, but wail his fall
Who I myself struck down: and thence it is
That I to your assistance do make love,
Masking the business from the common eye
For sundry weighty reasons.
SEC. MUR.   We shall, my lord,
Perform what you command us.
FIRST MUR.   Though our lives—
MACB.   Your spirits shine through you. Within this hour at most
I will advise you where to plant yourselves,
Acquaint you with the perfect spy o' the time,
The moment on 't; for 't must be done to-night,
And something[13] from the palace; always thought
That I require a clearness:[14] and with him—
To leave no rubs nor botches in the work—
Fleance his son, that keeps him company,
Whose absence is no less material to me
Than is his father's, must embrace the fate
Of that dark hour. Resolve yourselves apart:
I'll come to you anon.
BOTH MUR.   We are resolved, my lord.
MACB.   I'll call upon you straight: abide within. [*Exeunt Murderers.*
It is concluded: Banquo, thy soul's flight,
If it find heaven, must find it out to-night.   [*Exit.*

---

[13] *something*] somewhat.
[14] *clearness*] i e , alibi

SCENE II. *The palace.*

Enter LADY MACBETH *and a* Servant.

LADY M. Is Banquo gone from court?
SERV.   Ay, madam, but returns again to-night.
LADY M. Say to the king, I would attend his leisure
        For a few words.
SERV.   Madam, I will.   [*Exit.*
LADY M.   Nought's had, all's spent,
        Where our desire is got without content:
        'Tis safer to be that which we destroy
        Than by destruction dwell in doubtful joy.

Enter MACBETH.

        How now, my lord! why do you keep alone,
        Of sorriest fancies your companions making;
        Using those thoughts which should indeed have died
        With them they think on? Things without all remedy
        Should be without regard: what's done is done.
MACB.   We have scotch'd[1] the snake, not kill'd it:
        She'll close and be herself, whilst our poor malice
        Remains in danger of her former tooth.
        But let the frame of things disjoint, both the worlds suffer,
        Ere we will eat our meal in fear, and sleep
        In the affliction of these terrible dreams
        That shake us nightly: better be with the dead,
        Whom we, to gain our peace, have sent to peace,
        Than on the torture of the mind to lie
        In restless ecstasy.[2] Duncan is in his grave;
        After life's fitful fever he sleeps well;
        Treason has done his worst: nor steel, nor poison,
        Malice domestic, foreign levy, nothing,
        Can touch him further.

[1] *scotch'd*] slashed.
[2] *ecstasy*] mental alienation.

LADY M.   Come on;
                Gentle my lord, sleek o'er your rugged looks;
                Be bright and jovial among your guests to-night.
MACB.   So shall I, love; and so, I pray, be you:
                Let your remembrance apply to Banquo;
                Present him eminence, both with eye and tongue:
                Unsafe the while, that we
                Must lave our honours in these flattering streams,
                And make our faces visards to our hearts,
                Disguising what they are.
LADY M.   You must leave this.
MACB.   O, full of scorpions is my mind, dear wife!
                Thou know'st that Banquo, and his Fleance, lives.
LADY M.   But in them nature's copy's not eterne.
MACB.   There's comfort yet; they are assailable;
                Then be thou jocund: ere the bat hath flown
                His cloister'd flight; ere to black Hecate's summons
                The shard-borne³ beetle with his drowsy hums
                Hath rung night's yawning peal, there shall be done
                A deed of dreadful note.
LADY M.   What's to be done?
MACB.   Be innocent of the knowledge, dearest chuck,
                Till thou applaud the deed. Come, seeling⁴ night,
                Scarf up the tender eye of pitiful day,
                And with thy bloody and invisible hand
                Cancel and tear to pieces that great bond
                Which keeps me pale! Light thickens, and the crow
                Makes wing to the rooky wood:
                Good things of day begin to droop and drowse,
                Whiles night's black agents to their preys do rouse.
                Thou marvell'st at my words: but hold thee still;
                Things bad begun make strong themselves by ill:
                So, prithee, go with me.   [*Exeunt.*

---

³ *shard-borne*] borne on scaly wings.
¹ *seeling*] blinding. The term, from falconry, refers to the sewing together of the bird's eyelids.

SCENE III. *A park near the palace.*

Enter three MURDERERS.

FIRST MUR.   But who did bid thee join with us?
THIRD MUR.   Macbeth.
SEC. MUR.   He needs not our mistrust; since he delivers
        Our offices, and what we have to do,
        To the direction just. [1]
FIRST MUR.   Then stand with us.
        The west yet glimmers with some streaks of day:
        Now spurs the lated[2] traveller apace
        To gain the timely inn, and near approaches
        The subject of our watch.
THIRD MUR.   Hark! I hear horses.
BAN.   [*Within*] Give us a light there, ho!
SEC. MUR.   Then 'tis he: the rest
        That are within the note of expectation[3]
        Already are i' the court.
FIRST MUR.   His horses go about.
THIRD MUR.   Almost a mile: but he does usually—
        So all men do—from hence to the palace gate
        Make it their walk.
SEC. MUR.   A light, a light!

Enter BANQUO, *and* FLEANCE *with a torch.*

THIRD MUR.   'Tis he.
FIRST MUR.   Stand to 't.
BAN.   It will be rain to-night.
FIRST MUR.   Let it come down.
                            [*They set upon Banquo.*
BAN.   O, treachery! Fly, good Fleance, fly, fly, fly!
        Thou mayst revenge. O slave!   [*Dies. Fleance escapes.*
THIRD MUR.   Who did strike out the light?
FIRST MUR.   Was't not the way?

---

[1] *To the direction just*] according to Macbeth's instructions.
[2] *lated*] belated.
[3] *note of expectation*] list of those expected.

THIRD MUR.   There's but one down; the son is fled.
SEC. MUR.   We have lost
            Best half of our affair.
FIRST MUR.   Well, let's away and say how much is done.   [*Exeunt.*

SCENE IV. *Hall in the palace.*

A banquet prepared. Enter MACBETH, LADY MACBETH, ROSS, LENNOX,
Lords, *and* Attendants.

MACB.   You know your own degrees; sit down: at first
            And last the hearty welcome.
LORDS.   I hanks to your majesty.
MACB.   Ourself will mingle with society
            And play the humble host.
            Our hostess keeps her state,[1] but in best time
            We will require[2] her welcome.
LADY M.   Pronounce it for me, sir, to all our friends,
            For my heart speaks they are welcome.

Enter first Murderer *to the door.*

MACB.   See, they encounter thee with their hearts' thanks.
            Both sides are even: here I'll sit i' the midst:
            Be large[3] in mirth; anon we'll drink a measure
            The table round. [*Approaching the door*] There's blood upon
                thy face.
MUR.   'Tis Banquo's then.
MACB.   'Tis better thee without than he within.
            Is he dispatch'd?
MUR.   My lord, his throat is cut; that I did for him.
MACB.   Thou art the best o' the cut-throats: yet he's good
            That did the like for Fleance: if thou didst it,

---

[1] *state*] canopied chair of state.
[2] *require*] request.
[3] *luige*] liberal.

Thou art the nonpareil.[4]

MUR. Most royal sir,
Fleance is 'scaped.

MACB. [*Aside*] Then comes my fit again: I had else been perfect,
Whole as the marble, founded as the rock,
As broad and general as the casing air:[5]
But now I am cabin'd, cribb'd,[6] confined, bound in
To saucy[7] doubts and fears.—But Banquo's safe?

MUR. Ay, my good lord: safe in a ditch he bides,
With twenty trenched[8] gashes on his head;
The least a death to nature.

MACB. Thanks for that.
[*Aside*] There the grown serpent lies; the worm[9] that's fled
Hath nature that in time will venom breed,
No teeth for the present. Get thee gone: to-morrow
We'll hear ourselves again.[10] [*Exit Murderer.*

LADY M. My royal lord,
You do not give the cheer: the feast is sold
That is not often vouch'd,[11] while 'tis a-making,
'Tis given with welcome: to feed were best at home;
From thence[12] the sauce to meat is ceremony;
Meeting were bare without it.

MACB. Sweet remembrancer!
Now good digestion wait on appetite,
And health on both!

LEN. May't please your highness sit.

[*The Ghost of Banquo enters, and sits in Macbeth's place.*

MACB. Here had we now our country's honour roof'd,
Were the graced[13] person of our Banquo present;

---

[4] *nonpareil*] paragon.
[5] *broad . . . air*] free and unrestrained as the surrounding air.
[6] *cribb'd*] caged.
[7] *saucy*] unbounded.
[8] *trenched*] cut.
[9] *worm*] serpent.
[10] *hear ourselves again*] discuss things further.
[11] *vouch'd*] asserted.
[12] *From thence*] away from home.
[13] *graced*] dignified.

	Who may I rather challenge for unkindness
	Than pity for mischance!
Ross.	His absence, sir,
	Lays blame upon his promise. Please't your highness
	To grace us with your royal company.
Macb.	The table's full.
Len.	Here is a place reserved, sir.
Macb.	Where?
Len.	Here, my good lord. What is't that moves your highness?
Macb.	Which of you have done this?
Lords.	What, my good lord?
Macb.	Thou canst not say I did it: never shake
	Thy gory locks at me.
Ross.	Gentlemen, rise; his highness is not well
Lady M.	Sit, worthy friends: my lord is often thus,
	And hath been from his youth: pray you, keep seat;
	The fit is momentary; upon a thought[14]
	He will again be well: if much you note him,
	You shall offend him and extend his passion:
	Feed, and regard him not. Are you a man?
Macb.	Ay, and a bold one, that dare look on that
	Which might appal the devil.
Lady M.	O proper stuff!
	This is the very painting of your fear:
	This is the air-drawn dagger which, you said,
	Led you to Duncan. O, these flaws[15] and starts,
	Impostors to true fear, would well become
	A woman's story at a winter's fire,
	Authorized by her grandam. Shame itself!
	Why do you make such faces? When all's done,
	You look but on a stool.
Macb.	Prithee, see there! behold! look! lo! how say you?
	Why, what care I? If thou canst nod, speak too.
	If charnel-houses and our graves must send
	Those that we bury back, our monuments
	Shall be the maws of kites. [*Exit Ghost.*

[14] *upon a thought*] in no time.
[15] *flaws*] storms of passion.

LADY M.   What, quite unmann'd in folly?
MACB.   If I stand here, I saw him.
LADY M.   Fie, for shame!
MACB.   Blood hath been shed ere now, i' the olden time,
          Ere humane statute purged the gentle weal;
          Ay, and since too, murders have been perform'd
          Too terrible for the ear: the time has been,
          That, when the brains were out, the man would die,
          And there an end; but now they rise again,
          With twenty mortal murders[16] on their crowns,
          And push us from our stools: this is more strange
          Than such a murder is.
LADY M.   My worthy lord,
          Your noble friends do lack you.
MACB.   I do forget.
          Do not muse at me, my most worthy friends;
          I have a strange infirmity, which is nothing
          To those that know me. Come, love and health to all;
          Then I'll sit down. Give me some wine, fill full.
          I drink to the general joy o' the whole table,
          And to our dear friend Banquo, whom we miss;
          Would he were here! to all and him we thirst,
          And all to all.
LORDS.   Our duties, and the pledge.

Re-enter Ghost.

MACB.   Avaunt! and quit my sight! let the earth hide thee!
          Thy bones are marrowless, thy blood is cold;
          Thou hast no speculation[17] in those eyes
          Which thou dost glare with.
LADY M.   Think of this, good peers,
          But as a thing of custom: 'tis no other;
          Only it spoils the pleasure of the time.
MACB.   What man dare, I dare:
          Approach thou like the rugged Russian bear,
          The arm'd rhinoceros, or the Hyrcan tiger;

---

[16] *mortal murders*] fatal wounds.
[17] *speculation*] power of intelligent vision.

'Take any shape but that, and my firm nerves
Shall never tremble: or be alive again,
And dare me to the desert with thy sword;
If trembling I inhabit then, protest me
The baby of a girl. Hence, horrible shadow!
Unreal mockery, hence!   [*Exit Ghost.*
                              Why, so: being gone,
I am a man again. Pray you, sit still.

LADY M. You have displaced the mirth, broke the good meeting,
With most admired disorder.[18]

MACB.   Can such things be,
And overcome[19] us like a summer's cloud,
Without our special wonder? You make me strange
Even to the disposition that I owe,[20]
When now I think you can behold such sights,
And keep the natural ruby of your cheeks,
When mine is blanch'd with fear.

ROSS.   What sights, my lord?

LADY M. I pray you, speak not; he grows worse and worse;
Question enrages him: at once, good night:
Stand not upon the order of your going,
But go at once.

LEN.   Good night; and better health
Attend his majesty!

LADY M.   A kind good night to all!

                    [*Exeunt all but Macbeth and Lady M.*

MACB.   It will have blood: they say blood will have blood:
Stones have been known to move and trees to speak;
Augures[21] and understood relations have
By maggot-pies[22] and choughs and rooks brought forth
The secret'st man of blood. What is the night?

LADY M. Almost at odds with morning, which is which.

MACB.   How say'st thou, that Macduff denies his person

---

[18] *admired disorder*] amazing mental derangement.
[19] *overcome*] pass over.
[20] *owe*] possess.
[21] *Augures*] auguries.
[22] *maggot-pies*] magpies.

        At our great bidding?

LADY M.   Did you send to him, sir?

MACB.   I hear it by the way, but I will send:
        There's not a one of them but in his house
        I keep a servant fee'd. I will to-morrow,
        And betimes I will, to the weird sisters:
        More shall they speak, for now I am bent to know,
        By the worst means, the worst. For mine own good
        All causes shall give way: I am in blood
        Stepp'd in so far that, should I wade no more,
        Returning were as tedious as go o'er:
        Strange things I have in head that will to hand,
        Which must be acted ere they may be scann'd.

LADY M. You lack the season of all natures, sleep.

MACB.   Come, we'll to sleep. My strange and self-abuse[23]
        Is the initiate fear[24] that wants hard use:
        We are yet but young in deed.   [*Exeunt.*

SCENE V. *A heath.*

Thunder. Enter the three Witches, *meeting* HECATE.

FIRST WITCH.   Why, how now, Hecate! you look angerly.

HEC.   Have I not reason, beldams as you are,
        Saucy and over-bold? How did you dare
        To trade and traffic with Macbeth
        In riddles and affairs of death;
        And I, the mistress of your charms,
        The close contriver of all harms,
        Was never call'd to bear my part,
        Or show the glory of our art?
        And, which is worse, all you have done
        Hath been but for a wayward son,
        Spiteful and wrathful; who, as others do,

---

[23] *self-abuse*] delusion.
[24] *initiate fear*] novice's fear.

Loves for his own ends, not for you.
But make amends now: get you gone,
And at the pit of Acheron
Meet me i' the morning: thither he
Will come to know his destiny:
Your vessels and your spells provide,
Your charms and every thing beside.
I am for the air; this night I'll spend
Unto a dismal[1] and a fatal end:
Great business must be wrought ere noon:
Upon the corner of the moon
There hangs a vaporous drop profound;
I'll catch it ere it come to ground:
And that distill'd by magic sleights
Shall raise such artificial[2] sprites
As by the strength of their illusion
Shall draw him on to his confusion:
He shall spurn fate, scorn death, and bear
His hopes 'bove wisdom, grace and fear:
And you all know security[3]
Is mortals' chiefest enemy.

[*Music and a song within:* 'Come away, come away,' &c.

Hark! I am call'd; my little spirit, see,
Sits in a foggy cloud, and stays for me.   [*Exit.*
First Witch.   Come, let's make haste; she'll soon be back again.
                                                           [*Exeunt.*

Scene VI. *Forres. The palace.*

Enter Lennox *and another* Lord.

Len.   My former speeches have but hit your thoughts,
            Which can interpret farther: only I say

---

[1] *dismal*] disastrous.
[2] *artificial*] artful, cunning.
[3] *security*] overconfidence, carelessness.

Things have been strangely borne.[1] The gracious Duncan
Was pitied of Macbeth: marry, he was dead:
And the right-valiant Banquo walk'd too late;
Whom, you may say, if't please you, Fleance kill'd,
For Fleance fled: men must not walk too late.
Who cannot want the thought, how monstrous
It was for Malcolm and for Donalbain
To kill their gracious father? damned fact![2]
How it did grieve Macbeth! did he not straight,
In pious rage, the two delinquents tear,
That were the slaves of drink and thralls of sleep?
Was not that nobly done? Ay, and wisely too;
For 'twould have anger'd any heart alive
To hear the men deny't. So that, I say,
He has borne all things well: and I do think
That, had he Duncan's sons under his key—
As, an't please heaven, he shall not—they should find
What 'twere to kill a father; so should Fleance.
But, peace! for from broad words, and 'cause he fail'd
His presence at the tyrant's feast, I hear,
Macduff lives in disgrace: sir, can you tell
Where he bestows himself?

LORD.   The son of Duncan,
From whom this tyrant holds the due of birth,
Lives in the English court, and is received
Of the most pious Edward with such grace
That the malevolence of fortune nothing
Takes from his high respect. Thither Macduff
Is gone to pray the holy king, upon his aid
To wake Northumberland and warlike Siward:
That by the help of these, with Him above
To ratify the work, we may again
Give to our tables meat, sleep to our nights,
Free from our feasts and banquets bloody knives,
Do faithful homage and receive free honours:
All which we pine for now: and this report

---

[1] *borne*] conducted.
[2] *fact*] deed.

        · Hath so exasperate the king that he
        Prepares for some attempt of war.

LEN.   Sent he to Macduff?

LORD.   He did: and with an absolute 'Sir, not I,'
        The cloudy[3] messenger turns me his back,
        And hums, as who should say 'You'll rue the time
        That clogs me with this answer.'

LEN.   And that well might
        Advise him to a caution, to hold what distance
        His wisdom can provide. Some holy angel
        Fly to the court of England and unfold
        His message ere he come, that a swift blessing
        May soon return to this our suffering country
        Under a hand accursed!

LORD.   I'll send my prayers with him.
                                            [*Exeunt.*

---

3 *cloudy*] moroso.

ACT IV.

Scene I. *A cavern. In the middle, a boiling cauldron.*

Thunder. Enter the three Witches.

FIRST WITCH.   Thrice the brinded[1] cat hath mew'd.
SEC. WITCH.   Thrice and once the hedge-pig[2] whined.
THIRD WITCH.   Harpier cries ' 'Tis time, 'tis time.'
FIRST WITCH.   Round about the cauldron go:
      In the poison'd entrails throw.
      Toad, that under cold stone
      Days and nights has thirty one
      Swelter'd[3] venom sleeping got,
      Boil thou first i' the charmed pot.
ALL.   Double, double toil and trouble;
      Fire burn and cauldron bubble.
SEC. WITCH.   Fillet of a fenny snake,
      In the cauldron boil and bake;
      Eye of newt and toe of frog,
      Wool of bat and tongue of dog,
      Adder's fork[4] and blind-worm's sting,
      Lizard's leg and howlet's wing,
      For a charm of powerful trouble,
      Like a hell-broth boil and bubble.
ALL.   Double, double toil and trouble;
      Fire burn and cauldron bubble.
THIRD WITCH.   Scale of dragon, tooth of wolf,

---

[1] *brinded*] spotted, brindled.
[2] *hedge-pig*] hedgehog.
[3] *Swelter'd*] exuded.
[4] *fork*] forked tongue.

Witches' mummy, maw and gulf[5]
Of the ravin'd salt-sea shark,
Root of hemlock digg'd i' the dark,
Liver of blaspheming Jew,
Gall of goat and slips of yew
Sliver'd[6] in the moon's eclipse,
Nose of Turk and Tartar's lips,
Finger of birth-strangled babe
Ditch-deliver'd by a drab,
Make the gruel thick and slab:[7]
Add thereto a tiger's chaudron,[8]
For the ingredients of our cauldron.

ALL.　　Double, double toil and trouble;
Fire burn and cauldron bubble.

SEC. WITCH.　Cool it with a baboon's blood,
Then the charm is firm and good.

Enter HECATE *to the other three* Witches.

HEC.　　O, well done! I commend your pains;
And every one shall share i' the gains:
And now about the cauldron sing,
Like elves and fairies in a ring,
Enchanting all that you put in.

　　　　　　　　[*Music and a song:* 'Black spirits,' &c.
　　　　　　　　　　　　　　　　[*Hecate retires.*

SEC. WITCH.　By the pricking of my thumbs,
Something wicked this way comes:
Open, locks,
Whoever knocks!

Enter MACBETH.

MACB.　How now, you secret, black, and midnight hags!
What is't you do?

ALL.　　　　　　　A deed without a name.

---

[5] *gulf*] gullet.
[6] *Sliver'd*] broken off.
[7] *slab*] glutinous.
[8] *chaudron*] entrails.

MACB.   I conjure you, by that which you profess,
          Howe'er you come to know it, answer me:
          Though you untie the winds and let them fight
          Against the churches; though the yesty[9] waves
          Confound and swallow navigation up;
          Though bladed corn be lodged[10] and trees blown down;
          Though castles topple on their warders' heads;
          Though palaces and pyramids do slope
          Their heads to their foundations; though the treasure
          Of nature's germens[11] tumble all together,
          Even till destruction sicken; answer me
          To what I ask you.
FIRST WITCH.   Speak.
SEC. WITCH.   Demand
THIRD WITCH.   We'll answer.
FIRST WITCH.   Say, if thou'dst rather hear it from our mouths,
          Or from our masters?
MACB.   Call 'em, let me see 'em.
FIRST WITCH.   Pour in sow's blood, that hath eaten
          Her nine farrow;[12] grease that's sweaten
          From the murderer's gibbet throw
          Into the flame.
ALL.   Come, high or low;
          Thyself and office deftly show!

Thunder. First Apparition: an armed Head.

MACB.   Tell me, thou unknown power,—
FIRST WITCH.   He knows thy thought.
          Hear his speech, but say thou nought.
FIRST APP.   Macbeth! Macbeth! Macbeth! beware Macduff;
          Beware the thane of Fife. Dismiss me: enough. [*Descends.*
MACB.   Whate'er thou art, for thy good caution thanks;
          Thou hast harp'd[13] my fear aright: but one word more,—
FIRST WITCH.   He will not be commanded: here's another,

---

[9] *yesty*] foamy.
[10] *lodged*] beaten flat.
[11] *germens*] seeds.
[12] *farrow*] litter.
[13] *harp'd*] hit upon.

More potent than the first.

Thunder. Second Apparition: *a bloody Child.*

SEC. APP.   Macbeth! Macbeth! Macbeth!
MACB.   Had I three ears, I'ld hear thee.
SEC. APP.   Be bloody, bold and resolute; laugh to scorn
The power of man, for none of woman born
Shall harm Macbeth.   *[Descends.*
MACB.   Then live, Macduff: what need I fear of thee?
But yet I'll make assurance double sure,
And take a bond of fate: thou shalt not live;
That I may tell pale-hearted fear it lies,
And sleep in spite of thunder.

Thunder. Third Apparition: *a Child crowned, with a tree in his hand.*

What is this,
That rises like the issue of a king,
And wears upon his baby-brow the round
And top of sovereignty?
ALL.   Listen, but speak not to't.
THIRD APP.   Be lion-mettled, proud, and take no care
Who chafes, who frets, or where conspirers are:
Macbeth shall never vanquish'd be until
Great Birnam wood to high Dunsinane hill
Shall come against him.   *[Descends.*

MACB.   That will never be:
Who can impress the forest, bid the tree
Unfix his earth-bound root? Sweet bodements! good!
Rebellion's head, rise never, till the wood
Of Birnam rise, and our high-placed Macbeth
Shall live the lease of nature, pay his breath
To time and mortal custom. Yet my heart
Throbs to know one thing: tell me, if your art
Can tell so much: shall Banquo's issue ever
Reign in this kingdom?
ALL.   Seek to know no more.
MACB.   I will be satisfied: deny me this,
And an eternal curse fall on you! Let me know:

Why sinks that cauldron? and what noise[14] is this? [*Hautboys.*

FIRST WITCH.   Show!
SEC. WITCH.   Show!
THIRD WITCH.   Show!
ALL.   Show his eyes, and grieve his heart;
            Come like shadows, so depart!

A show of eight Kings, *the last with a glass in his hand; Banquo's Ghost following.*

MACB.   Thou art too like the spirit of Banquo: down!
            Thy crown does sear mine eye-balls. And thy hair,
            Thou other gold-bound brow, is like the first.
            A third is like the former. Filthy hags!
            Why do you show me this? A fourth! Start, eyes!
            What, will the line stretch out to the crack of doom?
            Another yet! A seventh! I'll see no more:
            And yet the eighth appears, who bears a glass
            Which shows me many more; and some I see
            That two-fold balls and treble sceptres carry:
            Horrible sight! Now I see 'tis true;
            For the blood-bolter'd[15] Banquo smiles upon me,
            And points at them for his. What, is this so?
FIRST WITCH.   Ay, sir, all this is so: but why
            Stands Macbeth thus amazedly?
            Come, sisters, cheer we up his sprites,
            And show the best of our delights:
            I'll charm the air to give a sound,
            While you perform your antic round,[16]
            That this great king may kindly say
            Our duties did his welcome pay.

            [*Music. The Witches dance, and then vanish, with Hecate.*

MACB.   Where are they? Gone? Let this pernicious hour
            Stand aye accursed in the calendar!
            Come in, without there!

---

[14] *noise*] music.
[15] *blood-bolter'd*] with blood-clotted hair.
[16] *antic round*] old and fantastic dance.

Enter LENNOX.

LEN.   What's your grace's will?
MACB.   Saw you the weird sisters?
LEN.   No, my lord.
MACB.   Came they not by you?
LEN.   No indeed, my lord.
MACB.   Infected be the air whereon they ride,
               And damn'd all those that trust them! I did hear
               The galloping of horse: who was't came by?
LEN.   'Tis two or three, my lord, that bring you word
               Macduff is fled to England.
MACB.   Fled to England!
LEN.   Ay, my good lord.
MACB.   [*Aside*] Time, thou anticipatest my dread exploits:
               The flighty purpose never is o'ertook
               Unless the deed go with it: from this moment
               The very firstlings of my heart shall be
               The firstlings of my hand. And even now,
               To crown my thoughts with acts, be it thought and done:
               The castle of Macduff I will surprise;
               Seize upon Fife; give to the edge o' the sword
               His wife, his babes, and all unfortunate souls
               That trace him in his line. No boasting like a fool;
               This deed I'll do before this purpose cool:
               But no more sights!—Where are these gentlemen?
               Come, bring me where they are.   [*Exeunt.*

SCENE II. *Fife. Macduff's castle.*

Enter LADY MACDUFF, *her* SON, *and* ROSS.

L. MACD.   What had he done, to make him fly the land?
ROSS.   You must have patience, madam.
L. MACD.   He had none:
               His flight was madness: when our actions do not,
               Our fears do make us traitors.

ROSS.   You know not
    Whether it was his wisdom or his fear.
L. MACD.   Wisdom! to leave his wife, to leave his babes,
     His mansion and his titles,[1] in a place
    From whence himself does fly? He loves us not;
    He wants the natural touch:[2] for the poor wren,
    The most diminutive of birds, will fight,
    Her young ones in her nest, against the owl.
    All is the fear and nothing is the love;
    As little is the wisdom, where the flight
    So runs against all reason.
ROSS.   My dearest coz,
    I pray you, school[3] yourself: but, for your husband,
    He is noble, wise, judicious, and best knows
    The fits o' the season. I dare not speak much further:
    But cruel are the times, when we are traitors
    And do not know ourselves; when we hold rumour
    From what we fear, yet know not what we fear,
    But float upon a wild and violent sea
    Each way and move. I take my leave of you:
    Shall not be long but I'll be here again:
    Things at the worst will cease, or else climb upward
    To what they were before. My pretty cousin,
    Blessing upon you!
L. MACD.   Father'd he is, and yet he's fatherless.
ROSS.   I am so much a fool, should I stay longer,
    It would be my disgrace and your discomfort:
    I take my leave at once.   *[Exit.*

L. MACD.   Sirrah, your father's dead:
    And what will you do now? How will you live?
SON.   As birds do, mother.
L. MACD.   What, with worms and flies?
SON.   With what I get, I mean; and so do they.
L. MACD.   Poor bird! thou'ldst never fear the net nor lime,
    The pitfall nor the gin.
SON.   Why should I, mother? Poor birds they are not set for.

---

[1] *titles*] possessions.
[2] *touch*] feeling, affection.
[3] *school*] control.

My father is not dead, for all your saying.

L. MACD. Yes, he is dead: how wilt thou do for a father?

SON. Nay, how will you do for a husband?

L. MACD. Why, I can buy me twenty at any market.

SON. Then you'll buy 'em to sell again.

L. MACD. Thou speak'st with all thy wit, and yet, i' faith,
With wit enough for thee.

SON. Was my father a traitor, mother?

L. MACD. Ay, that he was.

SON. What is a traitor?

L. MACD. Why, one that swears and lies.

SON. And be all traitors that do so?

L. MACD. Every one that does so is a traitor, and must be hanged.

SON. And must they all be hanged that swear and lie?

L. MACD. Every one.

SON. Who must hang them?

L. MACD. Why, the honest men.

SON. Then the liars and swearers are fools; for there are liars and
swearers enow to beat the honest men and hang up them.

L. MACD. Now, God help thee, poor monkey! But how wilt thou do for
a father?

SON. If he were dead, you'ld weep for him: if you would not, it were
a good sign that I should quickly have a new father.

L. MACD. Poor prattler, how thou talk'st!

Enter a Messenger.

MESS. Bless you, fair dame! I am not to you known,
Though, in your state of honour I am perfect.[4]
I doubt[5] some danger does approach you nearly:
If you will take a homely man's advice,
Be not found here; hence, with your little ones.
To fright you thus, methinks I am too savage;
To do worse to you were fell cruelty,
Which is too nigh your person. Heaven preserve you!
I dare abide no longer. *Exit.*

L. MACD. Whither should I fly?

---

[4] *perfect*] fully aware.
[5] *doubt*] fear.

I have done no harm. But I remember now
I am in this earthly world, where to do harm
Is often laudable, to do good sometime
Accounted dangerous folly: why then, alas,
Do I put up that womanly defence,
To say I have done no harm?—What are these faces?

Enter Murderers.

FIRST MUR.   Where is your husband?
L. MACD.   I hope, in no place so unsanctified
Where such as thou mayst find him.
FIRST MUR.   He's a traitor.
SON.   Thou liest, thou shag-ear'd villain!
FIRST MUR.   What, you egg!
                                                  [*Stabbing him.*

       Young fry of treachery!
SON.   He has kill'd me, mother:
       Run away, I pray you!   [*Dies.*
                              [*Exit Lady Macduff, crying* 'Murder!'
                              [*Exeunt murderers, following her.*

SCENE III. *England. Before the King's palace.*

Enter MALCOLM *and* MACDUFF.

MAL.   Let us seek out some desolate shade, and there
         Weep our sad bosoms empty.
MACD.   Let us rather
         Hold fast the mortal sword, and like good men
         Bestride our down-fall'n birthdom:[1] each new morn
         New widows howl, new orphans cry, new sorrows
         Strike heaven on the face, that it resounds
         As if it felt with Scotland and yell'd out
         Like syllable of dolour.

_____
[1] *birthdom*] motherland.

MAL.   What I believe, I'll wail;
What know, believe; and what I can redress,
As I shall find the time to friend, I will.
What you have spoke, it may be so perchance.
This tyrant, whose sole name blisters our tongues,
Was once thought honest: you have loved him well;
He hath not touch'd you yet. I am young; but something
You may deserve of him through me; and wisdom
To offer up a weak, poor, innocent lamb
To appease an angry god.

MACD.   I am not treacherous.

MAL.   But Macbeth is.
A good and virtuous nature may recoil
In an imperial charge.[2] But I shall crave your pardon;
That which you are, my thoughts cannot transpose:[3]
Angels are bright still, though the brightest fell:
Though all things foul would wear the brows of grace,
Yet grace must still look so.

MACD.   I have lost my hopes.

MAL.   Perchance even there where I did find my doubts.
Why in that rawness[4] left you wife and child,
Those precious motives, those strong knots of love,
Without leave-taking? I pray you,
Let not my jealousies[5] be your dishonours,
But mine own safeties. You may be rightly just,
Whatever I shall think.

MACD.   Bleed, bleed, poor country:
Great tyranny, lay thou thy basis sure,
For goodness dare not check thee: wear thou thy wrongs;
The title is affeer'd.[6] Fare thee well, lord:
I would not be the villain that thou think'st
For the whole space that's in the tyrant's grasp
And the rich East to boot.

MAL.   Be not offended:

---

[2] *charge*] command.
[3] *transpose*] alter.
[4] *rawness*] exposed condition.
[5] *jealousies*] suspicions.
[6] *affeer'd*] confirmed.

I speak not as in absolute fear of you.
I think our country sinks beneath the yoke;
It weeps, it bleeds, and each new day a gash
Is added to her wounds: I think withal
There would be hands uplifted in my right;
And here from gracious England[7] have I offer
Of goodly thousands: but for all this,
When I shall tread upon the tyrant's head,
Or wear it on my sword, yet my poor country
Shall have more vices than it had before,
More suffer and more sundry ways than ever,
By him that shall succeed.

MACD.   What should he be?

MAL.   It is myself I mean: in whom I know
All the particulars of vice so grafted
That, when they shall be open'd, black Macbeth
Will seem as pure as snow, and the poor state
Esteem him as a lamb, being compared
With my confineless[8] harms.

MACD.   Not in the legions
Of horrid hell can come a devil more damn'd
In evils to top Macbeth.

MAL.   I grant him bloody,
Luxurious,[9] avaricious, false, deceitful,
Sudden,[10] malicious, smacking of every sin
That has a name: but there's no bottom, none,
In my voluptuousness: your wives, your daughters,
Your matrons and your maids, could not fill up
The cistern of my lust, and my desire
All continent[11] impediments would o'erbear,
That did oppose my will: better Macbeth
Than such an one to reign.

MACD.   Boundless intemperance

---

[7] *England*] the King of England.
[8] *confineless*] boundless.
[9] *Luxurious*] lascivious.
[10] *Sudden*] violent, impetuous.
[11] *continent*] restraining, chaste.

In nature[12] is a tyranny; it hath been
The untimely emptying of the happy throne,
And fall of many kings. But fear not yet
To take upon you what is yours: you may
Convey[13] your pleasures in a spacious plenty,
And yet seem cold, the time you may so hoodwink:
We have willing dames enough; there cannot be
That vulture in you, to devour so many
As will to greatness dedicate themselves,
Finding it so inclined.

MAL.   With this there grows
In my most ill-composed affection[14] such
A stanchless[15] avarice that, were I king,
I should cut off the nobles for their lands,
Desire his[16] jewels and this other's house:
And my more-having would be as a sauce
To make me hunger more, that I should forge
Quarrels unjust against the good and loyal,
Destroying them for wealth.

MACD.   This avarice
Sticks deeper, grows with more pernicious root
Than summer-seeming[17] lust, and it hath been
The sword of our slain kings: yet do not fear;
Scotland hath foisons[18] to fill up your will
Of your mere own: all these are portable,
With other graces weigh'd.[19]

MAL.   But I have none: the king-becoming graces,
As justice, verity, temperance, stableness,
Bounty, perseverance, mercy, lowliness,
Devotion, patience, courage, fortitude,
I have no relish[20] of them, but abound

---

[12] *nature*] natural appetites.
[13] *Convey*] carry out secretly.
[14] *affection*] disposition.
[15] *stanchless*] insatiable.
[16] *his*] one person's.
[17] *summer-seeming*] summer-like, transitory.
[18] *foisons*] rich harvests, plenty.
[19] *weigh'd*] counterbalanced.
[20] *relish*] trace.

In the division[21] of each several crime,
Acting it many ways. Nay, had I power, I should
Pour the sweet milk of concord into hell,
Uproar[22] the universal peace, confound
All unity on earth.

MACD.   O Scotland, Scotland!
MAL.   If such a one be fit to govern, speak:
I am as I have spoken.
MACD.   Fit to govern!
No, not to live. O nation miserable!
With an untitled tyrant bloody-scepter'd,
When shalt thou see thy wholesome days again,
Since that the truest issue of thy throne
By his own interdiction stands accursed,
And does blaspheme[23] his breed? Thy royal father
Was a most sainted king: the queen that bore thee,
Oftener upon her knees than on her feet,
Died every day she lived. Fare thee well!
These evils thou repeat'st upon thyself
Have banish'd me from Scotland. O my breast,
Thy hope ends here!
MAL.   Macduff, this noble passion,
Child of integrity, hath from my soul
Wiped the black scruples, reconciled my thoughts
To thy good truth and honour. Devilish Macbeth
By many of these trains[24] hath sought to win me
Into his power; and modest wisdom plucks me
From over-credulous haste: but God above
Deal between thee and me! for even now
I put myself to thy direction, and
Unspeak mine own detraction; here abjure
The taints and blames I laid upon myself,
For strangers to my nature. I am yet
Unknown to woman, never was forsworn,
Scarcely have coveted what was mine own,

[21] *division*] variation.
[22] *Uproar*] disturb.
[23] *blaspheme*] slander.
[24] *trains*] stratagems, lures.

At no time broke my faith, would not betray
The devil to his fellow, and delight
No less in truth than life: my first false speaking
Was this upon myself: what I am truly,
Is thine and my poor country's to command:
Whither indeed, before thy here-approach,
Old Siward, with ten thousand warlike men,
Already at a point,[25] was setting forth.
Now we'll together, and the chance of goodness[26]
Be like our warranted quarrel! Why are you silent?

MACD. Such welcome and unwelcome things at once
'Tis hard to reconcile.

Enter a Doctor.

MAL. Well, more anon. Comes the king forth, I pray you?
DOCT. Ay, sir; there are a crew of wretched souls
That stay his cure: their malady convinces[27]
The great assay of art; but at his touch,
Such sanctity hath heaven given his hand,
They presently amend.
MAL.   I thank you, doctor. [*Exit Doctor.*
MACD. What's the disease he means?
MAL.   'Tis call'd the evil:[28]
A most miraculous work in this good king;
Which often, since my here-remain in England,
I have seen him do. How he solicits heaven,
Himself best knows: but strangely-visited people,
All swoln and ulcerous, pitiful to the eye,
The mere[29] despair of surgery, he cures,
Hanging a golden stamp[30] about their necks,
Put on with holy prayers: and 'tis spoken,
To the succeeding royalty he leaves
The healing benediction. With this strange virtue
He hath a heavenly gift of prophecy,

[25] *at a point*] prepared.
[26] *goodness*] good fortune.
[27] *convinces*] conquers.
[28] *the evil*] i.e., the king's evil (scrofula).
[29] *mere*] absolute.
[30] *stamp*] coin.

And sundry blessings hang about his throne
That speak him full of grace.

Enter Ross.

MACD.   See, who comes here?
MAL.   My countryman; but yet I know him not.
MACD.   My ever gentle cousin, welcome hither.
MAL.   I know him now: good God, betimes remove
The means that makes us strangers!
ROSS.   Sir, amen.
MACD.   Stands Scotland where it did?
ROSS.   Alas, poor country!
Almost afraid to know itself! It cannot
Be call'd our mother, but our grave: where nothing,
But who knows nothing, is once[31] seen to smile;
Where sighs and groans and shrieks that rend the air,
Are made, not mark'd; where violent sorrow seems
A modern ecstasy:[32] the dead man's knell
Is there scarce ask'd for who; and good men's lives
Expire before the flowers in their caps,
Dying or ere they sicken.
MACD.   O, relation
Too nice,[33] and yet too true!
MAL.   What's the newest grief?
ROSS.   That of an hour's age doth hiss the speaker;
Each minute teems a new one.
MACD.   How does my wife?
ROSS.   Why, well.
MACD.   And all my children?
ROSS.   Well too.
MACD.   The tyrant has not batter'd at their peace?
ROSS.   No; they were well at peace when I did leave 'em.
MACD.   Be not a niggard of your speech: how goes't?
ROSS.   When I came hither to transport the tidings,
Which I have heavily borne, there ran a rumour
Of many worthy fellows that were out;[34]

---

[31] *once*] ever.
[32] *modern ecstasy*] common emotion.
[33] *nice*] precise.
[34] *out*] in rebellion.

Which was to my belief witness'd the rather,
For that I saw the tyrant's power a-foot:
Now is the time of help; your eye in Scotland
Would create soldiers, make our women fight,
To doff their dire distresses.

MAL.   Be't their comfort
We are coming thither: gracious England hath
Lent us good Siward and ten thousand men;
An older and a better soldier none
That Christendom gives out.[35]

ROSS.   Would I could answer
This comfort with the like! But I have words
That would be howl'd out in the desert air,
Where hearing should not latch[36] them.

MACD.   What concern they?
The general cause? or is it a fee-grief[37]
Due to some single breast?

ROSS.   No mind that's honest
But in it shares some woe, though the main part
Pertains to you alone.

MACD.   If it be mine,
Keep it not from me, quickly let me have it.

ROSS.   Let not your ears despise my tongue for ever,
Which shall possess[38] them with the heaviest sound
That ever yet they heard.

MACD.   Hum! I guess at it.

ROSS.   Your castle is surprised; your wife and babes
Savagely slaughter'd: to relate the manner,
Were, on the quarry of these murder'd deer,
To add the death of you.

MAL.   Merciful heaven!
What, man! ne'er pull your hat upon your brows;
Give sorrow words: the grief that does not speak
Whispers the o'er-fraught heart, and bids it break.

MACD. My children too?

---

[35] *gives out*] proclaims.
[36] *latch*] catch.
[37] *fee-grief*] grief pertaining to an individual.
[38] *possess*] fill.

ROSS.   Wife, children, servants, all
That could be found.
MACD.   And I must be from thence!
My wife kill'd too?
ROSS.   I have said.
MAL.   Be comforted:
Let's make us medicines of our great revenge,
To cure this deadly grief.
MACD. He has no children. All my pretty ones?
Did you say all? O hell-kite! All?
What, all my pretty chickens and their dam
At one fell swoop?
MAL. Dispute it like a man.
MACD.   I shall do so;
But I must also feel it as a man:
I cannot but remember such things were,
That were most precious to me. Did heaven look on,
And would not take their part? Sinful Macduff,
They were all struck for thee! naught[39] that I am,
Not for their own demerits, but for mine,
Fell slaughter on their souls: heaven rest them now!
MAL. Be this the whetstone of your sword: let grief
Convert to anger; blunt not the heart, enrage it.
MACD. O, I could play the woman with mine eyes,
And braggart with my tongue! But, gentle heavens,
Cut short all intermission; front to front
Bring thou this fiend of Scotland and myself;
Within my sword's length set him; if he 'scape,
Heaven forgive him too!
MAL.   This tune goes manly.
Come, go we to the king; our power[40] is ready;
Our lack is nothing but our leave.[41] Macbeth
Is ripe for shaking, and the powers above
Put on their instruments. Receive what cheer you may;
The night is long that never finds the day. [*Exeunt.*

---

[39] *naught*] wicked.
[40] *power*] army.
[41] *leave*] leave-taking.

ACT V.

SCENE I. *Dunsinane. Ante-room in the castle.*

Enter a Doctor of Physic and a Waiting-Gentlewoman.

DOCT.   I have two nights watched with you, but can perceive no truth
in your report. When was it she last walked?

GENT.   Since his majesty went into the field, I have seen her rise from
her bed, throw her nightgown upon her, unlock her closet,
take forth paper, fold it, write upon't, read it, afterwards seal
it, and again return to bed; yet all this while in a most fast
sleep.

DOCT.   A great perturbation in nature, to receive at once the benefit of
sleep and do the effects of watching! In this slumbery agita-
tion, besides her walking and other actual performances,
what, at any time, have you heard her say?

GENT.   That, sir, which I will not report after her.

DOCT.   You may to me, and 'tis most meet you should.

GENT.   Neither to you nor any one, having no witness to confirm my
speech.

Enter LADY MACBETH, *with a taper.*

Lo you, here she comes! This is her very guise, and, upon my
life, fast asleep. Observe her; stand close.[1]

DOCT.   How came she by that light?

GENT.   Why, it stood by her: she has light by her continually; 'tis her
command.

DOCT.   You see, her eyes are open.

GENT.   Ay, but their sense is shut.

DOCT.   What is it she does now? Look, how she rubs her hands.

---

[1] *close*] hidden.

199

GENT.   It is an accustomed action with her, to seem thus washing her
        hands: I have known her continue in this a quarter of an
        hour.

LADY M. Yet here's a spot.

DOCT.   Hark! she speaks: I will set down what comes from her, to
        satisfy my remembrance the more strongly.

LADY M. Out, damned spot! out, I say! One: two: why, then 'tis time to
        do't. Hell is murky. Fie, my lord, fie! a soldier, and afeard?
        What need we fear who knows it, when none can call our
        power to account? Yet who would have thought the old man
        to have had so much blood in him?

DOCT.   Do you mark that?

LADY M. The thane of Fife had a wife; where is she now? What, will
        these hands ne'er be clean? No more o' that, my lord, no
        more o' that: you mar all with this starting.

DOCT.   Go to, go to; you have known what you should not.

GENT.   She has spoke what she should not, I am sure of that: heaven
        knows what she has known.

LADY M. Here's the smell of the blood still: all the perfumes of Arabia
        will not sweeten this little hand. Oh, oh, oh!

DOCT.   What a sigh is there! The heart is sorely charged.

GENT.   I would not have such a heart in my bosom for the dignity[2] of
        the whole body.

DOCT.   Well, well, well,—

GENT.   Pray God it be, sir.

DOCT.   This disease is beyond my practice:[3] yet I have known those
        which have walked in their sleep who have died holily in
        their beds.

LADY M. Wash your hands; put on your nightgown; look not so pale: I
        tell you yet again, Banquo's buried; he cannot come out on's
        grave.

DOCT.   Even so?

LADY M. To bed, to bed; there's knocking at the gate: come, come, come,
        come, give me your hand: what's done cannot be undone: to
        bed, to bed, to bed.   [*Exit.*

DOCT.   Will she go now to bed?

GENT.   Directly.

---

[2] *dignity*] worth.
[3] *practice*] art, skill.

DOCT.	Foul whisperings are abroad: unnatural deeds
	Do breed unnatural troubles: infected minds
	To their deaf pillows will discharge their secrets:
	More needs she the divine than the physician.
	God, God forgive us all! Look after her;
	Remove from her the means of all annoyance,[4]
	And still keep eyes upon her. So good night:
	My mind she has mated[5] and amazed my sight:
	I think, but dare not speak.
GENT.	Good night, good doctor. [*Exeunt.*

SCENE II. *The country near Dunsinane.*

Drum and colours. Enter MENTEITH, CAITHNESS, ANGUS, LENNOX, *and* Soldiers.

MENT.	The English power is near, led on by Malcolm,
	His uncle Siward and the good Macduff:
	Revenges burn in them; for their dear causes
	Would to the bleeding and the grim alarm
	Excite the mortified man.
ANG.	Near Birnam wood
	Shall we well meet them; that way are they coming.
CAITH.	Who knows if Donalbain be with his brother?
LEN.	For certain, sir, he is not: I have a file[1]
	Of all the gentry: there is Siward's son,
	And many unrough[2] youths, that even now
	Protest[3] their first of manhood.
MENT.	What does the tyrant?

---

[4] *annoyance*] injury.
[5] *mated*] confounded.

---

[1] *file*] list.
[2] *unrough*] unbearded.
[3] *protest*] proclaim.

CAITH. Great Dunsinane he strongly fortifies:
Some say he's mad; others, that lesser hate him,
Do call it valiant fury: but, for certain,
He cannot buckle his distemper'd cause
Within the belt of rule.

ANG. Now does he feel
His secret murders sticking on his hands;
Now minutely[4] revolts upbraid his faith-breach;
Those he commands move only in command,
Nothing in love: now does he feel his title
Hang loose about him, like a giant's robe
Upon a dwarfish thief.

MENT. Who then shall blame
His pester'd senses to recoil and start,
When all that is within him does condemn
Itself for being there?

CAITH. Well, march we on,
To give obedience where 'tis truly owed:
Meet we the medicine of the sickly weal,
And with him pour we, in our country's purge,
Each drop of us.

LEN. Or so much as it needs
To dew the sovereign flower and drown the weeds.
Make we our march towards Birnam. [*Exeunt, marching.*

SCENE III. *Dunsinane. A room in the castle.*

Enter MACBETH, Doctor, *and* Attendants.

MACB. Bring me no more reports; let them fly all:
Till Birnam wood remove to Dunsinane
I cannot taint[1] with fear. What's the boy Malcolm?
Was he not born of woman? The spirits that know
All mortal consequences have pronounced me thus:

---

[4] *minutely*] continual.

---

[1] *taint*] be infected.

       'Fear not, Macbeth; no man that's born of woman
       Shall e'er have power upon thee.' Then fly, false thanes,
       And mingle with the English epicures:
       The mind I sway[2] by and the heart I bear
       Shall never sag with doubt nor shake with fear.

Enter a Servant.

       The devil damn thee black, thou cream-faced loon![3]
       Where got'st thou that goose look?

SERV.   There is ten thousand—

MACB.   Geese, villain?

SERV.   Soldiers, sir.

MACB.   Go prick thy face and over-red thy fear,
       Thou lily-liver'd boy. What soldiers, patch?[4]
       Death of thy soul! those linen cheeks of thine
       Are counsellors to fear. What soldiers, whey-face?

SERV.   The English force, so please you.

MACB.   Take thy face hence.   *[Exit Servant.*
                 Seyton!—I am sick at heart,
       When I behold—Seyton, I say!—This push[5]
       Will cheer me ever, or disseat me now.
       I have lived long enough: my way[6] of life
       Is fall'n into the sear, the yellow leaf,
       And that which should accompany old age,
       As honour, love, obedience, troops of friends,
       I must not look to have; but, in their stead,
       Curses, not loud but deep, mouth-honour, breath,
       Which the poor heart would fain deny, and dare not.
       Seyton!

Enter SEYTON.

SEY.   What's your gracious pleasure?

---

[2] *sway*] rule myself.
[3] *loon*] brute, rogue.
[4] *patch*] clown, fool.
[5] *push*] attack.
[6] *way*] course, term.

MACB.   What news more?
SEY.   All is confirm'd, my lord, which was reported.
MACB.   I'll fight, till from my bones my flesh be hack'd.
            Give me my armour.
SEY.   'Tis not needed yet.
MACB.   I'll put it on.
            Send out moe[7] horses, skirr[8] the country round;
            Hang those that talk of fear. Give me mine armour.
            How does your patient, doctor?
DOCT.   Not so sick, my lord,
            As she is troubled with thick-coming fancies,
            That keep her from her rest.
MACB.   Cure her of that.
            Canst thou not minister to a mind diseased,
            Pluck from the memory a rooted sorrow,
            Raze out the written troubles of the brain,
            And with some sweet oblivious antidote
            Cleanse the stuff'd bosom of that perilous stuff
            Which weighs upon the heart?
DOCT.   Therein the patient
            Must minister to himself.
MACB.   Throw physic to the dogs, I'll none of it.
            Come, put mine armour on; give me my staff.
            Seyton, send out. Doctor, the thanes fly from me.
            Come, sir, dispatch. If thou couldst, doctor, cast
            The water[9] of my land, find her disease
            And purge it to a sound and pristine health,
            I would applaud thee to the very echo,
            That should applaud again. Pull't off, I say.
            What rhubarb, senna,[10] or what purgative drug,
            Would scour these English hence? Hear'st thou of them?
DOCT.   Ay, my good lord; your royal preparation
            Makes us hear something.
MACB.   Bring it[11] after me.

---

[7] *moe*] more.
[8] *skirr*] move rapidly, scour.
[9] *cast The water*] inspect the urine.
[10] *senna*] Cassia senna, a plant used as a purgative.
[11] *it*] i.e., a piece of Macbeth's armor.

I will not be afraid of death and bane
Till Birnam forest come to Dunsinane.
DOCT.   [*Aside*] Were I from Dunsinane away and clear,
Profit again should hardly draw me here.   [*Exeunt.*

SCENE IV. *Country near Birnam wood.*

Drum and colours. Enter MALCOLM, *old* SIWARD *and his·Son,* MAC-
DUFF, MENTEITH, CAITHNESS, ANGUS, LENNOX, ROSS, *and* Soldiers,
marching.

MAL.   Cousins, I hope the days are near at hand
    That chambers will be safe.
MENT.   We doubt it nothing.
SIW.   What wood is this before us?
MENT.   The wood of Birnam.
MAL.   Let every soldier hew him down a bough,
    And bear't before him: thereby shall we shadow
    The numbers of our host, and make discovery
    Err in report of us.
SOLDIERS.   It shall be done.
SIW.   We learn no other but the confident tyrant
    Keeps still in Dunsinane, and will endure
    Our setting down before't.
MAL.   'Tis his main hope:
    For where there is advantage[1] to be given,
    Both more and less have given him the revolt,
    And none serve with him but constrained things
    Whose hearts are absent too.
MACD.   Let our just censures
    Attend the true event, and put we on
    Industrious soldiership.

1 *advantage*] opportunity

SIW.   The time approaches,
      That will with due decision make us know
      What we shall say we have and what we owe.
      Thoughts speculative their unsure hopes relate,
      But certain issue strokes must arbitrate:
      Towards which advance the war.   *[Exeunt, marching.*

SCENE V. *Dunsinane. Within the castle.*

Enter MACBETH, SEYTON, *and* Soldiers, *with drum and colours.*

MACB.   Hang out our banners on the outward walls;
      The cry is still 'They come': our castle's strength
      Will laugh a siege to scorn: here let them lie
      Till famine and the ague eat them up:
      Were they not forced[1] with those that should be ours,
      We might have met them dareful,[2] beard to beard,
      And beat them backward home.   *[A cry of women within.*
                           What is that noise?
SEY.   It is the cry of women, my good lord.   *[Exit.*
MACB.   I have almost forgot the taste of fears:
      The time has been, my senses would have cool'd
      To hear a night-shriek, and my fell of hair[3]
      Would at a dismal treatise[4] rouse and stir
      As life were in't: I have supp'd full with horrors;
      Direness,[5] familiar to my slaughterous thoughts,
      Cannot once start me.

Re-enter SEYTON.

                      Wherefore was that cry?
SEY.   The queen, my lord, is dead.

---

[1] *forced*] reinforced.
[2] *dareful*] boldly.
[3] *fell of hair*] hairy skin.
[4] *treatise*] tale.
[5] *Direness*] horror.

MACB.　She should have died hereafter;
　　　There would have been a time for such a word.
　　　To-morrow, and to-morrow, and to-morrow,
　　　Creeps in this petty pace from day to day,
　　　To the last syllable of recorded time;
　　　And all our yesterdays have lighted fools
　　　The way to dusty death. Out, out, brief candle!
　　　Life's but a walking shadow, a poor player
　　　That struts and frets his hour upon the stage
　　　And then is heard no more: it is a tale
　　　Told by an idiot, full of sound and fury,
　　　Signifying nothing.

Enter a MESSENGER.

　　　Thou comest to use thy tongue; thy story quickly.
MESS.　Gracious my lord,
　　　I should report that which I say I saw,
　　　But know not how to do it.
MACB.　　　　　　　　　Well, say, sir.
MESS.　As I did stand my watch upon the hill,
　　　I look'd toward Birnam, and anon, methought,
　　　The wood began to move.
MACB.　　　　　　　　Liar and slave!
MESS.　Let me endure your wrath, if't be not so:
　　　Within this three mile may you see it coming;
　　　I say, a moving grove.
MACB.　　　　　　　If thou speak'st false,
　　　Upon the next tree shalt thou hang alive,
　　　Till famine cling[6] thee: if thy speech be sooth,
　　　I care not if thou dost for me as much.
　　　I pull in resolution, and begin
　　　To doubt the equivocation of the fiend
　　　That lies like truth: 'Fear not, till Birnam wood
　　　Do come to Dunsinane'; and now a wood
　　　Comes toward Dunsinane. Arm, arm, and out!
　　　If this which he avouches does appear,
　　　There is nor flying hence nor tarrying here.
　　　I 'gin to be a-weary of the sun,

[6] *cling*] shrivel.

And wish the estate o' the world were now undone.
Ring the alarum-bell! Blow, wind! come, wrack!
At least we'll die with harness on our back.   [*Exeunt.*

SCENE VI. *Dunsinane. Before the castle.*

Drum and colours. Enter MALCOLM, *old* SIWARD, MACDUFF, *and their* Army, *with boughs.*

MAL.   Now near enough; your leavy screens throw down,
          And show like those you are. You, worthy uncle,
          Shall, with my cousin, your right noble son,
          Lead our first battle:[1] worthy Macduff and we
          Shall take upon's what else remains to do,
          According to our order.
SIW.   Fare you well.
          Do we but find the tyrant's power to-night,
          Let us be beaten, if we cannot fight.
MACD.   Make all our trumpets speak; give them all breath,
          Those clamorous harbingers of blood and death.   [*Exeunt.*

SCENE VII. *Another part of the field.*

Alarums. Enter MACBETH.

MACB.   They have tied me to a stake; I cannot fly,
          But bear-like I must fight the course. What's he
          That was not born of woman? Such a one
          Am I to fear, or none.

Enter young SIWARD.

[1] *battle*] army.

Yo. Siw.	What is thy name?
Macb.	Thou'lt be afraid to hear it.
Yo. Siw.	No; though thou call'st thyself a hotter name
	Than any is in hell.
Macb.	My name's Macbeth.
Yo. Siw.	The devil himself could not pronounce a title
	More hateful to mine ear.
Macb.	No, nor more fearful.
Yo. Siw.	Thou liest, abhorred tyrant; with my sword
	I'll prove the lie thou speak'st.

                        [They fight, and young Siward is slain.

Macb.	Thou wast born of woman.
	But swords I smile at, weapons laugh to scorn,
	Brandish'd by man that's of a woman born. *[Exit.*

Alarums. Enter Macduff.

Macd.	That way the noise is. Tyrant, show thy face!
	If thou be'st slain and with no stroke of mine,
	My wife and children's ghosts will haunt me still.
	I cannot strike at wretched kerns,[1] whose arms
	Are hired to bear their staves:[2] either thou, Macbeth,
	Or else my sword, with an unbatter'd edge,
	I sheathe again undeeded. There thou shouldst be;
	By this great clatter, one of greatest note
	Seems bruited:[3] let me find him, fortune!
	And more I beg not. *[Exit. Alarums.*

Enter Malcolm *and old* Siward.

Siw.	This way, my lord; the castle's gently render'd:[4]
	The tyrant's people on both sides do fight;
	The noble thanes do bravely in the war;
	The day almost itself professes yours,
	And little is to do.
Mal.	We have met with foes

---

[1] *kerns*] Irish mercenaries.
[2] *staves*] spear shafts.
[3] *bruited*] reported.
[4] *gently render'd*] surrendered unreluctantly.

That strike beside us.

SIW.   Enter, sir, the castle. [*Exeunt. Alarum.*

SCENE VIII. *Another part of the field.*

Enter MACBETH.

MACB.   Why should I play the Roman fool, and die
         On mine own sword? whiles I see lives, the gashes
         Do better upon them.

Enter MACDUFF.

MACD.   Turn, hell-hound, turn!
MACB.   Of all men else I have avoided thee:
         But get thee back; my soul is too much charged
         With blood of thine already.
MACD.   I have no words:
         My voice is in my sword, thou bloodier villain
         Than terms can give thee out!   [*They fight.*
MACB.   Thou losest labour:
         As easy mayst thou the intrenchant[1] air
         With thy keen sword impress as make me bleed:
         Let fall thy blade on vulnerable crests;
         I bear a charmed life, which must not yield
         To one of woman born.
MACD.   Despair thy charm,
         And let the angel whom thou still hast served
         Tell thee, Macduff was from his mother's womb
         Untimely ripp'd.
MACB.   Accursed be that tongue that tells me so,
         For it hath cow'd my better part of man!
         And be these juggling fiends no more believed,
         That palter[2] with us in a double sense;
         That keep the word of promise to our ear,

---

[1] *intrenchant*] invulnerable.
[2] *palter*] shuffle, equivocate.

	And break it to our hope. I'll not fight with thee.
MACD.	Then yield thee, coward,
	And live to be the show and gaze o' the time:
	We'll have thee, as our rarer monsters are,
	Painted upon a pole, and underwrit,
	'Here may you see the tyrant.'
MACB.	I will not yield,

And break it to our hope. I'll not fight with thee.

MACD.   Then yield thee, coward,
And live to be the show and gaze o' the time:
We'll have thee, as our rarer monsters are,
Painted upon a pole, and underwrit,
'Here may you see the tyrant.'

MACB.   I will not yield,
To kiss the ground before young Malcolm's feet,
And to be baited with the rabble's curse.
Though Birnam wood be come to Dunsinane,
And thou opposed, being of no woman born,
Yet I will try the last: before my body
I throw my warlike shield: lay on, Macduff;
And damn'd be him that first cries 'Hold, enough!'

[*Exeunt, fighting. Alarums.*

Retreat. Flourish. Enter, with drum and colours, MALCOLM, *old*
SIWARD, ROSS, *the other* Thanes, *and* Soldiers.

MAL.   I would the friends we miss were safe arrived.
SIW.   Some must go off: and yet, by these I see,
So great a day as this is cheaply bought.
MAL.   Macduff is missing, and your noble son.
ROSS.   Your son, my lord, has paid a soldier's debt:
He only lived but till he was a man;
The which no sooner had his prowess confirm'd
In the unshrinking station where he fought,
But like a man he died.
SIW.   Then he is dead?
ROSS.   Ay, and brought off the field: your cause of sorrow
Must not be measured by his worth, for then
It hath no end.
SIW.   Had he his hurts before?
ROSS.   Ay, on the front.
SIW.   Why then, God's soldier be he!
Had I as many sons as I have hairs,
I would not wish them to a fairer death:
And so his knell is knoll'd.
MAL.   He's worth more sorrow,
And that I'll spend for him.

SIW.   He's worth no more:
     They say he parted well and paid his score:
     And so God be with him! Here comes newer comfort.

Re-enter MACDUFF, *with* MACBETH'S *head.*

MACD.   Hail, king! for so thou art: behold, where stands
     The usurper's cursed head: the time is free:
     I see thee compass'd with thy kingdom's pearl,
     That speak my salutation in their minds;
     Whose voices I desire aloud with mine:
     Hail, King of Scotland!

ALL.   Hail, King of Scotland!   [*Flourish.*

MAL.   We shall not spend a large expense of time
     Before we reckon with your several loves,
     And make us even with you. My thanes and kinsmen,
     Henceforth be earls, the first that ever Scotland
     In such an honour named. What's more to do,
     Which would be planted newly with the time,
     As calling home our exiled friends abroad
     That fled the snares of watchful tyranny,
     Producing forth the cruel ministers
     Of this dead butcher and his fiend-like queen,
     Who, as 'tis thought, by self and violent hands
     Took off her life; this, and what needful else
     That calls upon us, by the grace of Grace
     We will perform in measure, time and place:
     So thanks to all at once and to each one,
     Whom we invite to see us crown'd at Scone.
                             [*Flourish. Exeunt.*

Othello

Othello

SINCE ITS FIRST performance in 1604, *Othello* has proved one of Shakespeare's most enduring tragedies. The play, set against the backdrop of the Venetian-Turkish wars, features one of Shakespeare's most compelling villains, Iago. Ostensibly driven by a desire for revenge, Iago plots and schemes to bring about Othello's fall. But his malignancy appears incommensurate to the wrongs he claims Othello has done him. Indeed, Iago uses the fact that he was passed over for promotion to enlist Roderigo's aid rather than to offer a legitimate motive for his behavior. Even his offhand aside reporting a rumor that Othello slept with his wife seems implausible, and all we have is Iago's simple statement: "I hate the Moor."

Othello provides the perfect foil for Iago and the latter's description illustrates his contempt of the tragic hero. "The Moor is of a free and open nature," Iago tells us, "And will as tenderly be led by the nose / As asses are." Iago's comparison of Othello to an ass is one of many animal images he applies to his enemy. Othello is an "old black ram," a beast, a "Barbary horse." Sprung from Iago's hatred, these images of blackness and brutishness point up Othello's tenuous position in Venetian society. And Othello's reluctant but complete conviction of Desdemona's infidelity speaks of an insecurity born of his marginalized position.

For Desdemona, Othello's "wondrous pitiful" story strikes a sympathetic chord that arouses first her compassion, then her passion. Under Iago's direction, however, the lovers appear mere pawns, as easily manipulated as the less heroic characters in the play. And we are caught in Iago's plottings too, for despite our privileged access to his plans, we never learn "Why he hath thus ensnared [Othello's] soul and body." All we are left with, in the end, are Iago's last words: "What you know, you know."

CANDACE WARD

Dramatis Personæ

DUKE OF VENICE.
BRABANTIO, a senator.
Other Senators.
GRATIANO, brother to Brabantio.
LODOVICO, kinsman to Brabantio.
OTHELLO, a noble Moor in the service of the Venetian state.
CASSIO, his lieutenant.
IAGO, his ancient.
RODERIGO, a Venetian gentleman.
MONTANO, Othello's predecessor in the government of Cyprus.
Clown, servant to Othello.

DESDEMONA, daughter to Brabantio and wife to Othello.
EMILIA, wife to Iago.
BIANCA, mistress to Cassio.

Sailor, Messenger, Herald, Officers, Gentlemen, Musicians, and Attendants.

SCENE: *Venice: a seaport in Cyprus*

ACT I.

SCENE I. *Venice. A Street.*

Enter RODERIGO *and* IAGO

ROD.   Tush, never tell me;[1] I take it much unkindly
    That thou, Iago, who hast had my purse
    As if the strings were thine, shouldst know of this.
IAGO.   'Sblood, but you will not hear me:
    If ever I did dream of such a matter,
    Abhor me.
ROD.   Thou told'st me thou didst hold him in thy hate.
IAGO.   Despise me, if I do not. Three great ones of the city,
    In personal suit to make me his lieutenant,
    Off-capp'd to[2] him: and, by the faith of man,
    I know my price, I am worth no worse a place:
    But he, as loving his own pride and purposes,
    Evades them, with a bombast circumstance
    Horribly stuff'd with epithets of war;
    And, in conclusion,
    Nonsuits[3] my mediators; for, "Certes," says he,
    "I have already chose my officer."
    And what was he?
    Forsooth, a great arithmetician,
    One Michael Cassio, a Florentine,
    A fellow almost damn'd in a fair wife;
    That never set a squadron in the field,
    Nor the division of a battle knows
    More than a spinster; unless the bookish theoric,
    Wherein the toged[4] consuls can propose

---

1. *Tush . . . me*] The scene opens in the middle of a conversation about Othello's elopement with Desdemona.
2. *Off-capp'd to*] Stood cap in hand soliciting.
3. *Nonsuits*] To disappoint in a suit, not to comply with.
4. *toged*] wearing the "toga," the uniform of civil officers of state as opposed to military officers.

As masterly as he: mere prattle without practice
Is all his soldiership. But he, sir, had the election:
And I, of whom his eyes had seen the proof
At Rhodes, at Cyprus, and on other grounds
Christian and heathen, must be be-lee'd[5] and calm'd
By debitor and creditor: this counter-caster,[6]
He, in good time, must his lieutenant be,
And I — God bless the mark! — his Moorship's ancient.[7]
ROD.　By heaven, I rather would have been his hangman.
IAGO.　Why, there's no remedy; 'tis the curse of service,
Preferment goes by letter and affection,
And not by old gradation, where each second
Stood heir to the first. Now, sir, be judge yourself
Whether I in any just term am affined[8]
To love the Moor.
ROD.　　　　　　　　　I would not follow him then.
IAGO.　O, sir, content you;
I follow him to serve my turn upon him:
We cannot all be masters, nor all masters
Cannot be truly follow'd. You shall mark
Many a duteous and knee-crooking knave,
That doting on his own obsequious bondage
Wears out his time, much like his master's ass,
For nought but provender,[9] and when he's old, cashier'd:
Whip me such honest knaves. Others there are
Who, trimm'd in forms and visages of duty,
Keep yet their hearts attending on themselves,
And throwing but shows of service on their lords
Do well thrive by them, and when they have lined their coats
Do themselves homage: these fellows have some soul,
And such a one do I profess myself.
For, sir,
It is as sure as you are Roderigo,
Were I the Moor, I would not be Iago:
In following him, I follow but myself;
Heaven is my judge, not I for love and duty,
But seeming so, for my peculiar end:
For when my outward action doth demonstrate

---

5. *be-lee'd*] under the lee of another, out of the way of the wind, and so becalmed (as of a ship).
6. *counter-caster*] one who casts up counters; an old method of accountancy.
7. *ancient*] a colloquial mispronunciation of "ensign."
8. *affined*] bound by close terms of affinity, such as kin- or friendship.
9. *provender*] dry food for animals.

    The native act and figure of my heart
    In compliment extern,[10] 't is not long after
    But I will wear my heart upon my sleeve
    For daws to peck at: I am not what I am.
ROD.   What a full fortune does the thick-lips owe,
    If he can carry 't thus!
IAGO.   Call up her father,[11]
    Rouse him: make after him, poison his delight,
    Proclaim him in the streets; incense her kinsmen,
    And, though he in a fertile climate dwell,
    Plague him with flies: though that his joy be joy,
    Yet throw such changes of vexation on 't
    As it may lose some colour.
ROD.   Here is her father's house; I 'll call aloud.
IAGO.   Do; with like timorous accent and dire yell
    As when, by night and negligence, the fire
    Is spied in populous cities.
ROD.   What, ho, Brabantio! Signior Brabantio, ho!
IAGO.   Awake! what, ho, Brabantio! thieves! thieves! thieves!
    Look to your house, your daughter and your bags!
    Thieves! thieves!

BRABANTIO *appears above, at a window*

BRA.   What is the reason of this terrible summons?
    What is the matter there?
ROD.   Signior, is all your family within?
IAGO.   Are your doors lock'd?
BRA.   Why, wherefore ask you this?
IAGO.   'Zounds, sir, you're robb'd; for shame, put on your gown;
    Your heart is burst, you have lost half your soul;
    Even now, now, very now, an old black ram
    Is tupping your white ewe. Arise, arise;
    Awake the snorting citizens with the bell,
    Or else the devil will make a grandsire of you:
    Arise, I say.
BRA.   What, have you lost your wits?
ROD.   Most reverend signior, do you know my voice?
BRA.   Not I: what are you?
ROD.   My name is Roderigo.
BRA.   The worser welcome.

---

10. *In compliment extern*] In external etiquette or behaviour.
11. *her father*] i. e., Desdemona's father.

I have charged thee not to haunt about my doors:
In honest plainness thou hast heard me say
My daughter is not for thee; and now, in madness,
Being full of supper and distempering draughts,
Upon malicious bravery, dost thou come
To start my quiet.

ROD.   Sir, sir, sir, —

BRA.   But thou must needs be sure
My spirit and my place have in them power
To make this bitter to thee.

ROD.   Patience, good sir.

BRA.   What tell'st thou me of robbing? this is Venice;
My house is not a grange.

ROD.   Most grave Brabantio,
In simple and pure soul I come to you.

IAGO.   'Zounds, sir, you are one of those that will not serve God, if the
devil bid you. Because we come to do you service and you think
we are ruffians, you 'll have your daughter covered with a Barbary horse; you 'll have your nephews[12] neigh to you; you 'll have
coursers for cousins, and gennets for germans.[13]

BRA.   What profane wretch art thou?

IAGO.   I am one, sir, that comes to tell you your daughter and the Moor
are now making the beast with two backs.

BRA.   Thou art a villain.

IAGO.   You are — a senator.

BRA.   This thou shalt answer; I know thee, Roderigo.

ROD.   Sir, I will answer any thing. But, I beseech you,
If 't be your pleasure and most wise consent,
As partly I find it is, that your fair daughter,
At this odd-even and dull watch o' the night,
Transported with no worse nor better guard
But with a knave of common hire, a gondolier,
To the gross clasps of a lascivious Moor, —
If this be known to you, and your allowance,[14]
We then have done you bold and saucy wrongs;
But if you know not this, my manners tell me
We have your wrong rebuke. Do not believe
That, from the sense of all civility,
I thus would play and trifle with your reverence:
Your daughter, if you have not given her leave,

---

12. *nephews*] grandsons.
13. *gennets for germans*] (small Spanish) horses for kinsmen.
14. *allowance*] authorization, permission.

I say again, hath made a gross revolt,
Tying her duty, beauty, wit and fortunes,
In an extravagant and wheeling stranger
Of here and every where. Straight satisfy yourself:
If she be in her chamber or your house,
Let loose on me the justice of the state
For thus deluding you.

BRA.   Strike on the tinder, ho!
Give me a taper! call up all my people!
This accident is not unlike my dream:
Belief of it oppresses me already.
Light, I say! light!   [*Exit above.*]

IAGO.   Farewell; for I must leave you:
It seems not meet, nor wholesome to my place,
To be produced — as, if I stay, I shall —
Against the Moor: for I do know, the state,
However this may gall him with some check,[15]
Cannot with safety cast[16] him; for he 's embark'd
With such loud reason to the Cyprus wars,
Which even now stand in act, that, for their souls,
Another of his fathom[17] they have none
To lead their business: in which regard,
Though I do hate him as I do hell pains,
Yet for necessity of present life,
I must show out a flag and sign of love,
Which is indeed but sign. That you shall surely find him,
Lead to the Sagittary[18] the raised search;
And there will I be with him. So farewell.   [*Exit.*]

Enter, below, BRABANTIO, *in his night-gown, and* Servants *with torches*

BRA.   It is too true an evil: gone she is;
And what 's to come of my despised time
Is nought but bitterness. Now, Roderigo,
Where didst thou see her? O unhappy girl!
With the Moor, say'st thou? Who would be a father!
How didst thou know 't was she? O, she deceives me
Past thought! What said she to you? Get more tapers.
Raise all my kindred. Are they married, think you?

---

15. *check*] rebuke.
16. *cast*] dismiss, reject.
17. *fathom*] capacity.
18. *the Sagittary*] probably intended for the name of a well-known inn.

ROD. Truly, I think they are.

BRA. O heaven! How got she out? O treason of the blood!
Fathers, from hence trust not your daughters' minds
By what you see them act. Is there not charms
By which the property of youth and maidhood
May be abused? Have you not read, Roderigo,
Of some such thing?

ROD. Yes, sir, I have indeed.

BRA. Call up my brother. O, would you had had her!
Some one way, some another. Do you know
Where we may apprehend her and the Moor?

ROD. I think I can discover him, if you please
To get good guard and go along with me.

BRA. Pray you, lead on. At every house I 'll call;
I may command at most. Get weapons, ho!
And raise some special officers of night.
On, good Roderigo; I 'll deserve your pains. [*Exeunt.*]

SCENE II. *Another Street.*

Enter OTHELLO, IAGO, *and* Attendants *with torches*

IAGO. Though in the trade of war I have slain men,
Yet do I hold it very stuff o' the conscience
To do no contrived murder: I lack iniquity
Sometimes to do me service: nine or ten times
I had thought to have yerk'd[1] him here under the ribs.

OTH. 'T is better as it is.

IAGO. Nay, but he prated
And spoke such scurvy and provoking terms
Against your honour,
That, with the little godliness I have,
I did full hard forbear him. But I pray you, sir,
Are you fast married? Be assured of this,
That the magnifico is much beloved,
And hath in his effect a voice potential
As double as the duke's: he will divorce you,
Or put upon you what restraint and grievance

---

1. *yerk'd*] jerked; to have given a thrust with a sudden and quick motion.

The law, with all his might to enforce it on,
Will give him cable.[2]

OTH.   Let him do his spite:
My services, which I have done the signiory,
Shall out-tongue his complaints. 'T is yet to know —
Which, when I know that boasting is an honour,
I shall promulgate — I fetch my life and being
From men of royal siege, and my demerits
May speak unbonneted to as proud a fortune
As this that I have reach'd: for know, Iago,
But that I love the gentle Desdemona,
I would not my unhoused free condition
Put into circumscription and confine
For the sea's worth. But, look! what lights come yond?

IAGO.   Those are the raised father and his friends:
You were best go in.

OTH.   Not I; I must be found:
My parts, my title and my perfect soul,
Shall manifest me rightly. Is it they?

IAGO.   By Janus, I think no.

Enter CASSIO, *and certain* Officers *with torches*

OTH.   The servants of the duke, and my lieutenant.
The goodness of the night upon you, friends!
What is the news?

CAS.   The duke does greet you, general,
And he requires your haste-post-haste appearance,
Even on the instant.

OTH.   What is the matter, think you?

CAS.   Something from Cyprus, as I may divine:
It is a business of some heat: the galleys
Have sent a dozen sequent[3] messengers
This very night at one another's heels;
And many of the consuls, raised and met,
Are at the duke's already: you have been hotly call'd for;
When, being not at your lodging to be found,
The senate hath sent about three several quests[4]
To search you out.

OTH.   'T is well I am found by you.

---

2. *cable*] full means or opportunity.
3. *sequent*] following one another, one after the other.
4. *quests*] search parties.

I will but spend a word here in the house,
And go with you. [*Exit.*]
CAS. Ancient, what makes he here?
IAGO. Faith, he to-night hath boarded a land carack:[5]
If it prove lawful prize, he 's made for ever.
CAS. I do not understand.
IAGO. He 's married.
CAS. To who?

Re-enter OTHELLO

IAGO. Marry, to — Come, captain, will you go?
OTH. Have with you.[6]
CAS. Here comes another troop to seek for you.
IAGO. It is Brabantio: general, be advised;
He comes to bad intent.

Enter BRABANTIO, RODERIGO, *and* Officers *with torches and weapons*

OTH. Holla! stand there!
ROD. Signior, it is the Moor.
BRA. Down with him, thief!
[*They draw on both sides.*]
IAGO. You, Roderigo! come, sir, I am for you.
OTH. Keep up your bright swords, for the dew will rust them.
Good signior, you shall more command with years
Than with your weapons.
BRA. O thou foul thief, where hast thou stow'd my daughter?
Damn'd as thou art, thou hast enchanted her;
For I 'll refer me to all things of sense,
If she in chains of magic were not bound,
Whether a maid so tender, fair and happy,
So opposite to marriage that she shunn'd
The wealthy curled darlings of our nation,
Would ever have, to incur a general mock,
Run from her guardage[7] to the sooty bosom
Of such a thing as thou, to fear, not to delight.
Judge me the world, if 't is not gross in sense
That thou hast practised on her with foul charms,
Abused her delicate youth with drugs or minerals
That weaken motion: I 'll have 't disputed on;

---

5. *a land carack*] a ship of great burden on land.
6. *Have with you*] I am quite ready.
7. *guardage*] guardianship.

'T is probable, and palpable to thinking.
I therefore apprehend and do attach[8] thee
For an abuser of the world, a practiser
Of arts inhibited and out of warrant.[9]
Lay hold upon him: if he do resist,
Subdue him at his peril.

OTH.   Hold your hands,
Both you of my inclining and the rest:
Were it my cue to fight, I should have known it
Without a prompter. Where will you that I go
To answer this your charge?

BRA.   To prison, till fit time
Of law and course of direct session
Call thee to answer.

OTH.   What if I do obey?
How may the duke be therewith satisfied,
Whose messengers are here about my side,
Upon some present business of the state
To bring me to him?

FIRST OFF.   'T is true, most worthy signior;
The duke 's in council, and your noble self,
I am sure, is sent for.

BRA.   How! the duke in council!
In this time of the night! Bring him away:
Mine 's not an idle cause: the duke himself,
Or any of my brothers of the state,
Cannot but feel this wrong as 't were their own;
For if such actions may have passage free,
Bond-slaves and pagans shall our statesmen be.   [*Exeunt.*]

SCENE III. A *Council-Chamber.*

The Duke *and* Senators *sitting at a table*; Officers *attending*

DUKE.   There is no composition[1] in these news
That gives them credit.

FIRST SEN.   Indeed they are disproportion'd;
My letters say a hundred and seven galleys.

---

8. *attach*] arrest.
9. *inhibited . . . warrant*] prohibited and unauthorised.
1. *composition*] consistency, coherence.

DUKE.   And mine, a hundred and forty.

SEC. SEN.   And mine, two hundred:
    But though they jump not on a just account, — 2
    As in these cases, where the aim reports,
    'T is oft with difference, — yet do they all confirm
    A Turkish fleet, and bearing up to Cyprus.

DUKE.   Nay, it is possible enough to judgement:
    I do not so secure me in the error,
    But the main article I do approve3
    In fearful sense.

SAILOR.   [*Within*] What, ho! what, ho! what, ho!

FIRST OFF.   A messenger from the galleys.

Enter Sailor

DUKE.   Now, what's the business?

SAIL.   The Turkish preparation4 makes for Rhodes;
    So was I bid report here to the state
    By Signior Angelo.

DUKE.   How say you by this change?

FIRST SEN.   This cannot be,
    By no assay5 of reason: 't is a pageant
    To keep us in false gaze. When we consider
    The importancy of Cyprus to the Turk,
    And let ourselves again but understand
    That as it more concerns the Turk than Rhodes,
    So may he with more facile question bear it,6
    For that it stands not in such warlike brace,
    But altogether lacks the abilities
    That Rhodes is dress'd in: if we make thought of this,
    We must not think the Turk is so unskilful
    To leave that latest which concerns him first,
    Neglecting an attempt of ease and gain,
    To wake and wage7 a danger profitless.

DUKE.   Nay, in all confidence, he 's not for Rhodes.

FIRST OFF.   Here is more news.

---

2. *jump not . . . account*] agree not in an exact estimate.
3. *approve*] believe, give credit to.
4. *preparation*] force ready for action.
5. *assay*] test.
6. *with . . . bear it*] with less opposition contest it.
7. *wake and wage*] excite and challenge.

Enter a Messenger

MESS.   The Ottomites, reverend and gracious,
     Steering with due course toward the isle of Rhodes,
     Have there injointed them[8] with an after fleet.'
FIRST SEN.   Ay, so I thought. How many, as you guess?
MESS.   Of thirty sail: and now they do re-stem[9]
     Their backward course, bearing with frank appearance
     Their purposes toward Cyprus. Signior Montano,
     Your trusty and most valiant servitor,
     With his free duty recommends you thus,
     And prays you to believe him.
DUKE.   'T is certain then for Cyprus.
     Marcus Luccicos, is not he in town?
FIRST SEN.   He 's now in Florence.
DUKE.   Write from us to him; post post haste dispatch.
FIRST SEN.   Here comes Brabantio and the valiant Moor.

Enter BRABANTIO, OTHELLO, IAGO, RODERIGO, *and* Officers

DUKE.   Valiant Othello, we must straight employ you
     Against the general enemy Ottoman.
     [*To* BRABANTIO] I did not see you; welcome, gentle signior;
     We lack'd your counsel and your help to-night.
BRA.   So did I yours. Good your grace, pardon me;
     Neither my place nor aught I heard of business
     Hath raised me from my bed, nor doth the general care
     Take hold on me; for my particular grief
     Is of so flood-gate and o'erbearing nature
     That it engluts and swallows other sorrows,
     And it is still itself.
DUKE.   Why, what's the matter?
BRA.   My daughter! O, my daughter!
ALL.   Dead?
BRA.   Ay, to me;
     She is abused, stol'n from me and corrupted
     By spells and medicines bought of mountebanks;
     For nature so preposterously to err,
     Being not deficient, blind, or lame of sense,

---

8. *injointed them*] joined their forces, combined.
9. *re-stem*] retrace.

      Sans[10] witchcraft could not.
DUKE.   Whoe'er he be that in this foul proceeding
      Hath thus beguiled your daughter of herself
      And you of her, the bloody book of law
      You shall yourself read in the bitter letter
      After your own sense, yea, though our proper son
      Stood in your action.
BRA.   Humbly I thank your grace.
      Here is the man, this Moor; whom now, it seems,
      Your special mandate for the state-affairs
      Hath hither brought.
ALL.   We are very sorry for 't.
DUKE.   [*To* OTHELLO] What in your own part can you say to this?
BRA.   Nothing, but this is so.
OTH.   Most potent, grave, and reverend signiors,
      My very noble and approved good masters,
      That I have ta'en away this old man's daughter
      It is most true; true, I have married her:
      The very head and front of my offending
      Hath this extent, no more. Rude am I in my speech,
      And little blest with the soft phrase of peace;
      For since these arms of mine had seven years' pith,[11]
      Till now some nine moons wasted, they have used
      Their dearest action in the tented field;
      And little of this great world can I speak,
      More than pertains to feats of broil and battle;
      And therefore little shall I grace my cause
      In speaking for myself. Yet, by your gracious patience,
      I will a round[12] unvarnish'd tale deliver
      Of my whole course of love; what drugs, what charms,
      What conjuration and what mighty magic —
      For such proceeding I am charged withal —
      I won his daughter.
BRA.   A maiden never bold;
      Of spirit so still and quiet that her motion
      Blush'd at herself; and she — in spite of nature,
      Of years, of country, credit, every thing —
      To fall in love with what she fear'd to look on!
      It is a judgement maim'd and most imperfect,
      That will confess perfection so could err

---

10. *Sans*] Without.
11. *pith*] strength, force.
12. *round*] plain, direct.

     Against all rules of nature; and must be driven
     To find out practices of cunning hell,
     Why this should be. I therefore vouch again,
     That with some mixtures powerful o'er the blood,
     Or with some dram conjured to this effect,
     He wrought upon her.
DUKE.   To vouch this, is no proof,
     Without more certain and more overt test
     Than these thin habits and poor likelihoods
     Of modern[13] seeming do prefer against him.
FIRST SEN.   But, Othello, speak:
     Did you by indirect and forced courses
     Subdue and poison this young maid's affections?
     Or came it by request, and such fair question
     As soul to soul affordeth?
OTH   I do beseech you,
     Send for the lady to the Sagittary,
     And let her speak of me before her father:
     If you do find me foul in her report,
     The trust, the office I do hold of you,
     Not only take away, but let your sentence
     Even fall upon my life.
DUKE.   Fetch Desdemona hither.
OTH.   Ancient, conduct them; you best know the place.
                 [*Exeunt* IAGO *and* Attendants.]
     And till she come, as truly as to heaven
     I do confess the vices of my blood,
     So justly to your grave ears I'll present
     How I did thrive in this fair lady's love
     And she in mine.
DUKE.   Say it, Othello.
OTH.   Her father loved me, oft invited me,
     Still question'd me the story of my life
     From year to year, the battles, sieges, fortunes,
     That I have pass'd.
     I ran it through, even from my boyish days
     To the very moment that he bade me tell it:
     Wherein I spake of most disastrous chances,
     Of moving accidents by flood and field,
     Of hair-breadth 'scapes i' the imminent deadly breach,
     Of being taken by the insolent foe,
     And sold to slavery, of my redemption thence,

---

13. *modern*] commonplace, trivial.

And portance in my travels' history:
Wherein of antres[14] vast and deserts idle,
Rough quarries, rocks, and hills whose heads touch heaven,
It was my hint[15] to speak, — such was the process;
And of the Cannibals that each other eat,
The Anthropophagi, and men whose heads
Do grow beneath their shoulders. This to hear
Would Desdemona seriously incline:
But still the house-affairs would draw her thence;
Which ever as she could with haste dispatch,
She 'ld come again, and with a greedy ear
Devour up my discourse: which I observing,
Took once a pliant hour, and found good means
To draw from her a prayer of earnest heart
That I would all my pilgrimage dilate,[16]
Whereof by parcels she had something heard,
But not intentively:[17] I did consent,
And often did beguile her of her tears
When I did speak of some distressful stroke
That my youth suffer'd. My story being done,
She gave me for my pains a world of sighs:
She swore, in faith, 't was strange, 't was passing strange;
'T was pitiful, 't was wondrous pitiful:
She wish'd she had not heard it, yet she wish'd
That heaven had made her such a man: she thank'd me,
And bade me, if I had a friend that loved her,
I should but teach him how to tell my story,
And that would woo her. Upon this hint I spake:
She loved me for the dangers I had pass'd,
And I loved her that she did pity them.
This only is the witchcraft I have used.
Here comes the lady; let her witness it.

Enter DESDEMONA, IAGO, *and* Attendants

DUKE.   I think this tale would win my daughter too.
Good Brabantio,
Take up this mangled matter at the best:
Men do their broken weapons rather use

---

14. *antres*] caves or caverns.
15. *hint*] occasion.
16. *dilate*] relate in full.
17. *intentively*] with full attention, intently.

Than their bare hands.

BRA.   I pray you, hear her speak:
If she confess that she was half the wooer,
Destruction on my head, if my bad blame
Light on the man! Come hither, gentle mistress:
Do you perceive in all this noble company
Where most you owe obedience?

DES.   My noble father,
I do perceive here a divided duty:
To you I am bound for life and education;
My life and education both do learn me
How to respect you; you are the lord of duty,
I am hitherto your daughter: but here's my husband,
And so much duty as my mother show'd
To you, preferring you before her father,
So much I challenge that I may protest
Due to the Moor my lord.

BRA.   God be with you! I have done.
Please it your grace, on to the state-affairs:
I had rather to adopt a child than get it.
Come hither, Moor:
I here do give thee that with all my heart,
Which, but thou hast already, with all my heart
I would keep from thee. For your sake, jewel,
I am glad at soul I have no other child;
For thy escape[18] would teach me tyranny,
To hang clogs[19] on them. I have done, my lord.

DUKE.   Let me speak like yourself, and lay a sentence
Which, as a grise[20] or step, may help these lovers
Into your favour.
When remedies are past, the griefs are ended
By seeing the worst, which late on hopes depended.
To mourn a mischief that is past and gone
Is the next way to draw new mischief on.
What cannot be preserved when fortune takes,
Patience her injury a mockery makes.
The robb'd that smiles steals something from the thief;
He robs himself that spends a bootless grief.

BRA.   So let the Turk of Cyprus us beguile;
We lose it not so long as we can smile.

---

18. *escape*] escapade.
19. *clogs*] anything hung upon an animal to hinder motion.
20. *grise*] step.

He bears the sentence well, that nothing bears
But the free comfort which from thence he hears;
But he bears both the sentence and the sorrow,
That, to pay grief, must of poor patience borrow.
These sentences, to sugar or to gall,
Being strong on both sides, are equivocal:
But words are words; I never yet did hear
That the bruised heart was pierced through the ear.
I humbly beseech you, proceed to the affairs of state.

DUKE.   The Turk with a most mighty preparation makes for Cyprus.
Othello, the fortitude of the place is best known to you; and
though we have there a substitute of most allowed sufficiency,
yet opinion, a sovereign mistress of effects, throws a more safer
voice on you: you must therefore be content to slubber the gloss
of your new fortunes with this more stubborn and boisterous
expedition.

OTH.   The tyrant custom, most grave senators,
Hath made the flinty and steel couch of war
My thrice-driven bed of down: I do agnize[21]
A natural and prompt alacrity
I find in hardness; and do undertake
These present wars against the Ottomites.
Most humbly therefore bending to your state,
I crave fit disposition for my wife,
Due reference of place and exhibition,
With such accommodation and besort[22]
As levels with her breeding.

DUKE.   If you please,
Be 't at her father's.

BRA.   I 'll not have it so.

OTH.   Nor I.

DES.   Nor I, I would not there reside,
To put my father in impatient thoughts
By being in his eye. Most gracious duke,
To my unfolding lend your prosperous ear,
And let me find a charter in your voice
To assist my simpleness.

DUKE.   What would you, Desdemona?

DES.   That I did love the Moor to live with him,
My downright violence and storm of fortunes
May trumpet to the world: my heart 's subdued

---

21. *agnize*] confess, acknowledge.
22. *besort*] companionship, retinue.

Even to the very quality of my lord:
I saw Othello's visage in his mind,
And to his honours and his valiant parts
Did I my soul and fortunes consecrate.
So that, dear lords, if I be left behind,
A moth[23] of peace, and he go to the war,
The rites for which I love him are bereft me,
And I a heavy interim shall support
By his dear absence. Let me go with him.

OTH.   Let her have your voices.
Vouch with me, heaven, I therefore beg it not,
To please the palate of my appetite;
Nor to comply with heat — the young affects
In me defunct — and proper satisfaction;
But to be free and bounteous to her mind:
And heaven defend your good souls, that you think
I will your serious and great business scant
For she is with me. No, when light-wing'd toys
Of feather'd Cupid seel[24] with wanton dulness
My speculative and officed instruments,[25]
That my disports corrupt and taint my business,
Let housewives make a skillet of my helm,
And all indign[26] and base adversities
Make head against my estimation!

DUKE.   Be it as you shall privately determine,
Either for her stay or going: the affair cries haste,
And speed must answer 't; you must hence to-night.

DES.   To-night, my lord?

DUKE.   This night.

OTH.   With all my heart.

DUKE.   At nine i' the morning here we 'll meet again.
Othello, leave some officer behind,
And he shall our commission bring to you;
With such things else of quality and respect
As doth import you.

OTH.   So please your grace, my ancient;
A man he is of honesty and trust:
To his conveyance I assign my wife,

---

23. A moth] An idle parasite.
24. seel] close or sew up the eyes.
25. My . . . instruments] My faculties of thought or vision and of activity in the discharge of duty.
26. indign] unworthy, disgraceful.

With what else needful your good grace shall think
To be sent after me.
DUKE.   Let it be so.
   Good night to every one. [*To* BRAB.] And, noble signior,
   If virtue no delighted beauty lack,
   Your son-in-law is far more fair than black.
FIRST SEN.   Adieu, brave Moor; use Desdemona well.
BRA.   Look to her, Moor, if thou hast eyes to see:
   She has deceived her father, and may thee.
                         [*Exeunt* Duke, Senators, Officers, &c.]
OTH.   My life upon her faith! Honest Iago,
   My Desdemona must I leave to thee:
   I prithee, let thy wife attend on her;
   And bring them after in the best advantage.
   Come, Desdemona; I have but an hour
   Of love, of worldly matters and direction,
   To spend with thee: we must obey the time.
                         [*Exeunt* OTHELLO *and* DESDEMONA.]
ROD.   Iago!
IAGO.   What say'st thou, noble heart?
ROD.   What will I do, thinkest thou?
IAGO.   Why, go to bed and sleep.
ROD.   I will incontinently drown myself.
IAGO.   If thou dost, I shall never love thee after. Why, thou silly
   gentleman!
ROD.   It is silliness to live when to live is torment; and then have we a
   prescription to die when death is our physician.
IAGO.   O villanous! I have looked upon the world for four times seven
   years; and since I could distinguish betwixt a benefit and an injury, I never found man that knew how to love himself. Ere I
   would say I would drown myself for the love of a guinea-hen, I
   would change my humanity with a baboon.
ROD.   What should I do? I confess it is my shame to be so fond; but it
   is not in my virtue to amend it.
IAGO.   Virtue! a fig! 't is in ourselves that we are thus or thus. Our
   bodies are gardens; to the which our wills are gardeners: so that
   if we will plant nettles or sow lettuce, set hyssop and weed up
   thyme, supply it with one gender of herbs or distract it with
   many, either to have it sterile with idleness or manured with
   industry, why, the power and corrigible authority of this lies in
   our wills. If the balance of our lives had not one scale of reason
   to poise another of sensuality, the blood and baseness of our natures would conduct us to most preposterous conclusions: but
   we have reason to cool our raging motions, our carnal stings, our

unbitted lusts; whereof I take this, that you call love, to be a sect or scion.[27]

ROD.   It cannot be.

IAGO.   It is merely a lust of the blood and a permission of the will. Come, be a man: drown thyself! drown cats and blind puppies. I have professed me thy friend, and I confess me knit to thy deserving[28] with cables of perdurable toughness: I could never better stead thee than now. Put money in thy purse; follow thou the wars; defeat thy favour[29] with an usurped beard; I say, put money in thy purse. It cannot be that Desdemona should long continue her love to the Moor — put money in thy purse — nor he his to her: it was a violent commencement, and thou shalt see an answerable sequestration; put but money in thy purse. These Moors are changeable in their wills: — fill thy purse with money. The food that to him now is as luscious as locusts, shall be to him shortly as bitter as coloquintida.[30] She must change for youth: when she is sated with his body, she will find the error of her choice: she must have change, she must: therefore put money in thy purse. If thou wilt needs damn thyself, do it a more delicate way than drowning. Make all the money thou canst: if sanctimony and a frail vow betwixt an erring barbarian and a supersubtle Venetian be not too hard for my wits and all the tribe of hell, thou shalt enjoy her; therefore make money. A pox of drowning thyself! it is clean out of the way: seek thou rather to be hanged in compassing thy joy than to be drowned and go without her.

ROD.   Wilt thou be fast to my hopes, if I depend on the issue?

IAGO.   Thou art sure of me: go, make money: I have told thee often, and I re-tell thee again and again, I hate the Moor: my cause is hearted; thine hath no less reason. Let us be conjunctive in our revenge against him: if thou canst cuckold him, thou dost thyself a pleasure, me a sport. There are many events in the womb of time, which will be delivered. Traverse; go; provide thy money. We will have more of this to-morrow. Adieu.

ROD.   Where shall we meet i' the morning?

IAGO.   At my lodging.

ROD.   I'll be with thee betimes.

IAGO.   Go to; farewell. Do you hear, Roderigo?

---

27. *a sect or scion*] a cutting or graft
28. *thy deserving*] thy merits, deserts.
29. *defeat thy favour*] disfigure or disguise your countenance.
30. *coloquintida*] more familiarly known as "colocynth," made from "bitter" apples, a familiar ingredient in pills.

ROD. What say you?
IAGO. No more of drowning, do you hear?
ROD. I am changed: I 'll go sell all my land. [*Exit.*]
IAGO. Thus do I ever make my fool my purse;
    For I mine own gain'd knowledge should profane,
    If I would time expend with such a snipe
    But for my sport and profit. I hate the Moor;
    And it is thought abroad that 'twixt my sheets
    He has done my office: I know not if 't be true;
    But I for mere suspicion in that kind
    Will do as if for surety. He holds me well;[31]
    The better shall my purpose work on him.
    Cassio 's a proper[32] man: let me see now;
    To get his place, and to plume up my will
    In double knavery — How, how? — Let 's see: —
    After some time, to abuse Othello's ear
    That he is too familiar with his wife.
    He hath a person and a smooth dispose[33]
    To be suspected; framed to make women false.
    The Moor is of a free and open nature,
    That thinks men honest that but seem to be so;
    And will as tenderly be led by the nose
    As asses are.
    I have 't. It is engender'd. Hell and night
    Must bring this monstrous birth to the world's light. [*Exit.*]

ACT II.

SCENE I. *A Sea-Port in Cyprus. An Open Place Near the Quay.*

Enter MONTANO *and two* Gentlemen

MON. What from the cape can you discern at sea?
FIRST GENT. Nothing at all: it is a high-wrought flood;
    I cannot, 'twixt the heaven and the main,
    Descry a sail.

---

31. *He holds me well*] He thinks well of me.
32. *proper*] handsome.
33. *a smooth dispose*] a smooth or gentle disposition or manner.

MON.   Methinks the wind hath spoke aloud at land;
    A fuller blast ne'er shook our battlements:
    If it hath ruffian'd[1] so upon the sea,
    What ribs of oak, when mountains melt on them,
    Can hold the mortise? What shall we hear of this?
SEC. GENT.   A segregation of the Turkish fleet:
    For do but stand upon the foaming shore,
    The chidden billow seems to pelt the clouds;
    The wind-shaked surge, with high and monstrous mane,
    Seems to cast water on the burning bear,[2]
    And quench the guards of the ever-fixed pole:
    I never did like molestation view
    On the enchafed flood.
MON.   If that the Turkish fleet
    Be not enshelter'd and embay'd, they are drown'd;
    It is impossible to bear it out.

Enter a third Gentleman

THIRD GENT.   News, lads! our wars are done.
    The desperate tempest hath so bang'd the Turks,
    That their designment halts: a noble ship of Venice
    Hath seen a grievous wreck and sufferance
    On most part of their fleet.
MON.   How! is this true?
THIRD GENT.   The ship is here put in,
    A Veronesa; Michael Cassio,
    Lieutenant to the warlike Moor Othello,
    Is come on shore: the Moor himself at sea,
    And is in full commission here for Cyprus.
MON.   I am glad on 't; 't is a worthy governor.
THIRD GENT.   But this same Cassio, though he speak of comfort
    Touching the Turkish loss, yet he looks sadly
    And prays the Moor be safe; for they were parted
    With foul and violent tempest.
MON.   Pray heavens he be;
    For I have served him, and the man commands
    Like a full soldier. Let 's to the seaside, ho!
    As well to see the vessel that 's come in
    As to throw out our eyes for brave Othello,

---

  1. *ruffian'd*] blustered.
  2. *the burning bear*] the shining constellation of the Great Bear, the "ursa major" in the
     northern sky.

Even till we make the main and the aerial blue
An indistinct regard.
THIRD GENT.   Come, let 's do so;
For every minute is expectancy
Of more arrivance.

Enter CASSIO

CAS.   Thanks, you the valiant of this warlike isle,
That so approve the Moor! O, let the heavens
Give him defence against the elements,
For I have lost him on a dangerous sea.
MON.   Is he well shipp'd?
CAS.   His bark is stoutly timber'd, and his pilot
Of very expert and approved allowance;
Therefore my hopes, not surfeited to death,
Stand in bold cure.   [*A cry within:* "A sail, a sail, a sail!"]

Enter a fourth Gentleman

CAS.   What noise?
FOURTH GENT.   The town is empty; on the brow o' the sea
Stand ranks of people, and they cry "A sail!"
CAS.   My hopes do shape him for the governor.   [*Guns heard.*]
SEC. GENT.   They do discharge their shot of courtesy:
Our friends at least.
CAS.   I pray you, sir, go forth,
And give us truth who 't is that is arrived.
SEC. GENT.   I shall.   [*Exit.*]

MON.   But, good lieutenant, is your general wived?
CAS.   Most fortunately: he hath achieved a maid
That paragons description and wild fame;
One that excels the quirks of blazoning pens,
And in the essential vesture of creation
Does tire the ingener.[3]

Re-enter second Gentleman

                How now! who has put in?
SEC. GENT.   'T is one Iago, ancient to the general.
CAS.   He has had most favourable and happy speed:

---

3. *ingener*] designer, author.

Tempests themselves, high seas, and howling winds,
The gutter'd rocks, and congregated sands,
Traitors ensteep'd to clog the guiltless keel,
As having sense of beauty, do omit
Their mortal natures, letting go safely by
The divine Desdemona.
MON.   What is she?
CAS.   She that I spake of, our great captain's captain,
Left in the conduct of the bold Iago;
Whose footing here anticipates our thoughts
A se'nnight's speed. Great Jove, Othello guard,
And swell his sail with thine own powerful breath,
That he may bless this bay with his tall ship,
Make love's quick pants in Desdemona's arms,
Give renew'd fire to our extinced spirits,
And bring all Cyprus comfort.

Enter DESDEMONA, EMILIA, IAGO, RODERIGO, *and* Attendants

                              O, behold,
The riches of the ship is come on shore!
Ye men of Cyprus, let her have your knees.
Hail to thee, lady! and the grace of heaven,
Before, behind thee, and on every hand,
Enwheel thee round!
DES.   I thank you, valiant Cassio.
What tidings can you tell me of my lord?
CAS.   He is not yet arrived: nor know I aught
But that he 's well and will be shortly here.
DES.   O, but I fear — How lost you company?
CAS.   The great contention of the sea and skies
Parted our fellowship — But, hark! a sail.
                         [*A cry within:* "A sail, a sail!" *Guns heard.*]
SEC. GENT.   They give their greeting to the citadel:
This likewise is a friend.
CAS.   See for the news.   [*Exit* Gentleman.]
Good ancient, you are welcome. [*To* EMILIA] Welcome, mistress:
Let it not gall your patience, good Iago,
That I extend my manners; 't is my breeding
That gives me this bold show of courtesy.   [*Kissing her.*]
IAGO.   Sir, would she give you so much of her lips
As of her tongue she oft bestows on me,
You 'ld have enough.
DES.   Alas, she has no speech.

IAGO.   In faith, too much;
   I find it still when I have list[4] to sleep:
   Marry, before your ladyship, I grant,
   She puts her tongue a little in her heart
   And chides with thinking.
EMIL.   You have little cause to say so.
IAGO.   Come on, come on; you are pictures[5] out of doors,
   Bells in your parlours, wild-cats in your kitchens,
   Saints in your injuries,[6] devils being offended,
   Players in your housewifery, and housewives[7] in your beds.
DES.   O, fie upon thee, slanderer!
IAGO.   Nay, it is true, or else I am a Turk:
   You rise to play, and go to bed to work.
EMIL.   You shall not write my praise.
IAGO.   No, let me not.
DES.   What wouldst thou write of me, if thou shouldst praise me?
IAGO.   O gentle lady, do not put me to 't;
   For I am nothing if not critical.
DES.   Come on, assay — There 's one gone to the harbour?
IAGO.   Ay, madam.
DES.   I am not merry; but I do beguile
   The thing I am by seeming otherwise.
   Come, how wouldst thou praise me?
IAGO.   I am about it; but indeed my invention
   Comes from my pate as birdlime does from frize;[8]
   It plucks out brains and all: but my Muse labours,
   And thus she is deliver'd.
   If she be fair and wise, fairness and wit,
   The one 's for use, the other useth it.
DES.   Well praised! How if she be black and witty?
IAGO.   If she be black, and thereto have a wit,
   She 'll find a white that shall her blackness fit.
DES.   Worse and worse.
EMIL.   How if fair and foolish?
IAGO.   She never yet was foolish that was fair;
   For even her folly help'd her to an heir.

---

4. *have list*] have inclination.
5. *pictures*] beautiful painted objects.
6. *Saints in your injuries*] Assume the meek air of saints when you are bent on injuring others.
7. *housewives*] hussies, with an implication of wantonness.
8. *as birdlime . . . frize*] birdlime was a sticky substance used to trap birds; frize was a coarse woollen material.

DES.   These are old fond[9] paradoxes to make fools laugh i' the ale-
       house. What miserable praise hast thou for her that 's foul and
       foolish?

IAGO.   There's none so foul, and foolish thereunto,
      But does foul pranks which fair and wise ones do.

DES.   O heavy ignorance! thou praisest the worst best. But what praise
       couldst thou bestow on a deserving woman indeed, one that in
       the authority of her merit did justly put on the vouch of very
       malice itself?

IAGO.   She that was ever fair and never proud,
      Had tongue at will and yet was never loud,
      Never lack'd gold and yet went never gay,
      Fled from her wish and yet said "Now I may;"
      She that, being anger'd, her revenge being nigh,
      Bade her wrong stay and her displeasure fly;
      She that in wisdom never was so frail
      To change the cod's head for the salmon's tail;[10]
      She that could think and ne'er disclose her mind,
      See suitors following and not look behind;
      She was a wight, if ever such wight were, —

DES.   To do what?

IAGO.   To suckle fools and chronicle small beer.[11]

DES.   O most lame and impotent conclusion! Do not learn of him,
       Emilia, though he be thy husband. How say you, Cassio? is he
       not a most profane and liberal counsellor?

CAS.   He speaks home,[12] madam: you may relish him more in the
       soldier than in the scholar.

IAGO.   [*Aside*] He takes her by the palm: ay, well said, whisper: with as
       little a web as this will I ensnare as great a fly as Cassio. Ay, smile
       upon her, do; I will gyve thee in thine own courtship. You say
       true; 't is so, indeed: if such tricks as these strip you out of your
       lieutenantry, it had been better you had not kissed your three fin-
       gers so oft, which now again you are most apt to play the sir in.
       Very good; well kissed! an excellent courtesy! 't is so, indeed. Yet
       again your fingers to your lips? would they were clyster-pipes for
       your sake! — [*Trumpet within.*] The Moor! I know his trumpet.

CAS.   'T is truly so.

DES.   Let 's meet him and receive him.

CAS.   Lo, where he comes!

---

9. *fond*] silly.

10. *change . . . tail*] give up a delicacy (cod's head) in exchange for coarse fare (salmon's tail).

11. *chronicle small beer*] keep account of small household expenses.

12. *home*] to the quick, so as to make the intended effect.

Enter OTHELLO *and* Attendants.

OTH.   O my fair warrior!
DES.   My dear Othello!
OTH.   It gives me wonder great as my content
       To see you here before me. O my soul's joy!
       If after every tempest come such calms,
       May the winds blow till they have waken'd death!
       And let the labouring bark climb hills of seas
       Olympus-high, and duck again as low
       As hell 's from heaven! If it were now to die,
       'T were now to be most happy; for I fear,
       My soul hath her content so absolute
       That not another comfort like to this
       Succeeds in unknown fate.
DES.   The heavens forbid
       But that our loves and comforts should increase,
       Even as our days do grow!
OTH.   Amen to that, sweet powers!
       I cannot speak enough of this content;
       It stops me here; it is too much of joy:
       And this, and this, the greatest discords be   [*Kissing her.*]
       That e'er our hearts shall make!
IAGO.   [*Aside*]   O, you are well tuned now!
       But I 'll set down the pegs that make this music,
       As honest as I am.
OTH.   Come, let us to the castle.
       News, friends; our wars are done, the Turks are drown'd.
       How does my old acquaintance of this isle?
       Honey, you shall be well desired in Cyprus;
       I have found great love amongst them. O my sweet,
       I prattle out of fashion, and I dote
       In mine own comforts. I prithee, good Iago,
       Go to the bay, and disembark my coffers:
       Bring thou the master to the citadel;
       He is a good one, and his worthiness
       Does challenge much respect. Come, Desdemona,
       Once more well met at Cyprus.
                              [*Exeunt all but* IAGO *and* RODERIGO.]
IAGO.   Do thou meet me presently at the harbour. Come hither. If thou
       be'st valiant — as, they say, base men being in love have then a
       nobility in their natures more than is native to them — list me.
       The lieutenant to-night watches on the court of guard. First, I
       must tell thee this: Desdemona is directly in love with him.

ROD. With him! why, 't is not possible.

IAGO. Lay thy finger thus,[13] and let thy soul be instructed. Mark me
with what violence she first loved the Moor, but for bragging and
telling her fantastical lies: and will she love him still for prating?
let not thy discreet heart think it. Her eye must be fed; and what
delight shall she have to look on the devil? When the blood is
made dull with the act of sport, there should be, again to in-
flame it and to give satiety a fresh appetite, loveliness in favour,
sympathy in years, manners and beauties; all which the Moor is
defective in: now, for want of these required conveniences, her
delicate tenderness will find itself abused, begin to heave the
gorge, disrelish and abhor the Moor; very nature will instruct
her in it and compel her to some second choice. Now, sir, this
granted — as it is a most pregnant and unforced position — who
stands so eminently in the degree of this fortune as Cassio does?
a knave very voluble; no further conscionable than in putting
on the mere form of civil and humane seeming, for the better
compassing of his salt and most hidden loose affection? why,
none; why, none: a slipper[14] and subtle knave; a finder out of
occasions; that has an eye can stamp and counterfeit advantages,
though true advantage never present itself: a devilish knave! Besides, the knave is handsome, young, and hath all those requisites
in him that folly and green minds look after: a pestilent complete
knave; and the woman hath found him already.

ROD. I cannot believe that in her; she 's full of most blest condition.

IAGO. Blest fig's-end! the wine she drinks is made of grapes: if she had
been blest, she would never have loved the Moor: blest pudding!
Didst thou not see her paddle with the palm of his hand? didst
not mark that?

ROD. Yes, that I did; but that was but courtesy.

IAGO. Lechery, by this hand; an index and obscure prologue to the
history of lust and foul thoughts. They met so near with their
lips that their breaths embraced together. Villanous thoughts,
Roderigo! when these mutualities so marshal the way, hard at
hand comes the master and main exercise, the incorporate conclusion: pish! But, sir, be you ruled by me: I have brought you
from Venice. Watch you to-night; for the command, I 'll lay 't
upon you: Cassio knows you not: I 'll not be far from you: do you
find some occasion to anger Cassio, either by speaking too loud,
or tainting his discipline, or from what other course you please,
which the time shall more favourably minister.

---

13. *Lay thy finger thus*] Iago puts his finger to his lips, enjoining silence on Roderigo.
14. *slipper*] an old form of "slippery."

Rod. Well.

IAGO. Sir, he is rash and very sudden in choler, and haply may strike at you: provoke him, that he may; for even out of that will I cause these of Cyprus to mutiny; whose qualification shall come into no true taste again but by the displanting of Cassio. So shall you have a shorter journey to your desires by the means I shall then have to prefer them, and the impediment most profitably removed, without the which there were no expectation of our prosperity.

Rod. I will do this, if I can bring it to any opportunity.

IAGO. I warrant thee. Meet me by and by at the citadel: I must fetch his necessaries ashore. Farewell.

Rod. Adieu. [*Exit.*]

IAGO. That Cassio loves her, I do well believe it;
That she loves him, 't is apt and of great credit:[15]
The Moor, howbeit that I endure him not,
Is of a constant, loving, noble nature;
And I dare think he 'll prove to Desdemona
A most dear husband. Now, I do love her too,
Not out of absolute lust, though peradventure
I stand accountant for as great a sin,
But partly led to diet my revenge,
For that I do suspect the lusty Moor
Hath leap'd into my seat: the thought whereof
Doth like a poisonous mineral gnaw my inwards;
And nothing can or shall content my soul
Till I am even'd with him, wife for wife;
Or failing so, yet that I put the Moor
At least into a jealousy so strong
That judgement cannot cure. Which thing to do,
If this poor trash of Venice, whom I trash[16]
For his quick hunting, stand the putting on,
I 'll have our Michael Cassio on the hip,
Abuse him to the Moor in the rank garb;
For I fear Cassio with my night-cap too;
Make the Moor thank me, love me and reward me,
For making him egregiously an ass
And practising upon his peace and quiet
Even to madness. 'T is here,[17] but yet confused:
Knavery's plain face is never seen till used. [*Exit.*]

---

15. *apt . . . credit*] natural and most credible.
16. *trash . . . trash*] the noun "trash" here means worthless people; the verb "trash" is a hunting term, meaning to restrain with a leash.
17. *'T is here*] Iago raises his hand to his head.

SCENE II. *A Street.*

Enter a Herald *with a proclamation*; *People following*

HER. It is Othello's pleasure, our noble and valiant general, that upon
certain tidings now arrived, importing the mere perdition of
the Turkish fleet, every man put himself into triumph; some to
dance, some to make bonfires, each man to what sport and revels
his addiction leads him: for, besides these beneficial news, it is
the celebration of his nuptial. So much was his pleasure should
be proclaimed. All offices[1] are open, and there is full liberty
of feasting from this present hour of five till the bell have told
eleven. Heaven bless the isle of Cyprus and our noble general
Othello!   [*Exeunt.*]

SCENE III. *A Hall in the Castle.*

Enter OTHELLO, DESDEMONA, CASSIO, *and* Attendants

OTH.   Good Michael, look you to the guard to-night:
Let's teach ourselves that honourable stop,
Not to outsport discretion.
CAS.   Iago hath direction what to do;
But notwithstanding with my personal eye
Will I look to 't.
OTH.   Iago is most honest.
Michael, good night: to-morrow with your earliest
Let me have speech with you. Come, my dear love,
The purchase made, the fruits are to ensue;
That profit 's yet to come 'tween me and you.
Good night.   [*Exeunt* OTHELLO, DESDEMONA, *and* Attendants.]

Enter IAGO

CAS.   Welcome, Iago; we must to the watch.
IAGO.   Not this hour, lieutenant; 't is not yet ten o' the clock. Our general cast us thus early for the love of his Desdemona; who let us

---

1. *offices*] rooms in the castle where stores of food and drink were kept.

not therefore blame: he hath not yet made wanton the night with her, and she is sport for Jove.

CAS. She 's a most exquisite lady.

IAGO. And, I 'll warrant her, full of game.

CAS. Indeed she 's a most fresh and delicate creature.

IAGO. What an eye she has! methinks it sounds a parley to provocation.

CAS. An inviting eye; and yet methinks right modest.

IAGO. And when she speaks, is it not an alarum to love?

CAS. She is indeed perfection.

IAGO. Well, happiness to their sheets! Come, lieutenant, I have a stoup[1] of wine; and here without are a brace of Cyprus gallants that would fain have a measure to the health of black Othello.

CAS. Not to-night, good Iago: I have very poor and unhappy brains for drinking: I could well wish courtesy would invent some other custom of entertainment.

IAGO. O, they are our friends; but one cup: I 'll drink for you.

CAS. I have drunk but one cup to-night, and that was craftily qualified too, and behold what innovation it makes here: I am unfortunate in the infirmity, and dare not task my weakness with any more.

IAGO. What, man! 't is a night of revels: the gallants desire it.

CAS. Where are they?

IAGO. Here at the door; I pray you, call them in.

CAS. I 'll do 't; but it dislikes me.   [*Exit.*]

IAGO. If I can fasten but one cup upon him,
With that which he hath drunk to-night already,
He 'll be as full of quarrel and offence
As my young mistress' dog. Now my sick fool Roderigo,
Whom love hath turn'd almost the wrong side out,
To Desdemona hath to-night caroused
Potations pottle-deep;[2] and he 's to watch:
Three lads of Cyprus, noble swelling spirits,
That hold their honours in a wary distance,
The very elements of this warlike isle,
Have I to-night fluster'd with flowing cups,
And they watch too. Now, 'mongst this flock of drunkards,
Am I to put our Cassio in some action
That may offend the isle. But here they come:
If consequence do but approve my dream,

---

1. *a stoup*] a large tankard.
2. *pottle-deep*] a "pottle" was a measure of two quarts.

My boat sails freely, both with wind and stream.

Re-enter CASSIO; *with him* MONTANO *and* Gentlemen; *Servants following with wine*

CAS.   'Fore God, they have given me a rouse[3] already.
MON.   Good faith, a little one; not past a pint, as I am a soldier.
IAGO.   Some wine, ho!

    [*Sings*]   And let me the canakin clink, clink;
                 And let me the canakin clink:
                      A soldier 's a man;
                      A life 's but a span;
                 Why then let a soldier drink.

    Some wine, boys!
CAS.   'Fore God, an excellent song.
IAGO.   I learned it in England, where indeed they are most potent
           in potting: your Dane, your German, and your swag-bellied
           Hollander, — Drink, ho! — are nothing to your English.
CAS.   Is your Englishman so expert in his drinking?
IAGO.   Why, he drinks you with facility your Dane dead drunk; he
           sweats not to overthrow your Almain; he gives your Hollander a
           vomit ere the next pottle can be filled.
CAS.   To the health of our general!
MON.   I am for it, lieutenant, and I 'll do you justice.
IAGO.   O sweet England!

    [*Sings*]   King Stephen was a worthy peer,
                  His breeches cost him but a crown;
                 He held them sixpence all too dear,
                  With that he call'd the tailor lown.

                 He was a wight of high renown,
                  And thou art but of low degree:
                 'T is pride that pulls the country down;
                  Then take thine auld cloak about thee.

    Some wine, ho!
CAS.   Why, this is a more exquisite song than the other.
IAGO.   Will you hear 't again?
CAS.   No; for I hold him to be unworthy of his place that does those
           things. Well. God 's above all, and there be souls must be saved,
           and there be souls must not be saved.

---

3. *a rouse*] a full measure of liquor.

IAGO.　It's true, good lieutenant.

CAS.　For mine own part — no offence to the general, nor any man of
quality — I hope to be saved.

IAGO.　And so do I too, lieutenant.

CAS.　Ay, but, by your leave, not before me; the lieutenant is to be saved
before the ancient. Let's have no more of this; let's to our affairs.
God forgive us our sins! Gentlemen, let's look to our business.
Do not think, gentlemen, I am drunk: this is my ancient: this is
my right hand, and this is my left. I am not drunk now; I can
stand well enough, and speak well enough.

ALL.　Excellent well.

CAS.　Why, very well then; you must not think then that I am
drunk.　　　　　　　　　　　　　　　　　　　　　　　[*Exit.*]

MON.　To the platform, masters; come, let's set the watch.

IAGO.　You see this fellow that is gone before;
He is a soldier fit to stand by Cæsar
And give direction: and do but see his vice;
'T is to his virtue a just equinox,
The one as long as the other: 't is pity of him.
I fear the trust Othello puts him in
On some odd time of his infirmity
Will shake this island.

MON.　　　　　　　　　　But is he often thus?

IAGO.　'T is evermore the prologue to his sleep:
He 'll watch the horologe[4] a double set,
If drink rock not his cradle.

MON.　　　　　　　　　　It were well
The general were put in mind of it.
Perhaps he sees it not, or his good nature
Prizes the virtue that appears in Cassio
And looks not on his evils: is not this true?

Enter RODERIGO

IAGO.　[*Aside to him*] How now, Roderigo!
I pray you, after the lieutenant; go.　　　　　[*Exit* RODERIGO.]

MON.　And 't is great pity that the noble Moor
Should hazard such a place as his own second
With one of an ingraft[5] infirmity:
It were an honest action to say
So to the Moor.

---

4. *horologe*] clock.
5. *ingraft*] inveterate, rooted.

IAGO.　　　　　　　　　　Not I, for this fair island:
　　　I do love Cassio well, and would do much
　　　To cure him of this evil: — But, hark! what noise?
　　　　　　　　　　　　　　　　　[A cry within: "Help! help!"]

Re-enter CASSIO, driving in RODERIGO

CAS.　　'Zounds! you rogue! you rascal!
MON.　　What's the matter, lieutenant?
CAS.　　A knave teach me my duty! But I'll beat the knave into a wicker
　　　bottle.
ROD.　　Beat me!
CAS.　　Dost thou prate, rogue?　　　　　　　　[Striking RODERIGO.]
MON.　　Nay, good lieutenant; I pray you, sir, hold your hand.
CAS.　　Let me go, sir, or I'll knock you o'er the mazzard.[6]
MON.　　Come, come, you're drunk.
CAS.　　Drunk!　　　　　　　　　　　　　　　　[They fight.]
IAGO.　　[Aside to RODERIGO] Away, I say; go out, and cry a mutiny.
　　　　　　　　　　　　　　　　　　　　[Exit RODERIGO.]
　　　Nay, good lieutenant! God's will, gentlemen!
　　　Help, ho! — Lieutenant, — sir, — Montano, — sir; —
　　　Help, masters! — Here's a goodly watch indeed!　[A bell rings.]
　　　Who's that that rings the bell? — Diablo, ho!
　　　The town will rise: God's will, lieutenant, hold;
　　　You will be shamed for ever.

Re-enter OTHELLO and Attendants

OTH.　　　　　　　　　　　　What is the matter here?
MON.　　'Zounds, I bleed still; I am hurt to the death.　　[Faints.]
OTH.　　Hold, for your lives!
IAGO.　　Hold, ho! Lieutenant, — sir, — Montano, — gentlemen, —
　　　Have you forgot all sense of place and duty?
　　　Hold! the general speaks to you; hold, hold, for shame!
OTH.　　Why, how now, ho! from whence ariseth this?
　　　Are we turn'd Turks, and to ourselves do that
　　　Which heaven hath forbid the Ottomites?
　　　For Christian shame, put by this barbarous brawl:
　　　He that stirs next to carve for his own rage
　　　Holds his soul light; he dies upon his motion.
　　　Silence that dreadful bell: it frights the isle
　　　From her propriety. What is the matter, masters?

---

6. mazzard] head.

    Honest Iago, that look'st dead with grieving,
    Speak, who began this? on thy love, I charge thee.
IAGO.   I do not know: friends all but now, even now,
    In quarter, and in terms like bride and groom
    Devesting them for bed; and then, but now,
    As if some planet had unwitted men,
    Swords out, and tilting one at other's breast,
    In opposition bloody. I cannot speak
    Any beginning to this peevish odds;
    And would in action glorious I had lost
    Those legs that brought me to a part of it!
OTH.   How comes it, Michael, you are thus forgot?
CAS.   I pray you, pardon me; I cannot speak.
OTH.   Worthy Montano, you were wont be civil;
    The gravity and stillness of your youth
    The world hath noted, and your name is great
    In mouths of wisest censure: what 's the matter,
    That you unlace your reputation thus,
    And spend your rich opinion for the name
    Of a night-brawler? give me answer to it.
MON.   Worthy Othello, I am hurt to danger:
    Your officer, Iago, can inform you —
    While I spare speech, which something now offends me —
    Of all that I do know: nor know I aught
    By me that 's said or done amiss this night;
    Unless self-charity be sometimes a vice,
    And to defend ourselves it be a sin
    When violence assails us.
OTH.   Now, by heaven,
    My blood begins my safer guides to rule,
    And passion, having my best judgement collied,[7]
    Assays to lead the way: if I once stir,
    Or do but lift this arm, the best of you
    Shall sink in my rebuke. Give me to know
    How this foul rout began, who set it on,
    And he that is approved in this offence,
    Though he had twinn'd with me, both at a birth,
    Shall lose me. What! in a town of war,
    Yet wild, the people's hearts brimful of fear,
    To manage private and domestic quarrel,
    In night, and on the court and guard of safety!
    'T is monstrous. Iago, who began 't?

---

7. *collied*] blackened, darkened.

MON.   If partially affined,[8] or leagued in office,
     Thou dost deliver more or less than truth,
     Thou art no soldier.
IAGO.   Touch me not so near:
     I had rather have this tongue cut from my mouth
     Than it should do offence to Michael Cassio;
     Yet, I persuade myself, to speak the truth
     Shall nothing wrong him. Thus it is, general.
     Montano and myself being in speech,
     There comes a fellow crying out for help,
     And Cassio following him with determined sword,
     To execute upon him. Sir, this gentleman
     Steps in to Cassio and entreats his pause:
     Myself the crying fellow did pursue,
     Lest by his clamour — as it so fell out —
     The town might fall in fright: he, swift of foot,
     Outran my purpose; and I return'd the rather
     For that I heard the clink and fall of swords,
     And Cassio high in oath; which till to-night
     I ne'er might say before. When I came back —
     For this was brief — I found them close together,
     At blow and thrust; even as again they were
     When you yourself did part them.
     More of this matter cannot I report:
     But men are men; the best sometimes forget:
     Though Cassio did some little wrong to him,
     As men in rage strike those that wish them best,
     Yet surely Cassio, I believe, received
     From him that fled some strange indignity,
     Which patience could not pass.
OTH.   I know, Iago,
     Thy honesty and love doth mince this matter,
     Making it light to Cassio. Cassio, I love thee;
     But never more be officer of mine.

Re-enter DESDEMONA, *attended*

     Look, if my gentle love be not raised up!
     I 'll make thee an example.
DES.   What 's the matter?
OTH.   All 's well now, sweeting, come away to bed.

---

   8. *partially affined*] connected by close ties, which would result in a partial account of
the fight.

Sir, for your hurts, myself will be your surgeon:

[*To* MONTANO, *who is led off.*]

Lead him off.

Iago, look with care about the town,

And silence those whom this vile brawl distracted.

Come, Desdemona: 't is the soldiers' life

To have their balmy slumbers waked with strife.

[*Exeunt all but* IAGO *and* CASSIO.]

IAGO.   What, are you hurt, lieutenant?

CAS.   Ay, past all surgery.

IAGO.   Marry, heaven forbid!

CAS.   Reputation, reputation, reputation! O, I have lost my reputation! I have lost the immortal part of myself, and what remains is bestial. My reputation, Iago, my reputation!

IAGO.   As I am an honest man, I thought you had received some bodily wound; there is more sense in that than in reputation. Reputation is an idle and most false imposition; oft got without merit and lost without deserving: you have lost no reputation at all, unless you repute yourself such a loser. What, man! there are ways to recover the general again: you are but now cast in his mood, a punishment more in policy than in malice; even so as one would beat his offenceless dog to affright an imperious lion: sue to him again, and he 's yours.

CAS.   I will rather sue to be despised than to deceive so good a commander with so slight, so drunken, and so indiscreet an officer. Drunk? and speak parrot?[9] and squabble? swagger? swear? and discourse fustian[10] with one's own shadow? O thou invisible spirit of wine, if thou hast no name to be known by, let us call thee devil!

IAGO.   What was he that you followed with your sword? What had he done to you?

CAS.   I know not.

IAGO.   Is 't possible?

CAS.   I remember a mass of things, but nothing distinctly; a quarrel, but nothing wherefore. O God, that men should put an enemy in their mouths to steal away their brains! that we should, with joy, pleasance, revel and applause, transform ourselves into beasts!

IAGO.   Why, but you are now well enough: how came you thus recovered?

CAS.   It hath pleased the devil drunkenness to give place to the devil

---

9. *speak parrot?*] speak as senselessly as a parrot.

10. *fustian*] high-sounding nonsense.

wrath: one unperfectness shows me another, to make me frankly despise myself.

IAGO.   Come, you are too severe a moraler: as the time, the place, and the condition of this country stands, I could heartily wish this had not befallen; but since it is as it is, mend it for your own good.

CAS.   I will ask him for my place again; he shall tell me I am a drunkard! Had I as many mouths as Hydra, such an answer would stop them all. To be now a sensible man, by and by a fool, and presently a beast! O strange! Every inordinate cup is unblest, and the ingredient is a devil.

IAGO.   Come, come, good wine is a good familiar creature, if it be well used: exclaim no more against it. And, good lieutenant, I think you think I love you.

CAS.   I have well approved it, sir. I drunk!

IAGO.   You or any man living may be drunk at some time, man. I 'll tell you what you shall do. Our general's wife is now the general. I may say so in this respect, for that he hath devoted and given up himself to the contemplation, mark and denotement of her parts and graces: confess yourself freely to her; importune her help to put you in your place again: she is of so free, so kind, so apt, so blessed a disposition, she holds it a vice in her goodness not to do more than she is requested: this broken joint between you and her husband entreat her to splinter; and, my fortunes against any lay worth naming, this crack of your love shall grow stronger than it was before.

CAS.   You advise me well.

IAGO.   I protest, in the sincerity of love and honest kindness.

CAS.   I think it freely; and betimes in the morning I will beseech the virtuous Desdemona to undertake for me: I am desperate of my fortunes if they check me here.

IAGO.   You are in the right. Good night, lieutenant; I must to the watch.

CAS.   Good night, honest Iago.   [Exit.]

IAGO.   And what 's he then that says I play the villain?
When this advice is free I give and honest,
Probal[11] to thinking, and indeed the course
To win the Moor again? For 't is most easy
The inclining Desdemona to subdue
In any honest suit. She 's framed as fruitful[12]
As the free elements. And then for her
To win the Moor, were 't to renounce his baptism,
All seals and symbols of redeemed sin,

---

11. *Probal*] Contraction of "probable."
12. *fruitful*] bountiful, benign.

His soul is so enfetter'd to her love,
That she may make, unmake, do what she list,
Even as her appetite shall play the god
With his weak function. How am I then a villain
To counsel Cassio to this parallel course,
Directly to his good? Divinity of hell!
When devils will the blackest sins put on,
They do suggest at first with heavenly shows,
As I do now: for whiles this honest fool
Plies Desdemona to repair his fortunes,
And she for him pleads strongly to the Moor,
I 'll pour this pestilence into his ear,
That she repeals him for her body's lust;
And by how much she strives to do him good,
She shall undo her credit with the Moor.
So will I turn her virtue into pitch;
And out of her own goodness make the net
That shall enmesh them all.

Enter RODERIGO

        How now, Roderigo!
ROD. I do follow here in the chase, not like a hound that hunts, but one
  that fills up the cry.[13] My money is almost spent; I have been to-
  night exceedingly well cudgelled; and I think the issue will be,
  I shall have so much experience for my pains; and so, with no
  money at all and a little more wit, return again to Venice.
IAGO. How poor are they that have not patience!
  What wound did ever heal but by degrees?
  Thou know'st we work by wit and not by witchcraft,
  And wit depends on dilatory time.
  Does 't not go well? Cassio hath beaten thee,
  And thou by that small hurt hast cashier'd Cassio:
  Though other things grow fair against the sun,
  Yet fruits that blossom first will first be ripe:
  Content thyself awhile. By the mass, 't is morning;
  Pleasure and action make the hours seem short.
  Retire thee; go where thou art billeted:
  Away, I say; thou shalt know more hereafter:
  Nay, get thee gone. [*Exit* ROD.] Two things are to be done:
  My wife must move for Cassio to her mistress;
  I 'll set her on;

---

13. *the cry*] a common term for a pack of hounds.

Myself the while to draw the Moor apart,
And bring him jump[14] when he may Cassio find
Soliciting his wife: ay, that 's the way;
Dull not device by coldness and delay.   [*Exit.*]

ACT III.

SCENE I. *Before the Castle.*

Enter CASSIO *and some* Musicians

CAS.   Masters, play here; I will content your pains;
    Something that 's brief; and bid "Good morrow, general."
                                              [*Music.*]

Enter Clown

CLO.   Why, masters, have your instruments been in Naples, that they
    speak i' the nose thus?
FIRST MUS.   How, sir, how?
CLO.   Are these, I pray you, wind-instruments?
FIRST MUS.   Ay, marry, are they, sir.
CLO.   O, thereby hangs a tail.
FIRST MUS.   Whereby hangs a tale, sir?
CLO.   Marry, sir, by many a wind-instrument that I know. But, masters,
    here 's money for you: and the general so likes your music, that
    he desires you, for love's sake, to make no more noise with it.
FIRST MUS.   Well, sir, we will not.
CLO.   If you have any music that may not be heard, to 't again: but, as
    they say, to hear music the general does not greatly care.
FIRST MUS.   We have none such, sir.
CLO.   Then put up your pipes in your bag, for I 'll away: go; vanish into
    air; away!   [*Exeunt* Musicians.]
CAS.   Dost thou hear, my honest friend?
CLO.   No, I hear not your honest friend; I hear you.
CAS.   Prithee, keep up thy quillets.[1] There's a poor piece of gold for
    thee: if the gentlewoman that attends the general's wife be stir-
    ring, tell her there 's one Cassio entreats her a little favour of
    speech: wilt thou do this?

---

14. *jump*] just, at the very instant.
  1. *quillets*] niceties, verbal distinctions.

CLO.   She is stirring, sir: if she will stir hither, I shall seem to notify
       unto her.
CAS.   Do, good my friend.   [*Exit* Clown.]

Enter IAGO

                       In happy time, Iago.
IAGO.   You have not been a-bed, then?
CAS.   Why, no; the day had broke
       Before we parted. I have made bold, Iago,
       To send in to your wife: my suit to her
       Is, that she will to virtuous Desdemona
       Procure me some access.
IAGO.   I 'll send her to you presently;
       And I 'll devise a mean to draw the Moor
       Out of the way, that your converse and business
       May be more free.
CAS.   I humbly thank you for 't. [*Exit* IAGO.] I never knew
       A Florentine more kind and honest.

Enter EMILIA

EMIL.   Good morrow, good lieutenant: I am sorry
       For your displeasure; but all will sure be well.
       The general and his wife are talking of it,
       And she speaks for you stoutly: the Moor replies,
       That he you hurt is of great fame in Cyprus
       And great affinity, and that in wholesome wisdom
       He might not but refuse you; but he protests he loves you,
       And needs no other suitor but his likings
       To take the safest occasion by the front
       To bring you in again.
CAS.   Yet, I beseech you,
       If you think fit, or that it may be done,
       Give me advantage of some brief discourse
       With Desdemona alone.
EMIL.   Pray you, come in:
       I will bestow you where you shall have time
       To speak your bosom freely.
CAS.   I am much bound to you.   [*Exeunt.*]

SCENE II. *A Room in the Castle.*

Enter OTHELLO, IAGO, *and* Gentlemen

OTH.   These letters give, Iago, to the pilot;
      And by him do my duties to the senate:
      That done, I will be walking on the works;
      Repair there to me.
IAGO.   Well, my good lord, I 'll do 't.
OTH.   This fortification, gentlemen, shall we see 't?
GENT.   We 'll wait upon your lordship.   [*Exeunt.*]

SCENE III. *The Garden of the Castle.*

Enter DESDEMONA, CASSIO, *and* EMILIA

DES.   Be thou assured, good Cassio, I will do
      All my abilities in thy behalf.
EMIL.   Good madam, do: I warrant it grieves my husband
      As if the case were his.
DES.   O, that 's an honest fellow. Do not doubt, Cassio,
      But I will have my lord and you again
      As friendly as you were.
CAS.   Bounteous madam,
      Whatever shall become of Michael Cassio,
      He 's never any thing but your true servant.
DES.   I know 't: I thank you. You do love my lord:
      You have known him long; and be you well assured
      He shall in strangeness stand no farther off
      Than in a politic distance.
CAS.   Ay, but, lady,
      That policy may either last so long,
      Or feed upon such nice and waterish diet,
      Or breed itself so out of circumstance,
      That, I being absent and my place supplied,
      My general will forget my love and service.
DES.   Do not doubt[1] that; before Emilia here
      I give thee warrant of thy place: assure thee,
      If I do vow a friendship, I 'll perform it

---

1. *doubt*] fear.

To the last article: my lord shall never rest;
I 'll watch him tame[2] and talk him out of patience;
His bed shall seem a school, his board a shrift;
I 'll intermingle every thing he does
With Cassio's suit: therefore be merry, Cassio;
For thy solicitor shall rather die
Than give thy cause away.

Enter OTHELLO *and* IAGO, *at a distance*

EMIL.   Madam, here comes my lord.
CAS.   Madam, I 'll take my leave.
DES.   Nay, stay and hear me speak.
CAS.   Madam, not now: I am very ill at ease,
Unfit for mine own purposes.
DES.   Well, do your discretion.   [*Exit* CASSIO.]
IAGO.   Ha! I like not that.
OTH.   What dost thou say?
IAGO.   Nothing, my lord: or if — I know not what.
OTH.   Was not that Cassio parted from my wife?
IAGO.   Cassio, my lord! No, sure, I cannot think it,
That he would steal away so guilty-like,
Seeing you coming.
OTH.   I do believe 't was he.
DES.   How now, my lord!
I have been talking with a suitor here,
A man that languishes in your displeasure.
OTH.   Who is 't you mean?
DES.   Why, your lieutenant, Cassio. Good my lord,
If I have any grace or power to move you,
His present reconciliation take;
For if he be not one that truly loves you,
That errs in ignorance and not in cunning,
I have no judgement in an honest face:
I prithee, call him back.
OTH.   Went he hence now?
DES.   Ay, sooth; so humbled,
That he hath left part of his grief with me,
To suffer with him. Good love, call him back.
OTH.   Not now, sweet Desdemona; some other time.
DES.   But shall 't be shortly?
OTH.   The sooner, sweet, for you.

---

2. *I 'll watch him tame*] Falconers kept hawks awake in order to tame them and make them
obedient.

DES.   Shall 't be to-night at supper?
OTH.   No, not to-night.
DES.   To-morrow dinner then?
OTH.   I shall not dine at home;
     I meet the captains at the citadel.
DES.   Why then to-morrow night; or Tuesday morn;
     On Tuesday noon, or night; on Wednesday morn:
     I prithee, name the time; but let it not
     Exceed three days: in faith, he 's penitent;
     And yet his trespass, in our common reason —
     Save that, they say, the wars must make examples
     Out of their best — is not almost a fault
     To incur a private check. When shall he come?
     Tell me, Othello: I wonder in my soul,
     What you would ask me, that I should deny,
     Or stand so mammering[3] on. What! Michael Cassio,
     That came a-wooing with you, and so many a time
     When I have spoke of you dispraisingly
     Hath ta'en your part; to have so much to do
     To bring him in! Trust me, I could do much —
OTH.   Prithee, no more: let him come when he will;
     I will deny thee nothing.
DES.   Why, this is not a boon;
     'T is as I should entreat you wear your gloves,
     Or feed on nourishing dishes, or keep you warm,
     Or sue to you to do a peculiar profit
     To your own person: nay, when I have a suit
     Wherein I mean to touch[4] your love indeed,
     It shall be full of poise and difficult weight,
     And fearful to be granted.
OTH.   I will deny thee nothing:
     Whereon, I do beseech thee, grant me this,
     To leave me but a little to myself.
DES.   Shall I deny you? no: farewell, my lord.
OTH.   Farewell, my Desdemona: I 'll come to thee straight.
DES.   Emilia, come. Be as your fancies teach you;
     Whate'er you be, I am obedient.
                             [*Exeunt* DESDEMONA *and* EMILIA.]
OTH.   Excellent wretch! Perdition catch my soul,
     But I do love thee! and when I love thee not,
     Chaos is come again.

---

3. *mammering*] muttering hesitatingly.
4. *touch*] test, apply the touchstone to.

IAGO. My noble lord, —
OTH. What dost thou say, Iago?
IAGO. Did Michael Cassio, when you woo'd my lady,
    Know of your love?
OTH. He did, from first to last: why dost thou ask?
IAGO. But for a satisfaction of my thought;
   No further harm.
OTH. Why of thy thought, Iago?
IAGO. I did not think he had been acquainted with her.
OTH. O, yes, and went between us very oft.
IAGO. Indeed!
OTH. Indeed! ay, indeed: discern'st thou aught in that?
   Is he not honest?
IAGO. Honest, my lord!
OTH. Honest! ay, honest.
IAGO. My lord, for aught I know.
OTH. What dost thou think?
IAGO. Think, my lord!
OTH. Think, my lord! By heaven, he echoes me,
   As if there were some monster in his thought
   Too hideous to be shown. Thou dost mean something:
   I heard thee say even now, thou likedst not that,
   When Cassio left my wife: what didst not like?
   And when I told thee he was of my counsel
   In my whole course of wooing, thou criedst "Indeed!"
   And didst contract and purse thy brow together,
   As if thou then hadst shut up in thy brain
   Some horrible conceit: if thou dost love me,
   Show me thy thought.
IAGO. My lord, you know I love you.
OTH. I think thou dost;
   And for I know thou 'rt full of love and honesty
   And weigh'st thy words before thou givest them breath,
   Therefore these stops of thine fright me the more:
   For such things in a false disloyal knave
   Are tricks of custom; but in a man that 's just
   They 're close delations,[5] working from the heart,
   That passion cannot rule.
IAGO. For Michael Cassio,
   I dare be sworn I think that he is honest.
OTH. I think so too.
IAGO. Men should be what they seem;

---

5. *delations*] denunciations, accusations.

    Or those that be not, would they might seem none!

OTH.   Certain, men should be what they seem.

IAGO.   Why then I think Cassio 's an honest man.

OTH.   Nay, yet there 's more in this:
    I prithee, speak to me as to thy thinkings,
    As thou dost ruminate, and give thy worst of thoughts
    The worst of words.

IAGO.   Good my lord, pardon me:
    Though I am bound to every act of duty,
    I am not bound to that all slaves are free to.
    Utter my thoughts? Why, say they are vile and false;
    As where 's that palace whereinto foul things
    Sometimes intrude not? who has a breast so pure,
    But some uncleanly apprehensions
    Keep leets[6] and law-days, and in session sit
    With meditations lawful?

OTH.   Thou dost conspire against thy friend, Iago,
    If thou but think'st him wrong'd and makest his ear
    A stranger to thy thoughts.

IAGO.   I do beseech you —
    Though I perchance am vicious in my guess,
    As, I confess, it is my nature's plague
    To spy into abuses, and oft my jealousy
    Shapes faults that are not — that your wisdom yet,
    From one that so imperfectly conceits,
    Would take no notice, nor build yourself a trouble
    Out of his scattering[7] and unsure observance.
    It were not for your quiet nor your good,
    Nor for my manhood, honesty, or wisdom,
    To let you know my thoughts.

OTH.   What dost thou mean?

IAGO.   Good name in man and woman, dear my lord,
    Is the immediate jewel of their souls:
    Who steals my purse steals trash; 't is something, nothing;
    'T was mine, 't is his, and has been slave to thousands;
    But he that filches from me my good name
    Robs me of that which not enriches him
    And makes me poor indeed.

OTH.   By heaven, I 'll know thy thoughts.

IAGO.   You cannot, if my heart were in your hand;
    Nor shall not, whilst 't is in my custody.

---

6. *leets*] days on which private jurisdiction courts were held.

7. *scattering*] random.

OTH. Ha!

IAGO.   O, beware, my lord, of jealousy;
    It is the green-eyed monster, which doth mock
    The meat it feeds on: that cuckold lives in bliss
    Who, certain of his fate, loves not his wronger;[8]
    But, O, what damned minutes tells he o'er
    Who dotes, yet doubts, suspects, yet strongly loves!

OTH. O misery!

IAGO. Poor and content is rich, and rich enough;
    But riches fineless[9] is as poor as winter
    To him that ever fears he shall be poor:
    Good heaven, the souls of all my tribe defend
    From jealousy!

OTH.   Why, why is this?
    Think'st thou I 'ld make a life of jealousy,
    To follow still the changes of the moon
    With fresh suspicions? No; to be once in doubt
    Is once to be resolved: exchange me for a goat,
    When I shall turn the business of my soul
    To such exsufflicate[10] and blown surmises,
    Matching thy inference. 'T is not to make me jealous
    To say my wife is fair, feeds well, loves company,
    Is free of speech, sings, plays and dances well;
    Where virtue is, these are more virtuous:
    Nor from mine own weak merits will I draw
    The smallest fear or doubt of her revolt;
    For she had eyes, and chose me. No, Iago;
    I 'll see before I doubt; when I doubt, prove;
    And on the proof, there is no more but this,
    Away at once with love or jealousy!

IAGO. I am glad of it; for now I shall have reason
    To show the love and duty that I bear you
    With franker spirit: therefore, as I am bound,
    Receive it from me. I speak not yet of proof.
    Look to your wife: observe her well with Cassio;
    Wear your eye thus, not jealous nor secure:
    I would not have your free and noble nature
    Out of self-bounty be abused; look to 't:
    I know our country disposition well;
    In Venice they do let heaven see the pranks

---

8. *his wronger*] his faithless wife.
9. *fineless*] endless.
10. *exsufflicate*] swollen like a bubble, inflated.

      They dare not show their husbands; their best conscience
      Is not to leave 't undone, but keep 't unknown.
OTH.   Dost thou say so?
IAGO.   She did deceive her father, marrying you;
      And when she seem'd to shake and fear your looks,
      She loved them most.
OTH.   And so she did.
IAGO.   Why, go to then;
      She that so young could give out such a seeming,
      To seel her father's eyes up close as oak — [11]
      He thought 't was witchcraft — but I am much to blame;
      I humbly do beseech you of your pardon
      For too much loving you.
OTH.   I am bound to thee for ever.
IAGO.   I see this hath a little dash'd your spirits.
OTH.   Not a jot, not a jot.
IAGO.   I' faith, I fear it has.
      I hope you will consider what is spoke
      Comes from my love; but I do see you 're moved:
      I am to pray you not to strain my speech
      To grosser issues nor to larger reach
      Than to suspicion.
OTH.   I will not.
IAGO.   Should you do so, my lord,
      My speech should fall into such vile success
      As my thoughts aim not at. Cassio 's my worthy friend —
      My lord, I see you 're moved.
OTH.   No, not much moved:
      I do not think but Desdemona 's honest.
IAGO.   Long live she so! and long live you to think so!
OTH.   And yet, how nature erring from itself —
IAGO.   Ay, there 's the point: as — to be bold with you —
      Not to affect many proposed matches
      Of her own clime, complexion and degree,
      Whereto we see in all things nature tends —
      Foh! one may smell in such a will most rank,
      Foul disproportion, thoughts unnatural.
      But pardon me: I do not in position
      Distinctly speak of her; though I may fear
      Her will, recoiling to her better judgement,
      May fall to match you with her country forms,[12]

---

11. *close as oak*] close as the grain of oak.
12. *her country forms*] the form or outward aspect of her fellow-countrymen.

And happily repent.

OTH.   Farewell, farewell:
If more thou dost perceive, let me know more;
Set on thy wife to observe: leave me, Iago.

IAGO.   [*Going*] My lord, I take my leave.

OTH.   Why did I marry? This honest creature doubtless
Sees and knows more, much more, than he unfolds.

IAGO.   [*Returning*] My lord, I would I might entreat your honour
To scan this thing no further; leave it to time:
Though it be fit that Cassio have his place,
For sure he fills it up with great ability,
Yet, if you please to hold him off awhile,
You shall by that perceive him and his means:
Note if your lady strain his entertainment
With any strong or vehement importunity;
Much will be seen in that. In the mean time,
Let me be thought too busy in my fears —
As worthy cause I have to fear I am —
And hold her free, I do beseech your honour.

OTH.   Fear not my government.[13]

IAGO.   I once more take my leave.   [*Exit.*]

OTH.   This fellow 's of exceeding honesty,
And knows all qualities, with a learned spirit,
Of human dealings. If I do prove her haggard,
Though that her jesses[14] were my dear heart-strings,
I 'ld whistle her off and let her down the wind
To prey at fortune. Haply, for I am black
And have not those soft parts of conversation
That chamberers have, or for I am declined
Into the vale of years, — yet that 's not much —
She 's gone; I am abused, and my relief
Must be to loathe her. O curse of marriage,
That we can call these delicate creatures ours,
And not their appetites! I had rather be a toad,
And live upon the vapour of a dungeon,
Than keep a corner in the thing I love
For others' uses. Yet, 't is the plague of great ones;
Prerogatived are they less than the base;
'T is destiny unshunnable, like death:
Even then this forked plague[15] is fated to us

---

13. *government*] self-control.
14. *haggard . . . jesses*] a wild or untrained hawk, "haggard," is sometimes used for "courte-
san." "Jesses" are the leathern thongs which bind the hawk's foot to the falconer's wrist.
15. *forked plague*] a reference to the forked horns of a cuckolded husband.

When we do quicken.[16] Desdemona comes:

Re-enter DESDEMONA *and* EMILIA

If she be false, O, then heaven mocks itself!
I 'll not believe 't.
DES.   How now, my dear Othello!
Your dinner, and the generous islanders
By you invited, do attend your presence.
OTH.   I am to blame.
DES.   Why do you speak so faintly?
Are you not well?
OTH.   I have a pain upon my forehead here.
DES.   Faith, that 's with watching; 't will away again:
Let me but bind it hard, within this hour
It will be well.
OTH.   Your napkin is too little;
        [*He puts the handkerchief from him; and she drops it.*]
Let it alone. Come, I 'll go in with you.
DES.   I am very sorry that you are not well.
                          [*Exeunt* OTHELLO *and* DESDEMONA.]
EMIL.   I am glad I have found this napkin:
This was her first remembrance from the Moor:
My wayward husband hath a hundred times
Woo'd me to steal it; but she so loves the token,
For he conjured her she should ever keep it,
That she reserves it evermore about her
To kiss and talk to. I 'll have the work ta'en out,[17]
And give 't Iago: what he will do with it
Heaven knows, not I;
I nothing but to please his fantasy.

Re-enter IAGO

IAGO.   How now! what do you here alone?
EMIL.   Do not you chide; I have a thing for you.
IAGO.   A thing for me? it is a common thing —
EMIL.   Ha!
IAGO.   To have a foolish wife.
EMIL.   O, is that all? What will you give me now
    For that same handkerchief?

---

16. *When we do quicken*] When we are born.
17. *the work ta'en out*] the embroidery copied.

IAGO. What handkerchief?
EMIL. What handkerchief!
    Why, that the Moor first gave to Desdemona;
    That which so often you did bid me steal.
IAGO. Hast stol'n it from her?
EMIL. No, faith; she let it drop by negligence,
    And, to the advantage, I being here took 't up.
    Look, here it is.
IAGO. A good wench; give it me.
EMIL. What will you do with 't, that you have been so earnest
    To have me filch it?
IAGO. [*Snatching it*] Why, what 's that to you?
EMIL. If 't be not for some purpose of import,
    Give 't me again: poor lady, she 'll run mad
    When she shall lack it.
IAGO. Be not acknown[18] on 't; I have use for it.
    Go, leave me.   [*Exit* EMILIA.]
    I will in Cassio's lodging lose this napkin,
    And let him find it. Trifles light as air
    Are to the jealous confirmations strong
    As proofs of holy writ: this may do something.
    The Moor already changes with my poison:
    Dangerous conceits are in their natures poisons,
    Which at the first are scarce found to distaste,
    But with a little act upon the blood
    Burn like the mines of sulphur. I did say so:
    Look, where he comes!

Re-enter OTHELLO

              Not poppy, nor mandragora,[19]
    Nor all the drowsy syrups of the world,
    Shall ever medicine thee to that sweet sleep
    Which thou owedst yesterday.
OTH. Ha! ha! false to me?
IAGO. Why, how now, general! no more of that.
OTH. Avaunt! be gone! thou hast set me on the rack:
    I swear 't is better to be much abused
    Than but to know 't a little.
IAGO. How now, my lord!
OTH. What sense had I of her stol'n hours of lust?
    I saw 't not, thought it not, it harm'd not me:
    I slept the next night well, was free and merry;

18. *acknown*] knowing, acquainted with.
19. *mandragora*] an herb well known as a soporific or opiate.

I found not Cassio's kisses on her lips:
He that is robb'd, not wanting what is stol'n,
Let him not know 't and he 's not robb'd at all.
IAGO.   I am sorry to hear this.
OTH.   I had been happy, if the general camp,
Pioners and all, had tasted her sweet body,
So I had nothing known. O, now for ever
Farewell the tranquil mind! farewell content!
Farewell the plumed troop and the big wars
That make ambition virtue! O, farewell,
Farewell the neighing steed and the shrill trump,
The spirit-stirring drum, the ear-piercing fife,
The royal banner and all quality,
Pride, pomp and circumstance of glorious war!
And, O you mortal engines, whose rude throats
The immortal Jove's dread clamours counterfeit,
Farewell! Othello's occupation 's gone!
IAGO.   Is 't possible, my lord?
OTH.   Villain, be sure thou prove my love a whore;
Be sure of it; give me the ocular proof;
Or, by the worth of man's eternal soul,
Thou hadst been better have been born a dog
Than answer my waked wrath!
IAGO.   Is 't come to this?
OTH.   Make me to see 't; or at the least so prove it,
That the probation bear no hinge nor loop
To hang a doubt on; or woe upon thy life!
IAGO.   My noble lord, —
OTH.   If thou dost slander her and torture me,
Never pray more; abandon all remorse;
On horror's head horrors accumulate;
Do deeds to make heaven weep, all earth amazed;
For nothing canst thou to damnation add
Greater than that.
IAGO.   O grace! O heaven defend me!
Are you a man? have you a soul or sense?
God be wi' you; take mine office. O wretched fool,
That livest to make thine honesty a vice!
O monstrous world! Take note, take note, O world,
To be direct and honest is not safe.
I thank you for this profit, and from hence
I 'll love no friend sith[20] love breeds such offence.

---

20. *sith*] since.

OTH.　Nay, stay: thou shouldst be honest.
IAGO.　I should be wise; for honesty 's a fool,
　　And loses that it works for.
OTH.　　　　　　　　　　　　By the world,
　　I think my wife be honest, and think she is not;
　　I think that thou art just, and think thou art not:
　　I 'll have some proof. Her name, that was as fresh
　　As Dian's visage, is now begrimed and black
　　As mine own face. If there be cords, or knives,
　　Poison, or fire, or suffocating streams,
　　I 'll not endure it. Would I were satisfied!
IAGO.　I see, sir, you are eaten up with passion:
　　I do repent me that I put it to you.
　　You would be satisfied?
OTH.　　　　　　　　　　　Would! nay, I will.
IAGO.　And may: but, how? how satisfied, my lord?
　　Would you, the supervisor,[21] grossly gape on?
　　Behold her topp'd?
OTH.　　　　　　　　　　　Death and damnation! O!
IAGO.　It were a tedious difficulty, I think,
　　To bring them to that prospect: damn them then,
　　If ever mortal eyes do see them bolster
　　More than their own! What then? how then?
　　What shall I say? Where 's satisfaction?
　　It is impossible you should see this,
　　Were they as prime as goats, as hot as monkeys,
　　As salt as wolves in pride, and fools as gross
　　As ignorance made drunk. But yet, I say,
　　If imputation and strong circumstances,
　　Which lead directly to the door of truth,
　　Will give you satisfaction, you may have 't.
OTH.　Give me a living reason she 's disloyal.
IAGO.　I do not like the office:
　　But sith I am enter'd in this cause so far,
　　Prick'd to 't by foolish honesty and love,
　　I will go on. I lay with Cassio lately,
　　And being troubled with a raging tooth,
　　I could not sleep.
　　There are a kind of men so loose of soul,
　　That in their sleeps will mutter their affairs:
　　One of this kind is Cassio:
　　In sleep I heard him say "Sweet Desdemona,

---

21. *supervisor*] onlooker.

Let us be wary, let us hide our loves;"
And then, sir, would he gripe and wring my hand,
Cry "O sweet creature!" and then kiss me hard,
As if he pluck'd up kisses by the roots,
That grew upon my lips: then laid his leg
Over my thigh, and sigh'd and kiss'd, and then
Cried "Cursed fate that gave thee to the Moor!"

OTH.   O monstrous! monstrous!

IAGO.   Nay, this was but his dream.

OTH.   But this denoted a foregone conclusion:
'T is a shrewd doubt, though it be but a dream.

IAGO.   And this may help to thicken other proofs
That do demonstrate thinly.

OTH.   I 'll tear her all to pieces.

IAGO.   Nay, but be wise: yet we see nothing done;
She may be honest yet. Tell me but this,
Have you not sometimes seen a handkerchief
Spotted[22] with strawberries in your wife's hand?

OTH.   I gave her such a one; 't was my first gift.

IAGO.   I know not that: but such a handkerchief —
I am sure it was your wife's — did I to-day
See Cassio wipe his beard with.

OTH.   If it be that, —

IAGO.   If it be that, or any that was hers,
It speaks against her with the other proofs.

OTH.   O, that the slave had forty thousand lives!
One is too poor, too weak for my revenge.
Now do I see 't is true. Look here, Iago;
All my fond love thus do I blow to heaven:
'T is gone.
Arise, black vengeance, from thy hollow cell!
Yield up, O love, thy crown and hearted throne
To tyrannous hate! Swell, bosom, with thy fraught,[23]
For 't is of aspics'[24] tongues!

IAGO.   Yet be content.

OTH.   O, blood, blood, blood!

IAGO.   Patience, I say; your mind perhaps may change.

OTH.   Never, Iago. Like to the Pontic sea,[25]

---

22. *Spotted*] Embroidered.
23. *fraught*] burden, freight.
24. *aspics'*] asps'.
25. *the Pontic sea*] the Pontic, now the Black sea, according to Pliny and the ancient geog-
raphers, had only a flowing tide, and never ebbed, for ever flowing into the Propontic,
i. e., the sea of Marmora, and the Hellespont, *i. e.*, the Bosphorus.

Whose icy current and compulsive course
Ne'er feels retiring ebb, but keeps due on
To the Propontic and the Hellespont;
Even so my bloody thoughts, with violent pace,
Shall ne'er look back, ne'er ebb to humble love,
Till that a capable and wide revenge
Swallow them up. Now, by yond marble heaven,
In the due reverence of a sacred vow   [*Kneels.*]
I here engage my words.

IAGO.   Do not rise yet.   [*Kneels.*]
Witness, you ever-burning lights above,
You elements that clip[26] us round about,
Witness that here Iago doth give up
The execution of his wit, hands, heart,
To wrong'd Othello's service! Let him command,
And to obey shall be in me remorse,
What bloody business ever.   [*They rise.*]

OTH.   I greet thy love,
Not with vain thanks, but with acceptance bounteous,
And will upon the instant put thee to 't:
Within these three days let me hear thee say
That Cassio 's not alive.

IAGO.   My friend is dead; 't is done at your request:
But let her live.

OTH.   Damn her, lewd minx! O, damn her!
Come, go with me apart; I will withdraw,
To furnish me with some swift means of death
For the fair devil. Now art thou my lieutenant.

IAGO.   I am your own for ever.   [*Exeunt.*]

SCENE IV. *Before the Castle.*

Enter DESDEMONA, EMILIA, *and* Clown

DES.   Do you know, sirrah, where Lieutenant Cassio lies?
CLO.   I dare not say he lies any where.
DES.   Why, man?
CLO.   He 's a soldier; and for one to say a soldier lies, is stabbing.

---

26. *clip*] embrace.

DES.   Go to: where lodges he?
CLO.   To tell you where he lodges, is to tell you where I lie.
DES.   Can any thing be made of this?
CLO.   I know not where he lodges; and for me to devise a lodging, and
        say he lies here or he lies there, were to lie in mine own throat.
DES.   Can you inquire him out and be edified by report?
CLO.   I will catechize the world for him; that is, make questions and
        by them answer.
DES.   Seek him, bid him come hither: tell him I have moved my lord
        on his behalf and hope all will be well.
CLO.   To do this is within the compass of man's wit, and therefore I
        will attempt the doing it.   [*Exit.*]
DES.   Where should I lose that handkerchief, Emilia?
EMIL.   I know not, madam.
DES.   Believe me, I had rather have lost my purse
        Full of crusadoes:[1] and, but my noble Moor
        Is true of mind and made of no such baseness
        As jealous creatures are, it were enough
        To put him to ill thinking.
EMIL.   Is he not jealous?
DES.   Who, he? I think the sun where he was born
        Drew all such humours from him.
EMIL.   Look, where he comes.
DES.   I will not leave him now till Cassio
        Be call'd to him.

Enter OTHELLO

                        How is 't with you, my lord?
OTH.   Well, my good lady. [*Aside*] O, hardness to dissemble!
        How do you, Desdemona?
DES.   Well, my good lord.
OTH.   Give me your hand: this hand is moist,[2] my lady.
DES.   It yet has felt no age nor known no sorrow.
OTH.   This argues fruitfulness and liberal heart:
        Hot, hot, and moist: this hand of yours requires
        A sequester from liberty, fasting and prayer,
        Much castigation, exercise devout;
        For here 's a young and sweating devil here,
        That commonly rebels. 'T is a good hand,

---

1. *crusadoes*] gold coins of Portugal, marked with a cross.
2. *this hand is moist*] A moist hand was commonly held to be a sign of an amorous
   disposition, as a dry hand was held to be a sign of indifference to love.

A frank one.

DES.   You may, indeed, say so;
For 't was that hand that gave away my heart.

OTH.   A liberal hand: the hearts of old gave hands;
But our new heraldry is hands, not hearts.

DES.   I cannot speak of this. Come now, your promise.

OTH.   What promise, chuck?

DES.   I have sent to bid Cassio come speak with you.

OTH.   I have a salt and sorry rheum offends me;
Lend me thy handkerchief.

DES.   Here, my lord.

OTH.   That which I gave you.

DES.   I have it not about me.

OTH.   Not?

DES.   No, indeed, my lord.

OTH.   That 's a fault. That handkerchief
Did an Egyptian[3] to my mother give;
She was a charmer,[4] and could almost read
The thoughts of people: she told her, while she kept it
'T would make her amiable and subdue my father
Entirely to her love, but if she lost it
Or made a gift of it, my father's eye
Should hold her loathed and his spirits should hunt
After new fancies: she dying gave it me,
And bid me, when my fate would have me wive,
To give it her. I did so: and take heed on 't;
Make it a darling like your precious eye;
To lose 't or give 't away were such perdition
As nothing else could match.

DES.   Is 't possible?

OTH.   'T is true: there 's magic in the web of it:
A sibyl,[5] that had number'd in the world
The sun to course two hundred compasses,
In her prophetic fury sew'd the work;
The worms were hallow'd that did breed the silk;
And it was dyed in mummy which the skilful
Conserved of maidens' hearts.

DES.   Indeed! is 't true?

OTH.   Most veritable; therefore look to 't well.

DES.   Then would to God that I had never seen 't!

---

3. *Egyptian*] Gypsy.
4. *charmer*] a practiser of enchantments, a witch.
5. *sibyl*] prophetess, sorceress.

OTH.   Ha! wherefore?
DES.   Why do you speak so startingly and rash?
OTH.   Is 't lost? is 't gone? speak, is it out o' the way?
DES.   Heaven bless us!
OTH.   Say you?
DES.   It is not lost; but what an if it were?
OTH.   How!
DES.   I say, it is not lost.
OTH.   Fetch 't, let me see it.
DES.   Why, so I can, sir, but I will not now.
     This is a trick to put me from my suit:
     Pray you, let Cassio be received again.
OTH.   Fetch me the handkerchief: my mind misgives.
DES.   Come, come;
     You 'll never meet a more sufficient man.
OTH.   The handkerchief!
DES.   I pray, talk me of Cassio.
OTH.   The handkerchief!
DES.   A man that all his time
     Hath founded his good fortunes on your love,
     Shared dangers with you, —
OTH.   The handkerchief!
DES.   In sooth, you are to blame.
OTH.   Away!   [Exit.]
EMIL.   Is not this man jealous?
DES.   I ne'er saw this before.
     Sure there 's some wonder in this handkerchief:
     I am most unhappy in the loss of it.
EMIL.   'T is not a year or two shows us a man:
     They are all but stomachs and we all but food;
     They eat us hungerly, and when they are full
     They belch us. Look you, Cassio and my husband.

Enter CASSIO *and* IAGO

IAGO.   There is no other way; 't is she must do 't:
     And, lo, the happiness! go and importune her.
DES.   How now, good Cassio! what 's the news with you?
CAS.   Madam, my former suit: I do beseech you
     That by your virtuous means I may again
     Exist, and be a member of his love
     Whom I with all the office of my heart
     Entirely honour: I would not be delay'd.
     If my offence be of such mortal kind,

That nor my service past nor present sorrows
Nor purposed merit in futurity
Can ransom me into his love again,
But to know so must be my benefit;
So shall I clothe me in a forced content
And shut myself up in some other course
To fortune's alms.

DES.   Alas, thrice-gentle Cassio!
My advocation is not now in tune;
My lord is not my lord, nor should I know him
Were he in favour as in humour alter'd.
So help me every spirit sanctified,
As I have spoken for you all my best
And stood within the blank of his displeasure
For my free speech! You must awhile be patient:
What I can do I will; and more I will
Than for myself I dare: let that suffice you.

IAGO.   Is my lord angry?

EMIL.   He went hence but now,
And certainly in strange unquietness.

IAGO.   Can he be angry? I have seen the cannon,
When it hath blown his ranks into the air,
And, like the devil, from his very arm
Puff'd his own brother; and can he be angry?
Something of moment then: I will go meet him:
There 's matter in 't indeed if he be angry.

DES.   I prithee, do so.   [*Exit* IAGO.]
                Something sure of state,
Either from Venice or some unhatch'd practice
Made demonstrable here in Cyprus to him,
Hath puddled his clear spirit; and in such cases
Men's natures wrangle with inferior things,
Though great ones are their object. 'T is even so;
For let our finger ache, and it indues
Our other healthful members even to that sense
Of pain: nay, we must think men are not gods,
Nor of them look for such observancy
As fits the bridal. Beshrew me much, Emilia,
I was, unhandsome warrior as I am,
Arraigning his unkindness with my soul;
But now I find I had suborn'd the witness,
And he 's indicted falsely.

EMIL.   Pray heaven it be state-matters, as you think,
And no conception nor no jealous toy

Concerning you.

DES. Alas the day, I never gave him cause!

EMIL. But jealous souls will not be answer'd so;
  They are not ever jealous for the cause,
  But jealous for they are jealous: 't is a monster
  Begot upon itself, born on itself.

DES. Heaven keep that monster from Othello's mind!

EMIL. Lady, amen.

DES. I will go seek him. Cassio, walk hereabout:
  If I do find him fit, I 'll move your suit,
  And seek to effect it to my uttermost.

CAS. I humbly thank your ladyship.

                    [*Exeunt* DESDEMONA *and* EMILIA.]

Enter BIANCA

BIAN. Save you, friend Cassio!

CAS.   What make you from home?
  How is it with you, my most fair Bianca?
  I' faith, sweet love, I was coming to your house.

BIAN. And I was going to your lodging, Cassio.
  What, keep a week away? seven days and nights?
  Eight score eight hours? and lovers' absent hours,
  More tedious than the dial eight score times?
  O weary reckoning!

CAS.   Pardon me, Bianca:
  I have this while with leaden thoughts been press'd;
  But I shall in a more continuate time
  Strike off this score of absence. Sweet Bianca,
                    [*Giving her* DESDEMONA'S *handkerchief.*]
  Take me this work out.

BIAN.   O Cassio, whence came this?
  This is some token from a newer friend:
  To the felt absence now I feel a cause:
  Is 't come to this? Well, well.

CAS.   Go to, woman!
  Throw your vile guesses in the devil's teeth,
  From whence you have them. You are jealous now
  That this is from some mistress, some remembrance:
  No, by my faith, Bianca.

BIAN.   Why, whose is it?

CAS. I know not, sweet: I found it in my chamber.
  I like the work well: ere it be demanded —
  As like enough it will — I 'ld have it copied:

Take it, and do 't; and leave me for this time.
BIAN.   Leave you! wherefore?
CAS.   I do attend here on the general;
And think it no addition, nor my wish,
To have him see me woman'd.
BIAN.   Why, I pray you?
CAS.   Not that I love you not.
BIAN.   But that you do not love me.
I pray you, bring me on the way a little;
And say if I shall see you soon at night.
CAS.   'T is but a little way that I can bring you;
For I attend here: but I 'll see you soon.
BIAN.   'T is very good; I must be circumstance.   [*Exeunt.*]

ACT IV.

SCENE I. *Cyprus. Before the Castle.*

Enter OTHELLO *and* IAGO

IAGO.   Will you think so?
OTH.   Think so, Iago!
IAGO.   What,
To kiss in private?
OTH.   An unauthorized kiss.
IAGO.   Or to be naked with her friend in bed
An hour or more, not meaning any harm?
OTH.   Naked in bed, Iago, and not mean harm!
It is hypocrisy against the devil:
They that mean virtuously and yet do so,
The devil their virtue tempts and they tempt heaven.
IAGO.   So they do nothing, 't is a venial slip:
But if I give my wife a handkerchief —
OTH.   What then?
IAGO.   Why, then, 't is hers, my lord; and being hers,
She may, I think, bestow 't on any man.
OTH.   She is protectress of her honour too:
May she give that?
IAGO.   Her honour is an essence that 's not seen:
They have it very oft that have it not:
But for the handkerchief —

OTH.   By heaven, I would most gladly have forgot it:
    Thou said'st — O, it comes o'er my memory,
    As doth the raven o'er the infected house,
    Boding to all — he had my handkerchief.
IAGO.   Ay, what of that?
OTH.   That 's not so good now.
IAGO.   What,
    If I had said I had seen him do you wrong?
    Or heard him say — as knaves be such abroad,
    Who having, by their own importunate suit,
    Or voluntary dotage of some mistress,
    Convinced or supplied them, cannot choose
    But they must blab —
OTH.   Hath he said any thing?
IAGO.   He hath, my lord; but be you well assured,
    No more than he 'll unswear.
OTH.   What hath he said?
IAGO.   Faith, that he did — I know not what he did.
OTH.   What? what?
IAGO.   Lie —
OTH.   With her?
IAGO.   With her, on her; what you will.
OTH.   Lie with her! lie on her! — We say lie on her, when they belie
    her. — Lie with her! 'Zounds, that's fulsome! Handker-
    chief — confessions — handkerchief! — To confess, and be
    hanged for his labour; first, to be hanged, and then to con-
    fess. I tremble at it. Nature would not invest herself in such
    shadowing passion without some instruction. It is not words that
    shakes me thus. Pish! Noses, ears and lips. Is 't possible? — Con-
    fess? — Handkerchief? — O devil!   [Falls in a trance.]
IAGO.   Work on,
    My medicine, work! Thus credulous fools are caught;
    And many worthy and chaste dames even thus,
    All guiltless, meet reproach. What, ho! my lord!
    My lord, I say! Othello!

Enter CASSIO

                        How now, Cassio!
CAS.   What's the matter?
IAGO.   My lord is fall'n into an epilepsy:
    This is his second fit; he had one yesterday.
CAS.   Rub him about the temples.
IAGO.   No, forbear;

The lethargy must have his quiet course:
If not, he foams at mouth, and by and by
Breaks out to savage madness. Look, he stirs:
Do you withdraw yourself a little while,
He will recover straight: when he is gone,
I would on great occasion speak with you.   [*Exit* CASSIO.]
How is it, general? have you not hurt your head?

OTH.   Dost thou mock me?

IAGO.   I mock you! no, by heaven.
Would you would bear your fortune like a man!

OTH.   A horned man 's a monster and a beast.

IAGO.   There 's many a beast then in a populous city,
And many a civil monster.

OTH.   Did he confess it?

IAGO.   Good sir, be a man;
Think every bearded fellow that 's but yoked
May draw with you: there 's millions now alive
That nightly lie in those unproper beds
Which they dare swear peculiar: your case is better.
O, 't is the spite of hell, the fiend's arch-mock,
To lip[1] a wanton in a secure couch,
And to suppose her chaste! No, let me know;
And knowing what I am, I know what she shall be.

OTH.   O, thou art wise; 't is certain.

IAGO.   Stand you awhile apart;
Confine yourself but in a patient list.[2]
Whilst you were here o'erwhelmed with your grief —
A passion most unsuiting such a man —
Cassio came hither: I shifted him away,
And laid good 'scuse upon your ecstasy;
Bade him anon return and here speak with me;
The which he promised. Do but encave yourself,
And mark the fleers,[3] the gibes and notable scorns,
That dwell in every region of his face;
For I will make him tell the tale anew,
Where, how, how oft, how long ago and when
He hath and is again to cope your wife:
I say, but mark his gesture. Marry, patience;
Or I shall say you are all in all in spleen,
And nothing of a man.

---

1. *To lip*] To kiss.
2. *in a patient list*] within the bounds of patience.
3. *fleers*] sneers, looks of contempt.

OTH.   Dost thou hear, Iago?
  I will be found most cunning in my patience;
  But — dost thou hear? — most bloody.
IAGO.   That 's not amiss;
  But yet keep time[4] in all. Will you withdraw?   [OTHELLO *retires.*]
  Now will I question Cassio of Bianca,
  A housewife[5] that by selling her desires
  Buys herself bread and clothes: it is a creature
  That dotes on Cassio; as 't is the strumpet's plague
  To beguile many and be beguiled by one.
  He, when he hears of her, cannot refrain
  From the excess of laughter. Here he comes.

Re-enter CASSIO

  As he shall smile, Othello shall go mad;
  And his unbookish jealousy must construe
  Poor Cassio's smiles, gestures and light behaviour,
  Quite in the wrong. How do you now, lieutenant?
CAS.   The worser that you give me the addition[6]
  Whose want even kills me.
IAGO.   Ply Desdemona well, and you are sure on 't.
  Now, if this suit lay in Bianca's power,
  How quickly should you speed!
CAS.   Alas, poor caitiff!
OTH.   Look, how he laughs already!
IAGO.   I never knew a woman love man so.
CAS.   Alas, poor rogue! I think, i' faith, she loves me.
OTH.   Now he denies it faintly and laughs it out.
IAGO.   Do you hear, Cassio?
OTH.   Now he importunes him
  To tell it o'er: go to; well said, well said.
IAGO.   She gives it out that you shall marry her:
  Do you intend it?
CAS.   Ha, ha, ha!
OTH.   Do you triumph, Roman? do you triumph?
CAS.   I marry her! what, a customer![7] I prithee, bear some charity to
  my wit; do not think it so unwholesome. Ha, ha, ha!
OTH.   So, so, so, so: they laugh that win.

---

  4. *keep time*] be patient; avoid haste.
  5. *housewife*] used like "hussy."
  6. *addition*] title.
  7. *a customer*] a prostitute.

IAGO.   Faith, the cry goes that you shall marry her.

CAS.   Prithee, say true.

IAGO.   I am a very villain else.

OTH.   Have you scored me? Well.

CAS.   This is the monkey's own giving out: she is persuaded I will marry her, out of her own love and flattery, not out of my promise.

OTH.   Iago beckons me; now he begins the story.

CAS.   She was here even now: she haunts me in every place. I was the other day talking on the sea-bank with certain Venetians; and thither comes the bauble, and, by this hand, she falls me thus about my neck —

OTH.   Crying "O dear Cassio!" as it were: his gesture imports it.

CAS.   So hangs and lolls and weeps upon me; so hales and pulls me: ha, ha, ha!

OTH.   Now he tells how she plucked him to my chamber. O, I see that nose of yours, but not that dog I shall throw it to.

CAS.   Well, I must leave her company.

IAGO.   Before me! look, where she comes.

CAS.   'T is such another fitchew![8] marry, a perfumed one.

Enter BIANCA

     What do you mean by this haunting of me?

BIAN.   Let the devil and his dam haunt you! What did you mean by that same handkerchief you gave me even now? I was a fine fool to take it. I must take out the work? A likely piece of work, that you should find it in your chamber, and not know who left it there! This is some minx's token, and I must take out the work? There; give it your hobby-horse:[9] wheresoever you had it, I 'll take out no work on 't.

CAS.   How now, my sweet Bianca! how now! how now!

OTH.   By heaven, that should be my handkerchief!

BIAN.   An you 'll come to supper to-night, you may; an you will not, come when you are next prepared for.   [*Exit.*]

IAGO.   After her, after her.

CAS.   Faith, I must; she 'll rail i' the street else.

IAGO.   Will you sup there?

CAS.   Faith, I intend so.

IAGO.   Well, I may chance to see you; for I would very fain speak with you.

CAS.   Prithee, come; will you?

---

8. *fitchew*] a polecat, a term commonly applied to a wanton woman.
9. *hobby-horse*] a term of contempt for a frivolous woman.

IAGO.	Go to; say no more. [*Exit* CASSIO.]
OTH.	[*Advancing*] How shall I murder him, Iago?
IAGO.	Did you perceive how he laughed at his vice?
OTH.	O Iago!
IAGO.	And did you see the handkerchief?
OTH.	Was that mine?
IAGO.	Yours, by this hand: and to see how he prizes the foolish woman your wife! she gave it him, and he hath given it his whore.
OTH.	I would have him nine years a-killing. A fine woman! a fair woman! a sweet woman!
IAGO.	Nay, you must forget that.
OTH.	Ay, let her rot, and perish, and be damned to-night: for she shall not live: no, my heart is turned to stone; I strike it, and it hurts my hand. O, the world hath not a sweeter creature: she might lie by an emperor's side, and command him tasks.
IAGO.	Nay, that 's not your way.
OTH.	Hang her! I do but say what she is: so delicate with her needle: an admirable musician: O, she will sing the savageness out of a bear: of so high and plenteous wit and invention: —
IAGO.	She 's the worse for all this.
OTH.	O, a thousand thousand times: and then, of so gentle a condition!
IAGO.	Ay, too gentle.
OTH.	Nay, that 's certain: but yet the pity of it, Iago! O Iago, the pity of it, Iago!
IAGO.	If you are so fond over her iniquity, give her patent[10] to offend; for, if it touch not you, it comes near nobody.
OTH.	I will chop her into messes: cuckold me!
IAGO.	O, 't is foul in her.
OTH.	With mine officer!
IAGO.	That 's fouler.
OTH.	Get me some poison, Iago; this night. I 'll not expostulate with her, lest her body and beauty unprovide my mind again: this night, Iago.
IAGO.	Do it not with poison, strangle her in her bed, even the bed she hath contaminated.
OTH.	Good, good: the justice of it pleases: very good.
IAGO.	And for Cassio, let me be his undertaker:[11] you shall hear more by midnight.

10. *patent*] formal right, permission.
11. *let me . . . undertaker*] let me take up your cause of quarrel with him. "Undertaker" was the title commonly bestowed on such interveners in controversy.

OTH.   Excellent good. [*A trumpet within.*] What trumpet is that same?
IAGO.   Something from Venice, sure. 'T is Lodovico
  Come from the duke: and, see, your wife is with him.

Enter LODOVICO, DESDEMONA, *and* Attendants

LOD.   God save the worthy general!
OTH.   With all my heart, sir.
LOD.   The duke and senators of Venice greet you.
               [*Gives him a letter.*]
OTH.   I kiss the instrument of their pleasures.
           [*Opens the letter, and reads.*]
DES.   And what 's the news, good cousin Lodovico?
IAGO.   I am very glad to see you, signior;
  Welcome to Cyprus.
LOD.   I thank you. How does Lieutenant Cassio?
IAGO.   Lives, sir.
DES.   Cousin, there 's fall'n between him and my lord
  An unkind breach: but you shall make all well.
OTH.   Are you sure of that?
DES.   My lord?
OTH.   [*Reads*] "This fail you not to do, as you will — "
LOD.   He did not call; he 's busy in the paper.
  Is there division 'twixt my lord and Cassio?
DES.   A most unhappy one: I would do much
  To atone them, for the love I bear to Cassio.
OTH.   Fire and brimstone!
DES.   My lord?
OTH.   Are you wise?
DES.   What, is he angry?
LOD.   May be the letter moved him;
  For, as I think, they do command him home,
  Deputing Cassio in his government.
DES.   By my troth, I am glad on 't.
OTH.   Indeed!
DES.   My lord?
OTH.   I am glad to see you mad.
DES.   Why, sweet Othello?
OTH.   Devil!   [*Striking her.*]
DES.   I have not deserved this.
LOD.   My lord, this would not be believed in Venice,
  Though I should swear I saw 't: 't is very much:
  Make her amends; she weeps.
OTH.   O devil, devil!
  If that the earth could teem with woman's tears,

      Each drop she falls would prove a crocodile.[12]
      Out of my sight!
DES.   I will not stay to offend you.   [*Going.*]
LOD.   Truly, an obedient lady:
      I do beseech your lordship, call her back.
OTH.   Mistress!
DES.   My lord?
OTH.   What would you with her, sir?
LOD.   Who, I, my lord?
OTH.   Ay; you did wish that I would make her turn:
      Sir, she can turn and turn, and yet go on,
      And turn again; and she can weep, sir, weep;
      And she 's obedient, as you say, obedient,
      Very obedient. Proceed you in your tears.
      Concerning this, sir, — O well-painted passion! —
      I am commanded home. Get you away,
      I 'll send for you anon. Sir, I obey the mandate,
      And will return to Venice. Hence, avaunt!   [*Exit* DESDEMONA.]
      Cassio shall have my place. And, sir, to-night,
      I do entreat that we may sup together:
      You are welcome, sir, to Cyprus. Goats and monkeys!   [*Exit.*]
LOD.   Is this the noble Moor whom our full senate
      Call all in all sufficient? This the nature
      Whom passion could not shake? whose solid virtue
      The shot of accident nor dart of chance
      Could neither graze nor pierce?
IAGO.   He is much changed.
LOD.   Are his wits safe? is he not light of brain?
IAGO.   He 's that he is: I may not breathe my censure
      What he might be: if what he might he is not,
      I would to heaven he were!
LOD.   What, strike his wife!
IAGO.   Faith, that was not so well; yet would I knew
      That stroke would prove the worst!
LOD.   Is it his use?
      Or did the letters work upon his blood,
      And new create this fault?
IAGO.   Alas, alas!
      It is not honesty in me to speak
      What I have seen and known. You shall observe him,
      And his own courses will denote him so
      That I may save my speech: do but go after,

---

12. *tears . . . crocodile*] Feigned tears are commonly known as "crocodile's tears."

And mark how he continues.
LOD.   I am sorry that I am deceived in him.   [*Exeunt.*]

SCENE II. *A Room in the Castle.*

Enter OTHELLO *and* EMILIA

OTH.   You have seen nothing, then?
EMIL.   Nor ever heard, nor ever did suspect.
OTH.   Yes, you have seen Cassio and she together.
EMIL.   But then I saw no harm, and then I heard
        Each syllable that breath made up between them.
OTH.   What, did they never whisper?
EMIL.   Never, my lord.
OTH.   Nor send you out o' the way?
EMIL.   Never.
OTH.   To fetch her fan, her gloves, her mask, nor nothing?
EMIL.   Never, my lord.
OTH.   That 's strange.
EMIL.   I durst, my lord, to wager she is honest,
        Lay down my soul at stake: if you think other,
        Remove your thought; it doth abuse your bosom.
        If any wretch have put this in your head,
        Let heaven requite it with the serpent's curse!
        For if she be not honest, chaste and true,
        There 's no man happy; the purest of their wives
        Is foul as slander.
OTH.   Bid her come hither: go.   [*Exit* EMILIA.]
        She says enough: yet she 's a simple bawd
        That cannot say as much. This is a subtle whore,
        A closet lock and key of villanous secrets:
        And yet she 'll kneel and pray; I have seen her do 't.

Enter DESDEMONA *with* EMILIA

DES.   My lord, what is your will?
OTH.   Pray, chuck, come hither.
DES.   What is your pleasure?
OTH.   Let me see your eyes;
        Look in my face.
DES.   What horrible fancy 's this?

OTH.   [*To* EMILIA] Some of your function, mistress,
    Leave procreants alone and shut the door;
    Cough, or cry hem, if any body come:
    Your mystery, your mystery: nay, dispatch.   [*Exit* EMILIA.]
DES.   Upon my knees, what doth your speech import?
    I understand a fury in your words,
    But not the words.
OTH.   Why, what art thou?
DES.   Your wife, my lord; your true and loyal wife.
OTH.   Come, swear it, damn thyself;
    Lest, being like one of heaven, the devils themselves
    Should fear to seize thee: therefore be double-damn'd;
    Swear thou art honest.
DES.   Heaven doth truly know it.
OTH.   Heaven truly knows that thou art false as hell.
DES.   To whom, my lord? with whom? how am I false?
OTH.   O Desdemona! Away! away! away!
DES.   Alas the heavy day! Why do you weep?
    Am I the motive of these tears, my lord?
    If haply you my father do suspect
    An instrument of this your calling back,
    Lay not your blame on me: if you have lost him,
    Why, I have lost him too.
OTH.   Had it pleased heaven
    To try me with affliction; had they rain'd
    All kinds of sores and shames on my bare head,
    Steep'd me in poverty to the very lips,
    Given to captivity me and my utmost hopes,
    I should have found in some place of my soul
    A drop of patience: but, alas, to make me
    A fixed figure for the time of scorn
    To point his slow unmoving finger at!
    Yet could I bear that too; well, very well:
    But there, where I have garner'd up my heart,
    Where either I must live or bear no life,
    The fountain from which my current runs,
    Or else dries up; to be discarded thence!
    Or keep it as a cistern for foul toads
    To knot and gender in! Turn thy complexion there,
    Patience, thou young and rose-lipp'd cherubin,
    Ay, there, look grim as hell!
DES.   I hope my noble lord esteems me honest.
OTH.   O, ay; as summer flies are in the shambles,
    That quicken even with blowing. O thou weed,

Who art so lovely fair and smell'st so sweet
That the sense aches at thee, would thou hadst ne'er been born!

DES. Alas, what ignorant sin have I committed?

OTH. Was this fair paper, this most goodly book,
Made to write "whore" upon? What committed!
Committed! O thou public commoner!
I should make very forges of my cheeks,
That would to cinders burn up modesty,
Did I but speak thy deeds. What committed!
Heaven stops the nose at it, and the moon winks;
The bawdy wind, that kisses all it meets,
Is hush'd within the hollow mine of earth,
And will not hear it. What committed!
Impudent strumpet!

DES.   By heaven, you do me wrong.

OTH. Are not you a strumpet?

DES.   No, as I am a Christian:
If to preserve this vessel for my lord
From any other foul unlawful touch
Be not to be a strumpet, I am none.

OTH. What, not a whore?

DES.   No, as I shall be saved.

OTH. Is 't possible?

DES. O, heaven forgive us!

OTH.   I cry you mercy then:
I took you for that cunning whore of Venice
That married with Othello. [*Raising his voice*] You, mistress,
That have the office opposite to Saint Peter,
And keep the gate of hell!

Re-enter EMILIA

                            You, you, ay, you!
We have done our course; there 's money for your pains:
I pray you, turn the key, and keep our counsel.   [*Exit.*]

EMIL. Alas, what does this gentleman conceive?
How do you, madam? how do you, my good lady?

DES. Faith, half asleep.

EMIL. Good madam, what's the matter with my lord?

DES. With who?

EMIL. Why, with my lord, madam.

DES. Who is thy lord?

EMIL.   He that is yours, sweet lady.

DES. I have none: do not talk to me, Emilia;

I cannot weep, nor answer have I none
But what should go by water.[1] Prithee, to-night
Lay on my bed my wedding sheets: remember;
And call thy husband hither.

EMIL.   Here 's a change indeed!   [*Exit.*]
DES.   'T is meet I should be used so, very meet.
How have I been behaved, that he might stick
The small'st opinion on my least misuse?

Re-enter EMILIA *with* IAGO

IAGO.   What is your pleasure, madam? How is 't with you?
DES.   I cannot tell. Those that do teach young babes
Do it with gentle means and easy tasks:
He might have chid me so; for, in good faith,
I am a child to chiding.
IAGO.   What 's the matter, lady?
EMIL.   Alas, Iago, my lord hath so bewhored her,
Thrown such despite and heavy terms upon her,
As true hearts cannot bear.
DES.   Am I that name, Iago?
IAGO.   What name, fair lady?
DES.   Such as she says my lord did say I was.
EMIL.   He call'd her whore: a beggar in his drink
Could not have laid such terms upon his callet.[2]
IAGO.   Why did he so?
DES.   I do not know; I am sure I am none such.
IAGO.   Do not weep, do not weep. Alas the day!
EMIL.   Hath she forsook so many noble matches,
Her father and her country and her friends,
To be call'd whore? would it not make one weep?
DES.   It is my wretched fortune.
IAGO.   Beshrew him for 't!
How comes this trick upon him?
DES.   Nay, heaven doth know.
EMIL.   I will be hang'd, if some eternal villain,
Some busy and insinuating rogue,
Some cogging, cozening slave, to get some office,
Have not devised this slander; I 'll be hang'd else.
IAGO.   Fie, there is no such man; it is impossible.
DES.   If any such there be, heaven pardon him!

---

1. *go by water*] express itself in tears.
2. *callet*] a low prostitute.

EMIL. A halter pardon him! and hell gnaw his bones!
Why should he call her whore? who keeps her company?
What place? what time? what form? what likelihood?
The Moor 's abused by some most villainous knave,
Some base notorious knave, some scurvy fellow.
O heaven, that such companions thou 'ldst unfold,
And put in every honest hand a whip
To lash the rascals naked through the world
Even from the east to the west!

IAGO. Speak within door.[3]

EMIL. O, fie upon them! Some such squire he was
That turn'd your wit the seamy side without,
And made you to suspect me with the Moor.

IAGO. You are a fool; go to.

DES. O good Iago,
What shall I do to win my lord again?
Good friend, go to him; for, by this light of heaven,
I know not how I lost him. Here I kneel:
If e'er my will did trespass 'gainst his love
Either in discourse of thought or actual deed,
Or that mine eyes, mine ears, or any sense,
Delighted them in any other form,
Or that I do not yet, and ever did,
And ever will, though he do shake me off
To beggarly divorcement, love him dearly,
Comfort forswear me! Unkindness may do much;
And his unkindness may defeat my life,
But never taint my love. I cannot say "whore":
It doth abhor me now I speak the word;
To do the act that might the addition earn
Not the world's mass of vanity could make me.

IAGO. I pray you, be content; 't is but his humour:
The business of the state does him offence,
And he does chide with you.

DES. If 't were no other, —

IAGO. 'T is but so, I warrant. [*Trumpets within.*]
Hark, how these instruments summon to supper!
The messengers of Venice stay the meat:
Go in, and weep not; all things shall be well.

[*Exeunt* DESDEMONA *and* EMILIA.]

Enter RODERIGO

---

3. *Speak within door*] Don't speak so loud as to be heard outside the door.

How now, Roderigo!

ROD.   I do not find that thou dealest justly with me.

IAGO.   What in the contrary?

ROD.   Every day thou daffest me with some device, Iago; and rather, as it seems to me now, keepest from me all conveniency than suppliest me with the least advantage of hope. I will indeed no longer endure it; nor am I yet persuaded to put up in peace what already I have foolishly suffered.

IAGO.   Will you hear me, Roderigo?

ROD.   Faith, I have heard too much; for your words and performances are no kin together.

IAGO.   You charge me most unjustly.

ROD.   With nought but truth. I have wasted myself out of my means. The jewels you have had from me to deliver to Desdemona would half have corrupted a votarist:[4] you have told me she hath received them and returned me expectations and comforts of sudden respect and acquaintance; but I find none.

IAGO.   Well; go to; very well.

ROD.   Very well! go to! I cannot go to, man; nor 't is not very well: by this hand, I say 't is very scurvy, and begin to find myself fopped in it.

IAGO.   Very well.

ROD.   I tell you 't is not very well. I will make myself known to Desdemona: if she will return me my jewels, I will give over my suit and repent my unlawful solicitation; if not, assure yourself I will seek satisfaction of you.

IAGO.   You have said now.

ROD.   Ay, and said nothing but what I protest intendment of doing.

IAGO.   Why, now I see there 's mettle in thee; and even from this instant do build on thee a better opinion than ever before. Give me thy hand, Roderigo: thou hast taken against me a most just exception; but yet, I protest, I have dealt most directly in thy affair.

ROD.   It hath not appeared.

IAGO.   I grant indeed it hath not appeared, and your suspicion is not without wit and judgement. But, Roderigo, if thou hast that in thee indeed, which I have greater reason to believe now than ever, I mean purpose, courage and valour, this night show it: if thou the next night following enjoy not Desdemona, take me from this world with treachery and devise engines for my life.

ROD.   Well, what is it? is it within reason and compass?

IAGO.   Sir, there is especial commission come from Venice to depute Cassio in Othello's place.

---

4. *a votarist*] a nun.

ROD. Is that true? why then Othello and Desdemona return again to Venice.

IAGO. O, no; he goes into Mauritania, and takes away with him the fair Desdemona, unless his abode be lingered here by some accident: wherein none can be so determinate as the removing of Cassio.

ROD. How do you mean, removing of him?

IAGO. Why, by making him uncapable of Othello's place; knocking out his brains.

ROD. And that you would have me to do?

IAGO. Ay, if you dare do yourself a profit and a right. He sups to-night with a harlotry, and thither will I go to him: he knows not yet of his honourable fortune. If you will watch his going thence, which ·I will fashion to fall out between twelve and one, you may take him at your pleasure: I will be near to second your attempt, and he shall fall between us. Come, stand not amazed at it, but go along with me; I will show you such a necessity in his death that you shall think yourself bound to put it on him. It is now high supper-time, and the night grows to waste: about it.

ROD. I will hear further reason for this.

IAGO. And you shall be satisfied.   [*Exeunt.*]

SCENE III. *Another Room in the Castle.*

Enter OTHELLO, LODOVICO, DESDEMONA, EMILIA, *and* Attendants

LOD. I do beseech you, sir, trouble yourself no further.

OTH. O, pardon me; 't will do me good to walk.

LOD. Madam, good night; I humbly thank your ladyship.

DES. Your honour is most welcome.

OTH.   Will you walk,[1] sir?
  O, — Desdemona, —

DES. My lord?

OTH. Get you to bed on the instant; I will be returned forthwith: dismiss your attendant there: look it be done.

DES. I will, my lord. [*Exeunt* OTHELLO, LODOVICO, *and* Attendants.]

EMIL. How goes it now? he looks gentler than he did.

DES. He says he will return incontinent:[2]

---

1. *walk*] withdraw.
2. *incontinent*] immediately.

He hath commanded me to go to bed,
And bade me to dismiss you.
EMIL.   Dismiss me!
DES.   It was his bidding; therefore, good Emilia,
  Give me my nightly wearing, and adieu:
  We must not now displease him.
EMIL.   I would you had never seen him!
DES.   So would not I: my love doth so approve him,
  That even his stubbornness, his checks, his frowns, —
  Prithee, unpin me, — have grace and favour in them.
EMIL.   I have laid those sheets you bade me on the bed.
DES.   All 's one. Good faith, how foolish are our minds!
  If I do die before thee, prithee, shroud me
  In one of those same sheets.
EMIL.   Come, come, you talk.
DES.   My mother had a maid call'd Barbara:
  She was in love; and he she loved proved mad
  And did forsake her: she had a song of "willow;"
  An old thing 't was, but it express'd her fortune,
  And she died singing it: that song to-night
  Will not go from my mind; I have much to do
  But to go hang my head all at one side
  And sing it like poor Barbara. Prithee, dispatch.
EMIL.   Shall I go fetch your night-gown?
DES.   No, unpin me here.
  This Lodovico is a proper man.
EMIL.   A very handsome man.
DES.   He speaks well.
EMIL.   I know a lady in Venice would have walked barefoot to Palestine
  for a touch of his nether lip.

DES.   [*Singing*]   The poor soul sat sighing by a sycamore tree,
   Sing all a green willow;
  Her hand on her bosom, her head on her knee,
   Sing willow, willow, willow:
  The fresh streams ran by her, and murmur'd her moans;
   Sing willow, willow, willow;
  Her salt tears fell from her, and soften'd the stones; —

Lay by these: —

 [*Singing*]   Sing willow, willow, willow;

Prithee, hie thee; he 'll come anon: —

 [*Singing*]   Sing all a green willow must be my garland.

Let nobody blame him; his scorn I approve, —

Nay, that's not next. Hark! who is 't that knocks?
EMIL.   It 's the wind.

DES.   [*Singing*]   I call'd my love false love; but what said he then?
   Sing willow, willow, willow:
If I court moe³ women, you 'll couch with moe men.

So get thee gone; good night. Mine eyes do itch;
Doth that bode weeping?
EMIL.   'T is neither here nor there.
DES.   I have heard it said so. O, these men, these men!
Dost thou in conscience think, — tell me, Emilia, —
That there be women do abuse their husbands
In such gross kind?
EMIL.   There be some such, no question.
DES.   Wouldst thou do such a deed for all the world?
EMIL.   Why, would not you?
DES.   No, by this heavenly light!
EMIL.   Nor I neither by this heavenly light; I might do 't as well i' the
  dark.
DES.   Wouldst thou do such a deed for all the world?
EMIL.   The world 's a huge thing: it is a great price
  For a small vice.
DES.   In troth, I think thou wouldst not.
EMIL.   In troth, I think I should; and undo 't when I had done. Marry,
  I would not do such a thing for a joint-ring, nor for measures of
  lawn, nor for gowns, petticoats, nor caps, nor any petty exhibi-
  tion;⁴ but, for the whole world, — why, who would not make her
  husband a cuckold to make him a monarch? I should venture
  purgatory for 't.
DES.   Beshrew me, if I would do such a wrong
  For the whole world.
EMIL.   Why, the wrong is but a wrong i' the world; and having the world
  for your labour, 't is a wrong in your own world, and you might
  quickly make it right.
DES.   I do not think there is any such woman.
EMIL.   Yes, a dozen; and as many to the vantage⁵ as would store the
  world they played for.
  But I do think it is their husbands' faults

---

3. *moe*] more.
4. *exhibition*] allowance.
5. *to the vantage*] into the bargain.

If wives do fall: say that they slack their duties
And pour our treasures into foreign laps,
Or else break out in peevish jealousies,
Throwing restraint upon us, or say they strike us,
Or scant our former having[6] in despite,
Why, we have galls, and though we have some grace,
Yet have we some revenge. Let husbands know
Their wives have sense[7] like them: they see and smell
And have their palates both for sweet and sour,
As husbands have. What is it that they do
When they change us for others? Is it sport?
I think it is: and doth affection breed it?
I think it doth: is 't frailty that thus errs?
It is so too: and have not we affections,
Desires for sport, and frailty, as men have?
Then let them use us well: else let them know,
The ills we do, their ills instruct us so.

DES.   Good night, good night: heaven me such uses send,
Not to pick bad from bad, but by bad mend!   [*Exeunt.*]

ACT V

SCENE I. *Cyprus. A Street.*

Enter IAGO *and* RODERIGO

IAGO.   Here, stand behind this bulk; straight will he come:
Wear thy good rapier bare, and put it home:
Quick, quick; fear nothing; I 'll be at thy elbow:
It makes us, or it mars us; think on that,
And fix most firm thy resolution.

ROD.   Be near at hand; I may miscarry in 't.

IAGO.   Here, at thy hand: be bold, and take thy stand. [*Retires.*]

ROD.   I have no great devotion to the deed;
And yet he hath given me satisfying reasons:
'T is but a man gone. Forth, my sword: he dies.

IAGO.   I have rubb'd this young quat[1] almost to the sense,

---

6. *having*] allowance for expenses.
7. *sense*] sensual appetite.
1. *quat*] pustule, pimple.

And he grows angry. Now, whether he kill Cassio,
Or Cassio him, or each do kill the other,
Every way makes my gain: live Roderigo,
He calls me to a restitution large
Of gold and jewels that I bobb'd[2] from him,
As gifts to Desdemona:
It must not be: if Cassio do remain,
He hath a daily beauty in his life
That makes me ugly; and besides, the Moor
May unfold me to him; there stand I in much peril:
No, he must die. Be 't so. I hear him coming.

Enter CASSIO

ROD.   I know his gait; 't is he. Villain, thou diest!

                                          [*Makes a pass at* CASSIO.]
CAS.   That thrust had been mine enemy indeed,
But that my coat is better than thou know'st:
I will make proof of thine.   [*Draws, and wounds* RODERIGO.]
ROD.   O, I am slain!
        [IAGO *from behind wounds* CASSIO *in the leg, and exit.*]
CAS.   I am maim'd for ever. Help, ho! murder! murder!   [*Falls.*]

Enter OTHELLO

OTH.   The voice of Cassio: Iago keeps his word.
ROD.   O, villain that I am!
OTH.   It is even so.
CAS.   O, help, ho! light! a surgeon!
OTH.   'T is he. O brave Iago, honest and just,
That hast such noble sense of thy friend's wrong!
Thou teachest me. Minion, your dear lies dead,
And your unblest fate hies: strumpet, I come!
Forth of my heart those charms, thine eyes, are blotted;
Thy bed lust-stain'd shall with lust's blood be spotted.   [*Exit.*]

Enter LODOVICO *and* GRATIANO

CAS.   What, ho! no watch? no passage?[3] murder! murder!
GRA.   'T is some mischance; the cry is very direful.
CAS.   O, help!

---

2. *bobb'd*] cheated or swindled.
3. *passage*] traffic, passersby.

LOD.   Hark!
ROD.   O wretched villain!
LOD.   Two or three groan: it is a heavy night:
     These may be counterfeits: let 's think 't unsafe
     To come in to the cry without more help.
ROD.   Nobody come? then shall I bleed to death.
LOD.   Hark!

Re-enter IAGO, *with a light*

GRA.   Here 's one comes in his shirt, with light and weapons.
IAGO.   Who 's there? whose noise is this that cries on murder?
LOD.   We do not know.
IAGO.   Did not you hear a cry?
CAS.   Here, here! for heaven's sake, help me!
IAGO.   What 's the matter?
GRA.   This is Othello's ancient, as I take it.
LOD.   The same indeed; a very valiant fellow.
IAGO.   What are you here that cry so grievously?
CAS.   Iago? O, I am spoil'd, undone by villains!
     Give me some help.
IAGO.   O me, lieutenant! what villains have done this?
CAS.   I think that one of them is hereabout,
     And cannot make away.
IAGO.   O treacherous villains!
     What are you there? come in and give some help.
                        [*To* LODOVICO *and* GRATIANO.]
ROD.   O, help me here!
CAS.   That 's one of them.
IAGO.   O murderous slave! O villain!
                           [*Stabs* RODERIGO.]
ROD.   O damn'd Iago! O inhuman dog!
IAGO.   Kill men i' the dark! Where be these bloody thieves?
     How silent is this town! Ho! murder! murder!
     What may you be? are you of good or evil?
LOD.   As you shall prove us, praise us.
IAGO.   Signior Lodovico?
LOD.   He, sir.
IAGO.   I cry you mercy. Here 's Cassio hurt by villains.
GRA.   Cassio!
IAGO.   How is 't, brother?
CAS.   My leg is cut in two.
IAGO.   Marry, heaven forbid!
     Light, gentlemen: I 'll bind it with my shirt.

Enter BIANCA

BIAN. What is the matter, ho? who is 't that cried?
IAGO. Who is 't that cried!
BIAN. O my dear Cassio! my sweet Cassio! O Cassio, Cassio, Cassio!
IAGO. O notable strumpet! Cassio, may you suspect
    Who they should be that have thus mangled you?
CAS. No.
GRA. I am sorry to find you thus: I have been to seek you.
IAGO. Lend me a garter. So. O, for a chair,
    To bear him easily hence!
BIAN. Alas, he faints! O Cassio, Cassio, Cassio!
IAGO. Gentlemen all, I do suspect this trash
    To be a party in this injury.
    Patience awhile, good Cassio. Come, come;
    Lend me a light. Know we this face or no?
    Alas, my friend and my dear countryman
    Roderigo? no: — yes, sure: O heaven! Roderigo.
GRA. What, of Venice?
IAGO. Even he, sir: did you know him?
GRA.   Know him! ay.
IAGO. Signior Gratiano? I cry you gentle pardon;
    These bloody accidents must excuse my manners,
    That so neglected you.
GRA.   I am glad to see you.
IAGO. How do you, Cassio? O, a chair, a chair!
GRA. Roderigo!
IAGO. He, he, 't is he. [*A chair brought in.*] O, that 's well said; the chair:
    Some good man bear him carefully from hence;
    I 'll fetch the general's surgeon. [*To* BIANCA] For you, mistress,
    Save you your labour. He that lies slain here, Cassio,
    Was my dear friend: what malice was between you?
CAS. None in the world; nor do I know the man.
IAGO. [*To* BIAN.] What, look you pale? O, bear him out o' the
    air.   [CASSIO *and* RODERIGO *are borne off.*]
    Stay you, good gentlemen. Look you pale, mistress?
    Do you perceive the gastness[4] of her eye?
    Nay, if you stare, we shall hear more anon.
    Behold her well; I pray you, look upon her:
    Do you see, gentlemen? nay, guiltiness will speak,
    Though tongues were out of use.

Enter EMILIA

---

4. *gastness*] ghastliness, deadly paleness.

EMIL.   'Las, what 's the matter? what 's the matter, husband?
IAGO.   Cassio hath here been set on in the dark
    By Roderigo, and fellows that are 'scaped:
    He 's almost slain, and Roderigo dead.
EMIL.   Alas, good gentleman! alas, good Cassio!
IAGO.   This is the fruit of whoring. Prithee, Emilia,
    Go know of Cassio where he supp'd to-night.
    What, do you shake at that?
BIAN.   He supp'd at my house; but I therefore shake not.
IAGO.   O, did he so? I charge you, go with me.
EMIL.   Fie, fie upon thee, strumpet!
BIAN.   I am no strumpet; but of life as honest
    As you that thus abuse me.
EMIL.   As I! foh! fie upon thee!
IAGO.   Kind gentlemen, let 's go see poor Cassio dress'd.
    Come, mistress, you must tell 's another tale.
    Emilia, run you to the citadel,
    And tell my lord and lady what hath happ'd!
    Will you go on? I pray. [*Aside*] This is the night
    That either makes me or fordoes[5] me quite.   [*Exeunt.*]

SCENE II. A *Bedchamber in the Castle. Desdemona in Bed Asleep. A Light Burning.*

Enter OTHELLO

OTH.   It is the cause, it is the cause, my soul:
    Let me not name it to you, you chaste stars!
    It is the cause. Yet I 'll not shed her blood,
    Nor scar that whiter skin of hers than snow
    And smooth as monumental alabaster.
    Yet she must die, else she 'll betray more men.
    Put out the light, and then put out the light:
    If I quench thee, thou flaming minister,
    I can again thy former light restore,
    Should I repent me: but once put out thy light,
    Thou cunning'st pattern[1] of excelling nature,

---

5. *fordoes*] ruins, destroys.
1. *pattern*] model.

I know not where is that Promethean heat
That can thy light relume. When I have pluck'd the rose,
I cannot give it vital growth again,
It must needs wither: I 'll smell it on the tree.   [*Kissing her.*]
Ah, balmy breath, that dost almost persuade
Justice to break her sword! One more, one more:
Be thus when thou art dead, and I will kill thee,
And love thee after: one more, and this the last:
So sweet was ne'er so fatal. I must weep,
But they are cruel tears: this sorrow 's heavenly;
It strikes where it doth love. She wakes.

DES.   Who 's there? Othello?
OTH.   Ay, Desdemona.
DES.   Will you come to bed, my lord?
OTH.   Have you pray'd to-night, Desdemona?
DES.   Ay, my lord.
OTH.   If you bethink yourself of any crime
    Unreconciled as yet to heaven and grace,
    Solicit for it straight.
DES.   Alas, my lord, what may you mean by that?
OTH.   Well, do it, and be brief; I will walk by:
    I would not kill thy unprepared spirit;
    No; heaven forfend! I would not kill thy soul.
DES.   Talk you of killing?
OTH.   Ay, I do.
DES.   Then heaven have mercy on me!
OTH.   Amen, with all my heart!
DES.   If you say so, I hope you will not kill me.
OTH.   Hum!
DES.   And yet I fear you; for you are fatal then
    When your eyes roll so: why I should fear I know not,
    Since guiltiness I know not; but yet I feel I fear.
OTH.   Think on thy sins.
DES.   They are loves I bear to you.
OTH.   Ay, and for that thou diest.
DES.   That death 's unnatural that kills for loving.
    Alas, why gnaw you so your nether lip?
    Some bloody passion shakes your very frame:
    These are portents; but yet I hope, I hope,
    They do not point on me.
OTH.   Peace, and be still!
DES.   I will so. What 's the matter?
OTH.   That handkerchief which I so loved and gave thee
    Thou gavest to Cassio.

DES.   No, by my life and soul!
     Send for the man, and ask him.
OTH.   Sweet soul, take heed,
     Take heed of perjury; thou art on thy death-bed.
DES.   Ay, but not yet to die.
OTH.   Yes, presently:
     Therefore confess thee freely of thy sin;
     For to deny each article with oath
     Cannot remove nor choke the strong conception
     That I do groan withal. Thou art to die.
DES.   Then Lord have mercy on me!
OTH.   I say, amen.
DES.   And have you mercy too! I never did
     Offend you in my life; never loved Cassio
     But with such general warranty of heaven
     As I might love: I never gave him token.
OTH.   By heaven, I saw my handkerchief in 's hand.
     O perjured woman! thou dost stone my heart,
     And makest me call what I intend to do
     A murder, which I thought a sacrifice:
     I saw the handkerchief.
DES.   He found it then;
     I never gave it him: send for him hither;
     Let him confess a truth.
OTH.   He hath confess'd.
DES.   What, my lord?
OTH.   That he hath used thee.
DES.   How? unlawfully?
OTH.   Ay.
DES.   He will not say so.
OTH.   No, his mouth is stopp'd;
     Honest Iago hath ta'en order for 't.
DES.   O, my fear interprets! what, is he dead?
OTH.   Had all his hairs been lives, my great revenge
     Had stomach for them all.
DES.   Alas, he is betray'd, and I undone!
OTH.   Out, strumpet! weep'st thou for him to my face?
DES.   O, banish me, my lord, but kill me not!
OTH.   Down, strumpet!
DES.   Kill me to-morrow; let me live to-night!
OTH.   Nay, if you strive,
DES.   But half an hour!
OTH.   Being done, there is no pause.
DES.   But while I say one prayer!

OTH.   It is too late.   [*He stifles her.*]
EMIL.   [*Within*] My lord, my lord! what, ho! my lord, my lord!
OTH.   What noise is this? Not dead? not yet quite dead?
 I that am cruel am yet merciful;
 I would not have thee linger in thy pain:
 So, so.
EMIL.   [*Within*] What, ho! my lord, my lord!
OTH.   Who's there?
EMIL.   [*Within*] O, good my lord, I would speak a word with you!
OTH.   Yes: 't is Emilia. By and by. She 's dead.
 'T is like she comes to speak of Cassio's death.
 The noise was here. Ha! no more moving?
 Still as the grave. Shall she come in? were 't good?
 I think she stirs again. No. What 's best to do?
 If she come in, she 'll sure speak to my wife:
 My wife! my wife! what wife? I have no wife.
 O, insupportable! O heavy hour!
 Methinks it should be now a huge eclipse
 Of sun and moon, and that the affrighted globe
 Should yawn at alteration.
EMIL.   [*Within*] I do beseech you
 That I may speak with you, O, good my lord!
OTH.   I had forgot thee: O, come in, Emilia.
 Soft; by and by. Let me the curtains draw.
 Where art thou?   [*Unlocks the door.*]

Enter EMILIA

    What's the matter with thee now?
EMIL.   O, my good lord, yonder 's foul murders done!
OTH.   What, now?
EMIL.   But now, my lord.
OTH.   It is the very error of the moon;
 She comes more nearer earth than she was wont
 And makes men mad.
EMIL.   Cassio, my lord, hath kill'd a young Venetian
 Call'd Roderigo.
OTH.   Roderigo kill'd!
 And Cassio kill'd!
EMIL.   No, Cassio is not kill'd.
OTH.   Not Cassio kill'd! then murder 's out of tune,
 And sweet revenge grows harsh.
DES.   O, falsely, falsely murder'd!
EMIL.   Alas, what cry is that?

OTH.   That! what?

EMIL.   Out, and alas! that was my lady's voice.
    Help! help, ho! help! O lady, speak again!
    Sweet Desdemona! O sweet mistress, speak!

DES.   A guiltless death I die.

EMIL.   O, who hath done this deed?

DES.   Nobody; I myself. Farewell:
    Commend me to my kind lord: O, farewell!   [*Dies.*]

OTH.   Why, how should she be murder'd?

EMIL.   Alas, who knows?

OTH.   You heard her say herself, it was not I.

EMIL.   She said so: I must needs report the truth.

OTH.   She 's like a liar gone to burning hell:
    'T was I that kill'd her.

EMIL.   O, the more angel she,
    And you the blacker devil!

OTH.   She turn'd to folly, and she was a whore.

EMIL.   Thou dost belie her, and thou art a devil.

OTH.   She was false as water.

EMIL.   Thou art rash as fire, to say
    That she was false: O, she was heavenly true!

OTH.   Cassio did top her; ask thy husband else.
    O, I were damn'd beneath all depth in hell,
    But that I did proceed upon just grounds
    To this extremity. Thy husband knew it all.

EMIL.   My husband!

OTH.   Thy husband.

EMIL.   That she was false to wedlock?

OTH.   Ay, with Cassio. Nay, had she been true,
    If heaven would make me such another world
    Of one entire and perfect chrysolite,
    I 'ld not have sold her for it.

EMIL.   My husband!

OTH.   Ay, 't was he that told me first:
    An honest man he is, and hates the slime
    That sticks on filthy deeds.

EMIL.   My husband!

OTH.   What needs this iteration, woman? I say thy husband.

EMIL.   O mistress, villany hath made mocks with love!
    My husband say that she was false!

OTH.   He, woman;
    I say thy husband: dost understand the word?
    My friend, thy husband, honest, honest Iago.

EMIL.   If he say so, may his pernicious soul

Rot half a grain a day! he lies to the heart:
She was too fond of her most filthy bargain.
OTH.   Ha!
EMIL.   Do thy worst:
This deed of thine is no more worthy heaven
Than thou wast worthy her.
OTH.   Peace, you were best.
EMIL.   Thou hast not half that power to do me harm
As I have to be hurt. O gull! O dolt!
As ignorant as dirt! thou hast done a deed —
I care not for thy sword; I 'll make thee known,
Though I lost twenty lives. Help! help, ho! help!
The Moor hath kill'd my mistress! Murder! murder!

Enter MONTANO, GRATIANO, IAGO, *and others*

MON.   What is the matter? How now, general!
EMIL.   O, are you come, Iago? you have done well,
That men must lay their murders on your neck.
GRA.   What is the matter?
EMIL.   Disprove this villain, if thou be'st a man:
He says thou told'st him that his wife was false:
I know thou didst not, thou 'rt not such a villain.
Speak, for my heart is full.
IAGO.   I told him what I thought, and told no more
Than what he found himself was apt and true.
EMIL.   But did you ever tell him she was false?
IAGO.   I did.
EMIL.   You told a lie, an odious, damned lie;
Upon my soul, a lie, a wicked lie!
She false with Cassio! Did you say with Cassio?
IAGO.   With Cassio, mistress. Go to, charm your tongue.
EMIL.   I will not charm my tongue; I am bound to speak:
My mistress here lies murder'd in her bed, —
ALL.   O heavens forfend!
EMIL.   And your reports have set the murder on.
OTH.   Nay, stare not, masters: it is true indeed.
GRA.   'T is a strange truth.
MON.   O monstrous act!
EMIL.   Villany, villany, villany!
I think upon 't: I think: I smell 't: O villany!
I thought so then: I 'll kill myself for grief:
O villany, villany!
IAGO.   What, are you mad? I charge you, get you home.

EMIL.   Good gentlemen, let me have leave to speak:
    'T is proper I obey him, but not now.
    Perchance, Iago, I will ne'er go home.
OTH.   O! O! O!   [*Falling on the bed.*]
EMIL.   Nay, lay thee down and roar;
    For thou hast kill'd the sweetest innocent
    That e'er did lift up eye.
OTH.   [*Rising*]   O, she was foul!
    I scarce did know you, uncle: there lies your niece,
    Whose breath indeed these hands have newly stopp'd:
    I know this act shows horrible and grim.
GRA.   Poor Desdemona! I am glad thy father 's dead:
    Thy match was mortal to him, and pure grief
    Shore[2] his old thread in twain: did he live now,
    This sight would make him do a desperate turn,
    Yea, curse his better angel from his side,
    And fall to reprobation.
OTH.   'T is pitiful; but yet Iago knows
    That she with Cassio hath the act of shame
    A thousand times committed; Cassio confess'd it:
    And she did gratify his amorous works
    With that recognizance and pledge of love
    Which I first gave her; I saw it in his hand:
    It was a handkerchief, an antique token
    My father gave my mother.
EMIL.   O heaven! O heavenly powers!
IAGO.   'Zounds! hold your peace.
EMIL.   'T will out, 't will out. I peace!
    No, I will speak as liberal as the north:[3]
    Let heaven and men and devils, let them all,
    All, all, cry shame against me, yet I 'll speak.
IAGO.   Be wise, and get you home.
EMIL.   I will not.
             [IAGO *offers to stab* EMILIA.]
GRA.   Fie!
    Your sword upon a woman!
EMIL.   O thou dull Moor! that handkerchief thou speak'st of
    I found by fortune and did give my husband;
    For often with a solemn earnestness,
    More than indeed belong'd to such a trifle,
    He begg'd of me to steal it.

---

2. *Shore*] Cut.
3. *liberal as the north*] as free and as unrestrained as a blast of the north wind.

IAGO.   Villanous whore!

EMIL.   She give it Cassio! no, alas, I found it,
And I did give 't my husband.

IAGO.   Filth, thou liest!

EMIL.   By heaven, I do not, I do not, gentlemen.
O murderous coxcomb! what should such a fool
Do with so good a wife?

OTH.   Are there no stones in heaven
But what serve for the thunder? Precious villain!
        [*He runs at* IAGO: IAGO, *from behind, stabs* EMILIA, *and exit.*]

GRA.   The woman falls: sure, he hath kill'd his wife.

EMIL.   Ay, ay: O, lay me by my mistress' side.

GRA.   He 's gone, but his wife 's kill'd.

MON.   'T is a notorious villain. Take you this weapon,
Which I have here recover'd from the Moor:
Come, guard the door without; let him not pass,
But kill him rather. I 'll after that same villain,
For 't is a damned slave.   [*Exeunt all but* OTHELLO *and* EMILIA.]

OTH.   I am not valiant neither,
But every puny whipster[4] gets my sword.
But why should honour outlive honesty?
Let it go all.

EMIL.   What did thy song bode, lady?
Hark, canst thou hear me? I will play the swan,
And die in music.   [*Singing*] Willow, willow, willow.
Moor, she was chaste; she loved thee, cruel Moor;
So come my soul to bliss, as I speak true;
So speaking as I think, I die, I die.   [*Dies.*]

OTH.   I have another weapon in this chamber;
It is a sword of Spain, the ice-brook's temper. — [5]
O, here it is. Uncle, I must come forth.

GRA.   [*Within*] If thou attempt it, it will cost thee dear:
Thou hast no weapon, and perforce must suffer.

OTH.   Look in upon me then, and speak with me,
Or, naked[6] as I am, I will assault thee.

Re-enter GRATIANO

GRA.   What is the matter?

---

4. *whipster*] "whipper-snapper;" a term of contempt.

5. *a sword of Spain . . . temper*] The best swords came from Spain, and more especially
from Bilboa or Toledo. The steel blades were tempered by plunging the steel while it
was red-hot into ice-cold water.

6. *naked*] unarmed.

OTH.   Behold, I have a weapon;
 A better never did itself sustain
 Upon a soldier's thigh: I have seen the day
 That with this little arm and this good sword
 I have made my way through more impediments
 Than twenty times your stop:[7] but, O vain boast!
 Who can control his fate? 't is not so now.
 Be not afraid, though you do see me weapon'd;
 Here is my journey's end, here is my butt
 And very sea-mark of my utmost sail.
 Do you go back dismay'd? 't is a lost fear:
 Man but a rush against Othello's breast,
 And he retires. Where should Othello go?
 Now, how dost thou look now? O ill-starr'd wench!
 Pale as thy smock! when we shall meet at compt,[8]
 This look of thine will hurl my soul from heaven,
 And fiends will snatch at it. Cold, cold, my girl!
 Even like thy chastity. O cursed slave!
 Whip me, ye devils,
 From the possession of this heavenly sight!
 Blow me about in winds! roast me in sulphur!
 Wash me in steep-down gulfs of liquid fire!
 O Desdemona! Desdemona! dead!
 Oh! Oh! Oh!

Enter LODOVICO, MONTANO, CASSIO *carried in a chair, and* Officers *with*
IAGO, *prisoner*

LOD. Where is this rash and most unfortunate man?
OTH. That 's he that was Othello: here I am.
LOD. Where is that viper? bring the villain forth.
OTH. I look down towards his feet; but that 's a fable.[9]
 If that thou be'st a devil, I cannot kill thee.[10] [*Wounds* IAGO.]
LOD. Wrench his sword from him.
IAGO.   I bleed, sir, but not kill'd.
OTH. I am not sorry neither: I 'ld have thee live;
 For, in my sense, 't is happiness to die.
LOD. O thou Othello, that wert once so good,
 Fall'n in the practice of a damned slave,

---

 7. *your stop*] your power of resistance.
 8. *at compt*] at the day of reckoning or judgment.
 9. *I look down . . . fable*] a reference to the story that the Devil has cloven feet.
 10. *I cannot kill thee*] a reference to the belief that devils are immortal.

What shall be said to thee?

OTH.   Why, any thing:
An honourable murderer, if you will;
For nought did I in hate, but all in honour.

LOD.   This wretch hath part confess'd his villany:
Did you and he consent in Cassio's death?

OTH.   Ay.

CAS.   Dear general, I never gave you cause.

OTH.   I do believe it, and I ask your pardon.
Will you, I pray, demand that demi-devil
Why he hath thus ensnared my soul and body?

IAGO.   Demand me nothing; what you know, you know:
From this time forth I never will speak word.

LOD.   What, not to pray?

GRA.   Torments will ope your lips.

OTH.   Well, thou dost best.

LOD.   Sir, you shall understand what hath befall'n,
Which, as I think, you know not. Here is a letter
Found in the pocket of the slain Roderigo,
And here another: the one of them imports
The death of Cassio to be undertook
By Roderigo.

OTH.   O villain!

CAS.   Most heathenish and most gross!

LOD.   Now here's another discontented paper,
Found in his pocket too; and this, it seems,
Roderigo meant to have sent this damned villain;
But that, belike, Iago in the interim
Came in and satisfied him.

OTH.   O the pernicious caitiff!
How came you, Cassio, by that handkerchief
That was my wife's?

CAS.   I found it in my chamber:
And he himself confess'd but even now
That there he dropp'd it for a special purpose
Which wrought to his desire.

OTH.   O fool! fool! fool!

CAS.   There is besides in Roderigo's letter,
How he upbraids Iago, that he made him
Brave me upon the watch; whereon it came
That I was cast: and even but now he spake
After long seeming dead, Iago hurt him,
Iago set him on.

LOD.   You must forsake this room, and go with us:

Your power and your command is taken off,
And Cassio rules in Cyprus. For this slave,
If there be any cunning cruelty
That can torment him much and hold him long,
It shall be his. You shall close prisoner rest,
Till that the nature of your fault be known
To the Venetian state. Come, bring away.

OTH.   Soft you; a word or two before you go.
I have done the state some service, and they know 't.
No more of that. I pray you, in your letters
When you shall these unlucky deeds relate,
Speak of me as I am; nothing extenuate,
Nor set down aught in malice: then must you speak
Of one that loved not wisely but too well;
Of one not easily jealous, but, being wrought,
Perplex'd in the extreme; of one whose hand,
Like the base Indian, threw a pearl away
Richer than all his tribe; of one whose subdued eyes,
Albeit unused to the melting mood,
Drop tears as fast as the Arabian trees
Their medicinal gum. Set you down this;
And say besides, that in Aleppo once,
Where a malignant and a turban'd Turk
Beat a Venetian and traduced the state,
I took by the throat the circumcised dog
And smote him, thus.   [*Stabs himself.*]

LOD.   O bloody period!
GRA.   All that 's spoke is marr'd.
OTH.   I kiss'd thee ere I kill'd thee: no way but this,
Killing myself, to die upon a kiss.   [*Falls on the bed, and dies.*]

CAS.   This did I fear, but thought he had no weapon;
For he was great of heart.

LOD.   [*To* IAGO]   O Spartan dog,
More fell than anguish, hunger, or the sea!
Look on the tragic loading of this bed;
This is thy work: the object poisons sight;
Let it be hid. Gratiano, keep the house,
And seize upon the fortunes of the Moor,
For they succeed on you. To you, lord governor,
Remains the censure of this hellish villain,
The time, the place, the torture: O, enforce it!
Myself will straight aboard, and to the state
This heavy act with heavy heart relate.   [*Exeunt.*]

Romeo and Juliet

Romeo and Juliet

SHAKESPEARE is thought to have written *Romeo and Juliet* in the mid-1590s. The play, a tragedy of young love become sacrificial in an adverse environment of family feuds and mischance, is one of Shakespeare's earliest efforts in the tragic genre and bears many of the traits of the lyric poetry and romantic comedies with which it is contemporaneous. The immediate source for the play was Arthur Brooke's narrative poem *The Tragical History of Romeus and Juliet* (1562), which was in turn derived from a late-fifteenth-century Italian novella. With its rich Petrarchan strains, its stock characters, and the breadth of poetic forms it employs, *Romeo and Juliet* reveals a Shakespeare still coming to terms with his own technical virtuosity and originality. Yet one's critical reservations tend to be swept aside by the play's moments of comic vitality and its winning vision of innocent love doomed to an untimely end.

SHANE WELLER

Dramatis Personae

ESCALUS, Prince of Verona.
PARIS, a young nobleman, kinsman to the Prince.
MONTAGUE,
CAPULET, heads of two houses at variance with each other.
An old man, of the Capulet family.
ROMEO, son to Montague.
MERCUTIO, kinsman to the Prince, and friend to Romeo.
BENVOLIO, nephew to Montague, and friend to Romeo.
TYBALT, nephew to Lady Capulet.
FRIAR LAURENCE, a Franciscan.
FRIAR JOHN, of the same order.
BALTHASAR, servant to Romeo.
SAMPSON,
GREGORY, servants to Capulet.
PETER, servant to Juliet's nurse.
ABRAHAM, servant to Montague.
An Apothecary.
Three Musicians.
Page to Paris; another Page; an Officer.

LADY MONTAGUE, wife to Montague.
LADY CAPULET, wife to Capulet.
JULIET, daughter to Capulet.
Nurse to Juliet.

Citizens of Verona; kinsfolk of both houses; Maskers, Guards, Watchmen, and Attendants.

Chorus.

SCENE: *Verona; Mantua.*

PROLOGUE.

Enter Chorus.

Chor.   Two households, both alike in dignity,
  In fair Verona, where we lay our scene,
From ancient grudge break to new mutiny,
  Where civil blood makes civil hands unclean.
From forth the fatal loins of these two foes
  A pair of star-cross'd lovers take their life;
Whose misadventured piteous overthrows
  Do with their death bury their parents' strife.
The fearful passage of their death-mark'd love,
  And the continuance of their parents' rage,
Which, but their children's end, nought could remove,
  Is now the two hours' traffic of our stage;
The which if you with patient ears attend,
What here shall miss, our toil shall strive to mend.

ACT I.

SCENE I. *Verona. A public place.*

Enter SAMPSON *and* GREGORY, *of the house of Capulet, with swords and bucklers.*

SAM.   Gregory, on my word, we'll not carry coals.[1]

GRE.   No, for then we should be colliers.

SAM.   I mean, an we be in choler, we'll draw.

GRE.   Ay, while you live, draw your neck out o' the collar.[2]

SAM.   I strike quickly, being moved.

GRE.   But thou art not quickly moved to strike.

SAM.   A dog of the house of Montague moves me.

GRE.   To move is to stir, and to be valiant is to stand: therefore, if thou art moved, thou runn'st away.

SAM.   A dog of that house shall move me to stand: I will take the wall[3] of any man or maid of Montague's.

GRE.   That shows thee a weak slave; for the weakest goes to the wall.

SAM.   'Tis true; and therefore women, being the weaker vessels, are ever thrust to the wall: therefore I will push Montague's men from the wall and thrust his maids to the wall.

GRE.   The quarrel is between our masters and us their men.

SAM.   'Tis all one, I will show myself a tyrant: when I have fought with the men, I will be civil with the maids; I will cut off their heads.

GRE.   The heads of the maids?

SAM.   Ay, the heads of the maids, or their maidenheads; take it in what sense thou wilt.

GRE.   They must take it in sense that feel it.

---

[1] *carry coals*] tolerate insults.
[2] *collar*] hangman's noose.
[3] *take the wall*] walk on the side of the street nearest the wall; thus, insult.

SAM.   Me they shall feel while I am able to stand: and 'tis known I am a pretty piece of flesh.

GRE.   'Tis well thou art not fish; if thou hadst, thou hadst been poor John.[4] Draw thy tool; here comes two of the house of Montagues.

Enter ABRAHAM *and* BALTHASAR.

SAM.   My naked weapon is out: quarrel; I will back thee.

GRE.   How! turn thy back and run?

SAM.   Fear me not.

GRE.   No, marry: I fear thee!

SAM.   Let us take the law of our sides; let them begin.

GRE.   I will frown as I pass by, and let them take it as they list.

SAM.   Nay, as they dare. I will bite my thumb at them; which is a disgrace to them, if they bear it.

ABR.   Do you bite your thumb at us, sir?

SAM.   I do bite my thumb, sir.

ABR.   Do you bite your thumb at us, sir?

SAM.   [*Aside to* GRE.] Is the law of our side, if I say ay?

GRE.   No.

SAM.   No, sir, I do not bite my thumb at you, sir; but I bite my thumb, sir.

GRE.   Do you quarrel, sir?

ABR.   Quarrel, sir! no, sir.

SAM.   But if you do, sir, I am for you: I serve as good a man as you.

ABR.   No better.

SAM.   Well, sir.

Enter BENVOLIO.

GRE.   [*Aside to* SAM.] Say 'better': here comes one of my master's kinsmen.

SAM.   Yes, better, sir.

ABR.   You lie.

SAM.   Draw, if you be men. Gregory, remember thy swashing[5] blow.
                                      [*They fight.*

BEN.   Part, fools!   [*Beating down their weapons.*
Put up your swords; you know not what you do.

---

[4] *poor John*] salted and dried hake, a coarse kind of fish.
[5] *swashing*] smashing.

Enter TYBALT.

TYB.   What, art thou drawn among these heartless hinds?[6] ·
  Turn thee, Benvolio, look upon thy death.
BEN.   I do but keep the peace: put up thy sword,
  Or manage it to part these men with me.
TYB.   What, drawn, and talk of peace! I hate the word,
  As I hate hell, all Montagues, and thee:
  Have at thee, coward!   [*They fight.*

Enter several of both houses, who join the fray; then enter Citizens *and* Peace-officers, *with clubs.*

FIRST OFF.   Clubs, bills,[7] and partisans! strike! beat them down!
  Down with the Capulets! down with the Montagues!

Enter old CAPULET *in his gown, and* LADY CAPULET.

CAP.   What noise is this? Give me my long sword, ho!
LA. CAP.   A crutch, a crutch! why call you for a sword?
CAP.   My sword, I say! Old Montague is come,
  And flourishes his blade in spite of me.

Enter old MONTAGUE *and* LADY MONTAGUE.

MON.   Thou villain Capulet!—Hold me not, let me go.
LA. MON.   Thou shalt not stir one foot to seek a foe.

Enter PRINCE ESCALUS, *with his train.*

PRIN.   Rebellious subjects, enemies to peace,
  Profaners of this neighbour-stained steel,—
  Will they not hear? What, ho! you men, you beasts,
  That quench the fire of your pernicious rage
  With purple fountains issuing from your veins,
  On pain of torture, from those bloody hands
  Throw your mistemper'd weapons to the ground,
  And hear the sentence of your moved prince.
  Three civil brawls, bred of an airy word,
  By thee, old Capulet, and Montague,
  Have thrice disturb'd the quiet of our streets,
  And made Verona's ancient citizens

---

[6] *heartless hinds*] (1) cowardly menials; (2) female deer unprotected by a hart.
[7] *bills*] a kind of pike or halberd.

Cast by their grave beseeming ornaments,
To wield old partisans, in hands as old,
Canker'd with peace, to part your canker'd hate:
If ever you disturb our streets again,
Your lives shall pay the forfeit of the peace.
For this time, all the rest depart away:
You, Capulet, shall go along with me;
And, Montague, come you this afternoon,
To know our farther pleasure in this case,
To old Free-town, our common judgement-place.
Once more, on pain of death, all men depart.

   [*Exeunt all but* MONTAGUE, LADY MONTAGUE, *and* BENVOLIO.

MON.   Who set this ancient quarrel new abroach?
   Speak, nephew, were you by when it began?
BEN.   Here were the servants of your adversary
   And yours close fighting ere I did approach:
   I drew to part them: in the instant came
   The fiery Tybalt, with his sword prepared;
   Which, as he breathed defiance to my ears,
   He swung about his head, and cut the winds,
   Who, nothing hurt withal, hiss'd him in scorn:
   While we were interchanging thrusts and blows,
   Came more and more, and fought on part and part,[8]
   Till the Prince came, who parted either part.
LA. MON.   O, where is Romeo? saw you him to-day?
   Right glad I am he was not at this fray.
BEN.   Madam, an hour before the worshipp'd sun
   Peer'd forth the golden window of the east,
   A troubled mind drave me to walk abroad;
   Where, underneath the grove of sycamore
   That westward rooteth from the city's side,
   So early walking did I see your son:
   Towards him I made; but he was ware of me,
   And stole into the covert of the wood:
   I, measuring his affections[9] by my own,
   Which then most sought where most might not be found,
   Being one too many by my weary self,

[8] *on part and part*] on one side and the other.
[9] *affections*] wishes, inclination.

> Pursued my humour, not pursuing his,
> And gladly shunn'd who gladly fled from me.

MON.　Many a morning hath he there been seen,
> With tears augmenting the fresh morning's dew,
> Adding to clouds more clouds with his deep sighs:
> But all so soon as the all-cheering sun
> Should in the farthest east begin to draw
> The shady curtains from Aurora's bed,
> Away from light steals home my heavy son,
> And private in his chamber pens himself,
> Shuts up his windows, locks fair daylight out,
> And makes himself an artificial night:
> Black and portentous must this humour prove,
> Unless good counsel may the cause remove.

BEN.　My noble uncle, do you know the cause?

MON.　I neither know it nor can learn of him.

BEN.　Have you importuned him by any means?

MON.　Both by myself and many other friends:
> But he, his own affections' counsellor,
> Is to himself—I will not say how true—
> But to himself so secret and so close,
> So far from sounding and discovery,
> As is the bud bit with an envious worm,
> Ere he can spread his sweet leaves to the air,
> Or dedicate his beauty to the sun.
> Could we but learn from whence his sorrows grow,
> We would as willingly give cure as know.

Enter ROMEO.

BEN.　See, where he comes: so please you step aside;
> I'll know his grievance, or be much denied.

MON.　I would thou wert so happy by thy stay,
> To hear true shrift. Come, madam, let's away.

　　　　　　　　　　　　[Exeunt MONTAGUE *and* LADY.

BEN.　Good morrow, cousin.

ROM.　　　　　　　　　　Is the day so young?

BEN.　But new struck nine.

ROM.　　　　　　　　　Ay me! sad hours seem long.
> Was that my father that went hence so fast?

BEN.　It was. What sadness lengthens Romeo's hours?

ROM.　Not having that which, having, makes them short.

BEN.　In love?

Rom.   Out—
Ben.   Of love?
Rom.   Out of her favour, where I am in love.
Ben.   Alas, that love, so gentle in his view,
    Should be so tyrannous and rough in proof![10]
Rom.   Alas, that love, whose view is muffled still,
    Should without eyes see pathways to his will!
    Where shall we dine? O me! What fray was here?
    Yet tell me not, for I have heard it all.
    Here's much to do with hate, but more with love:
    Why, then, O brawling love! O loving hate!
    O any thing, of nothing first create!
    O heavy lightness! serious vanity!
    Mis-shapen chaos of well-seeming forms!
    Feather of lead, bright smoke, cold fire, sick health!
    Still-waking sleep, that is not what it is!
    This love feel I, that feel no love in this.
    Dost thou not laugh?
Ben.   No, coz, I rather weep.
Rom.   Good heart, at what?
Ben.   At thy good heart's oppression.
Rom.   Why, such is love's transgression.
    Griefs of mine own lie heavy in my breast;
    Which thou wilt propagate,[11] to have it prest
    With more of thine: this love that thou hast shown
    Doth add more grief to too much of mine own.
    Love is a smoke raised with the fume of sighs;
    Being purged, a fire sparkling in lovers' eyes;
    Being vex'd, a sea nourish'd with lovers' tears:
    What is it else? a madness most discreet,
    A choking gall and a preserving sweet.
    Farewell, my coz.
Ben.   Soft! I will go along:
    An if you leave me so, you do me wrong.
Rom.   Tut, I have lost myself; I am not here;
    This is not Romeo, he's some other where.
Ben.   Tell me in sadness,[12] who is that you love?
Rom.   What, shall I groan and tell thee?

---

[10] *proof*] experience.
[11] *propagate*] increase.
[12] *sadness*] seriousness.

BEN.   Groan! why, no;
    But sadly tell me who.
ROM.   Bid a sick man in sadness make his will:
    Ah, word ill urged to one that is so ill!
    In sadness, cousin, I do love a woman.
BEN.   I aim'd so near when I supposed you loved.
ROM.   A right good mark-man! And she's fair I love.
BEN.   A right fair mark, fair coz, is soonest hit.
ROM.   Well, in that hit you miss: she'll not be hit
    With Cupid's arrow; she hath Dian's wit,
    And in strong proof[13] of chastity well arm'd,
    From love's weak childish bow she lives unharm'd.
    She will not stay[14] the siege of loving terms,
    Nor bide the encounter of assailing eyes,
    Nor ope her lap to saint-seducing gold:
    O, she is rich in beauty, only poor
    That, when she dies, with beauty dies her store.
BEN.   Then she hath sworn that she will still[15] live chaste?
ROM.   She hath, and in that sparing makes huge waste;
    For beauty, starved with her severity,
    Cuts beauty off from all posterity.
    She is too fair, too wise, wisely too fair,
    To merit bliss by making me despair:
    She hath forsworn to love; and in that vow
    Do I live dead, that live to tell it now.
BEN.   Be ruled by me, forget to think of her.
ROM.   O, teach me how I should forget to think.
BEN.   By giving liberty unto thine eyes;
    Examine other beauties.
ROM.   'Tis the way
    To call hers, exquisite, in question more:[16]
    These happy masks that kiss fair ladies' brows,
    Being black, put us in mind they hide the fair;
    He that is strucken blind cannot forget
    The precious treasure of his eyesight lost:
    Show me a mistress that is passing[17] fair,

---

[13] *proof*] impenetrable armor.
[14] *stay*] undergo, endure.
[15] *still*] always.
[16] *in question more*] even more strongly to mind.
[17] *passing*] exceedingly.

What doth her beauty serve but as a note
Where I may read who pass'd that passing fair?
Farewell: thou canst not teach me to forget.
BEN.   I'll pay that doctrine,[18] or else die in debt.   [*Exeunt.*

SCENE II. *A street.*

Enter CAPULET, PARIS, *and* Servant.

CAP.   But Montague is bound as well as I,
In penalty alike; and 'tis not hard, I think,
For men so old as we to keep the peace.
PAR.   Of honourable reckoning[1] are you both;
And pity 'tis you lived at odds so long.
But now, my lord, what say you to my suit?
CAP.   But saying o'er what I have said before:
My child is yet a stranger in the world;
She hath not seen the change of fourteen years:
Let two more summers wither in their pride
Ere we may think her ripe to be a bride.
PAR.   Younger than she are happy mothers made.
CAP.   And too soon marr'd are those so early made.
The earth hath swallow'd all my hopes but she,
She is the hopeful lady of my earth:[2]
But woo her, gentle Paris, get her heart;
My will to her consent is but a part;
An she agree, within her scope of choice
Lies my consent and fair according voice.
This night I hold an old accustom'd feast,
Whereto I have invited many a guest,
Such as I love; and you among the store,
One more, most welcome, makes my number more.
At my poor house look to behold this night
Earth-treading stars that make dark heaven light:
Such comfort as do lusty young men feel
When well-apparell'd April on the heel

[18] *pay that doctrine*] give that instruction.

---

[1] *reckoning*] repute.
[2] *hopeful . . . earth*] heir of my property and line.

Of limping winter treads, even such delight
Among fresh female buds shall you this night
Inherit at my house; hear all, all see,
And like her most whose merit most shall be:
Which on more view, of many mine being one
May stand in number, though in reckoning none.
Come, go with me. [*To Servant*] Go, sirrah, trudge about
Through fair Verona; find those persons out
Whose names are written there, and to them say,
My house and welcome on their pleasure stay.

[*Exeunt* CAPULET *and* PARIS.

SERV. Find them out whose names are written here! It is written that the
shoemaker should meddle with his yard and the tailor with his last,[3]
the fisher with his pencil and the painter with his nets; but I am sent
to find those persons whose names are here writ, and can never find
what names the writing person hath here writ. I must to the learned.
In good time.

Enter BENVOLIO *and* ROMEO.

BEN. Tut, man, one fire burns out another's burning.
    One pain is lessen'd by another's anguish;
  Turn giddy, and be holp by backward turning;
    One desperate grief cures with another's languish:
  Take thou some new infection to thy eye,
  And the rank poison of the old will die.
ROM. Your plantain-leaf is excellent for that.
BEN. For what, I pray thee?
ROM.   For your broken shin.
BEN. Why, Romeo, art thou mad?
ROM. Not mad, but bound more than a madman is;
    Shut up in prison, kept without my food,
    Whipt and tormented and— God-den,[4] good fellow.
SERV. God gi' god-den. I pray, sir, can you read?
ROM. Ay, mine own fortune in my misery.
SERV. Perhaps you have learned it without book: but, I pray, can you
    read any thing you see?
ROM. Ay, if I know the letters and the language.
SERV. Ye say honestly: rest you merry!
ROM. Stay, fellow; I can read.

[*Reads.*

---

[3] *last*] the mold on which shoes are made.
[4] *God-den*] Good evening.

'Signior Martino and his wife and daughters; County Anselme and his
beauteous sisters; the lady widow of Vitruvio; Signior Placentio and
his lovely nieces; Mercutio and his brother Valentine; mine uncle
Capulet, his wife, and daughters; my fair niece Rosaline; Livia;
Signior Valentio and his cousin Tybalt; Lucio and the lively Helena.'

A fair assembly: whither should they come?

SERV.   Up. [5]

ROM.   Whither? to supper?

SERV.   To our house.

ROM.   Whose house?

SERV.   My master's.

ROM.   Indeed, I should have ask'd you that before.

SERV.   Now I'll tell you without asking: my master is the great rich
        Capulet; and if you be not of the house of Montagues, I pray, come
        and crush a cup of wine. Rest you merry!   [*Exit.*

BEN.   At this same ancient feast of Capulet's
        Sups the fair Rosaline whom thou so lovest,
        With all the admired beauties of Verona:
        Go thither, and with unattainted[6] eye
        Compare her face with some that I shall show,
        And I will make thee think thy swan a crow.

ROM.   When the devout religion of mine eye
            Maintains such falsehood, then turn tears to fires;
        And these, who, often drown'd, could never die,
            Transparent heretics, be burnt for liars!
        One fairer than my love! the all-seeing sun
        Ne'er saw her match since first the world begun.

BEN.   Tut, you saw her fair, none else being by,
        Herself poised with herself in either eye:
        But in that crystal scales let there be weigh'd
        Your lady's love against some other maid,
        That I will show you shining at this feast,
        And she shall scant show well that now seems best.

ROM.   I'll go along, no such sight to be shown,
        But to rejoice in splendour of mine own.   [*Exeunt.*

---

[5] *come . . . Up*] The servant is quibbling, "come up" being a vulgar phrase.
[6] *unattainted*] not infected, impartial.

Scene III. *A room in Capulet's house.*

Enter Lady Capulet *and* Nurse.

La. Cap. Nurse, where's my daughter? call her forth to me.
Nurse. Now, by my maidenhead at twelve year old,
    I bade her come. What, lamb! what, lady-bird!
    God forbid!—Where's this girl? What, Juliet!

Enter Juliet.

Jul. How now! who calls?
Nurse. Your mother.
Jul. Madam, I am here. What is your will?
La. Cap. This is the matter. Nurse, give leave awhile,
    We must talk in secret:—Nurse, come back again;
    I have remember'd me, thou's[1] hear our counsel.
    Thou know'st my daughter's of a pretty age.
Nurse. Faith, I can tell her age unto an hour.
La. Cap. She's not fourteen.
Nurse.   I'll lay fourteen of my teeth,—
    And yet, to my teen[2] be it spoken, I have but four,—
    She is not fourteen. How long is it now
    To Lammas-tide?
La. Cap. A fortnight and odd days.
Nurse. Even or odd, of all days in the year,
    Come Lammas-eve at night shall she be fourteen.
    Susan and she—God rest all Christian souls!—
    Were of an age: well, Susan is with God;
    She was too good for me:—but, as I said,
    On Lammas-eve at night shall she be fourteen;
    That shall she, marry; I remember it well.
    'Tis since the earthquake now eleven years;
    And she was wean'd,—I never shall forget it—
    Of all the days of the year, upon that day:
    For I had then laid wormwood[3] to my dug,
    Sitting in the sun under the dove-house wall;

---

[1] *thou's*] thou shalt.
[2] *teen*] grief, pain.
[3] *wormwood*] *Artemisia absinthium*, proverbial for its bitterness and medicinal properties.

My lord and you were then at Mantua:—
Nay, I do bear a brain:—but, as I said,
When it did taste the wormwood on the nipple
Of my dug, and felt it bitter, pretty fool,
To see it tetchy, and fall out with the dug!
Shake, quoth the dove-house: 'twas no need, I trow,
To bid me trudge.
And since that time it is eleven years;
For then she could stand high-lone;[4] nay, by the rood,
She could have run and waddled all about;
For even the day before, she broke her brow:[5]
And then my husband,—God be with his soul!
A' was a merry man—took up the child:
'Yea,' quoth he, 'dost thou fall upon thy face?
Thou wilt fall backward when thou hast more wit;
Wilt thou not, Jule?' and, by my holidame,[6]
The pretty wretch left crying, and said 'Ay.'
To see now how a jest shall come about!
I warrant, an I should live a thousand years,
I never should forget it: 'Wilt thou not, Jule?' quoth he;
And, pretty fool, it stinted,[7] and said 'Ay.'

LA. CAP.   Enough of this; I pray thee, hold thy peace.

NURSE.   Yes, madam: yet I cannot choose but laugh,
To think it should leave crying, and say 'Ay':
And yet, I warrant, it had upon it brow
A bump as big as a young cockerel's stone;[8]
A perilous knock; and it cried bitterly:
'Yea,' quoth my husband, 'fall'st upon thy face?
Thou wilt fall backward when thou comest to age;
Wilt thou not, Jule?' It stinted, and said 'Ay.'

JUL.   And stint thou too, I pray thee, Nurse, say I.

NURSE.   Peace, I have done. God mark thee to his grace!
Thou wast the prettiest babe that e'er I nursed:
An I might live to see thee married once,[9]
I have my wish.

LA. CAP.   Marry, that 'marry' is the very theme

---

[4] *high-lone*] on her own feet, unsupported.
[5] *broke her brow*] (fell and) cut her head.
[6] *holidame*] halldom, salvation.
[7] *stinted*] ceased.
[8] *stone*] testicle.
[9] *once*] ever, at some time.

    I came to talk of. Tell me, daughter Juliet,
    How stands your disposition to be married?
JUL.   It is an honour that I dream not of.
NURSE.   An honour! were not I thine only nurse,
    I would say thou hadst suck'd wisdom from thy teat.
LA. CAP.   Well, think of marriage now; younger than you
    Here in Verona, ladies of esteem,
    Are made already mothers. By my count,
    I was your mother much upon these years
    That you are now a maid. Thus then in brief;
    The valiant Paris seeks you for his love.
NURSE.   A man, young lady! lady, such a man
    As all the world—why, he's a man of wax. [10]
LA. CAP.   Verona's summer hath not such a flower.
NURSE.   Nay, he's a flower; in faith, a very flower.
LA. CAP.   What say you? can you love the gentleman?
    This night you shall behold him at our feast:
    Read o'er the volume of young Paris' face,
    And find delight writ there with beauty's pen;
    Examine every married[11] lineament,
    And see how one another lends content;
    And what obscured in this fair volume lies
    Find written in the margent of his eyes.
    This precious book of love, this unbound lover,
    To beautify him, only lacks a cover:
    The fish lives in the sea; and 'tis much pride
    For fair without the fair within to hide:
    That book in many's eyes doth share the glory,
    That in gold clasps locks in the golden story:
    So shall you share all that he doth possess,
    By having him making yourself no less.
NURSE.   No less! nay, bigger: women grow by men.
LA. CAP.   Speak briefly, can you like of Paris' love?
JUL.   I'll look to like, if looking liking move:
    But no more deep will I endart mine eye
    Than your consent gives strength to make it fly.

Enter a Servingman.

---

[10] *a man of wax*] as handsome as if modeled in wax.
[11] *married*] proportioned.

SERV.   Madam, the guests are come, supper served up, you called, my
        young lady asked for, the Nurse cursed in the pantry, and every
        thing in extremity. I must hence to wait; I beseech you, follow
        straight.
LA. CAP.   We follow thee. [*Exit* Servingman.] Juliet, the County stays.
NURSE.   Go, girl, seek happy nights to happy days.   [*Exeunt.*

SCENE IV. *A street.*

Enter ROMEO, MERCUTIO, BENVOLIO, *with five or six other* Maskers, *and*
Torch-bearers.

ROM.   What, shall this speech be spoke for our excuse?
        Or shall we on without apology?
BEN.   The date is out of such prolixity:
        We'll have no Cupid hoodwink'd[1] with a scarf,
        Bearing a Tartar's painted bow of lath,
        Scaring the ladies like a crow-keeper;[2]
        Nor no without-book prologue, faintly spoke
        After the prompter, for our entrance:
        But, let them measure us by what they will,
        We'll measure them a measure,[3] and be gone.
ROM.   Give me a torch: I am not for this ambling;[4]
        Being but heavy, I will bear the light.
MER.   Nay, gentle Romeo, we must have you dance.
ROM.   Not I, believe me: you have dancing shoes
        With nimble soles: I have a soul of lead
        So stakes me to the ground, I cannot move.
MER.   You are a lover; borrow Cupid's wings,
        And soar with them above a common bound.
ROM.   I am too sore enpierced with his shaft
        To soar with his light feathers, and so bound,
        I cannot bound a pitch[5] above dull woe:
        Under love's heavy burthen do I sink.

---

[1] *hoodwink'd*] blindfolded.
[2] *crow-keeper*] scarecrow.
[3] *measure them a measure*] dance.
[4] *ambling*] affected movement, as in a dance.
[5] *pitch*] height to which the falcon soars before swooping down for the kill.

MER. And, to sink in it, should you burthen love;
   Too great oppression for a tender thing.
ROM. Is love a tender thing? it is too rough,
   Too rude, too boisterous, and it pricks like thorn.
MER. If love be rough with you, be rough with love;
   Prick love for pricking, and you beat love down.
   Give me a case[6] to put my visage in:
   A visor for a visor! what care I
   What curious eye doth quote[7] deformities?
   Here are the beetle-brows shall blush for me.
BEN. Come, knock and enter, and no sooner in
   But every man betake him to his legs.
ROM. A torch for me: let wantons light of heart
   Tickle the senseless rushes with their heels;
   For I am proverb'd with a grandsire phrase;
   I'll be a candle-holder, and look on.
   The game was ne'er so fair, and I am done.
MER. Tut, dun's the mouse,[8] the constable's own word:
   If thou art dun, we'll draw thee from the mire
   Of this sir-reverence[9] love, wherein thou stick'st
   Up to the ears. Come, we burn daylight, ho.
ROM. Nay, that's not so.
MER.   I mean, sir, in delay
   We waste our lights in vain, like lamps by day.
   Take our good[10] meaning, for our judgement sits
   Five times in that ere once in our five wits.
ROM. And we mean well, in going to this mask;
   But 'tis no wit to go.
MER.   Why, may one ask?
ROM. I dreamt a dream to-night.
MER.   And so did I.
ROM. Well, what was yours?
MER.   That dreamers often lie.
ROM. In bed asleep, while they do dream things true.
MER. O, then, I see Queen Mab hath been with you.
   She is the fairies' midwife, and she comes
   In shape no bigger than an agate-stone

---

   [6] *case*] mask.
   [7] *quote*] perceive.
   [8] *dun's the mouse*] a proverbial expression meaning "stay still."
   [9] *sir-reverence*] a corruption of "save your reverence," a form of apology.
   [10] *good*] intended.

On the fore-finger of an alderman,
Drawn with a team of little atomies[11]
Athwart men's noses as they lie asleep:
Her waggon-spokes made of long spinners' legs;
The cover, of the wings of grasshoppers;
Her traces, of the smallest spider's web;
Her collars, of the moonshine's watery beams;
Her whip, of cricket's bone; the lash, of film;[12]
Her waggoner, a small grey-coated gnat,
Not half so big as a round little worm
Prick'd from the lazy finger of a maid:
Her chariot is an empty hazel-nut,
Made by the joiner squirrel or old grub,
Time out o' mind the fairies' coachmakers.
And in this state she gallops night by night
Through lovers' brains, and then they dream of love;
O'er courtiers' knees, that dream on court'sies straight;[13]
O'er lawyers' fingers, who straight dream on fees;
O'er ladies' lips, who straight on kisses dream,
Which oft the angry Mab with blisters plagues,
Because their breaths with sweetmeats tainted are:
Sometime she gallops o'er a courtier's nose,
And then dreams he of smelling out a suit;
And sometime comes she with a tithe-pig's tail
Tickling a parson's nose as a' lies asleep,
Then dreams he of another benefice:
Sometime she driveth o'er a soldier's neck,
And then dreams he of cutting foreign throats,
Of breaches, ambuscadoes, Spanish blades,
Of healths five fathom deep; and then anon
Drums in his ear, at which he starts and wakes,
And being thus frighted swears a prayer or two,
And sleeps again. This is that very Mab
That plats the manes of horses in the night,
And bakes the elf-locks[14] in foul sluttish hairs,
Which once untangled much misfortune bodes:
This is the hag, when maids lie on their backs,
That presses them and learns them first to bear,

[11] *atomies*] tiny creatures.
[12] *film*] gossamer.
[13] *straight*] immediately.
[14] *elf-locks*] tangles.

Making them women of good carriage:
This is she—

ROM.   Peace, peace, Mercutio, peace!
Thou talk'st of nothing.

MER.   True, I talk of dreams;
Which are the children of an idle brain,
Begot of nothing but vain fantasy,
Which is as thin of substance as the air,
And more inconstant than the wind, who wooes
Even now the frozen bosom of the north,
And, being anger'd, puffs away from thence,
Turning his face to the dew-dropping south.

BEN.   This wind you talk of blows us from ourselves;
Supper is done, and we shall come too late.

ROM.   I fear, too early: for my mind misgives
Some consequence, yet hanging in the stars,
Shall bitterly begin his fearful date[15]
With this night's revels, and expire the term
Of a despised life closed in my breast,
By some vile forfeit of untimely death:
But He, that hath the steerage of my course,
Direct my sail! On, lusty gentlemen.

BEN.   Strike, drum.   *[Exeunt.*

SCENE V. *A hall in Capulet's house.*

Musicians *waiting. Enter* Servingmen, *with napkins.*

FIRST SERV.   Where's Potpan, that he helps not to take away? he shift a
trencher![1] he scrape a trencher!

SEC. SERV.   When good manners shall lie all in one or two men's hands,
and they unwashed too, 'tis a foul thing.

FIRST SERV.   Away with the joint-stools,[2] remove the court-cupboard,[3]
look to the plate. Good thou, save me a piece of marchpane;[4] and,
as thou lovest me, let the porter let in Susan Grindstone and Nell.
Antony, and Potpan!

---

[15] *date*] time, duration.

---

[1] *trencher*] plate.
[2] *joint-stools*] wooden stools.
[3] *court-cupboard*] movable buffet or closet.
[4] *marchpane*] sweet biscuit made of sugar and almonds.

SEC. SERV.   Ay, boy, ready.

FIRST SERV.   You are looked for and called for, asked for and sought for,
in the great chamber.

THIRD SERV.   We cannot be here and there too. Cheerly, boys; be brisk a
while, and the longer liver take all.   *   [*They retire behind.*

Enter CAPULET, *with* JULIET *and others of his house, meeting the* Guests
and Maskers.

CAP.   Welcome, gentlemen! ladies that have their toes
Unplagued with corns will have a bout with you:
Ah ha, my mistresses! which of you all
Will now deny to dance? she that makes dainty,
She, I'll swear, hath corns; am I come near ye now?
Welcome, gentlemen! I have seen the day .
That I have worn a visor, and could tell
A whispering tale in a fair lady's ear,
Such as would please: 'tis gone, 'tis gone, 'tis gone:
You are welcome, gentlemen! Come, musicians, play.
A hall, a hall! give room! and foot it, girls.
                              [*Music plays, and they dance.*
More light, you knaves; and turn the tables up,
And quench the fire, the room is grown too hot.
Ah, sirrah, this unlook'd-for sport comes well.
Nay, sit, nay, sit, good cousin Capulet;
For you and I are past our dancing days:
How long is't now since last yourself and I
Were in a mask?

SEC. CAP.   By'r lady, thirty years.

CAP.   What, man! 'tis not so much, 'tis not so much:
'Tis since the nuptial of Lucentio,
Come Pentecost as quickly as it will,
Some five and twenty years; and then we mask'd.

SEC. CAP.   'Tis more, 'tis more: his son is elder, sir;
His son is thirty.

CAP.   Will you tell me that?
His son was but a ward two years ago.

ROM.   [*To a* Servingman] What lady's that, which doth enrich the hand
Of yonder knight?

SERV.   I know not, sir.

ROM.   O, she doth teach the torches to burn bright!
It seems she hangs upon the cheek of night

Like a rich jewel in an Ethiop's ear;
Beauty too rich for use, for earth too dear!
So shows a snowy dove trooping with crows,
As yonder lady o'er her fellows shows.
The measure done, I'll watch her place of stand,
And, touching hers, make blessed my rude hand.
Did my heart love till now? forswear it, sight!
For I ne'er saw true beauty till this night.

TYB. This, by his voice, should be a Montague.
Fetch me my rapier, boy. What dares the slave
Come hither, cover'd with an antic face, [5]
To fleer[6] and scorn at our solemnity?
Now, by the stock and honour of my kin,
To strike him dead I hold it not a sin.

CAP. Why, how now, kinsman! wherefore storm you so?

TYB. Uncle, this is a Montague, our foe;
A villain, that is hither come in spite,
To scorn at our solemnity this night.

CAP. Young Romeo is it?

TYB.   'Tis he, that villain Romeo.

CAP. Content thee, gentle coz, let him alone,
He bears him like a portly[7] gentleman;
And, to say truth, Verona brags of him
To be a virtuous and well-govern'd youth:
I would not for the wealth of all this town
Here in my house do him disparagement:
Therefore be patient, take no note of him:
It is my will, the which if thou respect,
Show a fair presence and put off these frowns,
An ill-beseeming semblance for a feast.

TYB. It fits, when such a villain is a guest:
I'll not endure him.

CAP.   He shall be endured:
What, goodman[8] boy! I say, he shall: go to;
Am I the master here, or you? go to.
You'll not endure him! God shall mend my soul,

---

[5] *antic face*] odd-looking mask.
[6] *fleer*] grin mockingly.
[7] *portly*] well-bred, dignified.
[8] *goodman*] below the rank of gentleman.

You'll make a mutiny among my guests!
You will set cock-a-hoop!⁹ you'll be the man!

TYB.   Why, uncle, 'tis a shame.

CAP.   Go to, go to;
You are a saucy boy: is't so, indeed?
This trick may chance to scathe you, I know what:
You must contrary me! marry, 'tis time.
Well said, my hearts! You are a princox; go:
Be quiet, or— More light, more light! For shame!
I'll make you quiet. What, cheerly, my hearts!

TYB.   Patience perforce with wilful choler meeting
Makes my flesh tremble in their different greeting.
I will withdraw: but this intrusion shall,
Now seeming sweet, convert to bitterest gall.   [Exit.

ROM.   [To JULIET] If I profane with my unworthiest hand
This holy shrine, the gentle fine is this,
My lips, two blushing pilgrims, ready stand
To smooth that rough touch with a tender kiss.

JUL.   Good pilgrim, you do wrong your hand too much,
Which mannerly devotion shows in this;
For saints have hands that pilgrims' hands do touch,
And palm to palm is holy palmers' kiss.

ROM.   Have not saints lips, and holy palmers too?

JUL.   Ay, pilgrim, lips that they must use in prayer.

ROM.   O, then, dear saint, let lips do what hands do;
They pray, grant thou, lest faith turn to despair.

JUL.   Saints do not move, though grant for prayers' sake.

ROM.   Then move not, while my prayer's effect I take.
Thus from my lips by thine my sin is purged.   [Kissing her.

JUL.   Then have my lips the sin that they have took.

ROM.   Sin from my lips? O trespass sweetly urged!
Give me my sin again.

JUL.   You kiss by the book.

NURSE.   Madam, your mother craves a word with you.

ROM.   What is her mother?

NURSE.   Marry, bachelor,
Her mother is the lady of the house,
And a good lady, and a wise and virtuous:
I nursed her daughter, that you talk'd withal;

⁹ set cock-a-hoop] pick a quarrel.

I tell you, he that can lay hold of her
Shall have the chinks.[10]

ROM.   Is she a Capulet?
O dear account! my life is my foe's debt.

BEN.   Away, be gone; the sport is at the best.

ROM.   Ay, so I fear; the more is my unrest.

CAP.   Nay, gentlemen, prepare not to be gone;
We have a trifling foolish[11] banquet towards.[12]
Is it e'en so? why, then, I thank you all;
I thank you, honest gentlemen; good night.
More torches here! Come on then, let's to bed.
Ah, sirrah, by my fay, it waxes late:
I'll to my rest.   [*Exeunt all but* JULIET *and* NURSE.

JUL.   Come hither, Nurse. What is yond gentleman?

NURSE.   The son and heir of old Tiberio.

JUL.   What's he that now is going out of door?

NURSE.   Marry, that, I think, be young Petruchio.

JUL.   What's he that follows there, that would not dance?

NURSE.   I know not.

JUL.   Go ask his name. If he be married,
My grave is like to be my wedding bed.

NURSE.   His name is Romeo, and a Montague,
The only son of your great enemy.

JUL.   My only love sprung from my only hate!
Too early seen unknown, and known too late!
Prodigious birth of love it is to me,
That I must love a loathed enemy.

NURSE.   What's this? what's this?

JUL.   A rhyme I learn'd even now
Of one I danced withal.   [*One calls within 'Juliet.'*

NURSE.   Anon, anon!
Come, let's away; the strangers all are gone.   [*Exeunt.*

---

[10] *have the chinks*] acquire a financial fortune.
[11] *foolish*] small-scale.
[12] *towards*] in preparation.

ACT II.

PROLOGUE.

Enter Chorus.

CHOR.　Now old desire doth in his death-bed lie,
　　　And young affection gapes to be his heir;
　　That fair for which love groan'd for and would die,
　　　With tender Juliet match'd, is now not fair.
　　Now Romeo is beloved and loves again,
　　　Alike bewitched by the charm of looks,
　　But to his foe supposed he must complain,
　　　And she steal love's sweet bait from fearful hooks:
　　Being held a foe, he may not have access
　　　To breathe such vows as lovers use to swear;
　　And she as much in love, her means much less
　　　To meet her new beloved any where:
　　But passion lends them power, time means, to meet,
　　Tempering extremities with extreme sweet.　　　　　　|*Exit.*

SCENE I. *A lane by the wall of Capulet's orchard.*

Enter ROMEO, *alone.*

ROM.　Can I go forward when my heart is here?
　　Turn back, dull earth, and find thy centre out.
　　　　　　　[*He climbs the wall, and leaps down within it.*

Enter BENVOLIO *with* MERCUTIO.

BEN.　Romeo! my cousin Romeo!
MER.　　　　　　　　　　　　　He is wise;

    And, on my life, hath stol'n him home to bed.
BEN.   He ran this way, and leap'd this orchard wall:
    Call, good Mercutio.
MER.   Nay, I'll conjure too.
    Romeo! humours! madman! passion! lover!
    Appear thou in the likeness of a sigh:
    Speak but one rhyme, and I am satisfied;
    Cry but 'ay me!' pronounce but 'love' and 'dove';
    Speak to my gossip Venus one fair word,
    One nick-name for her purblind son and heir,
    Young Adam Cupid, he that shot so trim
    When King Cophetua[1] loved the beggar-maid!
    He heareth not, he stirreth not, he moveth not;
    The ape[2] is dead, and I must conjure him.
    I conjure thee by Rosaline's bright eyes,
    By her high forehead and her scarlet lip,
    By her fine foot, straight leg and quivering thigh,
    And the demesnes that there adjacent lie,
    That in thy likeness thou appear to us!
BEN.   An if he hear thee, thou wilt anger him.
MER.   This cannot anger him: 'twould anger him
    To raise a spirit in his mistress' circle
    Of some strange[3] nature, letting it there stand
    Till she had laid it and conjured it down;
    That were some spite: my invocation
    Is fair and honest, and in his mistress' name
    I conjure only but to raise up him.
BEN.   Come, he hath hid himself among these trees,
    To be consorted[4] with the humorous[5] night:
    Blind is his love, and best befits the dark.
MER.   If love be blind, love cannot hit the mark.
    Now will he sit under a medlar-tree,
    And wish his mistress were that kind of fruit
    As maids call medlars when they laugh alone.
    O, Romeo, that she were, O, that she were
    An open et cetera, thou a poperin pear![6]

---

[1] *King Cophetua*] a legendary figure who married a beggar.
[2] *ape*] a term of endearment.
[3] *strange*] other person's.
[4] *consorted*] associated.
[5] *humorous*] damp and inducing strange moods.
[6] *medlars . . . poperin pear*] the fruits are euphemisms for sexual organs.

Romeo, good night: I'll to my truckle-bed;[7]
This field-bed is too cold for me to sleep:
Come, shall we go?

BEN.   Go then, for 'tis in vain.
To seek him here that means not to be found.   [*Exeunt.*

SCENE II. *Capulet's orchard.*

Enter ROMEO.

ROM.   He jests at scars that never felt a wound.

                  [JULIET *appears above at a window.*
But, soft! what light through yonder window breaks?
It is the east, and Juliet is the sun!
Arise, fair sun, and kill the envious moon,
Who is already sick and pale with grief,
That thou her maid art far more fair than she:
Be not her maid, since she is envious;
Her vestal livery is but sick and green,
And none but fools do wear it; cast it off.
It is my lady; O, it is my love!
O, that she knew she were!
She speaks, yet she says nothing: what of that?
Her eye discourses, I will answer it.
I am too bold, 'tis not to me she speaks:
Two of the fairest stars in all the heaven,
Having some business, do intreat her eyes
To twinkle in their spheres till they return.
What if her eyes were there, they in her head?
The brightness of her cheek would shame those stars,
As daylight doth a lamp; her eyes in heaven
Would through the airy region stream so bright
That birds would sing and think it were not night.
See, how she leans her cheek upon her hand!
O, that I were a glove upon that hand,
That I might touch that cheek!

JUL.   Ay me!

ROM.   She speaks:

---

[7] *truckle-bed*] a bed on casters that could be pushed under another bed.

    O, speak again, bright angel! for thou art
    As glorious to this night, being o'er my head,
    As is a winged messenger of heaven
    Unto the white-upturned wondering eyes
    Of mortals that fall back to gaze on him,
    When he bestrides the lazy-pacing clouds
    And sails upon the bosom of the air.

JUL.   O Romeo, Romeo! wherefore art thou Romeo?
    Deny thy father and refuse thy name;
    Or, if thou wilt not, be but sworn my love,
    And I'll no longer be a Capulet.

ROM.   [*Aside*] Shall I hear more, or shall I speak at this?

JUL.   'Tis but thy name that is my enemy;
    Thou art thyself, though not a Montague.
    What's Montague? it is nor hand, nor foot,
    Nor arm, nor face, nor any other part
    Belonging to a man. O, be some other name!
    What's in a name? that which we call a rose
    By any other name would smell as sweet;
    So Romeo would, were he not Romeo call'd,
    Retain that dear perfection which he owes[1]
    Without that title. Romeo, doff thy name,
    And for thy name, which is no part of thee,
    Take all myself.

ROM.   I take thee at thy word:
    Call me but love, and I'll be new baptized;
    Henceforth I never will be Romeo.

JUL.   What man art thou, that, thus bescreen'd in night,
    So stumblest on my counsel?

ROM.   By a name
    I know not how to tell thee who I am:
    My name, dear saint, is hateful to myself,
    Because it is an enemy to thee;
    Had I it written, I would tear the word.

JUL.   My ears have yet not drunk a hundred words
    Of thy tongue's uttering, yet I know the sound:
    Art thou not Romeo, and a Montague?

ROM.   Neither, fair maid, if either thee dislike.

JUL.   How camest thou hither, tell me, and wherefore?

---

[1] *owes*] possesses.

The orchard walls are high and hard to climb,
And the place death, considering who thou art,
If any of my kinsmen find thee here.

ROM.   With love's light wings did I o'er-perch these walls,
For stony limits cannot hold love out:
And what love can do, that dares love attempt;
Therefore thy kinsmen are no let[2] to me.

JUL.   If they do see thee, they will murder thee.

ROM.   Alack, there lies more peril in thine eye
Than twenty of their swords: look thou but sweet,
And I am proof against their enmity.

JUL.   I would not for the world they saw thee here.

ROM.   I have night's cloak to hide me from their eyes;
And but thou love me, let them find me here:
My life were better ended by their hate,
Than death prorogued,[3] wanting of thy love.

JUL.   By whose direction found'st thou out this place?

ROM.   By love, that first did prompt me to inquire;
He lent me counsel, and I lent him eyes.
I am no pilot; yet, wert thou as far
As that vast shore wash'd with the farthest sea,
I would adventure for such merchandise.

JUL.   Thou know'st the mask of night is on my face,
Else would a maiden blush bepaint my cheek
For that which thou hast heard me speak to-night.
Fain would I dwell on form, fain, fain deny
What I have spoke: but farewell compliment![4]
Dost thou love me? I know thou wilt say 'Ay,'
And I will take thy word: yet, if thou swear'st,
Thou mayst prove false: at lovers' perjuries,
They say, Jove laughs. O gentle Romeo,
If thou dost love, pronounce it faithfully:
Or if thou think'st I am too quickly won,
I'll frown and be perverse and say thee nay,
So thou wilt woo; but else, not for the world.
In truth, fair Montague, I am too fond;[5]

---

2 *let*] hindrance.
3 *prorogued*] postponed.
4 *compliment*] formality.
5 *fond*] foolish.

And therefore thou mayst think my 'havior light:
But trust me, gentleman, I'll prove more true
Than those that have more cunning to be strange.[6]
I should have been more strange, I must confess,
But that thou overheard'st, ere I was ware,
My true love's passion: therefore pardon me,
And not impute this yielding to light love,
Which the dark night hath so discovered.

ROM. Lady, by yonder blessed moon I swear,
That tips with silver all these fruit-tree tops,—

JUL. O, swear not by the moon, th' inconstant moon,
That monthly changes in her circled orb,
Lest that thy love prove likewise variable.

ROM. What shall I swear by?

JUL.   Do not swear at all;
Or, if thou wilt, swear by thy gracious self,
Which is the god of my idolatry,
And I'll believe thee.

ROM.   If my heart's dear love—

JUL. Well, do not swear: although I joy in thee,
I have no joy of this contract to-night:
It is too rash, too unadvised, too sudden,
Too like the lightning, which doth cease to be
Ere one can say 'It lightens.' Sweet, good night!
This bud of love, by summer's ripening breath,
May prove a beauteous flower when next we meet.
Good night, good night! as sweet repose and rest
Come to thy heart as that within my breast!

ROM. O, wilt thou leave me so unsatisfied?

JUL. What satisfaction canst thou have to-night?

ROM. The exchange of thy love's faithful vow for mine.

JUL. I gave thee mine before thou didst request it:
And yet I would it were to give again.

ROM. Wouldst thou withdraw it? for what purpose, love?

JUL. But to be frank,[7] and give it thee again.
And yet I wish but for the thing I have:
My bounty is as boundless as the sea,
My love as deep; the more I give to thee,

---

[6] *strange*] reserved, distant.
[7] *frank*] bountiful.

    The more I have, for both are infinite.
    I hear some noise within; dear love, adieu! [NURSE *calls within.*
    Anon, good Nurse! Sweet Montague, be true.
    Stay but a little, I will come again.   [*Exit.*
ROM.   O blessed, blessed night! I am afeard,
    Being in night, all this is but a dream,
    Too flattering-sweet to be substantial.

Re-enter JULIET, *above.*

JUL.   Three words, dear Romeo, and good night indeed.
    If that thy bent of love be honourable,
    Thy purpose marriage, send me word to-morrow,
    By one that I'll procure to come to thee,
    Where and what time thou wilt perform the rite,
    And all my fortunes at thy foot I'll lay,
    And follow thee my lord throughout the world.
NURSE.   [*Within*] Madam!
JUL.   I come, anon.—But if thou mean'st not well,
    I do beseech thee—
NURSE.   [*Within*] Madam!
JUL.   By and by, I come:—
    To cease thy suit, and leave me to my grief:
    To-morrow will I send.
ROM.   So thrive my soul,—
JUL.   A thousand times good night!   [*Exit.*
ROM.   A thousand times the worse, to want thy light.
    Love goes toward love, as schoolboys from their books,
    But love from love, toward school with heavy looks. [*Retiring slowly.*

Re-enter JULIET, *above.*

JUL.   Hist! Romeo, hist!—O, for a falconer's voice,
    To lure this tassel-gentle[8] back again!
    Bondage is hoarse, and may not speak aloud;
    Else would I tear the cave where Echo lies,
    And make her airy tongue more hoarse than mine,
    With repetition of my Romeo's name.
    Romeo!
ROM.   It is my soul that calls upon my name:
    How silver-sweet sound lovers' tongues by night,
    Like softest music to attending ears!

---

[8] *tassel-gentle*] male goshawk.

JUL.   Romeo!

ROM.   My dear?

JUL.   At what o'clock to-morrow
     Shall I send to thee?

ROM.   At the hour of nine.

JUL.   I will not fail: 'tis twenty years till then.
     I have forgot why I did call thee back.

ROM.   Let me stand here till thou remember it.

JUL.   I shall forget, to have thee still stand there,
     Remembering how I love thy company.

ROM.   And I'll still stay, to have thee still forget,
     Forgetting any other home but this.

JUL.   'Tis almost morning; I would have thee gone:
     And yet no farther than a wanton's bird,
     Who lets it hop a little from her hand,
     Like a poor prisoner in his twisted gyves,
     And with a silk thread plucks it back again,
     So loving-jealous of his liberty.

ROM.   I would I were thy bird.

JUL.   Sweet, so would I:
     Yet I should kill thee with much cherishing.
     Good night, good night! parting is such sweet sorrow
     That I shall say good night till it be morrow.   [*Exit.*

ROM.   Sleep dwell upon thine eyes, peace in thy breast!
     Would I were sleep and peace, so sweet to rest!
     Hence will I to my ghostly[9] father's cell,
     His help to crave and my dear hap[10] to tell.   [*Exit.*

SCENE III. *Friar Laurence's cell.*

Enter FRIAR LAURENCE, *with a basket.*

FRI. L.   The grey-eyed morn smiles on the frowning night,
     Chequering the eastern clouds with streaks of light;
     And flecked darkness like a drunkard reels
     From forth day's path and Titan's[1] fiery wheels:
     Now, ere the sun advance his burning eye,

---

[9] *ghostly*] spiritual.
[10] *hap*] fortune.

---

[1] *Titan's*] the Titan Helios, god of the sun.

The day to cheer and night's dank dew to dry,
I must up-fill this osier cage of ours
With baleful weeds and precious-juiced flowers.
The earth that's nature's mother is her tomb;
What is her burying grave, that is her womb:
And from her womb children of divers kind
We sucking on her natural bosom find,
Many for many virtues excellent,
None but for some, and yet all different.
O, mickle[2] is the powerful grace that lies
In herbs, plants, stones, and their true qualities:
For nought so vile that on the earth doth live,
But to the earth some special good doth give;
Nor aught so good, but, strain'd from that fair use,
Revolts from true birth, stumbling on abuse:
Virtue itself turns vice, being misapplied,
And vice sometime 's by action dignified.
Within the infant rind of this small flower
Poison hath residence, and medicine power:
For this, being smelt, with that part cheers each part,
Being tasted, slays all senses with the heart.
Two such opposed kings encamp them still
In man as well as herbs, grace and rude will;
And where the worser is predominant,
Full soon the canker death eats up that plant.

Enter ROMEO.

ROM.   Good morrow, father.
FRI. L.   Benedicite!
What early tongue so sweet saluteth me?
Young son, it argues a distemper'd head
So soon to bid good morrow to thy bed:
Care keeps his watch in every old man's eye,
And where care lodges, sleep will never lie;
But where unbruised youth with unstuff'd brain
Doth couch his limbs, there golden sleep doth reign:
Therefore thy earliness doth me assure
Thou art up-roused by some distemperature;
Or if not so, then here I hit it right,
Our Romeo hath not been in bed to-night.

[2] *mickle*] great.

ROM.   That last is true; the sweeter rest was mine.
FRI. L.   God pardon sin! wast thou with Rosaline?
ROM.   With Rosaline, my ghostly father? no;
    I have forgot that name and that name's woe.
FRI. L.   That's my good son: but where hast thou been then?
ROM.   I'll tell thee ere thou ask it me again.
    I have been feasting with mine enemy;
    Where on a sudden one hath wounded me,
    That's by me wounded: both our remedies
    Within thy help and holy physic lies:
    I bear no hatred, blessed man, for, lo,
    My intercession likewise steads[3] my foe.
FRI. L.   Be plain, good son, and homely in thy drift;
    Riddling confession finds but riddling shrift.
ROM.   Then plainly know my heart's dear love is set
    On the fair daughter of rich Capulet:
    As mine on hers, so hers is set on mine;
    And all combined, save what thou must combine
    By holy marriage: when, and where, and how,
    We met, we woo'd and made exchange of vow,
    I'll tell thee as we pass; but this I pray,
    That thou consent to marry us to-day.
FRI. L.   Holy Saint Francis, what a change is here!
    Is Rosaline, that thou didst love so dear,
    So soon forsaken? young men's love then lies
    Not truly in their hearts, but in their eyes.
    Jesu Maria, what a deal of brine
    Hath wash'd thy sallow cheeks for Rosaline!
    How much salt water thrown away in waste,
    To season love, that of it doth not taste!
    The sun not yet thy sighs from heaven clears,
    Thy old groans ring yet in mine ancient ears;
    Lo, here upon thy cheek the stain doth sit
    Of an old tear that is not wash'd off yet:
    If e'er thou wast thyself and these woes thine,
    Thou and these woes were all for Rosaline:
    And art thou changed? pronounce this sentence then:
    Women may fall when there's no strength in men.
ROM.   Thou chid'st me oft for loving Rosaline.

---

[3] *steads*] benefits.

FRI. L.   For doting, not for loving, pupil mine.
ROM.   And bad'st me bury love.
FRI. L.   Not in a grave,
    To lay one in, another out to have.
ROM.   I pray thee, chide not: she whom I love now
    Doth grace for grace and love for love allow;
    The other did not so.
FRI. L.   O, she knew well
    Thy love did read by rote and could not spell.
    But come, young waverer, come, go with me,
    In one respect I'll thy assistant be;
    For this alliance may so happy prove,
    To turn your households' rancour to pure love.
ROM.   O, let us hence; I stand on sudden haste.
FRI. L.   Wisely and slow; they stumble that run fast.   [*Exeunt.*

SCENE IV. *A street.*

Enter BENVOLIO *and* MERCUTIO.

MER.   Where the devil should this Romeo be? Came he not home to-
    night?
BEN.   Not to his father's; I spoke with his man.
MER.   Ah, that same pale hard-hearted wench, that Rosaline,
    Torments him so that he will sure run mad.
BEN.   Tybalt, the kinsman to old Capulet,
    Hath sent a letter to his father's house.
MER.   A challenge, on my life.
BEN.   Romeo will answer it.
MER.   Any man that can write may answer a letter.
BEN.   Nay, he will answer the letter's master, how he dares, being dared.
MER.   Alas, poor Romeo, he is already dead! stabbed with a white
    wench's black eye; shot thorough[1] the ear with a love-song; the very
    pin[2] of his heart cleft with the blind bow-boy's butt-shaft:[3] and is he a
    man to encounter Tybalt?
BEN.   Why, what is Tybalt?

---

[1] *thorough*] through.
[2] *pin*] center, middle of a target.
[3] *butt-shaft*] barbless arrow.

MER. More than prince of cats,[4] I can tell you. O, he's the courageous captain of compliments.[5] He fights as you sing prick-song,[6] keeps time, distance and proportion;[7] rests me his minim rest, one, two, and the third in your bosom: the very butcher of a silk button, a duellist, a duellist; a gentleman of the very first house,[8] of the first and second cause:[9] ah, the immortal passado! the punto reverso! the hai![10]

BEN. The what?

MER. The pox of such antic, lisping, affecting fantasticoes;[11] these new tuners of accents! 'By Jesu, a very good blade! a very tall[12] man! a very good whore!' Why, is not this a lamentable thing, grandsire, that we should be thus afflicted with these strange flies,[13] these fashion-mongers, these perdona-mi's, who stand so much on the new form that they cannot sit at ease on the old bench? O, their bones,[14] their bones!

Enter ROMEO.

BEN. Here comes Romeo, here comes Romeo.

MER. Without his roe, like a dried herring: O flesh, flesh, how art thou fishified! Now is he for the numbers that Petrarch flowed in: Laura to his lady was but a kitchen-wench; marry, she had a better love to be-rhyme her; Dido, a dowdy; Cleopatra, a gipsy; Helen and Hero, hildings[15] and harlots; Thisbe, a grey eye or so, but not to the purpose. Signior Romeo, bon jour! there's a French salutation to your French slop.[16] You gave us the counterfeit fairly last night.

ROM. Good morrow to you both. What counterfeit did I give you?

MER. The slip,[17] sir, the slip; can you not conceive?

ROM. Pardon, good Mercutio, my business was great; and in such a case as mine a man may strain courtesy.

[4] *prince of cats*] The prince of cats in *Reynard the Fox* is named Tybert.
[5] *captain of compliments*] master of ceremony.
[6] *prick-song*] sheet music.
[7] *proportion*] rhythm.
[8] *house*] rank, fencing school.
[9] *cause*] i.e., to take up a quarrel.
[10] *passado . . . punto reverso . . . hai*] fencing terms: forward thrust; backhanded stroke; home thrust.
[11] *fantasticoes*] coxcombs.
[12] *tall*] valiant.
[13] *strange flies*] parasites.
[14] *bones*] French *bon* pronounced to create an English pun.
[15] *hildings*] wretches.
[16] *slop*] large trousers.
[17] *slip*] a counterfeit coin.

MER.   That's as much as to say, Such a case as yours constrains a man to bow in the hams

ROM.   Meaning, to court'sy.

MER.   Thou hast most kindly hit it.

ROM.   A most courteous exposition.

MER.   Nay, I am the very pink of courtesy.

ROM.   Pink for flower.

MER.   Right.

ROM.   Why, then is my pump[18] well flowered.

MER.   Well said: follow me this jest now, till thou hast worn out thy pump, that, when the single sole of it is worn, the jest may remain, after the wearing, solely singular.

ROM.   O single-soled jest, solely singular for the singleness![19]

MER.   Come between us, good Benvolio; my wits faint.

ROM.   Switch and spurs, switch and spurs; or I'll cry a match.[20]

MER.   Nay, if thy wits run the wild-goose chase,[21] I have done; for thou hast more of the wild-goose in one of thy wits than, I am sure, I have in my whole five: was I with you there for the goose?

ROM.   Thou wast never with me for any thing when thou wast not there for the goose.[22]

MER.   I will bite thee by the ear for that jest.

ROM.   Nay, good goose, bite not.

MER.   Thy wit is a very bitter sweeting;[23] it is a most sharp sauce.

ROM.   And is it not well served in to a sweet goose?

MER.   O, here's a wit of cheveril,[24] that stretches from an inch narrow to an ell broad!

ROM.   I stretch it out for that word 'broad'; which added to the goose, proves thee far and wide a broad goose.

MER.   Why, is not this better now than groaning for love? now art thou sociable, now art thou Romeo; now art thou what thou art, by art as well as by nature: for this drivelling love is like a great natural,[25] that runs lolling up and down to hide his bauble[26] in a hole.

BEN.   Stop there, stop there.

---

[18] *pump*] a light shoe (often decorated with ribbons shaped as flowers).

[19] *singleness*] silliness.

[20] *cry a match*] claim victory.

[21] *wild-goose chase*] a horse race in which the leader chooses whatever course he wishes.

[22] *goose*] prostitute.

[23] *sweeting*] apple sauce.

[24] *cheveril*] kid leather.

[25] *natural*] idiot, fool.

[26] *bauble*] the fool's club, here with a bawdy quibble.

MER.   Thou desirest me to stop in my tale against the hair. [27]
BEN.   Thou wouldst else have made thy tale large.
MER.   O, thou art deceived; I would have made it short: for I was come
to the whole depth of my tale, and meant indeed to occupy the
argument no longer.
ROM.   Here's goodly gear!

Enter NURSE *and* PETER.

MER.   A sail, a sail!
BEN.   Two, two; a shirt and a smock. [28]
NURSE.   Peter!
PETER.   Anon.
NURSE.   My fan, Peter.
MER.   Good Peter, to hide her face; for her fan's the fairer of the two.
NURSE.   God ye good morrow, gentlemen.
MER.   God ye good den, fair gentlewoman.
NURSE.   Is it good den?
MER.   'Tis no less, I tell you; for the bawdy hand of the dial is now upon
the prick of noon.
NURSE.   Out upon you! what a man [29] are you?
ROM.   One, gentlewoman, that God hath made himself to mar.
NURSE.   By my troth, it is well said; 'for himself to mar,' quoth a'?
Gentlemen, can any of you tell me where I may find the young
Romeo?
ROM.   I can tell you; but young Romeo will be older when you have
found him than he was when you sought him: I am the youngest of
that name, for fault of a worse.
NURSE.   You say well.
MER.   Yea, is the worst well? very well took, i' faith; wisely, wisely.
NURSE.   If you be he, sir, I desire some confidence [30] with you.
BEN.   She will indite [31] him to some supper.
MER.   A bawd, a bawd, a bawd! So ho!
ROM.   What hast thou found?
MER.   No hare, sir; unless a hare, sir, in a lenten pie, that is something
stale and hoar [32] ere it be spent.   [*Sings.*

---

[27] *against the hair*] against the grain, with quibbling.
[28] *a shirt . . . smock*] i.e., a man and a woman.
[29] *what a man*] what sort of a man.
[30] *confidence*] the Nurse's malapropism for "conference."
[31] *indite*] a deliberate malapropism for "invite."
[32] *hoar*] moldy, punning on "whore."

> An old hare hoar,
> And an old hare hoar,
> Is very good meat in lent:
> But a hare that is hoar,
> Is too much for a score,
> When it hoars ere it be spent.

Romeo, will you come to your father's? we'll to dinner thither.

ROM.   I will follow you.

MER.   Farewell, ancient lady; farewell, [*singing*] 'lady, lady, lady.'

> [*Exeunt* MERCUTIO *and* BENVOLIO.

NURSE.   Marry, farewell! I pray you, sir, what saucy merchant[33] was this, that was so full of his ropery?[34]

ROM.   A gentleman, nurse, that loves to hear himself talk, and will speak more in a minute than he will stand to in a month.

NURSE.   An a' speak any thing against me, I'll take him down, an a' were lustier than he is, and twenty such Jacks;[35] and if I cannot, I'll find those that shall. Scurvy knave! I am none of his flirt-gills;[36] I am none of his skains-mates.[37] [*Turning to* PETER] And thou must stand by too, and suffer every knave to use me at his pleasure?

PETER.   I saw no man use you at his pleasure; if I had, my weapon should quickly have been out, I warrant you: I dare draw as soon as another man, if I see occasion in a good quarrel and the law on my side.

NURSE.   Now, afore God, I am so vexed that every part about me quivers. Scurvy knave! Pray you, sir, a word: and as I told you, my young lady bade me inquire you out; what she bade me say, I will keep to myself: but first let me tell ye, if ye should lead her into a fool's paradise, as they say, it were a very gross kind of behaviour, as they say: for the gentlewoman is young, and therefore, if you should deal double with her, truly it were an ill thing to be offered to any gentlewoman, and very weak[38] dealing.

ROM.   Nurse, commend me to thy lady and mistress. I protest unto thee—

---

[33] *merchant*] fellow.
[34] *ropery*] malapropism for "roguery."
[35] *Jacks*] term of contempt for an impudent fellow.
[36] *flirt-gills*] loose women.
[37] *skains-mates*] cutthroats.
[38] *weak*] contemptible.

NURSE.   Good heart, and, i' faith, I will tell her as much: Lord, Lord, she will be a joyful woman.

ROM.   What wilt thou tell her, Nurse? thou dost not mark me.

NURSE.   I will tell her, sir, that you do protest; which, as I take it, is a gentlemanlike offer.

ROM.   Bid her devise
Some means to come to shrift this afternoon;
And there she shall at Friar Laurence' cell
Be shrived and married. Here is for thy pains.

NURSE.   No, truly, sir; not a penny.

ROM.   Go to; I say you shall.

NURSE.   This afternoon, sir? well, she shall be there.

ROM.   And stay, good nurse, behind the abbey-wall:
Within this hour my man shall be with thee,
And bring thee cords made like a tackled stair;[39]
Which to the high top-gallant of my joy
Must be my convoy in the secret night.
Farewell; be trusty, and I'll quit[40] thy pains:
Farewell; commend me to thy mistress.

NURSE.   Now God in heaven bless thee! Hark you, sir.

ROM.   What say'st thou, my dear nurse?

NURSE.   Is your man secret? Did you ne'er hear say,
Two may keep counsel, putting one away?

ROM.   I warrant thee, my man's as true as steel.

NURSE.   Well, sir; my mistress is the sweetest lady—Lord, Lord! when 'twas a little prating thing—O, there is a nobleman in town, one Paris, that would fain lay knife aboard; but she, good soul, had as lieve see a toad, a very toad, as see him. I anger her sometimes, and tell her that Paris is the properer man; but, I'll warrant you, when I say so, she looks as pale as any clout[41] in the versal[42] world. Doth not rosemary and Romeo begin both with a[43] letter?

ROM.   Ay, nurse; what of that? both with an R.

NURSE.   Ah, mocker! that's the dog's name; R is for the—No; I know it begins with some other letter—and she hath the prettiest sententious[44] of it, of you and rosemary, that it would do you good to hear it.

---

[39] *tackled stair*] rope ladder.
[40] *quit*] reward.
[41] *clout*] piece of cloth.
[42] *versal*] universal, whole.
[43] *a*] one and the same.
[44] *sententious*] a malapropism, probably for "sentence," pithy saying.

Rom.   Commend me to thy lady.
Nurse.   Ay, a thousand times. [*Exit* Romeo.] Peter!
Pet.   Anon.
Nurse.   Peter, take my fan, and go before, and apace.   [*Exeunt*.

Scene V. *Capulet's orchard.*

Enter Juliet.

Jul.   The clock struck nine when I did send the Nurse;
In half an hour she promised to return.
Perchance she cannot meet him: that's not so.
O, she is lame! love's heralds should be thoughts,
Which ten times faster glide than the sun's beams,
Driving back shadows over louring hills.
Therefore do nimble-pinion'd doves draw love, [1]
And therefore hath the wind-swift Cupid wings.
Now is the sun upon the highmost hill
Of this day's journey, and from nine till twelve
Is three long hours; yet she is not come.
Had she affections and warm youthful blood,
She would be as swift in motion as a ball;
My words would bandy[2] her to my sweet love,
And his to me:
But old folks, many feign as they were dead;
Unwieldy, slow, heavy and pale as lead.

Enter Nurse, *with* Peter.

O God, she comes! O honey Nurse, what news?
Hast thou met with him? Send thy man away.
Nurse.   Peter, stay at the gate.   [*Exit* Peter.
Jul.   Now, good sweet Nurse,—O Lord, why look'st thou sad?
Though news be sad, yet tell them merrily;
If good, thou shamest the music of sweet news
By playing it to me with so sour a face.
Nurse.   I am a-weary; give me leave a while.
Fie how my bones ache! what a jaunce[3] have I had!

---

[1] *love*] Venus, goddess of love, whose chariot was drawn by doves.
[2] *bandy*] strike (as a ball).
[3] *jaunce*] hard journey.

JUL.   I would thou hadst my bones and I thy news:
    Nay, come, I pray thee, speak; good, good Nurse, speak.
NURSE.   Jesu, what haste? can you not stay a while?
    Do you not see that I am out of breath?
JUL.   How art thou out of breath, when thou hast breath
    To say to me that thou art out of breath?
    The excuse that thou dost make in this delay
    Is longer than the tale thou dost excuse.
    Is thy news good, or bad? answer to that;
    Say either, and I'll stay the circumstance:[4]
    Let me be satisfied, is't good or bad?
NURSE.   Well, you have made a simple choice; you know not how to choose a man: Romeo! no, not he; though his face be better than any man's, yet his leg excels all men's; and for a hand, and a foot, and a body, though they be not to be talked on, yet they are past compare: he is not the flower of courtesy, but, I'll warrant him, as gentle as a lamb. Go thy ways, wench; serve God. What, have you dined at home?
JUL.   No, no: but all this did I know before.
    What says he of our marriage? what of that?
NURSE.   Lord, how my head aches! what a head have I!
    It beats as it would fall in twenty pieces.
    My back o' t' other side,—ah, my back, my back!
    Beshrew your heart for sending me about,
    To catch my death with jauncing up and down!
JUL.   I' faith, I am sorry that thou art not well.
    Sweet, sweet, sweet Nurse, tell me, what says my love?
NURSE.   Your love says, like an honest gentleman, and a courteous, and a kind, and a handsome, and, I warrant, a virtuous,—Where is your mother?
JUL.   Where is my mother! why, she is within;
    Where should she be? How oddly thou repliest!
    'Your love says, like an honest gentleman,
    Where is your mother?'
NURSE.   O God's lady dear!
    Are you so hot? marry, come up, I trow;
    Is this the poultice for my aching bones?
    Henceforward do your messages yourself.

---

[4] *stay the circumstance*] wait until later for the details.

JUL.   Here's such a coil![5] come, what says Romeo?

NURSE.   Have you got leave to go to shrift to-day?

JUL.   I have.

NURSE.   Then hie you hence to Friar Laurence' cell;
      There stays a husband to make you a wife:
      Now comes the wanton blood up in your cheeks,
      They'll be in scarlet straight at any news.
      Hie you to church; I must another way,
      To fetch a ladder, by the which your love
      Must climb a bird's nest soon when it is dark;
      I am the drudge, and toil in your delight;
      But you shall bear the burthen soon at night.
      Go; I'll to dinner; hie you to the cell.

JUL.   Hie to high fortune! Honest Nurse, farewell.   [*Exeunt.*

SCENE VI. *Friar Laurence's cell.*

Enter FRIAR LAURENCE *and* ROMEO.

FRI. L.   So smile the heavens upon this holy act
      That after-hours with sorrow chide us not!

ROM.   Amen, amen! but come what sorrow can,
      It cannot countervail[1] the exchange of joy
      That one short minute gives me in her sight:
      Do thou but close our hands with holy words,
      Then love-devouring death do what he dare,
      It is enough I may but call her mine.

FRI. L.   These violent delights have violent ends,
      And in their triumph die; like fire and powder
      Which as they kiss consume: the sweetest honey
      Is loathsome in his own deliciousness,
      And in the taste confounds[2] the appetite:
      Therefore, love moderately; long love doth so;
      Too swift arrives as tardy as too slow.

Enter JULIET.

[5] *coil*] turmoil, confusion.

---

[1] *countervail*] equal.
[2] *confounds*] destroys, does away with.

Here comes the lady. O, so light a foot
Will ne'er wear out the everlasting flint.
A lover may bestride the gossamer
That idles in the wanton summer air,
And yet not fall; so light is vanity.

JUL.   Good even to my ghostly confessor.

FRI. L.   Romeo shall thank thee, daughter, for us both.

JUL.   As much to him, else is his thanks too much.

ROM.   Ah, Juliet, if the measure of thy joy
Be heap'd like mine, and that thy skill be more
To blazon it, then sweeten with thy breath
This neighbour air, and let rich music's tongue
Unfold the imagined happiness that both
Receive in either by this dear encounter.

JUL.   Conceit,[3] more rich in matter than in words,
Brags of his substance, not of ornament:
They are but beggars that can count their worth;
But my true love is grown to such excess,
I cannot sum up sum of half my wealth.

FRI. L.   Come, come with me, and we will make short work;
For, by your leaves, you shall not stay alone
Till holy church incorporate two in one.   [*Exeunt.*

---

[3] *Conceit*] Imagination.

ACT III.

Scene I. A *public place*.

Enter Mercutio, Benvolio, Page, *and* Servants.

Ben.   I pray thee, good Mercutio, let's retire:
    The day is hot, the Capulets abroad,
    And, if we meet, we shall not 'scape a brawl;
    For now these hot days is the mad blood stirring.

Mer.   Thou art like one of those fellows that when he enters the confines of a tavern claps me his sword upon the table, and says 'God send me no need of thee!' and by the operation of the second cup draws it on the drawer,[1] when indeed there is no need.

Ben.   Am I like such a fellow?

Mer.   Come, come, thou art as hot a Jack in thy mood as any in Italy, and as soon moved to be moody,[2] and as soon moody to be moved.

Ben.   And what to?

Mer.   Nay, an there were two such, we should have none shortly, for one would kill the other. Thou! why, thou wilt quarrel with a man that hath a hair more, or a hair less, in his beard than thou hast: thou wilt quarrel with a man for cracking nuts, having no other reason but because thou hast hazel eyes; what eye, but such an eye, would spy out such a quarrel? thy head is as full of quarrels as an egg is full of meat, and yet thy head hath been beaten as addle as an egg for quarrelling: thou hast quarrelled with a man for coughing in the street, because he hath wakened thy dog that hath lain asleep in the sun: didst thou not fall out with a tailor for wearing his new doublet before Easter? with another, for tying his new shoes with old riband? and yet thou wilt tutor me from quarrelling!

[1] *drawer*] waiter.
[2] *moody*] angry.

BEN.   An I were so apt to quarrel as thou art, any man should buy the
fee-simple of my life for an hour and a quarter.

MER.   The fee-simple! O simple!

Enter TYBALT *and others.*

BEN.   By my head, here come the Capulets.

MER.   By my heel, I care not.

TYB.   Follow me close, for I will speak to them.
Gentlemen, good den: a word with one of you.

MER.   And but one word with one of us? couple it with something;
make it a word and a blow.

TYB.   You shall find me apt enough to that, sir, an you will give me
occasion.

MER.   Could you not take some occasion without giving?

TYB.   Mercutio, thou consort'st with Romeo,—

MER.   Consort! what, dost thou make us minstrels? an thou make
minstrels of us, look to hear nothing but discords: here's my fid-
dlestick; here's that shall make you dance. 'Zounds, consort!

BEN.   We talk here in the public haunt of men:
Either withdraw unto some private place,
Or reason coldly of your grievances,
Or else depart; here all eyes gaze on us.

MER.   Men's eyes were made to look, and let them gaze;
I will not budge for no man's pleasure, I.

Enter ROMEO.

TYB.   Well, peace be with you, sir: here comes my man.

MER.   But I'll be hang'd, sir, if he wear your livery:
Marry, go before to field, he'll be your follower;
Your worship in that sense may call him man.

TYB.   Romeo, the love I bear thee can afford
No better term than this,—thou art a villain.

ROM.   Tybalt, the reason that I have to love thee
Doth much excuse the appertaining rage
To such a greeting: villain am I none;
Therefore farewell; I see thou know'st me not.

TYB.   Boy, this shall not excuse the injuries
That thou hast done me; therefore turn and draw.

ROM.   I do protest, I never injured thee,
But love thee better than thou canst devise
Till thou shalt know the reason of my love:

  And so, good Capulet,—which name I tender
  As dearly as mine own,—be satisfied.
MER. O calm, dishonourable, vile submission!
  Alla stoccata[3] carries it away.   *[Draws.*
  Tybalt, you rat-catcher, will you walk?
TYB. What wouldst thou have with me?
MER. Good king of cats, nothing but one of your nine lives, that I
  mean to make bold withal, and, as you shall use me hereafter, dry-
  beat[4] the rest of the eight. Will you pluck your sword out of his
  pilcher[5] by the ears? make haste, lest mine be about your ears ere it
  be out.
TYB. I am for you.   *[Drawing.*
ROM. Gentle Mercutio, put thy rapier up.
MER. Come, sir, your passado.   *[They fight.*
ROM. Draw, Benvolio, beat down their weapons.
  Gentlemen, for shame, forbear this outrage!
  Tybalt, Mercutio, the prince expressly hath
  Forbid this bandying in Verona streets:
  Hold, Tybalt! good Mercutio!
  [TYBALT *under* ROMEO'S *arm stabs* MERCUTIO *and*
               flies with his followers.

MER.   I am hurt;
  A plague o' both your houses! I am sped:[6]
  Is he gone, and hath nothing?
BEN.   What, art thou hurt?
MER. Ay, ay, a scratch, a scratch; marry, 'tis enough.
  Where is my page? Go, villain, fetch a surgeon. *[Exit Page.*
ROM. Courage, man; the hurt cannot be much.
MER. No, 'tis not so deep as a well, nor so wide as a church-door; but
  'tis enough, 'twill serve: ask for me to-morrow, and you shall find me
  a grave man. I am peppered, I warrant, for this world. A plague o'
  both your houses! 'Zounds, a dog, a rat, a mouse, a cat, to scratch a
  man to death! a braggart, a rogue, a villain, that fights by the book
  of arithmetic![7] Why the devil came you between us? I was hurt
  under your arm.
ROM. I thought all for the best.

  [3] *Alla stoccata*] a technical term for a fencing thrust.
  [4] *dry-beat*] cudgel.
  [5] *pilcher*] scabbard.
  [6] *sped*] done for.
  [7] *book of arithmetic*] fencing manual.

MER.   Help me into some house, Benvolio,
  Or I shall faint. A plague o' both your houses!
  They have made worms' meat of me: I have it,
  And soundly too: your houses!

       [*Exeunt* MERCUTIO *and* BENVOLIO.

ROM.   This gentleman, the Prince's near ally,[8]
  My very friend, hath got this mortal hurt
  In my behalf; my reputation stain'd
  With Tybalt's slander,—Tybalt, that an hour
  Hath been my kinsman: O sweet Juliet,
  Thy beauty hath made me effeminate,
  And in my temper soften'd valour's steel!

Re-enter BENVOLIO.

BEN.   O Romeo, Romeo, brave Mercutio's dead!
  That gallant spirit hath aspired the clouds,
  Which too untimely here did scorn the earth.
ROM.   This day's black fate on more days doth depend;
  This but begins the woe others must end.

Re-enter TYBALT.

BEN.   Here comes the furious Tybalt back again.
ROM.   Alive, in triumph! and Mercutio slain!
  Away to heaven, respective lenity,[9]
  And fire-eyed fury be my conduct[10] now!
  Now, Tybalt, take the 'villain' back again
  That late thou gavest me; for Mercutio's soul
  Is but a little way above our heads,
  Staying for thine to keep him company:
  Either thou, or I, or both, must go with him.
TYB.   Thou, wretched boy, that didst consort him here,
  Shalt with him hence.
ROM.   This shall determine that.

       [*They fight*; TYBALT *falls*.

BEN.   Romeo, away, be gone!
  The citizens are up, and Tybalt slain:
  Stand not amazed: the Prince will doom thee death
  If thou art taken: hence, be gone, away!

 [8] *ally*] relative.
 [9] *respective lenity*] concern for mildness.
 [10] *conduct*] guide.

ROM.   O, I am fortune's fool!
BEN.   Why dost thou stay?   [*Exit* ROMEO.

Enter Citizens, &c.

FIRST CIT.   Which way ran he that kill'd Mercutio?
        Tybalt, that murderer, which way ran he?
BEN.   There lies that Tybalt.
FIRST CIT.   Up, sir, go with me;
        I charge thee in the Prince's name, obey.

Enter PRINCE, *attended*; MONTAGUE, CAPULET, *their* Wives, *and others.*

PRIN.   Where are the vile beginners of this fray?
BEN.   O noble Prince, I can discover[11] all
        The unlucky manage of this fatal brawl:
        There lies the man, slain by young Romeo,
        That slew thy kinsman, brave Mercutio.
LA. CAP.   Tybalt, my cousin! O my brother's child!
        O Prince! O cousin! husband! O, the blood is spilt
        Of my dear kinsman! Prince, as thou art true,
        For blood of ours, shed blood of Montague.
        O cousin, cousin!
PRIN.   Benvolio, who began this bloody fray?
BEN.   Tybalt, here slain, whom Romeo's hand did slay;
        Romeo that spoke him fair, bid him bethink
        How nice[12] the quarrel was, and urged withal
        Your high displeasure: all this uttered
        With gentle breath, calm look, knees humbly bow'd,
        Could not take truce with the unruly spleen[13]
        Of Tybalt deaf to peace, but that he tilts
        With piercing steel at bold Mercutio's breast;
        Who, all as hot, turns deadly point to point,
        And, with a martial scorn, with one hand beats
        Cold death aside, and with the other sends
        It back to Tybalt, whose dexterity
        Retorts it: Romeo he cries aloud,
        'Hold, friends! friends, part!' and, swifter than his tongue,
        His agile arm beats down their fatal points,

---

[11] *discover*] reveal.
[12] *nice*] trivial.
[13] *take . . . spleen*] make peace with the uncontrollable rage.

And 'twixt them rushes; underneath whose arm
An envious thrust from Tybalt hit the life
Of stout Mercutio, and then Tybalt fled:
But by and by comes back to Romeo,
Who had but newly entertain'd revenge,
And to't they go like lightning: for, ere I
Could draw to part them, was stout Tybalt slain;
And, as he fell, did Romeo turn and fly;
This is the truth, or let Benvolio die.

LA. CAP.   He is a kinsman to the Montague,
Affection makes him false, he speaks not true:
Some twenty of them fought in this black strife,
And all those twenty could but kill one life.
I beg for justice, which thou, Prince, must give;
Romeo slew Tybalt, Romeo must not live.

PRIN.   Romeo slew him, he slew Mercutio;
Who now the price of his dear blood doth owe?

MON.   Not Romeo, Prince, he was Mercutio's friend;
His fault concludes but what the law should end,
The life of Tybalt.

PRIN.   And for that offence
Immediately we do exile him hence:
I have an interest in your hate's proceeding,
My blood for your rude brawls doth lie a-bleeding;
But I'll amerce[14] you with so strong a fine,
That you shall all repent the loss of mine:
I will be deaf to pleading and excuses;
Nor tears nor prayers shall purchase out abuses:[15]
Therefore use none: let Romeo hence in haste,
Else, when he's found, that hour is his last.
Bear hence this body, and attend our will:
Mercy but murders, pardoning those that kill.   [*Exeunt.*

---

[14] *amerce*] punish by imposing a fine.
[15] *purchase out abuses*] buy off the fine for misdeeds.

SCENE II. *Capulet's orchard.*

Enter JULIET.

JUL.   Gallop apace, you fiery-footed steeds,
     Towards Phoebus' lodging: such a waggoner
     As Phaethon would whip you to the west,
     And bring in cloudy night immediately.
     Spread thy close curtain, love-performing night,
     That runaways' eyes may wink, and Romeo
     Leap to these arms, untalk'd of and unseen.
     Lovers can see to do their amorous rites
     By their own beauties; or, if love be blind,
     It best agrees with night. Come, civil night,
     Thou sober-suited matron, all in black,
     And learn me how to lose a winning match,
     Play'd for a pair of stainless maidenhoods:
     Hood my unmann'd[1] blood bating in my cheeks
     With thy black mantle, till strange love grown bold
     Think true love acted simple modesty.
     Come, night, come, Romeo, come, thou day in night;
     For thou wilt lie upon the wings of night
     Whiter than new snow on a raven's back.
     Come, gentle night, come, loving, black-brow'd night,
     Give me my Romeo; and, when he shall die,
     Take him and cut him out in little stars,
     And he will make the face of heaven so fine,
     That all the world will be in love with night,
     And pay no worship to the garish sun.
     O, I have bought the mansion of a love,
     But not possess'd it, and, though I am sold,
     Not yet enjoy'd; so tedious is this day
     As is the night before some festival
     To an impatient child that hath new robes
     And may not wear them. O, here comes my Nurse,
     And she brings news, and every tongue that speaks
     But Romeo's name speaks heavenly eloquence.

---

[1] *unmann'd*] (1) untrained; (2) still without husband.

Enter NURSE, *with cords.*

> Now, Nurse, what news? What hast thou there? the cords
> That Romeo bid thee fetch?

NURSE.   Ay, ay, the cords. [*Throws them down.*

JUL.   Ay me! what news? why dost thou wring thy hands?

NURSE.   Ah, well-a-day! he's dead, he's dead, he's dead.
> We are undone, lady, we are undone.
> Alack the day! he's gone, he's kill'd, he's dead.

JUL.   Can heaven be so envious?

NURSE.   Romeo can,
> Though heaven cannot. O Romeo, Romeo!
> Who ever would have thought it? Romeo!

JUL.   What devil art thou that dost torment me thus?
> This torture should be roar'd in dismal hell.
> Hath Romeo slain himself? say thou but 'I,'[2]
> And that bare vowel 'I' shall poison more
> Than the death-darting eye of cockatrice:
> I am not I, if there be such an I,
> Or those eyes shut, that make thee answer 'I.'
> If he be slain, say 'I'; or if not, no:
> Brief sounds determine of my weal or woe.

NURSE.   I saw the wound, I saw it with mine eyes—
> God save the mark!—here on his manly breast:
> A piteous corse, a bloody piteous corse;
> Pale, pale as ashes, all bedaub'd in blood,
> All in gore[3] blood: I swounded at the sight.

JUL.   O, break, my heart! poor bankrupt, break at once!
> To prison, eyes, ne'er look on liberty!
> Vile earth, to earth resign, end motion here,
> And thou and Romeo press one heavy bier!

NURSE.   O Tybalt, Tybalt, the best friend I had!
> O courteous Tybalt! honest gentleman!
> That ever I should live to see thee dead!

JUL.   What storm is this that blows so contrary?
> Is Romeo slaughter'd, and is Tybalt dead?
> My dear-loved cousin, and my dearer lord?
> Then, dreadful trumpet, sound the general doom!
> For who is living, if those two are gone?

[2] 'I'] ay, yes.
[3] *gore*] clotted.

NURSE.   Tybalt is gone, and Romeo banished;
  Romeo that kill'd him, he is banished.
JUL.   O God! did Romeo's hand shed Tybalt's blood?
NURSE.   It did, it did; alas the day, it did!
JUL.   O serpent heart, hid with a flowering face!
  Did ever dragon keep so fair a cave?
  Beautiful tyrant! fiend angelical!
  Dove-feather'd raven! wolvish-ravening lamb!
  Despised substance of divinest show!
  Just opposite to what thou justly seem'st,
  A damned saint, an honourable villain!
  O nature, what hadst thou to do in hell,
  When thou didst bower the spirit of a fiend
  In mortal paradise of such sweet flesh?
  Was ever book containing such vile matter
  So fairly bound? O, that deceit should dwell
  In such a gorgeous palace!
NURSE.   There's no trust,
  No faith, no honesty in men; all perjured,
  All forsworn, all naught,[4] all dissemblers.
  Ah, where's my man? give me some aqua vitae:
  These griefs, these woes, these sorrows make me old.
  Shame come to Romeo!
JUL.   Blister'd be thy tongue
  For such a wish! he was not born to shame:
  Upon his brow shame is ashamed to sit;
  For 'tis a throne where honour may be crown'd
  Sole monarch of the universal earth.
  O, what a beast was I to chide at him!
NURSE.   Will you speak well of him that kill'd your cousin?
JUL.   Shall I speak ill of him that is my husband?
  Ah, poor my lord, what tongue shall smooth thy name,
  When I, thy three-hours wife, have mangled it?
  But wherefore, villain, didst thou kill my cousin?
  That villain cousin would have kill'd my husband:
  Back, foolish tears, back to your native spring;
  Your tributary drops belong to woe,
  Which you mistaking offer up to joy.
  My husband lives, that Tybalt would have slain;

---

[4] naught] worthless, wicked.

And Tybalt's dead, that would have slain my husband:
All this is comfort; wherefore weep I then?
Some word there was, worser than Tybalt's death,
That murder'd me: I would forget it fain;
But, O, it presses to my memory,
Like damned guilty deeds to sinners' minds:
'Tybalt is dead, and Romeo banished';
That 'banished,' that one word 'banished,'
Hath slain ten thousand Tybalts. Tybalt's death
Was woe enough, if it had ended there:
Or, if sour woe delights in fellowship,
And needly[5] will be rank'd with other griefs,
Why follow'd not, when she said 'Tybalt's dead,'
Thy father, or thy mother, nay, or both,
Which modern[6] lamentation might have moved?
But with a rear-ward[7] following Tybalt's death,
'Romeo is banished': to speak that word,
Is father, mother, Tybalt, Romeo, Juliet,
All slain, all dead. 'Romeo is banished.'
There is no end, no limit, measure, bound,
In that word's death; no words can that woe sound.
Where is my father, and my mother, Nurse?

NURSE.   Weeping and wailing over Tybalt's corse:
Will you go to them? I will bring you thither.

JUL.   Wash they his wounds with tears: mine shall be spent,
When theirs are dry, for Romeo's banishment.
Take up those cords: poor ropes, you are beguiled,
Both you and I; for Romeo is exiled:
He made you for a highway to my bed;
But I, a maid, die maiden-widowed.
Come, cords; come, Nurse; I'll to my wedding-bed;
And death, not Romeo, take my maidenhead!

NURSE.   Hie to your chamber: I'll find Romeo
To comfort you: I wot[8] well where he is.
Hark ye, your Romeo will be here at night:
I'll to him; he is hid at Laurence' cell.

JUL.   O, find him! give this ring to my true knight,
And bid him come to take his last farewell.   [*Exeunt.*

---

[5] *needly*] necessarily.
[6] *modern*] commonplace, ordinary.
[7] *rear-ward*] rear guard.
[8] *wot*] know.

SCENE III. *Friar Laurence's cell.*

Enter FRIAR LAURENCE.

FRI. L.   Romeo, come forth; come forth, thou fearful man:
     Affliction is enamour'd of thy parts,
     And thou art wedded to calamity.

Enter ROMEO.

ROM.   Father, what news? what is the Prince's doom?
     What sorrow craves acquaintance at my hand,
     That I yet know not?
FRI. L.   Too familiar
     Is my dear son with such sour company:
     I bring thee tidings of the Prince's doom.
ROM.   What less than dooms-day is the Prince's doom?
FRI. L.   A gentler judgement vanish'd[1] from his lips,
     Not body's death, but body's banishment.
ROM.   Ha, banishment! be merciful, say 'death';
     For exile hath more terror in his look,
     Much more than death: do not say 'banishment.'
FRI. L.   Here from Verona art thou banished:
     Be patient, for the world is broad and wide.
ROM.   There is no world without Verona walls,
     But purgatory, torture, hell itself.
     Hence banished is banish'd from the world,
     And world's exile is death: then 'banished'
     Is death mis-term'd: calling death 'banished,'
     Thou cut'st my head off with a golden axe,
     And smilest upon the stroke that murders me.
FRI. L.   O deadly sin! O rude unthankfulness!
     Thy fault our law calls death; but the kind Prince,
     Taking thy part, hath rush'd[2] aside the law,
     And turn'd that black word death to banishment:
     This is dear mercy, and thou seest it not.
ROM.   'Tis torture, and not mercy: heaven is here,
     Where Juliet lives; and every cat and dog

---

[1] *vanish'd*] issued.
[2] *rush'd*] violently thrust.

And little mouse, every unworthy thing,
Live here in heaven and may look on her,
But Romeo may not: more validity,[3]
More honourable state,[4] more courtship[5] lives
In carrion-flies than Romeo: they may seize
On the white wonder of dear Juliet's hand,
And steal immortal blessing from her lips;
Who, even in pure and vestal modesty,
Still blush, as thinking their own kisses sin;
But Romeo may not; he is banished:
This may flies do, but I from this must fly:
They are free men, but I am banished:
And say'st thou yet, that exile is not death?
Hadst thou no poison mix'd, no sharp-ground knife,
No sudden mean of death, though ne'er so mean,
But 'banished' to kill me?—'Banished'?
O Friar, the damned use that word in hell;
Howling attends it: how hast thou the heart,
Being a divine, a ghostly confessor,
A sin-absolver, and my friend profess'd,
To mangle me with that word 'banished'?

Fri. L.   Thou fond mad man, hear me but speak a word.

Rom.   O, thou wilt speak again of banishment.

Fri. L.   I'll give thee armour to keep off that word;
Adversity's sweet milk, philosophy,
To comfort thee, though thou art banished.

Rom.   Yet 'banished'? Hang up philosophy!
Unless philosophy can make a Juliet,
Displant a town, reverse a prince's doom,
It helps not, it prevails not: talk no more.

Fri. L.   O, then I see that madmen have no ears.

Rom.   How should they, when that wise men have no eyes?

Fri. L.   Let me dispute with thee of thy estate.[6]

Rom.   Thou canst not speak of that thou dost not feel:
Wert thou as young as I, Juliet thy love,
An hour but married, Tybalt murdered,
Doting like me, and like me banished,

---

[3] *validity*] value.
[4] *state*] rank.
[5] *courtship*] (1) civility befitting a courtier; (2) wooing.
[6] *dispute . . . estate*] discuss your situation with you.

    Then mightst thou speak, then mightst thou tear thy hair,
    And fall upon the ground, as I do now,
    Taking the measure of an unmade grave.   *[Knocking within.*
FRI. L.   Arise; one knocks; good Romeo, hide thyself.
ROM.   Not I; unless the breath of heart-sick groans
    Mist-like infold me from the search of eyes.   *[Knocking.*
FRI. L.   Hark, how they knock! Who's there? Romeo, arise;
    Thou wilt be taken.—Stay awhile!—Stand up;   *[Knocking.*
    Run to my study.—By and by!—God's will,
    What simpleness is this!—I come, I come!   *[Knocking.*
    Who knocks so hard? whence come you? what's your will?
NURSE.   *[Within]* Let me come in, and you shall know my errand;
    I come from Lady Juliet.
FRI. L.   Welcome, then.

Enter NURSE.

NURSE.   O holy Friar, O, tell me, holy Friar,
    Where is my lady's lord, where's Romeo?
FRI. L.   There on the ground, with his own tears made drunk.
NURSE.   O, he is even in my mistress' case,
    Just in her case!
FRI. L.   O woeful sympathy!
    Piteous predicament!
NURSE.   Even so lies she,
    Blubbering and weeping, weeping and blubbering.
    Stand up, stand up; stand, an you be a man:
    For Juliet's sake, for her sake, rise and stand;
    Why should you fall into so deep an O?
ROM.   Nurse!
NURSE.   Ah sir! ah sir! Well, death's the end of all.
ROM.   Spakest thou of Juliet? how is it with her?
    Doth she not think me an old murderer,
    Now I have stain'd the childhood of our joy
    With blood removed but little from her own?
    Where is she? and how doth she? and what says
    My conceal'd lady to our cancell'd love?
NURSE.   O, she says nothing, sir, but weeps and weeps;
    And now falls on her bed; and then starts up,
    And Tybalt calls; and then on Romeo cries,
    And then down falls again.
ROM.   As if that name,

Shot from the deadly level[7] of a gun,
Did murder her, as that name's cursed hand
Murder'd her kinsman. O, tell me, Friar, tell me,
In what vile part of this anatomy
Doth my name lodge? tell me, that I may sack
The hateful mansion.   [*Drawing his sword.*

FRI. L.   Hold thy desperate hand:
Art thou a man? thy form cries out thou art:
Thy tears are womanish; thy wild acts denote
The unreasonable fury of a beast:
Unseemly woman in a seeming man!
Or ill-beseeming beast in seeming both!
Thou hast amazed me: by my holy order,
I thought thy disposition better temper'd.
Hast thou slain Tybalt? wilt thou slay thyself?
And slay thy lady that in thy life lives,
By doing damned hate upon thyself?
Why rail'st thou on thy birth, the heaven and earth?
Since birth and heaven and earth, all three do meet
In thee at once, which thou at once wouldst lose.
Fie, fie, thou shamest thy shape, thy love, thy wit;
Which, like a usurer, abound'st in all,
And usest none in that true use indeed
Which should bedeck thy shape, thy love, thy wit:
Thy noble shape is but a form of wax,
Digressing from the valour of a man;
Thy dear love sworn, but hollow perjury,
Killing that love which thou hast vow'd to cherish;
Thy wit, that ornament to shape and love,
Mis-shapen in the conduct of them both,
Like powder in a skilless soldier's flask,
Is set a-fire by thine own ignorance,
And thou dismember'd with thine own defence.
What, rouse thee, man! thy Juliet is alive,
For whose dear sake thou wast but lately dead;
There art thou happy: Tybalt would kill thee,
But thou slew'st Tybalt; there art thou happy too:
The law, that threaten'd death, becomes thy friend,
And turns it to exile; there art thou happy:

[7-*level*] aim.

A pack of blessings lights upon thy back;
Happiness courts thee in her best array;
But, like a misbehaved and sullen wench,
Thou pout'st upon thy fortune and thy love:
Take heed, take heed, for such die miserable.
Go, get thee to thy love, as was decreed,
Ascend her chamber, hence and comfort her:
But look thou stay not till the watch be set,
For then thou canst not pass to Mantua;
Where thou shalt live till we can find a time
To blaze[8] your marriage, reconcile your friends,
Beg pardon of the Prince, and call thee back
With twenty hundred thousand times more joy
Than thou went'st forth in lamentation.
Go before, Nurse: commend me to thy lady,
And bid her hasten all the house to bed,
Which heavy sorrow makes them apt unto:
Romeo is coming.

NURSE.   O Lord, I could have stay'd here all the night
To hear good counsel: O, what learning is!
My lord, I'll tell my lady you will come.

ROM.   Do so, and bid my sweet prepare to chide.

NURSE.   Here, sir, a ring she bid me give you, sir:
Hie you, make haste, for it grows very late.   [*Exit.*

ROM.   How well my comfort is revived by this!

FRI. L.   Go hence; good night; and here stands all your state:
Either be gone before the watch be set,
Or by the break of day disguised from hence.
Sojourn in Mantua; I'll find out your man,
And he shall signify from time to time
Every good hap to you that chances here:
Give me thy hand; 'tis late: farewell; good night.

ROM.   But that a joy past joy calls out on me,
It were a grief, so brief to part with thee:
Farewell.   [*Exeunt.*

---

[8] *blaze*] make public.

SCENE IV. *A room in Capulet's house.*

Enter CAPULET, LADY CAPULET, *and* PARIS.

CAP.   Things have fall'n out, sir, so unluckily,
     That we have had no time to move our daughter.
     Look you, she loved her kinsman Tybalt dearly,
     And so did I. Well, we were born to die.
     'Tis very late; she'll not come down to-night:
     I promise you, but for your company,
     I would have been a-bed an hour ago.

PAR.   These times of woe afford no time to woo.
     Madam, good night: commend me to your daughter.

LA. CAP.   I will, and know her mind early to-morrow;
     To-night she's mew'd up to her heaviness.

CAP.   Sir Paris, I will make a desperate tender[1]
     Of my child's love: I think she will be ruled
     In all respects by me; nay more, I doubt it not.
     Wife, go you to her ere you go to bed;
     Acquaint her here of my son Paris' love;
     And bid her, mark you me, on Wednesday next—
     But, soft! what day is this?

PAR.   Monday, my lord.

CAP.   Monday! ha, ha! Well, Wednesday is too soon;
     O' Thursday let it be: o' Thursday, tell her,
     She shall be married to this noble earl.
     Will you be ready? do you like this haste?
     We'll keep no great ado; a friend or two;
     For, hark you, Tybalt being slain so late,
     It may be thought we held him carelessly,
     Being our kinsman, if we revel much:
     Therefore we'll have some half-a-dozen friends,
     And there an end. But what say you to Thursday?

PAR.   My lord, I would that Thursday were to-morrow.

CAP.   Well, get you gone: o' Thursday be it then.
     Go you to Juliet ere you go to bed,

---

[1] *desperate tender*] reckless offer.

Prepare her, wife, against this wedding-day.
Farewell, my lord. Light to my chamber, ho!
Afore me,[2] it is so very very late,
That we may call it early by and by:
Good night.   [*Exeunt.*

SCENE V. *Capulet's orchard.*

Enter ROMEO *and* JULIET, *above, at the window.*

JUL.   Wilt thou be gone? it is not yet near day:
        It was the nightingale, and not the lark,
        That pierced the fearful hollow of thine ear;
        Nightly she sings on yond pomegranate-tree:
        Believe me, love, it was the nightingale.
ROM.   It was the lark, the herald of the morn,
        No nightingale: look, love, what envious streaks
        Do lace the severing clouds in yonder east:
        Night's candles are burnt out, and jocund day
        Stands tiptoe on the misty mountain tops:
        I must be gone and live, or stay and die.
JUL.   Yond light is not day-light, I know it, I:
        It is some meteor that the sun exhales,
        To be to thee this night a torch-bearer,
        And light thee on thy way to Mantua:
        Therefore stay yet; thou need'st not to be gone.
ROM.   Let me be ta'en, let me be put to death;
        I am content, so thou wilt have it so.
        I'll say yon grey is not the morning's eye,
        'Tis but the pale reflex of Cynthia's[1] brow;
        Nor that is not the lark, whose notes do beat
        The vaulty heaven so high above our heads:
        I have more care to stay than will to go:
        Come, death, and welcome! Juliet wills it so.
        How is't, my soul? let's talk: it is not day.
JUL.   It is, it is: hie hence, be gone, away!
        It is the lark that sings so out of tune,
        Straining harsh discords and unpleasing sharps.

---

[2] *Afore me*] by my life.

---

[1] *Cynthia's*] the moon's.

Some say the lark makes sweet division;[2]
This doth not so, for she divideth us:
Some say the lark and loathed toad change eyes;
O, now I would they had changed voices too!
Since arm from arm that voice doth us affray,[3]
Hunting thee hence with hunts-up[4] to the day.
O, now be gone; more light and light it grows.

ROM.   More light and light: more dark and dark our woes!

Enter NURSE, *to the chamber.*

NURSE.   Madam!
JUL.   Nurse?
NURSE.   Your lady mother is coming to your chamber:
The day is broke; be wary, look about.   [*Exit.*
JUL.   Then, window, let day in, and let life out.
ROM.   Farewell, farewell! one kiss, and I'll descend.   [*Descends.*
JUL.   Art thou gone so? my lord, my love, my friend!
I must hear from thee every day in the hour,
For in a minute there are many days:
O, by this count I shall be much in years
Ere I again behold my Romeo!
ROM.   Farewell!
I will omit no opportunity
That may convey my greetings, love, to thee.
JUL.   O, think'st thou we shall ever meet again?
ROM.   I doubt it not; and all these woes shall serve
For sweet discourses in our time to come.
JUL.   O God! I have an ill-divining soul.
Methinks I see thee, now thou art below,
As one dead in the bottom of a tomb:
Either my eyesight fails or thou look'st pale.
ROM.   And trust me, love, in my eye so do you:
Dry sorrow drinks our blood. Adieu, adieu!   [*Exit.*
JUL.   O fortune, fortune! all men call thee fickle:
If thou art fickle, what dost thou with him
That is renown'd for faith? Be fickle, fortune;
For then, I hope, thou wilt not keep him long,
But send him back.

---

[2] *division*] melodic variation.
[3] *affray*] frighten.
[4] *hunts-up*] a tune played to awaken huntsmen.

LA. CAP.   [*Within*] Ho, daughter! are you up?

JUL.   Who is't that calls? it is my lady mother!
. Is she not down⁵ so late, or up so early?
What unaccustom'd cause procures her hither?

Enter LADY CAPULET.

LA. CAP.   Why, how now, Juliet!

JUL.   Madam, I am not well.

LA. CAP.   Evermore weeping for your cousin's death?
What, wilt thou wash him from his grave with tears?
An if thou couldst, thou couldst not make him live;
Therefore have done: some grief shows much of love,
But much of grief shows still some want of wit.

JUL.   Yet let me weep for such a feeling loss.

LA. CAP.   So shall you feel the loss, but not the friend
Which you weep for.

JUL.   Feeling so the loss,
I cannot choose but ever weep the friend.

LA. CAP.   Well, girl, thou weep'st not so much for his death
As that the villain lives which slaughter'd him.

JUL.   What villain, madam?

LA. CAP.   That same villain, Romeo.

JUL.   [*Aside*] Villain and he be many miles asunder.
God pardon him! I do, with all my heart;
And yet no man like he doth grieve my heart.

LA. CAP.   That is because the traitor murderer lives.

JUL.   Ay, madam, from the reach of these my hands:
Would none but I might venge my cousin's death!

LA. CAP.   We will have vengeance for it, fear thou not:
Then weep no more. I'll send to one in Mantua,
Where that same banish'd runagate doth live,
Shall give him such an unaccustom'd dram
That he shall soon keep Tybalt company:
And then, I hope, thou wilt be satisfied.

JUL.   Indeed, I never shall be satisfied
With Romeo, till I behold him—dead—
Is my poor heart so for a kinsman vex'd.
Madam, if you could find out but a man
To bear a poison, I would temper it,

⁵ *down*] in bed.

That Romeo should, upon receipt thereof,
Soon sleep in quiet. O, how my heart abhors
To hear him named, and cannot come to him,
To wreak the love I bore my cousin
Upon his body that hath slaughter'd him!

LA. CAP. Find thou the means, and I'll find such a man.
But now I'll tell thee joyful tidings, girl.

JUL. And joy comes well in such a needy time:
What are they, I beseech your ladyship?

LA. CAP. Well, well, thou hast a careful[6] father, child;
One who, to put thee from thy heaviness,
Hath sorted out a sudden day of joy,
That thou expect'st not, nor I look'd not for.

JUL. Madam, in happy time, what day is that?

LA. CAP. Marry, my child, early next Thursday morn,
The gallant, young, and noble gentleman,
The County Paris, at Saint Peter's Church,
Shall happily make thee there a joyful bride.

JUL. Now, by Saint Peter's Church, and Peter too,
He shall not make me there a joyful bride.
I wonder at this haste; that I must wed
Ere he that should be husband comes to woo.
I pray you, tell my lord and father, madam,
I will not marry yet; and, when I do, I swear,
It shall be Romeo, whom you know I hate,
Rather than Paris. These are news indeed!

LA. CAP. Here comes your father; tell him so yourself,
And see how he will take it at your hands.

Enter CAPULET *and* NURSE.

CAP. When the sun sets, the air doth drizzle dew;
But for the sunset of my brother's son
It rains downright.
How now! a conduit,[7] girl? what, still in tears?
Evermore showering? In one little body
Thou counterfeit'st a bark, a sea, a wind:
For still thy eyes, which I may call the sea,
Do ebb and flow with tears; the bark thy body is,

---

[6] *careful*] provident, attentive.
[7] *conduit*] water pipe.

　　　　Sailing in this salt flood; the winds, thy sighs;
　　　　Who raging with thy tears, and they with them,
　　　　Without a sudden calm will overset
　　　　Thy tempest-tossed body. How now, wife!
　　　　Have you deliver'd to her our decree?
LA. CAP.　　Ay, sir; but she will none, she gives you thanks.
　　　　I would the fool were married to her grave!
CAP.　　Soft! take me with you,[8] take me with you, wife.
　　　　How! will she none? doth she not give us thanks?
　　　　Is she not proud? doth she not count her blest,
　　　　Unworthy as she is, that we have wrought
　　　　So worthy a gentleman to be her bridegroom?
JUL.　　Not proud, you have, but thankful that you have:
　　　　Proud can I never be of what I hate;
　　　　But thankful even for hate that is meant love.
CAP.　　How, how! how, how! chop-logic! What is this?
　　　　'Proud,' and 'I thank you,' and 'I thank you not';
　　　　And yet 'not proud': mistress minion,[9] you,
　　　　Thank me no thankings, nor proud me no prouds,
　　　　But fettle[10] your fine joints 'gainst Thursday next,
　　　　To go with Paris to Saint Peter's Church,
　　　　Or I will drag thee on a hurdle[11] thither.
　　　　Out, you green-sickness[12] carrion! out, you baggage!
　　　　You tallow-face!
LA. CAP.　　　　　　Fie, fie! what, are you mad?
JUL.　　Good father, I beseech you on my knees,
　　　　Hear me with patience but to speak a word.
CAP.　　Hang thee, young baggage! disobedient wretch!
　　　　I tell thee what: get thee to church o' Thursday,
　　　　Or never after look me in the face:
　　　　Speak not, reply not, do not answer me;
　　　　My fingers itch. Wife, we scarce thought us blest
　　　　That God had lent us but this only child;
　　　　But now I see this one is one too much,
　　　　And that we have a curse in having her:

---

[8] *take me with you*] let me understand you.
[9] *minion*] spoiled minx.
[10] *fettle*] prepare.
[11] *hurdle*] a conveyance on which criminals were taken to the place of execution.
[12] *green-sickness*] anemic. Anemia was considered a young woman's ailment. Thus here the implication is "immature," "foolish."

Out on her, hilding!

NURSE.   God in heaven bless her!
 You are to blame, my lord, to rate[13] her so.

CAP.   And why, my lady wisdom? hold your tongue,
 Good prudence; smatter[14] with your gossips, go.

NURSE.   I speak no treason.

CAP.   O, God ye god-den.

NURSE.   May not one speak?

CAP.   Peace, you mumbling fool!
 Utter your gravity[15] o'er a gossip's bowl;
 For here we need it not.

LA. CAP.   You are too hot.

CAP.   God's bread! it makes me mad:
 Day, night, hour, tide, time, work, play,
 Alone, in company, still my care hath been
 To have her match'd: and having now provided
 A gentleman of noble parentage,
 Of fair demesnes, youthful, and nobly train'd,
 Stuff'd, as they say, with honourable parts,
 Proportion'd as one's thought would wish a man;
 And then to have a wretched puling fool,
 A whining mammet,[16] in her fortune's tender,
 To answer 'I'll not wed; I cannot love,
 I am too young; I pray you, pardon me.'
 But, an you will not wed, I'll pardon you:
 Graze where you will, you shall not house with me:
 Look to't, think on't, I do not use to jest.
 Thursday is near; lay hand on heart, advise:
 An you be mine, I'll give you to my friend;
 An you be not, hang, beg, starve, die in the streets,
 For, by my soul, I'll ne'er acknowledge thee,
 Nor what is mine shall never do thee good:
 Trust to't, bethink you; I'll not be forsworn.   [*Exit.*

JUL.   Is there no pity sitting in the clouds,
 That sees into the bottom of my grief?
 O, sweet my mother, cast me not away!
 Delay this marriage for a month, a week;

---

[13] *rate*] berate, scold.
[14] *smatter*] chatter, prattle.
[15] *gravity*] wisdom.
[16] *mammet*] doll, puppet.

Or, if you do not, make the bridal bed
In that dim monument where Tybalt lies.

LA. CAP.   Talk not to me, for I'll not speak a word:
Do as thou wilt, for I have done with thee.   [*Exit.*

JUL.   O God!—O Nurse, how shall this be prevented?
My husband is on earth, my faith in heaven;
How shall that faith return again to earth,
Unless that husband send it me from heaven
By leaving earth? comfort me, counsel me.
Alack, alack, that heaven should practise stratagems
Upon so soft a subject as myself!
What say'st thou? hast thou not a word of joy?
Some comfort, Nurse.

NURSE.   Faith, here it is.
Romeo is banish'd, and all the world to nothing,[17]
That he dares ne'er come back to challenge you;
Or, if he do, it needs must be by stealth.
Then, since the case so stands as now it doth,
I think it best you married with the County.
O, he's a lovely gentleman!
Romeo's a dishclout to him: an eagle, madam,
Hath not so green, so quick, so fair an eye
As Paris hath. Beshrew my very heart,
I think you are happy in this second match,
For it excels your first: or if it did not,
Your first is dead, or 'twere as good he were
As living here and you no use of him.

JUL.   Speakest thou from thy heart?
NURSE.   And from my soul too; else beshrew them both.
JUL.   Amen!
NURSE.   What?
JUL.   Well, thou hast comforted me marvellous much.
Go in, and tell my lady I am gone,
Having displeased my father, to Laurence' cell,
To make confession and to be absolved.
NURSE.   Marry, I will, and this is wisely done.   [*Exit.*
JUL.   Ancient damnation![18] O most wicked fiend!
Is it more sin to wish me thus forsworn,

---

[17] *all the world to nothing*] the odds are overwhelmingly against you.
[18] *Ancient damnation*] evil old woman.

Or to dispraise my lord with that same tongue
Which she hath praised him with above compare
So many thousand times? Go, counsellor;
Thou and my bosom henceforth shall be twain.
I'll to the Friar, to know his remedy:
If all else fail, myself have power to die.   [*Exit.*

ACT IV.

SCENE I. *Friar Laurence's cell.*

Enter FRIAR LAURENCE *and* PARIS.

FRI. L.   On Thursday, sir? the time is very short.
PAR.   My father Capulet will have it so;
    And I am nothing slow to slack his haste.
FRI. L.   You say you do not know the lady's mind:
    Uneven is the course; I like it not.
PAR.   Immoderately she weeps for Tybalt's death,
    And therefore have I little talk'd of love,
    For Venus smiles not in a house of tears.
    Now, sir, her father counts it dangerous
    That she doth give her sorrow so much sway,
    And in his wisdom hastes our marriage,
    To stop the inundation of her tears,
    Which, too much minded by herself alone,
    May be put from her by society:
    Now do you know the reason of this haste.
FRI. L.   [*Aside*] I would I knew not why it should be slow'd.
    Look, sir, here comes the lady toward my cell.

Enter JULIET.

PAR.   Happily met, my lady and my wife!
JUL.   That may be, sir, when I may be a wife.
PAR.   That may be must be, love, on Thursday next,
JUL.   What must be shall be.
FRI. L.   That's a certain text.
PAR.   Come you to make confession to this father?

379

JUL.   To answer that, I should confess to you.
PAR.   Do not deny to him that you love me.
JUL.   I will confess to you that I love him.
PAR.   So will ye, I am sure, that you love me.
JUL.   If I do so, it will be of more price,
      Being spoke behind your back, than to your face.
PAR.   Poor soul, thy face is much abused with tears.
JUL.   The tears have got small victory by that;
      For it was bad enough before their spite.
PAR.   Thou wrong'st it more than tears with that report.
JUL.   That is no slander, sir, which is a truth,
      And what I spake, I spake it to my face.
PAR.   Thy face is mine, and thou hast slander'd it.
JUL.   It may be so, for it is not mine own.
      Are you at leisure, holy father, now;
      Or shall I come to you at evening mass?
FRI. L.   My leisure serves me, pensive daughter, now.
      My lord, we must entreat the time alone.
PAR.   God shield I should disturb devotion!
      Juliet, on Thursday early will I rouse ye:
      Till then, adieu, and keep this holy kiss.   [*Exit.*
JUL.   O, shut the door, and when thou hast done so,
      Come weep with me; past hope, past cure, past help!
FRI. L.   Ah, Juliet, I already know thy grief;
      It strains me past the compass of my wits:
      I hear thou must, and nothing may prorogue it,
      On Thursday next be married to this County.
JUL.   Tell me not, Friar, that thou hear'st of this,
      Unless thou tell me how I may prevent it:
      If in thy wisdom thou canst give no help,
      Do thou but call my resolution wise,
      And with this knife I'll help it presently. [1]
      God join'd my heart and Romeo's, thou our hands;
      And ere this hand, by thee to Romeo's seal'd,
      Shall be the label to another deed,
      Or my true heart with treacherous revolt
      Turn to another, this shall slay them both:
      Therefore, out of thy long-experienced time,
      Give me some present counsel; or, behold,

---

[1] *presently*] instantly.

'Twixt my extremes² and me this bloody knife
Shall play the umpire, arbitrating that
Which the commission of³ thy years and art
Could to no issue of true honour bring.
Be not so long to speak; I long to die,
If what thou speak'st speak not of remedy.

FRI. L.   Hold, daughter: I do spy a kind of hope,
Which craves as desperate an execution
As that is desperate which we would prevent.
If, rather than to marry County Paris,
Thou hast the strength of will to slay thyself,
Then is it likely thou wilt undertake
A thing like death to chide away this shame,
That copest⁴ with death himself to 'scape from it;
And, if thou darest, I'll give thee remedy.

JUL.   O, bid me leap, rather than marry Paris,
From off the battlements of yonder tower;
Or walk in thievish ways; or bid me lurk
Where serpents are; chain me with roaring bears;
Or shut me nightly in a charnel-house,
O'er-cover'd quite with dead men's rattling bones,
With reeky shanks and yellow chapless⁵ skulls;
Or bid me go into a new-made grave,
And hide me with a dead man in his shroud;
Things that to hear them told, have made me tremble;
And I will do it without fear or doubt,
To live an unstain'd wife to my sweet love.

FRI. L.   Hold, then; go home, be merry, give consent
To marry Paris: Wednesday is to-morrow;
To-morrow night look that thou lie alone,
Let not thy nurse lie with thee in thy chamber:
Take thou this vial, being then in bed,
And this distilled liquor drink thou off:
When presently through all thy veins shall run
A cold and drowsy humour; for no pulse
Shall keep his native progress, but surcease:
No warmth, no breath, shall testify thou livest;

---

² *extremes*] extreme difficulties.
³ *commission of*] authority deriving from.
⁴ *copest*] associates.
⁵ *chapless*] without the lower jaw.

The roses in thy lips and cheeks shall fade
To paly ashes; thy eyes' windows fall,
Like death, when he shuts up the day of life;
Each part, deprived of supple government,
Shall, stiff and stark and cold, appear like death:
And in this borrow'd likeness of shrunk death
Thou shalt continue two and forty hours,
And then awake as from a pleasant sleep.
Now, when the bridegroom in the morning comes
To rouse thee from thy bed, there art thou dead:
Then, as the manner of our country is,
In thy best robes uncover'd on the bier
Thou shalt be borne to that same ancient vault
Where all the kindred of the Capulets lie.
In the mean time, against thou shalt awake,
Shall Romeo by my letters know our drift;
And hither shall he come: and he and I
Will watch thy waking, and that very night
Shall Romeo bear thee hence to Mantua.
And this shall free thee from this present shame,
If no inconstant toy[6] nor womanish fear
Abate thy valour in the acting it.

JUL.   Give me, give me! O, tell not me of fear!

FRI. L.   Hold; get you gone, be strong and prosperous
In this resolve: I'll send a friar with speed
To Mantua, with my letters to thy lord.

JUL.   Love give me strength! and strength shall help afford.
Farewell, dear father!   [*Exeunt.*

SCENE **II.** *Hall in Capulet's house.*

Enter CAPULET, LADY CAPULET, NURSE, *and two* Servingmen.

CAP.   So many guests invite as here are writ.   [*Exit* First Servant.
Sirrah, go hire me twenty cunning cooks.

SEC. SERV.   You shall have none ill, sir, for I'll try if they can lick their
fingers.

CAP.   How canst thou try them so?

---

[6] *toy*] whim, idle fancy.

SEC. SERV.   Marry, sir, 'tis an ill cook that cannot lick his own fingers:
    therefore he that cannot lick his fingers goes not with me.
CAP.   Go, be gone.   [*Exit* Sec. Servant.
    We shall be much unfurnish'd[1] for this time.
    What, is my daughter gone to Friar Laurence?
NURSE.   Ay, forsooth.
CAP.   Well, he may chance to do some good on her:
    A peevish self-will'd harlotry[2] it is.

Enter JULIET.

NURSE.   See where she comes from shrift with merry look.
CAP.   How now, my headstrong! where have you been gadding?
JUL.   Where I have learn'd me to repent the sin
    Of disobedient opposition
    To you and your behests, and am enjoin'd
    By holy Laurence to fall prostrate here,
    To beg your pardon: pardon, I beseech you!
    Henceforward I am ever ruled by you.
CAP.   Send for the County; go tell him of this:
    I'll have this knot knit up to-morrow morning.
JUL.   I met the youthful lord at Laurence' cell,
    And gave him what becomed[3] love I might,
    Not stepping o'er the bounds of modesty.
CAP.   Why, I am glad on 't; this is well: stand up:
    This is as 't should be. Let me see the County;
    Ay, marry, go, I say, and fetch him hither.
    Now, afore God, this reverend holy Friar,
    All our whole city is much bound to him.
JUL.   Nurse, will you go with me into my closet,[4]
    To help me sort such needful ornaments
    As you think fit to furnish me to-morrow?
LA. CAP.   No, not till Thursday; there is time enough.
CAP.   Go, Nurse, go with her: we'll to church to-morrow.
                     [*Exeunt* JULIET *and* NURSE.
LA. CAP.   We shall be short in our provision:
    'Tis now near night.
CAP.   Tush, I will stir about,

    [1] *unfurnish'd*] unprepared.
    [2] *harlotry*] good-for-nothing.
    [3] *becomed*] becoming, befitting.
    [4] *closet*] private room.

And all things shall be well, I warrant thee, wife:
Go thou to Juliet, help to deck up her;
I'll not to bed to-night; let me alone;
I'll play the housewife for this once. What, ho!
They are all forth: well, I will walk myself
To County Paris, to prepare him up
Against to-morrow: my heart is wondrous light,
Since this same wayward girl is so reclaim'd.   [*Exeunt.*

SCENE III. *Juliet's chamber.*

Enter JULIET *and* NURSE.

JUL.   Ay, those attires are best: but, gentle Nurse,
I pray thee, leave me to myself to-night;
For I have need of many orisons
To move the heavens to smile upon my state,
Which, well thou know'st, is cross[1] and full of sin.

Enter LADY CAPULET.

LA. CAP.   What, are you busy, ho? need you my help?
JUL.   No, madam; we have cull'd such necessaries
As are behoveful for our state to-morrow:
So please you, let me now be left alone,
And let the Nurse this night sit up with you,
For I am sure you have your hands full all
In this so sudden business.
LA. CAP.   Good night:
Get thee to bed and rest, for thou hast need.
                     [*Exeunt* LADY CAPULET *and* NURSE.
JUL.   Farewell! God knows when we shall meet again.
I have a faint cold fear thrills through my veins,
That almost freezes up the heat of life:
I'll call them back again to comfort me.
Nurse!—What should she do here?
My dismal scene I needs must act alone.
Come, vial.
What if this mixture do not work at all?

---

[1] *cross*] perverse.

Shall I be married then to-morrow morning?
No, no: this shall forbid it. Lie thou there. [*Laying down a dagger.*
What if it be a poison, which the Friar
Subtly hath minister'd to have me dead,
Lest in this marriage he should be dishonour'd,
Because he married me before to Romeo?
I fear it is: and yet, methinks, it should not,
For he hath still been tried a holy man.
How if, when I am laid into the tomb,
I wake before the time that Romeo
Come to redeem me? there's a fearful point.
Shall I not then be stifled in the vault,
To whose foul mouth no healthsome air breathes in,
And there die strangled ere my Romeo comes?
Or, if I live, is it not very like,
The horrible conceit of death and night,
Together with the terror of the place,
As in a vault, an ancient receptacle,
Where for this many hundred years the bones
Of all my buried ancestors are pack'd;
Where bloody Tybalt, yet but green in earth,
Lies festering in his shroud; where, as they say,
At some hours in the night spirits resort;
Alack, alack, is it not like that I
So early waking, what with loathsome smells
And shrieks like mandrakes' torn out of the earth,
That living mortals hearing them run mad:
O, if I wake, shall I not be distraught,
Environed with all these hideous fears?
And madly play with my forefathers' joints?
And pluck the mangled Tybalt from his shroud?
And, in this rage,[2] with some great kinsman's bone,
As with a club, dash out my desperate brains?
O, look! methinks I see my cousin's ghost
Seeking out Romeo, that did spit his body
Upon a rapier's point: stay, Tybalt, stay!
Romeo, I come! this do I drink to thee.

                         [*She falls upon her bed, within the curtains.*

---

[2] *rage*] madness.

SCENE IV. *Hall in Capulet's house.*

Enter LADY CAPULET *and* NURSE.

LA. CAP.   Hold, take these keys, and fetch more spices, Nurse.
NURSE.   They call for dates and quinces in the pastry.[1]

Enter CAPULET.

CAP.   Come, stir, stir, stir! the second cock hath crow'd,
     The curfew-bell hath rung, 'tis three o'clock:
     Look to the baked meats, good Angelica:
     Spare not for cost.
NURSE.   Go, you cot-quean,[2] go,
     Get you to bed; faith, you'll be sick to-morrow
     For this night's watching.
CAP.   No, not a whit: what! I have watch'd ere now
     All night for lesser cause, and ne'er been sick.
LA. CAP.   Ay, you have been a mouse-hunt[3] in your time;
     But I will watch you from such watching now.
                     [*Exeunt* LADY CAPULET *and* NURSE.
CAP.   A jealous-hood,[4] a jealous-hood!
Enter three or four Servingmen, *with spits, and logs, and baskets.*

                     Now, fellow,
     What's there?
FIRST SERV.   Things for the cook, sir, but I know not what.
CAP.   Make haste, make haste. [*Exit* First Serv.] Sirrah, fetch drier logs:
     Call Peter, he will show thee where they are.
SEC. SERV.   I have a head, sir, that will find out logs,
     And never trouble Peter for the matter.
CAP.   Mass, and well said; a merry whoreson, ha!
     Thou shalt be logger-head.[5] [*Exit* Sec. Serv.] Good faith, 'tis day:
     The County will be here with music straight,

---

[1] *pastry*] room in which pies were made.
[2] *cot-quean*] a man who plays the housewife.
[3] *mouse-hunt*] woman chaser.
[4] *jealous-hood*] jealousy.
[5] *logger-head*] blockhead.

For so he said he would. [*Music within.*] I hear him near.
Nurse! Wife! What, ho! What, Nurse, I say!

Re-enter NURSE.

Go waken Juliet, go and trim her up;
I'll go and chat with Paris: hie, make haste,
Make haste: the bridegroom he is come already:
Make haste, I say.   [*Exeunt.*

SCENE V. *Juliet's chamber.*

Enter NURSE.

NURSE.   Mistress! what, mistress! Juliet! fast,[1] I warrant her, she:
     Why, lamb! why, lady! fie, you slug-a-bed!
     Why, love, I say! madam! sweet-heart! why, bride!
     What, not a word? you take your pennyworths[2] now;
     Sleep for a week; for the next night, I warrant,
     The County Paris hath set up his rest[3]
     That you shall rest but little. God forgive me,
     Marry, and amen, how sound is she asleep!
     I needs must wake her. Madam, madam, madam!
     Ay, let the County take you in your bed;
     He'll fright you up, i' faith. Will it not be? [*Undraws the curtains.*
     What, dress'd! and in your clothes! and down again!
     I must needs wake you. Lady! lady! lady!
     Alas, alas! Help, help! my lady's dead!
     O, well-a-day, that ever I was born!
     Some aqua-vitae, ho! My lord! my lady!

Enter LADY CAPULET.

LA. CAP.   What noise is here?
NURSE.   O lamentable day!
LA. CAP.   What is the matter?
NURSE.   Look, look! O heavy day!
LA. CAP.   O me, O me! My child, my only life,
     Revive, look up, or I will die with thee.

---

[1] *fast*] fast asleep.
[2] *pennyworths*] small quantities (of sleep).
[3] *set up his rest*] determined, with a bawdy innuendo of couching the lance for the charge.

Help, help! call help.

Enter CAPULET.

CAP. For shame, bring Juliet forth; her lord is come.
NURSE. She's dead, deceased, she's dead; alack the day!
LA. CAP. Alack the day, she's dead, she's dead, she's dead!
CAP. Ha! let me see her. Out, alas! she's cold;
 Her blood is settled and her joints are stiff;
 Life and these lips have long been separated.
 Death lies on her like an untimely frost
 Upon the sweetest flower of all the field.
NURSE. O lamentable day!
LA. CAP.   O woeful time!
CAP. Death, that hath ta'en her hence to make me wail,
 Ties up my tongue and will not let me speak.

Enter FRIAR LAURENCE *and* PARIS, *with* Musicians.

FRI. L. Come, is the bride ready to go to church?
CAP. Ready to go, but never to return.
 O son, the night before thy wedding-day
 Hath Death lain with thy wife: see, there she lies,
 Flower as she was, deflowered by him.
 Death is my son-in-law, Death is my heir;
 My daughter he hath wedded: I will die,
 And leave him all; life, living, all is Death's.
PAR. Have I thought long to see this morning's face,
 And doth it give me such a sight as this?
LA. CAP. Accurst, unhappy, wretched, hateful day!
 Most miserable hour that e'er time saw
 In lasting labour of his pilgrimage!
 But one, poor one, one poor and loving child,
 But one thing to rejoice and solace in,
 And cruel death hath catch'd it from my sight!
NURSE. O woe! O woeful, woeful, woeful day!
 Most lamentable day, most woeful day,
 That ever, ever, I did yet behold!
 O day! O day! O day! O hateful day!
 Never was seen so black a day as this:
 O woeful day, O woeful day!
PAR. Beguiled, divorced, wronged, spited, slain!
 Most detestable death, by thee beguiled,

By cruel cruel thee quite overthrown!
O love! O life! not life, but love in death!

CAP.   Despised, distressed, hated, martyr'd, kill'd!
Uncomfortable[4] time, why camest thou now
To murder, murder our solemnity?[5]
O child! O child! my soul, and not my child!
Dead art thou! Alack, my child is dead;
And with my child my joys are buried!

FRI. L.   Peace, ho, for shame! confusion's[6] cure lives not
In these confusions. Heaven and yourself
Had part in this fair maid; now heaven hath all,
And all the better is it for the maid:
Your part in her you could not keep from death;
But heaven keeps his part in eternal life.
The most you sought was her promotion,
For 'twas your heaven she should be advanced:
And weep ye now, seeing she is advanced
Above the clouds, as high as heaven itself?
O, in this love, you love your child so ill,
That you run mad, seeing that she is well:
She's not well married that lives married long,
But she's best married that dies married young.
Dry up your tears, and stick your rosemary
On this fair corse, and, as the custom is,
In all her best array bear her to church:
For though fond nature bids us all lament,
Yet nature's tears are reason's merriment.

CAP.   All things that we ordained festival,
Turn from their office to black funeral:
Our instruments to melancholy bells;
Our wedding cheer to a sad burial feast;
Our solemn hymns to sullen dirges change;
Our bridal flowers serve for a buried corse,
And all things change them to the contrary.

FRI. L.   Sir, go you in; and, madam, go with him;
And go, Sir Paris; every one prepare
To follow this fair corse unto her grave:

---

[4] *Uncomfortable*] joyless.
[5] *solemnity*| celebration, ceremony.
[6] *confusion's*| calamity's.

   The heavens do lour upon you for some ill;
   Move them no more by crossing their high will.

             [*Exeunt* CAPULET, LADY CAPULET, PARIS, *and* FRIAR.

FIRST MUS.   Faith, we may put up our pipes, and be gone.

NURSE.   Honest good fellows, ah, put up, put up;
   For, well you know, this is a pitiful case.   [*Exit.*

FIRST MUS.   Ay, by my troth, the case may be amended.

Enter PETER.

PET.   Musicians, O, musicians, 'Heart's ease,[7] Heart's ease': O, an you
   will have me live, play 'Heart's ease.'

FIRST MUS.   Why 'Heart's ease'?

PET.   O, musicians, because my heart itself plays 'My heart is full of
   woe': O, play me some merry dump,[8] to comfort me.

FIRST MUS.   Not a dump we; 'tis no time to play now.

PET.   You will not then?

FIRST MUS.   No.

PET.   I will then give it you soundly.

FIRST MUS.   What will you give us?

PET.   No money, on my faith, but the gleek;[9] I will give you the
   minstrel.

FIRST MUS.   Then will I give you the serving-creature.

PET.   Then will I lay the serving-creature's dagger on your pate. I will
   carry no crotchets:[10] I'll re you, I'll fa you; do you note me?

FIRST MUS.   An you re us and fa us, you note us.

SEC. MUS.   Pray you, put up your dagger, and put out[11] your wit.

PET.   Then have at you with my wit! I will dry-beat you with an iron
   wit, and put up my iron dagger. Answer me like men:

                'When griping grief the heart doth wound
                And doleful dumps the mind oppress,
                Then music with her silver sound'—

why 'silver sound'? why 'music with her silver sound'?—What say
you, Simon Catling?[12]

---

[7] '*Heart's ease*'] a popular tune of the time.
[8] *dump*] melancholy tune.
[9] *gleek*] gesture of scorn.
[10] *carry no crotchets*] endure none of your whims (with the musical pun).
[11] *put out*] display.
[12] *Catling*] a lute string.

FIRST MUS.   Marry, sir, because silver hath a sweet sound.

PET.   Pretty! What say you, Hugh Rebeck?[13]

SEC. MUS.   I say, 'silver sound,' because musicians sound for silver.

PET.   Pretty too! What say you, James Soundpost?

THIRD MUS.   Faith, I know not what to say.

PET.   O, I cry you mercy; you are the singer: I will say for you. It is 'music with her silver sound,' because musicians have no gold for sounding:

> 'Then music with her silver sound
> With speedy help doth lend redress.'   [*Exit*.

FIRST MUS.   What a pestilent knave is this same!

SEC. MUS.   Hang him, Jack! Come, we'll in here; tarry for the mourners, and stay dinner.   [*Exeunt*.

---

[13] *Rebeck*] a three-stringed fiddle.

ACT V.

Scene I. *Mantua. A street.*

Enter ROMEO.

ROM.   If I may trust the flattering truth of sleep,
    My dreams presage some joyful news at hand:
    My bosom's lord sits lightly in his throne,
    And all this day an unaccustom'd spirit
    Lifts me above the ground with cheerful thoughts.
    I dreamt my lady came and found me dead—
    Strange dream, that gives a dead man leave to think!—
    And breathed such life with kisses in my lips,
    That I revived and was an emperor.
    Ah me! how sweet is love itself possess'd,
    When but love's shadows are so rich in joy!

Enter BALTHASAR, *booted.*

    News from Verona! How now, Balthasar!
    Dost thou not bring me letters from the Friar?
    How doth my lady? Is my father well?
    How fares my Juliet? that I ask again;
    For nothing can be ill, if she be well.
BAL.   Then she is well, and nothing can be ill:
    Her body sleeps in Capels' monument,
    And her immortal part with angels lives.
    I saw her laid low in her kindred's vault,
    And presently took post to tell it you:
    O, pardon me for bringing these ill news,
    Since you did leave it for my office, sir.
ROM.   Is it e'en so? then I defy you, stars!

    Thou know'st my lodging: get me ink and paper,
    And hire post-horses; I will hence to-night.
BAL.   I do beseech you, sir, have patience:
    Your looks are pale and wild, and do import
    Some misadventure.
ROM.   Tush, thou art deceived:
    Leave me, and do the thing I bid thee do.
    Hast thou no letters to me from the Friar?
BAL.   No, my good lord.
ROM.   No matter: get thee gone,
    And hire those horses; I'll be with thee straight. [*Exit* BALTHASAR.
    Well, Juliet, I will lie with thee to-night.
    Let's see for means:—O mischief, thou art swift
    To enter in the thoughts of desperate men!
    I do remember an apothecary,
    And hereabouts a' dwells, which late I noted
    In tatter'd weeds, with overwhelming[1] brows,
    Culling of simples;[2] meagre were his looks;
    Sharp misery had worn him to the bones:
    And in his needy shop a tortoise hung,
    An alligator stuff'd and other skins
    Of ill-shaped fishes; and about his shelves
    A beggarly account of empty boxes,
    Green earthen pots, bladders and musty seeds,
    Remnants of packthread and old cakes of roses,[3]
    Were thinly scatter'd, to make up a show.
    Noting this penury, to myself I said,
    An if a man did need a poison now,
    Whose sale is present death in Mantua,
    Here lives a caitiff wretch would sell it him.
    O, this same thought did but forerun my need,
    And this same needy man must sell it me.
    As I remember, this should be the house:
    Being holiday, the beggar's shop is shut.
    What, ho! apothecary!

Enter Apothecary.

---

[1] *overwhelming*] jutting out, overhanging.
[2] *Culling of simples*] gathering medicinal herbs.
[3] *cakes of roses*] rose petals compressed into cakes to be used as perfume.

AP.   Who calls so loud?

ROM.   Come hither, man. I see that thou art poor;
     Hold, there is forty ducats: let me have
     A dram of poison; such soon-speeding gear
     As will disperse itself through all the veins,
     That the life-weary taker may fall dead,
     And that the trunk may be discharged of breath
     As violently as hasty powder fired
     Doth hurry from the fatal cannon's womb.

AP.   Such mortal drugs I have; but Mantua's law
     Is death to any he that utters[4] them.

ROM.   Art thou so bare and full of wretchedness,
     And fear'st to die? famine is in thy cheeks,
     Need and oppression starveth in thy eyes,
     Contempt and beggary hangs upon thy back,
     The world is not thy friend, nor the world's law:
     The world affords no law to make thee rich;
     Then be not poor, but break it, and take this.

AP.   My poverty, but not my will, consents.

ROM.   I pay thy poverty and not thy will.

AP.   Put this in any liquid thing you will,
     And drink it off; and, if you had the strength
     Of twenty men, it would dispatch you straight.

ROM.   There is thy gold, worse poison to men's souls,
     Doing more murder in this loathsome world,
     Than these poor compounds that thou mayst not sell:
     I sell thee poison, thou hast sold me none.
     Farewell: buy food, and get thyself in flesh.
     Come, cordial and not poison, go with me
     To Juliet's grave; for there must I use thee.   [*Exeunt.*

---

[4] *utters*] dispenses.

SCENE II. *Friar Laurence's cell.*

Enter FRIAR JOHN.

FRI. J.   Holy Franciscan friar! brother, ho!

Enter FRIAR LAURENCE.

FRI. L.   This same should be the voice of Friar John.
       Welcome from Mantua: what says Romeo?
       Or, if his mind be writ, give me his letter.
FRI. J.   Going to find a bare-foot brother out,
       One of our order, to associate[1] me,
       Here in this city visiting the sick,
       And finding him, the searchers of the town,[2]
       Suspecting that we both were in a house
       Where the infectious pestilence did reign,
       Seal'd up the doors and would not let us forth;
       So that my speed to Mantua there was stay'd.
FRI. L.   Who bare my letter then to Romeo?
FRI. J.   I could not send it,—here it is again,—
       Nor get a messenger to bring it thee,
       So fearful were they of infection.
FRI. L.   Unhappy fortune! by my brotherhood,
       The letter was not nice,[3] but full of charge
       Of dear import, and the neglecting it
       May do much danger. Friar John, go hence;
       Get me an iron crow[4] and bring it straight
       Unto my cell.
FRI. J.   Brother, I'll go and bring it thee.   [*Exit.*
FRI. L.   Now must I to the monument alone;
       Within this three hours will fair Juliet wake:
       She will beshrew me much that Romeo
       Hath had no notice of these accidents;
       But I will write again to Mantua,

---

[1] *associate*] accompany.
[2] *searchers of the town*] officers of the town responsible for public health during a
    plague.
[3] *nice*] trivial.
[4] *crow*] crowbar.

And keep her at my cell till Romeo come:
Poor living corse, closed in a dead man's tomb!   [*Exit.*

SCENE III. *A churchyard; in it a monument belonging to the Capulets.*

Enter PARIS *and his* Page, *bearing flowers and a torch.*

PAR.   Give me thy torch, boy: hence, and stand aloof:
Yet put it out, for I would not be seen.
Under yond yew-trees lay thee all along, [1]
Holding thine ear close to the hollow ground;
So shall no foot upon the churchyard tread,
Being loose, unfirm, with digging up of graves,
But thou shalt hear it: whistle then to me,
As signal that thou hear'st something approach.
Give me those flowers. Do as I bid thee, go.
PAGE.   [*Aside*] I am almost afraid to stand alone
Here in the churchyard; yet I will adventure.   [*Retires.*
PAR.   Sweet flower, with flowers thy bridal bed I strew,—
O woe! thy canopy is dust and stones;—
Which with sweet water nightly I will dew,
Or, wanting that, with tears distill'd by moans:
The obsequies that I for thee will keep
Nightly shall be to strew thy grave and weep. [*The* Page *whistles.*
The boy gives warning something doth approach.
What cursed foot wanders this way to-night,
To cross my obsequies and true love's rite?
What, with a torch! Muffle me, night, a while.   [*Retires.*

Enter ROMEO *and* BALTHASAR, *with a torch, mattock, &c.*

ROM.   Give me that mattock and the wrenching iron.
Hold, take this letter; early in the morning
See thou deliver it to my lord and father.
Give me the light: upon thy life, I charge thee,
Whate'er thou hear'st or seest, stand all aloof,
And do not interrupt me in my course.
Why I descend into this bed of death
Is partly to behold my lady's face,
But chiefly to take thence from her dead finger

---

[1] *all along*] at full length.

A precious ring, a ring that I must use
In dear employment: therefore hence, be gone:
But if thou, jealous,[2] dost return to pry
In what I farther shall intend to do,
By heaven, I will tear thee joint by joint
And strew this hungry churchyard with thy limbs:
The time and my intents are savage-wild,
More fierce and more inexorable far
Than empty tigers or the roaring sea.

BAL.   I will be gone, sir, and not trouble you.

ROM.   So shalt thou show me friendship. Take thou that:
Live, and be prosperous: and farewell, good fellow.

BAL.   [*Aside*] For all this same, I'll hide me hereabout:
His looks I fear, and his intents I doubt.   [*Retires.*

ROM.   Thou detestable maw, thou womb of death,
Gorged with the dearest morsel of the earth,
Thus I enforce thy rotten jaws to open,
And in despite I'll cram thee with more food. [*Opens the tomb.*

PAR.   This is that banish'd haughty Montague
That murder'd my love's cousin, with which grief,
It is supposed, the fair creature died,
And here is come to do some villanous shame
To the dead bodies: I will apprehend him.   [*Comes forward.*
Stop thy unhallow'd toil, vile Montague!
Can vengeance be pursued further than death?
Condemned villain, I do apprehend thee:
Obey, and go with me; for thou must die.

ROM.   I must indeed, and therefore came I hither.
Good gentle youth, tempt not a desperate man;
Fly hence and leave me: think upon these gone;
Let them affright thee. I beseech thee, youth,
Put not another sin upon my head,
By urging me to fury: O, be gone!
By heaven, I love thee better than myself,
For I come hither arm'd against myself:
Stay not, be gone: live, and hereafter say,
A madman's mercy bid thee run away.

PAR.   I do defy thy conjurations[3]
And apprehend thee for a felon here.

---

[2] *jealous*] suspicious.
[3] *conjurations*] solemn appeals.

ROM.   Wilt thou provoke me? then have at thee, boy!   [*They fight.*
PAGE.   O Lord, they fight! I will go call the watch.   [*Exit.*
PAR.   O, I am slain! [*Falls.*] If thou be merciful,
    Open the tomb, lay me with Juliet.   [*Dies.*
ROM.   In faith, I will. Let me peruse this face:
    Mercutio's kinsman, noble County Paris!
    What said my man, when my betossed soul
    Did not attend him as we rode? I think
    He told me Paris should have married Juliet:
    Said he not so? or did I dream it so?
    Or am I mad, hearing him talk of Juliet,
    To think it was so? O, give me thy hand,
    One writ with me in sour misfortune's book!
    I'll bury thee in a triumphant grave;
    A grave? O, no, a lantern,[4] slaughter'd youth;
    For here lies Juliet, and her beauty makes
    This vault a feasting presence[5] full of light.
    Death, lie thou there, by a dead man interr'd.

                    [*Laying* PARIS *in the monument.*
    How oft when men are at the point of death
    Have they been merry! which their keepers call
    A lightning before death: O, how may I
    Call this a lightning? O my love! my wife!
    Death, that hath suck'd the honey of thy breath,
    Hath had no power yet upon thy beauty:
    Thou art not conquer'd; beauty's ensign yet
    Is crimson in thy lips and in thy cheeks,
    And death's pale flag is not advanced there.
    Tybalt, liest thou there in thy bloody sheet?
    O, what more favour can I do to thee
    Than with that hand that cut thy youth in twain
    To sunder his that was thine enemy?
    Forgive me, cousin! Ah, dear Juliet,
    Why art thou yet so fair? shall I believe
    That unsubstantial death is amorous,
    And that the lean abhorred monster keeps
    Thee here in dark to be his paramour?
    For fear of that, I still will stay with thee,

[4] *lantern*] turret full of windows.
[5] *presence*] presence chamber.

And never from this palace of dim night
Depart again: here, here will I remain
With worms that are thy chamber-maids; O, here
Will I set up my everlasting rest,
And shake the yoke of inauspicious stars
From this world-wearied flesh. Eyes, look your last!
Arms, take your last embrace! and, lips, O you
The doors of breath, seal with a righteous kiss
A dateless[6] bargain to engrossing death!
Come, bitter conduct, come, unsavoury guide!
Thou desperate pilot, now at once run on
The dashing rocks thy sea-sick weary bark.
Here's to my love! [*Drinks.*] O true apothecary!
Thy drugs are quick. Thus with a kiss I die.   [*Dies.*

Enter, at the other end of the churchyard, FRIAR LAURENCE, *with a lantern, crow, and spade.*

FRI. L.   Saint Francis be my speed![7] how oft to-night
Have my old feet stumbled at graves! Who's there?
BAL.   Here's one, a friend, and one that knows you well.
FRI. L.   Bliss be upon you! Tell me, good my friend,
What torch is yond that vainly lends his light
To grubs and eyeless skulls? as I discern,
It burneth in the Capels' monument.
BAL.   It doth so, holy sir; and there's my master,
One that you love.
FRI. L.   Who is it?
BAL.   Romeo.
FRI. L.   How long hath he been there?
BAL.   Full half an hour.
FRI. L.   Go with me to the vault.
BAL.   I dare not, sir:
My master knows not but I am gone hence;
And fearfully did menace me with death,
If I did stay to look on his intents.
FRI. L.   Stay, then; I'll go alone: fear comes upon me;
O, much I fear some ill unlucky thing.
BAL.   As I did sleep under this yew-tree here,

---

[6] *dateless*] eternal.
[7] *speed*] protecting and assisting power.

I dreamt my master and another fought,
And that my master slew him.

FRI. L. Romeo! [*Advances.*
Alack, alack, what blood is this, which stains
The stony entrance of this sepulchre?
What mean these masterless and gory swords
To lie discolour'd by this place of peace? [*Enters the tomb.*
Romeo! O, pale! Who else? what, Paris too?
And steep'd in blood? Ah, what an unkind hour
Is guilty of this lamentable chance!
The lady stirs. [JULIET *wakes.*

JUL. O comfortable Friar! where is my lord?
I do remember well where I should be,
And there I am: where is my Romeo? [*Noise within.*

FRI. L. I hear some noise. Lady, come from that nest
Of death, contagion and unnatural sleep:
A greater power than we can contradict
Hath thwarted our intents: come, come away:
Thy husband in thy bosom there lies dead;
And Paris too: come, I'll dispose of thee
Among a sisterhood of holy nuns:
Stay not to question, for the watch is coming;
Come, go, good Juliet; I dare no longer stay.

JUL. Go, get thee hence, for I will not away. [*Exit* FRI. L.
What's here? a cup, closed in my true love's hand?
Poison, I see, hath been his timeless end:
O churl! drunk all, and left no friendly drop
To help me after? I will kiss thy lips;
Haply some poison yet doth hang on them,
To make me die with a restorative. [*Kisses him.*
Thy lips are warm.

FIRST WATCH. [*Within*] Lead, boy: which way?

JUL. Yea, noise? then I'll be brief. O happy dagger!
[*Snatching* ROMEO'S *dagger.*
This is thy sheath [*Stabs herself*]; there rust, and let me die.
[*Falls on* ROMEO'S *body, and dies.*

Enter Watch, *with the* Page *of* PARIS.

PAGE. This is the place; there, where the torch doth burn.

FIRST WATCH. The ground is bloody; search about the churchyard:

Go, some of you, whoe'er you find attach.[8]
Pitiful sight! here lies the County slain; ·
And Juliet bleeding, warm, and newly dead,
Who here hath lain this two days buried.
Go, tell the Prince: run to the Capulets:
Raise up the Montagues: some others search:
We see the ground whereon these woes do lie;
But the true ground of all these piteous woes
We cannot without circumstance[9] descry.

Re-enter some of the Watch, *with* BALTHASAR.

SEC. WATCH.   Here's Romeo's man; we found him in the churchyard.
FIRST WATCH.   Hold him in safety, till the Prince come hither.

Re-enter FRIAR LAURENCE, *and another* Watchman.

THIRD WATCH.   Here is a friar, that trembles, sighs and weeps:
    We took this mattock and this spade from him,
    As he was coming from this churchyard's side.
FIRST WATCH.   A great suspicion: stay the friar too.

Enter the PRINCE *and* Attendants.

PRINCE.   What misadventure is so early up,
    That calls our person from our morning rest?

Enter CAPULET, LADY CAPULET, *and others.*

CAP.   What should it be that they so shriek abroad?
LA. CAP.   The people in the street cry Romeo,
    Some Juliet, and some Paris, and all run
    With open outcry toward our monument.
PRINCE.   What fear is this which startles in our ears?
FIRST WATCH.   Sovereign, here lies the County Paris slain;
    And Romeo dead; and Juliet, dead before,
    Warm and new kill'd.
PRINCE.   Search, seek, and know how this foul murder comes.
FIRST WATCH.   Here is a friar, and slaughter'd Romeo's man,
    With instruments upon them fit to open
    These dead men's tombs.
CAP.   O heavens! O wife, look how our daughter bleeds!

---

[8] *attach*] arrest.
[9] *circumstance*] detailed information.

This dagger hath mista'en, for, lo, his house
Is empty on the back of Montague,
And it mis-sheathed in my daughter's bosom!

LA. CAP.　O me! this sight of death is as a bell
That warns my old age to a sepulchre.

Enter MONTAGUE *and others.*

PRINCE.　Come, Montague; for thou art early up,
To see thy son and heir more early down.

MON.　Alas, my liege, my wife is dead to-night;
Grief of my son's exile hath stopp'd her breath:
What further woe conspires against mine age?

PRINCE.　Look, and thou shalt see.

MON.　O thou untaught! what manners is in this,
To press before thy father to a grave?

PRINCE.　Seal up the mouth of outrage[10] for a while,
Till we can clear these ambiguities,
And know their spring, their head, their true descent;
And then will I be general of your woes,
And lead you even to death: meantime forbear,
And let mischance be slave to patience.
Bring forth the parties of suspicion.

FRI. L.　I am the greatest, able to do least,
Yet most suspected, as the time and place
Doth make against me, of this direful murder;
And here I stand, both to impeach and purge
Myself condemned and myself excused.

PRINCE.　Then say at once what thou dost know in this.

FRI. L.　I will be brief, for my short date of breath
Is not so long as is a tedious tale.
Romeo, there dead, was husband to that Juliet;
And she, there dead, that Romeo's faithful wife:
I married them; and their stol'n marriage-day
Was Tybalt's dooms-day, whose untimely death
Banish'd the new-made bridegroom from this city;
For whom, and not for Tybalt, Juliet pined.
You, to remove that siege of grief from her,
Betroth'd and would have married her perforce
To County Paris: then comes she to me,

---

[10] *outrage*] outcry.

And with wild looks bid me devise some mean
To rid her from this second marriage,
Or in my cell there would she kill herself.
Then gave I her, so tutor'd by my art,
A sleeping potion; which so took effect
As I intended, for it wrought on her
The form of death: meantime I writ to Romeo,
That he should hither come as this dire night,
To help to take her from her borrow'd grave,
Being the time the potion's force should cease.
But he which bore my letter, Friar John,
Was stay'd by accident, and yesternight
Return'd my letter back. Then all alone
At the prefixed hour of her waking
Came I to take her from her kindred's vault,
Meaning to keep her closely[11] at my cell
Till I conveniently could send to Romeo:
But when I came, some minute ere the time
Of her awaking, here untimely lay
The noble Paris and true Romeo dead.
She wakes, and I entreated her come forth,
And bear this work of heaven with patience:
But then a noise did scare me from the tomb,
And she too desperate would not go with me,
But, as it seems, did violence on herself.
All this I know; and to the marriage
Her nurse is privy: and, if aught in this
Miscarried by my fault, let my old life
Be sacrificed some hour before his time
Unto the rigour of severest law.
PRINCE. We still[12] have known thee for a holy man.
 Where's Romeo's man? what can he say in this?
BAL. I brought my master news of Juliet's death,
 And then in post he came from Mantua
 To this same place, to this same monument.
 This letter he early bid me give his father,
 And threaten'd me with death, going in the vault,
 If I departed not and left him there.

---

[11] *closely*] in secret.
[12] *still*] always.

PRINCE.   Give me the letter; I will look on it.
     Where is the County's page, that raised the watch?
     Sirrah, what made your master in this place?
PAGE.   He came with flowers to strew his lady's grave;
     And bid me stand aloof, and so I did:
     Anon comes one with light to ope the tomb;
     And by and by my master drew on him;
     And then I ran away to call the watch.
PRINCE.   This letter doth make good the Friar's words,
     Their course of love, the tidings of her death:
     And here he writes that he did buy a poison
     Of a poor 'pothecary, and therewithal
     Came to this vault to die and lie with Juliet.
     Where be these enemies? Capulet! Montague!
     See, what a scourge is laid upon your hate,
     That heaven finds means to kill your joys with love!
     And I, for winking at your discords too,
     Have lost a brace of kinsmen: all are punish'd.
CAP.   O brother Montague, give me thy hand:
     This is my daughter's jointure,[13] for no more
     Can I demand.
MON.   But I can give thee more:
     For I will raise her statue in pure gold;
     That whiles Verona by that name is known,
     There shall no figure at such rate[14] be set
     As that of true and faithful Juliet.
CAP.   As rich shall Romeo's by his lady's lie;
     Poor sacrifices of our enmity!
PRINCE.   A glooming peace this morning with it brings;
     The sun for sorrow will not show his head:
     Go hence, to have more talk of these sad things;
     Some shall be pardon'd and some punished:
     For never was a story of more woe
     Than this of Juliet and her Romeo.

                                       [Exeunt.

[13] *jointure*] the marriage portion supplied by the bridegroom.
[14] *rate*] value.

DOVER · THRIFT · EDITIONS

PLAYS

THE MIKADO, William Schwenck Gilbert. 64pp. 27268-0
FAUST, PART ONE, Johann Wolfgang von Goethe. 192pp. 28046-2
THE INSPECTOR GENERAL, Nikolai Gogol. 80pp. 28500-6
SHE STOOPS TO CONQUER, Oliver Goldsmith. 80pp. 26867-5
A DOLL'S HOUSE, Henrik Ibsen. 80pp. 27062-9
GHOSTS, Henrik Ibsen. 64pp. 29852-3
HEDDA GABLER, Henrik Ibsen. 80pp. 26469-6
THE WILD DUCK, Henrik Ibsen. 96pp. 41116-8
VOLPONE, Ben Jonson. 112pp. 28049-7
DR. FAUSTUS, Christopher Marlowe. 64pp. 28208-2
THE MISANTHROPE, Molière. 64pp. 27065-3
ANNA CHRISTIE, Eugene O'Neill. 80pp. 29985-6
BEYOND THE HORIZON, Eugene O'Neill. 96pp. 29085-9
THE EMPEROR JONES, Eugene O'Neill. 64pp. 29268-1
THE LONG VOYAGE HOME AND OTHER PLAYS, Eugene O'Neill. 80pp. 28755-6
RIGHT YOU ARE, IF YOU THINK YOU ARE, Luigi Pirandello. 64pp. (Not available in Europe or United Kingdom.) 29576-1
SIX CHARACTERS IN SEARCH OF AN AUTHOR, Luigi Pirandello. 64pp. (Not available in Europe or United Kingdom.) 29992-9
PHÈDRE, Jean Racine. 64pp. 41927-4
HANDS AROUND, Arthur Schnitzler. 64pp. 28724-6
ANTONY AND CLEOPATRA, William Shakespeare. 128pp. 40062-X
AS YOU LIKE IT, William Shakespeare. 80pp. 40432-3
HAMLET, William Shakespeare. 128pp. 27278-8
HENRY IV, William Shakespeare. 96pp. 29584-2
JULIUS CAESAR, William Shakespeare. 80pp. 26876-4
KING LEAR, William Shakespeare. 112pp. 28058-6
LOVE'S LABOUR'S LOST, William Shakespeare. 64pp. 41929-0
MACBETH, William Shakespeare. 96pp. 27802-6
MEASURE FOR MEASURE, William Shakespeare. 96pp. 40889-2
THE MERCHANT OF VENICE, William Shakespeare. 96pp. 28492-1
A MIDSUMMER NIGHT'S DREAM, William Shakespeare. 80pp. 27067-X
MUCH ADO ABOUT NOTHING, William Shakespeare. 80pp. 28272-4
OTHELLO, William Shakespeare. 112pp. 29097-2
RICHARD III, William Shakespeare. 112pp. 28747-5
ROMEO AND JULIET, William Shakespeare. 96pp. 27557-4
THE TAMING OF THE SHREW, William Shakespeare. 96pp. 29765-9
THE TEMPEST, William Shakespeare. 96pp. 40658-X
TWELFTH NIGHT; OR, WHAT YOU WILL, William Shakespeare. 80pp. 29290-8
ARMS AND THE MAN, George Bernard Shaw. 80pp. (Not available in Europe or United Kingdom.) 26476-9
HEARTBREAK HOUSE, George Bernard Shaw. 128pp. (Not available in Europe or United Kingdom.) 29291-6
PYGMALION, George Bernard Shaw. 96pp. (Available in U.S. only.) 28222-8
THE RIVALS, Richard Brinsley Sheridan. 96pp. 40433-1
THE SCHOOL FOR SCANDAL, Richard Brinsley Sheridan. 96pp. 26687-7
ANTIGONE, Sophocles. 64pp. 27804-2
OEDIPUS AT COLONUS, Sophocles. 64pp. 40659-8
OEDIPUS REX, Sophocles. 64pp. 26877-2

DOVER·THRIFT·EDITIONS

PLAYS

ELECTRA, Sophocles. 64pp. 28482-4

MISS JULIE, August Strindberg. 64pp. 27281-8

THE PLAYBOY OF THE WESTERN WORLD AND RIDERS TO THE SEA, J. M. Synge. 80pp. 27562-0

THE DUCHESS OF MALFI, John Webster. 96pp. 40660-1

THE IMPORTANCE OF BEING EARNEST, Oscar Wilde. 64pp. 26478-5

LADY WINDERMERE'S FAN, Oscar Wilde. 64pp. 40078-6

BOXED SETS

FAVORITE JANE AUSTEN NOVELS: *Pride and Prejudice, Sense and Sensibility* and *Persuasion* (Complete and Unabridged), Jane Austen. 800pp. 29748-9

BEST WORKS OF MARK TWAIN: Four Books, Dover. 624pp. 40226-6

EIGHT GREAT GREEK TRAGEDIES: Six Books, Dover. 480pp. 40203-7

FIVE GREAT ENGLISH ROMANTIC POETS, Dover. 496pp. 27893-X

FIVE GREAT PLAYS, Dover. 368pp. 27179-X

47 GREAT SHORT STORIES: Stories by Poe, Chekhov, Maupassant, Gogol, O. Henry, and Twain, Dover. 688pp. 27178-1

GREAT AFRICAN-AMERICAN WRITERS: Seven Books, Dover. 704pp. 29995-3

GREAT AMERICAN NOVELS, Dover. 720pp. 28665-7

GREAT ENGLISH NOVELS, Dover. 704pp. 28666-5

GREAT IRISH WRITERS: Five Books, Dover. 672pp. 29996-1

GREAT MODERN WRITERS: Five Books, Dover. 720pp. (Available in U.S. only.) 29458-7

GREAT WOMEN POETS: 4 Complete Books, Dover. 256pp. (Available in U.S. only.) 28388-7

MASTERPIECES OF RUSSIAN LITERATURE: Seven Books, Dover. 880pp. 40665-2

SEVEN GREAT ENGLISH VICTORIAN POETS: Seven Volumes, Dover. 592pp. 40204-5

SIX GREAT AMERICAN POETS: Poems by Poe, Dickinson, Whitman, Longfellow, Frost, and Millay, Dover. 512pp. (Available in U.S. only.) 27425-X

38 SHORT STORIES BY AMERICAN WOMEN WRITERS: Five Books, Dover. 512pp. 29459-5

26 GREAT TALES OF TERROR AND THE SUPERNATURAL, Dover. 608pp. (Available in U.S. only.) 27891-3

All books complete and unabridged. All 5³⁄₁₆" x 8¹⁄₄," paperbound. Available at your book dealer, online at **www.doverpublications.com**, or by writing to Dept. GI, Dover Publications, Inc., 31 East 2nd Street, Mineola, NY 11501. For current price information or for free catalogs (please indicate field of interest), write to Dover Publications or log on to **www.doverpublications.com** and see every Dover book in print. Dover publishes more than 500 books each year on science, elementary and advanced mathematics, biology, music, art, literary history, social sciences, and other areas.